To Deborah

CW00588638

Unspoken Truths

By Liz Mistry

Lovely to see you again

Hope you enjoy

Best Wishes

Dec 2018

Print ISBN: 978-1-912604-92-0

Dedication

As always, with love, for my family;
Nilesh, Ravi, Kasi and Jimi

Haiku

Truths buried deeply
Under frozen hearts of ice
Unspoken. Dormant.

Prologue

Alice had been beasting it up in the pit. Today, she'd gone for progressive overload on the skull crusher, followed by ten reps of kettlebell swings, deadlifts and hanging knee raises. Since being incarcerated she'd needed to sharpen her focus – keep her senses on continual high alert. This was the one environment where *she* regained control. Surrounded by the grunts of women stacking weights and the clank of metal on metal, her gym time allowed her to escape from herself... for a short time at least. The rhythmic thump on the punch bags – leather on leather – whop, whop, whop... left, right, left... whop, whop, whop, allowed her to channel her anger.

Until her imprisonment, Alice had worked out in mixed gyms and the absence of testosterone, where only female sweat was broken, gave it a different vibe. It was the smell. Until now she hadn't considered that female perspiration smelt any different from men's. But it did. Or maybe it was just her imagination. It wasn't so in your face, so overpowering. *Mad, huh?* She'd always made the choice to avoid the single-sex joints, preferring to assert her independence, her lack of fear, her right to train in mixed company. Maybe it was the challenge. Maybe it was her competitive streak. The prison gym was a basic, no frills space. Its main aim being to dispel the stir crazy – and it worked. Well, it did for Alice. It kept her sane.

Tired and aching, body pushed to its limit, she wiped the sweat from her brow and left the gym. Not breaking stride, she sent a cursory glance at the other two prisoners who, like her, seemed to work out to combat their demons. She never spoke to them, nor they to her, despite that, they shared an unspoken appreciation of each other's dedication and stamina.

All too aware of her stalkers loitering by the exercise balls, Alice walked past. Haudit and Daudit, names she'd borrowed from Gus' old man, were sprawled on the mats – massive pink lycra-clad watermelons, ready to burst apart, spewing their innards out like venom. Their leader, Hairy Mary, leaned against the wall, one foot resting on an inflated turquoise ball, rolling it back and forth, an unlit cigarette hanging from the corner of her mouth. She'd had dealings with Hairy Mary and her crew before now and wondered at their sudden interest in the gym.

Before entering the shower area, Alice took a quick glance in the wall mirrors to check where everyone was; officers in a huddle near the punch bags, Hairy Mary's goons flattening the equipment to her right – no other threat in sight. Inside, she stripped off her kit and chucked it on the bench before stepping into the cubicle. Not bothering with the slimy plastic splash sheet, she banged her palm against the button and raised her face to meet the lukewarm water. An officer should have accompanied her inside, but who was she to interrupt their gossiping. One of them would notice her absence soon and catch up with her – for now though, Alice welcomed being alone. She rested her brow against the wall and savoured the water cooling her, washing the sweat away. The door clicked open and a quick smirk tugged at Alice's lips for a second. *Big Brother was on her case!*

As she lifted her forehead from the wall, she sensed movement right behind her, too close to be a guard. Whirling round on one leg, her hands flew up to the tiled walls on either side. Bracing herself against them, she kicked, connecting with pink lycra'd flab that elicited an 'oomph' before slipping on the wet floor and landing on its backside. Fists up, bobbing on the balls of her feet, Alice flicked water from her face. *Bitches! Trust them to start when I'm naked!* Eyes darting round the room, she saw two more adversaries; Hairy bloody Mary and her last remaining sidekick. *Where were the officers? Surely, they'd noticed her absence by now?*

Alice weighed up the odds. Neither of her opponents were in peak physical condition, so she reckoned she could dodge them. It all depended on whether the prison officers were actually going to put in an appearance or, as she suspected, had just turned a blind eye. *Fuck! She should've known better than to sneak off on her own.*

Narrowing her eyes, Alice unclenched her fists and dropped them to waist height, her palms up. Wiggling her fingers in a 'come on then' gesture, she raised her chin, glowering. 'What you waiting for? Better odds?'

Adrenalin surged through her, chasing her earlier fatigue away. Her eyes flitted between her opponents wondering which one would attack first. Hairy Mary laughed, her hair fanned around her face like a henna-maned lion. Jiggling a towel in front of Alice, her voice a childish sing song, said 'Here, you want this, ya slut?'

She took a step towards Alice, 'Fucking got ya now, Cooper. Fucking got ya.'

Ignoring the thought that being naked in a fight wasn't the best scenario she'd faced, Alice held her ground. Mary's pasty arms lunged towards her throat. Alice sidestepped which brought her closer to Mary's mate – the one she'd named Haudit. She'd already disposed of Daudit who was still sprawled on the ground, moaning. A fleeting expression of wide-eyed panic crossed Haudit's spotty face as Alice lifted her arms and stepped closer. It was then that the slow clapping began. Alice halted. A huge grin replaced Haudit's earlier anxious expression and a quick glance showed that Hairy Mary's face was now blooming – a Cheshire lion with spots and a mangy mane.

Alice's eyes flitted to the right and her stomach plummeted. How the *hell* had she not noticed Baby Jane Inflictor of Pain enter the arena? Not much bigger than Alice, Baby Jane, nonetheless, made Hannibal Lector seem sane. Glancing around, she looked for a way out. Wherever Baby Jane was, her goons wouldn't be far behind and she didn't want to wait around to see what was in store for her.

Taking a sideways step, she grabbed Haudit by the shoulders and – despite the excessive poundage the other woman carried – she swung her round with ease before catapulting her toward Baby Jane. Not waiting to witness the impact, Alice dodged back, her eye on the shower room door. She was within arm's reach of it when a vice-like grip settled on her upper arms, yanking her backwards and slamming her against the wall.

A hand round her throat kept her in place, her toes only just skimming the floor. From what seemed like miles above her, rotten teeth were bared in a halitosis grin. *Aw shit, Baby Jane's enforcer was here.* Alice's entire body tensed as Hairy Mary and her team sidled over to block the door. She was on her own. The Enforcer released Alice's throat and, knowing better than to show weakness, she raised her chin and stared straight at Baby Jane, aware that, with her arms held by her sides, her options were limited.

Baby Jane's eyes were as blue as a winter's sky, cold and empty. She smiled. The only person Alice had ever met with a similar expression was The Matchmaker. Whatever she wanted with her, it would *not* be in Alice's best interests. She shivered and Jane's enforcer, nostrils flared, yowled like a hound about to be let loose on a fox. Alice swallowed down her nausea and did the only thing she could…

Utilising the firmness of her attackers' hold on her arms, she waited till Jane was close enough. She pulled down on them, swung up with her legs and rammed her feet right into Baby Jane's chest. Baby Jane stumbled backwards. A yelp of pure rage hung in the cubicle. The goons increased the pressure on Alice's arms, smashing her back against the wall. Her head cracked against the tiles. Alice flinched, her eyesight clouded. She forced herself to shake off the dizziness. Baby Jane was coming for her, mouth open in a feral growl. Backing up, the cold tiles pressed against her bare buttocks, there was nothing she could do, nowhere to go.

Baby Jane, breathing heavily, crashed into her body. Alice's breath pouffed, her bones shuddered and then agonising pain. Her eyes flew open. Jane danced in front of her, something bloody gripped between her teeth, blood dripping down her chin. Eyes fastened on Alice, she snarled, baring her teeth. With one finger, she pushed Alice's nipple into her mouth. Two chews... still grinning, she gave an exaggerated swallow before opening her mouth wide, as if she was on *I'm a Celebrity Get Me Out Of Here.* 'All gone!'

Alice looked down at her bloody breast and vomited.

Leaning over, Baby Jane banged the shower button and a cascade of water spouted over all of them. 'Let her go!'

The goons released Alice, who landed on her back. Straddling her, Baby Jane leaned in close and in a final act of defiance, Alice – one hand cupped round her injured breast – stared her out. Baby Jane extended an arm to one of her goons who gave her a pink Barbie toothbrush. The handle had been fashioned into a home-made shiv, honed to a point with a blade inserted for good measure. Alice knew what was coming next.

Sean had finally got to her... she'd always known he would – even in here.

The water pounded her body, warm prickles fading to cold. Cowering in the foetal position, trickles of pink-tinged liquid flowed towards the plughole where it swirled momentarily – a silent gurgle before eddying away. She was numb. The shiv had fallen out of the wound and her blood leaked onto the shower room tiles, yet... no pain.

After she'd been stabbed, Alice had waited, anticipating another thrust. None had come. Just a combination of foul-smelling cigarettes, caffeine and the remnants of that evening's boiled veg concoction. It wasn't the foulness of her attacker's breath that made her blood run cold though, it was the whispered husky words... the threat.

Alice screamed, clutching her side. The strange disconnect between her blood, warm as it left her body coupled with the coolness of the shower, made her dizzy. She had to hold on. Had to survive this. For, if she didn't, the worst thing imaginable would happen and she *couldn't* be responsible for more deaths. Her eyelids flickered, her hand pressed to her side, weak and shaking.

Voices, hollow and echoey drifted above her. Shadows floated like phantoms and hands touched her skin. She clenched, trying to protest as pressure was applied to the puncture site and gentle fingers skimmed across her forehead. She recognised the voice -Lulu. Footsteps running, the shower's pounding stopped, softness replaced the hardness under her head... nothing.

February 2018

Thursday

Chapter 1

19:15 Heaton Woods

The Beast from the East that had been promised for days, hung heavy in the air with the odd flurry of snow turning vague threats into distinct possibility. The darkness was alleviated only by the moonlight and Gus' torch. He and Patti had chosen to walk up through Heaton woods to get to his parents' farmhouse on Shay Lane. This section was far enough away from the roads to have its own quiet. Not silence, but rather the gentle noises of wildlife settling in for the night. The trees, still bare from their winter hibernation, creaked in the breeze. In the undergrowth, a faint scuttling told them they weren't alone, whilst above them, an occasional hoot or the flutter of wings kept them company. Underfoot the path was uneven and sludgy. Rain followed by snow, followed by ice, followed by rain, made it squelch round their feet as they tramped uphill. Gus' cheeks were cold and he wished he'd picked up his scarf before he left Mariner's Drive.

He whistled to Bingo, who had his nose stuck in a bundle of something no doubt odorous and appealing only to dogs. The Wheaten Scottie wagged his tale good-naturedly, his entire rear end wobbling in rhythm, before turning and running back to Gus and Patti. At the back of Gus' mind was the thought that, one of these days, Bingo would turn over a bigger, more sinister corpse than those of the dead rabbits, mice and foxes he'd found to date. He didn't share the statistics concerning the number of murder victims discovered by dog walkers with Patti. No

3

way was he going to spoil the precious time he had with her by being all maudlin. Since before Christmas, with everything that had happened with Alice and Sampson, Patti had become more and more of a fixture in his life. Pulling himself up short for allowing his mind to wander, he focussed on the story she was telling him about a kid who'd brought a bag of weed into school.

'Ranjit searched her locker, found the baggie and trundled the kid along to my office.' Patti laughed, her cheeks shining in the torchlight. 'I gave her detentions for the rest of the week.' Giggling, she grabbed Gus' arm. 'But *wait* till you hear the best part! The dozy cow had actually bought a bag of parsley.' Gales of laughter halted their progress and, amused, Gus observed her as – still grinning – she mopped her eyes. He loved the way she laughed so unselfconsciously. Her face framed by her hair – loose for once, with a woolly hat covering her jet-black straightened tresses. The red of her hat complimenting her golden-brown complexion. It made her look like a warrior elf from Lord of the Rings. His heart stuttered. *This is all happening too fast for me. What if I mess it up like I always do?*

'*Parsley* – do you believe it? Dozy cow paid ten quid for a bag of parsley. I almost wish we'd been able to make her smoke it. That would've taught her.'

Still laughing, she snuggled closer to him. 'Lucky for her that it was a garden herb, cos if it *had* been marijuana, I'd have been obliged to exclude her. This way, she got in trouble with her parents, lost face with her mates, but *didn't* have an exclusion on her school record. She'll be pleased about that in five years' time.'

He loved hearing the stories she brought back from the school she ran. She was firm but fair and he wished *his* high school headteacher had been more like her. Instead, he'd been stern and unyielding and, in retrospect, more than a bit racist. How things had changed in Bradford – and some of it, at least, was for the better.

4

'... and she told us who'd supplied her. Of course, I passed that information onto your lot.'

'Yeah, heard about that. It was one of Bazza the Bampot Green's scrotes. The little turd was keeping it for his personal use and selling the herbs instead. We couldn't link it back to Bazza with real evidence so, as usual, he'll get off scot-free, and the lad'll get a slap on the wrists. Hopefully, he won't try to deal near your school next time.'

Patti shrugged, 'There's always another one waiting to take his place. We try our best, but they still manage to find a way in.'

Trouble was, weed was the least of their worries. There were all sorts of new concoctions out there and more and more kids were falling victim to them – Vallies, Spice, Oxy, Ecstasy. You name it, it was on the streets somewhere. Gus squeezed her arm. 'Come on, let's get a move on before we freeze.' He whistled for Bingo and set off again. 'Sooner I've updated the auld yins on Alice, the sooner we can get home and order a takeaway.'

Patti bit her lip and slowed down. Gus took a couple of extra steps before he realised she'd stopped and glanced back. Recognising her shame-faced look, he quirked an eyebrow, 'Go on. Spit it out.'

The enormous pom-pom on top of her hat wobbled endearingly when she moved her head, avoiding his look. As she shuffled her boots in the sludge, all thoughts of a curry from Aman's disappeared. 'Oh no, Patti. *Please* say you haven't.'

Having the grace to look a little chastised, Patti scrunched up her nose, stepped forward and linked her arm through his. 'What was I supposed to say? She asked and she sounded so keen, I hadn't the heart to say no. We'll survive.'

Gus had serious doubts on that score. Patti hadn't had much experience of his mum's cooking, yet surely, she realised by now that it was a miracle no one in the McGuire household had yet succumbed to a serious case of food poisoning. He scowled, and with an *'On your head be it'* sort of sniff, marched on.

Passing through the kissing gate onto Shay Lane, the sounds of the woods faded and street lights brightened their path. As they reached the McGuire seniors' residence, Gus took off one glove. Prompted by an attack on Gus' mum the previous year, the premises now had state-of-the-art security around it; cameras, motion sensor lights, biometric finger pads to open the metal gates to the drive – everything! Pressing his thumb to the pad next to the side gate, he waited till it swung open and he and Patti, preceded by an over-excited Bingo, entered. As soon as they'd cleared the sensor, the gate swung shut and they approached the house which was well lit in welcome.

Once inside they settled in front of a large fire, a glass of whisky in Gus' hand and a mug of hot chocolate in Patti's. Corrine and Fergus sat on a large sofa opposite. Gus smiled. When he saw his parent's together they always looked like such a mismatched couple. His dad, tall and broad, with a slight sprinkling of ginger through his greying beard. He had the sparkliest, shiniest blue eyes Gus had ever seen. People said he'd inherited his blue eyes from his dad. By contrast Gus' mum was petite, her tight curls moulded to her skull, her skin a gorgeous golden brown, like wet sand on a sunny day. In fact, everything about Corrine McGuire spoke of sunny days. She leaned forward, 'What's the update on Alice, Angus?'

Although her tone was upbeat, she wore her anxious frown and Gus wished he had something positive to say. He hated to see his folks so worried. All afternoon he'd been trying to think of a way to break the news of Alice's injuries to them. Now, looking at their concerned expressions, his mother's small hand dwarfed inside his father's shovel-like one, he realised there was no way to sugar-coat it. He just had to tell them. Alice had become like a second daughter to them over the last few years and they deserved to know the truth.

Desperate not to betray his own emotions, he kept his tone level and matter-of-fact. The brutality of it still made him want to punch a wall, to storm down to the prison and hold someone accountable, however that wouldn't do Alice any good. For her sake, he had to let the authorities do their thing. So, he explained to them about her injury, her refusal to have reconstructive surgery at this point, the stab wound that damaged her spleen, two broken ribs, a concussion and other minor bruising and lacerations.

'Surely someone saw something?'

Gus glanced at his dad, who gave an almost imperceptible shake of the head. Gus understood his motivation. He too would do anything to protect his mother from unpleasantnessries, but some things just *had* to be told. He shrugged an apology. 'As far as the other prisoners are concerned, not only is she a copper, she's a bent one and so she's fair game.' As his mother's eyes welled up, he continued, 'We've got her the best solicitor there is and we'll get her moved. This won't happen again and, for now, she's safe in hospital. I'm going to see her tomorrow.'

Corrine McGuire dabbed her tears with a tissue. 'That poor child. You've got to get her out of there, Angus. You've just *got* to.'

Fergus patted his wife's hand, 'There, there, Hen. I'm sure the lad's doing the very best he can.' And he looked at his son, his eyes less blue and sparkly than they'd been when Gus and Patti had arrived.

Shit, No pressure then! He hadn't explained fully to his parents about Alice pulling away from him and Nancy. Or about her refusal to see anyone from his team. It was becoming increasingly difficult to help her. Perhaps now she was in hospital things *would* be easier. He certainly hoped so. The silence sat heavy in the room for a few minutes. Corrine jumped to her feet, '*The oven!*' and scurried out of the room.

As the unmistakeable smell of burning drifted through the open door, Gus turned to

Patti, with an *I told you so* look.

7

Friday

Chapter 2

Jess sighed and directed her best retired school teacher frown at the young man sitting opposite her. It was irritating enough that the train was running late, but being forced to listen to the thrum of bass from the lad's headphones was just too much. *Surprised he's got any eardrums left!* The lad seemed oblivious to her annoyance, his head bopping to some annoying rhythm, his head, no doubt filled with inane thoughts of sweaty encounters or drug deals. She'd looked forward to having this time to read her book, now he'd gone and spoiled it. No more than she'd come to expect from the youth of today. Resigned, she slipped a bookmark between the pages of her romantic novel and closed it. Leaning back against the headrest to watch the countryside pass by, she tried to ignore his greasy blond head bobbing at the edge of her vision. His extra-long fringe flopped over his eyes making her want to cut it off. The train rattled, the lad's knee bounced and his fingers drummed on the Formica surface, making his empty Costa cup dance across the table top – well, she hoped it was empty.

Jess glared at the offending cup and then at the boy.

His spotty face broke into a lopsided grin and he pulled his headphones off. 'Just love that song.' He leaned both elbows on the table and looked straight at her. 'It's just brilliant. Wicked. Y'know?'

In the face of his enthusiasm, Jess' earlier irritation ebbed and she risked a small smile in return. No point in being overly

11

friendly, she didn't want to be engaged in a long blown-out conversation with a teenager. 'I probably wouldn't know the song, love. Nor the band, come to that.'

'Course you would…' He laughed. 'Everyone's heard of the Beatles.' And he raised his hand in the air to high five her.

Jess hesitated for a second, until with a small laugh – hoping no one was witnessing this strange encounter – she lifted her own hand to reciprocate. 'Yes, you're right. Even *I've* heard of the Beatles.'

The lad nodded, pulled his headphones on again and was soon lost in the rhythm.

As the train clattered towards Rawsforth, Jess hummed along to the now identifiable strains of *Norwegian Woods* fading into *Maxwell's Silver Hammer*.

Helen struggled to settle her two-year-old. Sammy had a slight cold and was tetchy. But, with her husband away, she'd decided to brave the one-and-a-half-hour journey to her mum's rather than be home alone. Now, she wished she hadn't bothered. A fluey headache pounded at her temples, her sinuses were blocked and she was sure she'd caught it from Sammy. The only thing worse than trying to entertain a poorly toddler on a train was trying to do it while you felt poorly yourself. The thought that when she reached Bradford, she could hand Sammy over to her parents until she felt better, helped her to hold it together.

After tantrums and tears and grumpy throwing of toys across the carriage, Sammy's head drooped against her shoulder in a deep sleep as he sucked on his dummy. Helen breathed a sigh of relief and for the first time glanced around at her fellow passengers. Her lips tightened when she noticed that the young man opposite, so engrossed in his phone, was Asian. Would you bloody credit it? She'd left Bradford and moved to Midforth to get away from the Pakis and yet, still in the leafy suburbs, she was surrounded by them.

Well, okay it was only one of them, but still, they weren't in Bradford yet. Everything about the man annoyed her, from his overgrown bushy beard down to his expensive trainers. God, she hated Pakis – everyone knew you couldn't trust them but everyone was just too scared to say it out loud. Perhaps spending a few days with her parents wasn't such a great idea after all. Maybe she should have struggled on at home on her own. Her grip on Sammy tightened a little and she angled her son away from him and tried to look out the window to distract herself. God, she felt rough.

Seconds later, she jumped when he muttered '*fuck*' under his breath and threw his phone on the table. Almost at once, he snatched it up again and frowning, turned to glare out the window. Helen's lips tightened. Her baby might only be small, but she didn't want him hearing *that* sort of language. Sammy was heavy and, combined with the tension across her shoulders, she thought her arms would break. Pulling her handbag onto her knee she shuffled closer to the edge of her seat. That's when she noticed the horrible black and white Paki scarf lying on top of his rucksack. Helen glanced anxiously at her watch; another forty minutes to go. After the arena attack, who knew what might be in that rucksack? And why the hell was he fiddling with his phone so much? In a decisive move she stood up, hoisted Sammy up to lean against one shoulder and swung his changing bag and her hand bag onto the other. A quick glance round the carriage and, decision made, she moved nearer to the exit, where the blind man and his dog sat.

Mike pretended to tap away on his laptop, yet all the while he was really eyeing up the woman opposite him. He'd noticed her at the station in Manchester and decided that she'd be a good person to chat to on the tedious journey to Bradford. Of course, her blonde hair, long legs and mini skirt had nothing to do with his decision to find a seat near her… or so he told himself. Truth was, a bit of female company wouldn't go amiss. His wife was in one of her never-ending moods because the fertility treatment had failed yet again. Didn't she get it that it was hard for him too? All the jokes about his 'manhood', about 'firing blanks', his friends who were dads gloating and sneering, his boss tutting when he had to take time off for the endless appointments. It was okay for her; she got all the sympathy, all the kind words. Her boss was fine about the time off, but shit, if he lost his job they'd be in so much debt… and now, he wasn't even sure if he wanted a kid or not.

An hour into the journey Mike was truly pissed off. Despite numerous smiles and many conversational gambits, the blonde refused to be drawn into conversation. She was perfectly polite but each reply was monosyllabic and uttered in a sexy foreign accent. Her half smile was strained and her eyes seemed to focus somewhere above his left shoulder. *Bloody snooty cow! Sitting there gripping on to her purse like she thinks I'm going grab her tits. As if – they're not all that. Well she can swivel on one!*

Jake sat near the carriage door, his guide dog by his feet. Listening to what was going on around him, he patted the dog's head. He'd counted exactly how many people shared the carriage and was content to pass the journey forming his own images of them in his mind. He knew that the young mother with the grizzly child had moved to sit opposite him. She seemed slightly breathless and he could hear her wriggling about in her seat.

Smiling, he listened as the man with the expensive aftershave, who was tapping on his laptop, attempted to chat up the woman in the high heels with the foreign accent. Her responses were lukewarm, but Jake judged that the young man would not give up. He was right. Laptop man persisted until, finally, Jake heard her cross her legs and change position. He guessed that she'd angled her body away from her would-be suitor. Jake smiled as the women at the back hummed quietly to the tune that escaped from the young lad's earphones. He liked The Beatles too.

10:55

2018 had roared in with a growl, stuttered around for a bit and by February had settled into a freezing freshness, only to be threatened by The Beast from the East. Of course, the upcoming weather would play havoc with Paddy Toner's job. *Nothing worse than snow and ice on the tracks…*

'Fuck!'

Paddy's final words as the train hurtled towards the lime green Toyota Corolla that sat abandoned in the middle of Rawsforth Level Crossing were: *'Oh, for the love of God, who left that there?'*

His final actions were to apply the brakes, close his eyes and cross himself.

His final memory was of his wife's flushed cheeks as she shuddered beneath him that morning – and he knew he'd never see her again.

The train's brakes squealed and the passengers screamed as they were sent flying from their seats, floundering as the carriage began to tip to the right. Metal screeched against metal as the train hit the car and was followed by a muted explosion and overpowering burning petrol fumes… silence.

Chapter 3

What had happened to the weather? Gus had expected it to be a bit warmer in the South, but no – Surrey was as damn cold as Bradford had been when he'd left home that morning. Tension played along his shoulders as he walked up the ramp to the entrance of the hospital. The last visit he'd made to see Alice hadn't gone well and he didn't have high hopes for this one either. He took the last slug from his Irn Bru, squashed the can and tossed it in the recycling. Having Patti with him last time had given him the confidence he needed. This time though, he was on his own. A pulse beat at his temple, promising him a raging headache to follow later in the evening. This was a new phenomenon for Gus. One that had started only after his previous investigation into the deaths of two teenage girls at a house party gone wrong. It hadn't only been the outcome of the investigation that had left him suffering these cluster headaches. It had been the loss of two close friends during the culmination of the case.

His fledgling relationship with Patti had begun just before the second most traumatic series of events in Gus' life and he still wasn't sure how it had survived it. She had been a large part of his coping mechanism. November had been hellish and had laid him bare. Raging against the world – the job he loved, the people he cared about – Gus was aware that he'd changed. A brittle patina created a barrier between him and the rest of the world and the only people who managed to get under that barrier were his mother and Patti. He hadn't intended to erect it, it had happened without him noticing at first, and as he became used to it – it sat easily on his shoulders; armour, a way to distance himself from feelings that were too raw and too sharp to examine right now.

On top of all that, he hated hospitals. Hated the clinical smell, the echoey hallways and the despair that lurked like an anxious patient. A sign pointed him in the direction of ward eighty-five. He took a deep breath and registered that his heartbeat had lowered a notch. *That was good.* The anger bubbling just beneath the surface had to be controlled if he was going to be of any use to Alice. He stepped into the lift and pressed the button.

When the doors slid open, releasing him onto a sterile pale blue painted corridor, he walked out and looked along its length. Alice, he'd been told, was in a side room. His lips tightened. He didn't need to ask directions because near the end of the corridor, a prison officer sat outside a room. Bastards had even put a fucking guard on her door. *What the hell? Did they expect her to make a great escape with her arse hanging out of a hospital gown and a drip attached? Idiots! She'd had her spleen removed, her ribs were broken and what they'd done to her nipple was just vile.* Alice was no more able to make a bid for freedom than his mum was likely to provide an edible Sunday lunch.

Well-aware that he was being touchy, Gus grimaced. It was procedure to have one officer outside, but still it rankled. Alice was a police officer but the adage 'innocent until proven guilty' didn't seem to apply to her.

From the flurry of activity further along on the main ward, Gus surmised the doctors were doing their rounds. White coated kids with stethoscopes dangling round their necks like a fashion accessory, were huddled round an older woman, their gazes intent, leaving their mentor's face only to dart down to the charts they carried in their hands. As he walked towards the officer, he tried to adjust his expression. It wasn't the officer's fault, he was just doing his job. Seeming to sense Gus' presence, the man stopped swinging on the chair, lowered its legs to the floor and stood up, his arms pulled out to the sides as if to emphasise his bulk. With a curt nod, Gus flipped open his warrant card and moved towards the closed door. The officer, grinning like an arse, stopped him, fat fingers moving in a 'gimme' gesture. 'I'll take that.'

Whilst Mr Arsey inspected his ID with unnecessary dedication, Gus gazed through the small window in the door. Alice was lying on a bed her head turned away from him. She had a drip and was attached to various monitors with blinking lights and beeps. Her hair was shorter than Gus had ever seen it. She'd taken a razor to it, for she now wore it as a buzz cut. With a sheet pulled up to her chest, she looked frail. Gus followed her frame down the bed and a spurt of anger made him close his eyes and count to ten. There was another officer in the room with her! *What the actual fuck?*

Chapter 4

12:45 Rawsforth level crossing

S now fell, getting steadily heavier as DCI Mickey Swanson, short hair spiked around her head, her ill-fitting suit just a little too tight, looked at the train wreck from the embankment. The cries of a baby reached her ears and the smell of smoke was stringent. She was glad she wasn't too near it. Two ambulances were parked, their back doors open as the paramedics attended the people on the ground. *Thank God it hadn't been a busy train.*

It wasn't usually her remit to attend this sort of incident but the car that had been positioned on the level crossing was owned by a known dealer. As soon as the number plate had been run, it had come to the attention of Mickey's vice team. Not the dealer's usual sort of stunt and he *had* reported the car stolen last week, still, it needed to be checked out. On impact the boot had sprung open revealing its contents which necessitated Mickey's presence – a few thousand pounds worth of heroin. She sighed. That was a drop in the ocean, but better locked up than polluting the streets of Bradford and Leeds.

There had been one fatality... the train driver. The engine had smashed into the car, pulverising it and pushing it beyond the level crossing, trapping it under its fender in the process. Catholic by birth, Mickey's fingers did a quick dance from forehead to chest and to each shoulder and she cursed – she'd not been to church in decades yet old habits die hard.

According to the crime scene officers, there was evidence that the train driver had applied the brakes, however the distance between his first sighting of the car after the train rounded the bend, had been too short for any effective preventative action. *Poor sod!* They'd removed his body and Mickey was glad she wasn't responsible for the death call this time. Meanwhile the CSIs were working against the elements. A layer of the falling white stuff was already covering the upended carriages and they were struggling to erect a cover over the Toyota in order to preserve evidence.

Body turned side on, she half ran, half slipped through the sludge to the bottom of the incline. The train's two carriages lay at an angle against the embankment. Chunks of metal had peeled from the carriage sides as they'd scraped against fences and pylons before skidding to a halt. Broken glass scattered the tracks and pungent smoke filled the air. Further down the track, away from the train's carcass, a small group of dishevelled people had gathered. There weren't many of them and she'd been told they'd only suffered minor injuries, so they'd soon be on their way to get checked over. Hopefully before this weather got any worse.

Mickey walked towards the two police constables who were keeping the log and a quick glance round told her they'd secured the area well. Crime scene tape sealed off an inner cordon and the passengers were now positioned between it and the wider, outer cordon they'd created. Beyond the level crossing, in the distance, she saw other officers re-directing traffic and questioning the small crowds that had gathered.

'Good job, you two. Scene's secured nicely. Now, go and find out what the good folk of Rawsforth have to offer.'

As they left, a paramedic carrying a clip board, approached. Mickey showed the paramedic her ID. 'What's the damage?'

The medic looked over at the engine. 'Well, as you'd expect the train driver's dead but other than him, they've been lucky. No other fatalities. Mainly minor bruising and cuts. Here's a list of their names and contact details. We're taking them into Bradford Royal Infirmary, if you want to catch up with them there.' She blew on her hands, 'Oh, hey… you might be interested to know that one of them is accusing the young Asian lad of being a terrorist. I've made a note of it on the back of that list.'

Mickey snorted. If there had been the merest hint of this being a suspected terrorist incident then the super ops team would have been all over it like a swarm of bloody bees. Besides… really…? She looked around at the vast expanse of rapidly whitening countryside, punctuated only by the train line and a couple of minor roads. 'Terrorist my arse. What terrorist would target a country train in the middle of nowhere?' She headed towards the CSIs and identified the manager. 'What you got?'

'Driver's dead.'

Mickey waved her hand in front of her in a 'get on with it' movement. 'Yeah, tell me something I haven't been told fifty times already.'

The CSI rolled her eyes and pulled her mask from her lower face and in a mild tone said, 'No need to be a cow bag, is there? I'm telling you what I know which, incidentally, is what you asked for.'

Mickey exhaled, 'Yeah, yeah you're right. I am a cow bag. Bloody HRT is doing me in. Let's back space. Apart from the deceased train driver and the presence of a car on the level crossing with a shed load of heroin in the boot, have you got anything?'

The CSI grinned. 'We've almost processed the car. You'll get that info when you get it, okay? We've got a backlog of lab work, so this,' she waved her hand to encompass the surrounding crime scene, 'will just have to join the never-ending queue. Nobody reported breaking down on the level crossing so I'm assuming it was deliberate.'

Mickey thought so too. She just couldn't work out why though. Who would leave a car chock full of heroin on a level crossing in sheep-shagging land? Didn't make bloody sense. She turned her gaze to the train and frowned. *Who in their right minds would want to derail a cross country train? What possible motivation could there be for that?* She glanced down at the list in her hand and then over at the line of passengers who were now being helped up the embankment to a waiting ambulance. Maybe one of them would have the answer for her. She certainly hoped so. Her thought process was interrupted by the CSI.

'This your boss coming?'

Mickey turned and saw a tall man in a suit walking towards her. Although she didn't recognise *him*, she did recognise the type and she swallowed a frustrated sigh. She could do without a pissing contest right now. 'Never seen him before.'

The man raised his arm and waved. 'DCI Swanson?'

Mickey walked to meet him, her face schooled to blandness. 'And you are?'

He smiled a Colgate smile and winked, 'I'm your fairy godmother.'

Bloody tosser! Mickey kept her expression neutral though she suspected what was coming. 'Sorry?'

'Just my little joke. I'm Detective Chief Inspector Hawes from the anti-terrorist unit. This scene is very sensitive, so I've come to take over.'

Ten minutes previously, Mickey had been fed up with being lumbered with another crime scene, now she was just as determined to fight for it. 'This scene has *not* been identified as a terrorist incident. In fact, it seems unlikely that it is.'

Hawes held his hands out in a placatory gesture. 'Now, now, don't get all agitated. Just leave all this to the experts. You head back to Bradford and I'll take over here. We need to involve the bomb squad and liaise with the arson team. It's all very technical and we have protocols in place.'

Mickey flushed. 'I head up Bradford's vice unit *and…* you know what?' She didn't wait for his reply, but instead lowered her voice, so he had to lean in a little to catch what she said, 'I'm well aware of all the protocols. Got it?'

Hawes' face melted into toddler's sulk, bottom lip protruding, brows pulled together, lips turned down. Mickey shook her head. Why the hell did these youngsters feel the need to patronise women who'd sucked eggs for longer than they'd been out of nappies? Okay, okay mixed metaphors, but she knew what she meant. Deciding there and then not to embark on a pissing contest, she took a step back and pasted an insincere smile on her lips, 'You can have the scene. I've seen all I need to.' No need to tell Hawes that she was off to speak to the passengers because that, she was sure, was where the answers lay – not in some imaginary terrorist attack.

By the time Mickey arrived at the Bradford Royal Infirmary, the passengers had all been released with minor injuries and were sitting together with cups of tea, in a room adjoining the Accident and Emergency waiting room. This room was usually designated for officers to keep prisoners needing medical help who may disturb the other waiting patients, but today it served to offer privacy to the still shocked passengers whilst they were interviewed.

After introductions, Mickey looked round the group. 'I bet you didn't expect this when you got on the train this morning, huh?'

The woman with the toddler on her lap mumbled something that elicited a tut from the older woman beside her. Glancing between the two women, Mickey noticed that the younger woman was glaring at the Asian lad sitting opposite. Remembering what the paramedic had told her earlier, Mickey sat next to the Asian lad, and leaned forward, arms resting on her knees, her gaze directed towards the woman who was bouncing the baby, in an attempt to keep him from crying. 'Sorry, I didn't catch that?'

The woman paused her bouncing, resulting in the baby's face crumpling into a cry not dissimilar to the expression Mickey had seen earlier on DCI Hawes' face. The woman, a Helen North, spoke in a venomous tone. 'I said, *most* of us didn't expect it,' and she looked pointedly at the man Mickey had identified from her list as Munir Rehman.

Munir slouched in his chair, and seemingly oblivious of Helen's toxicity, was texting frantically. However, when he looked up and saw her staring at him, his brows drew together for a second before throwing his head back, releasing a humourless bark. 'What's up?' He sat up straight, 'Oh, I get it. An abandoned car and a train wreck means the Paki must have done it? What? You think I'm a fucking terrorist or summat, do you?'

Mickey stood up. 'Mr. Rehman that is *not* what we think.' She turned to the others. 'There was no indication of a detonator of any kind. The impact of the train hitting the car caused the damage and, as yet, we have no explanation of why the car was left there.'

The other young man, headphones hanging round his neck, cleared his throat. 'Who in heaven's name would want to terrorise the sheep on Rawsforth Moor like? It's obviously some stupid prank gone drastically wrong. It's that poor driver I feel sorry for.'

Everyone nodded, yet Helen still looked unconvinced and continued to eye Munir with suspicion whilst attempting to twist her body away from him. This was thwarted by the fact that her baby seemed to have taken a liking to Munir and held out his chubby hands in his direction, saying, 'Da-da'

Mickey noticed a few of the passengers smirking and could empathise with them. Perhaps the mother needed to learn a few things from her baby. Knowing that they'd been interviewed by officers prior to her arrival and conscious of how weary they all looked, Mickey was keen to let them go home. She did a quick head count and frowned, 'Is someone missing? I was told there were eight of you and I've got eight names here, but there are only seven.'

The older lady looked up, revealing a bruised cheek and a neat row of stitches above her eyebrow, 'Oh, you mean the blonde? The one with the foreign accent? I don't think she came to the hospital with us.'

The blind man nodded. 'You're right. She climbed up the embankment whilst the paramedics were checking the baby. Think she got into the car that was idling at the top.'

Mickey noticed the guide dog that lay placidly beside the man and checked his name on her list; Jake Brown. 'I don't mean to be disrespectful, Mr Brown, but I'm wondering how you know this?'

Jake laughed. 'I'm used to people forgetting that sight isn't the only sense we have. The car tooted and seconds later she brushed past me, I smelled her rose perfume. She mumbled sorry and I recognised her accent. She also dislodged some stones as she went.'

Mickey looked at him. 'Well, Sir – that answers that query doesn't it?'

She turned to the others. 'Did any of you notice her going?'

No-one had. 'What about the car, Mr Brown heard. Did any of you see it?'

No one, bar the blind man, seemed to have noticed the foreign woman who'd given her name as Rose English leaving the group and all at once Mickey's sensors were on high alert. The name Rose English was clearly a play on English Rose and was more than likely a false name. She'd get it checked. She'd also get CCTV from Manchester Victoria checked too and any from the Rawsforth area around that time – not that it would do her any good without a make or model for the car, but who knew what would come in handy further down the line? She had a feeling that the train wreck and the idling car were all to do with this mysterious woman, but for now, these witnesses had nothing more to offer. 'Okay, I'll let you get home. Someone will come to take an official statement tomorrow. Just let me check I have your correct details. I have the blonde down here as Rose English, does anyone know if that's right?'

The cocky man in a suit who reeked of aftershave, laughed. According to Mickey's list, his name was Mike Borthwick. 'Well, *that's* not the name she gave *me* on the train.'

'No? What name did she give you Mr Borthwick?'

'Izzie. That's what she told me her name was. Stuck up cow!'

Having had her fill of testosterone-loaded males for one day, Mickey could sympathise with the missing woman if this tosser was bothering her. She frowned and put an asterisk next to Rose English's name and wished that Rawsforth Moor had some semblance of ANPR coverage. She was really interested in the car that was idling at the top of the embankment so soon after the train crash. The death of the train driver made this a murder investigation, despite Hawes' hopes of a juicy terrorist incident landing in his lap. Still, wasn't really in her remit though. The only tangible link to Vice was the drug haul in the boot of the car and murder trumped Vice every time.

Mickey was reluctant to pass this over to the anti-terrorist unit just yet and wondered if she could pull a few strings to get Gus McGuire on the case. She'd been impressed by how he'd handled himself when they'd worked together before Christmas. Shame how that whole thing panned out for him and his team though. Anyway, as far as she could see, Hawes had even less claim on this case than she did. Besides, her interest was piqued now and if you couldn't follow your gut as a DCI, then when the hell could you? She'd stick with this one for a while.

Chapter 5

Hospital radio was getting on Alice's nerves – cheesy songs intermingled with doom and gloom reports about the supposed Beast from the East – like it was going to come to much.

'Now to take your mind off the reports from the Met office that the

UK is set to receive the worst weather in decades here's Cliff Richard

and 'Summer Holiday' to keep you thinking past the storm.'

Idiot – half the people in this joint wouldn't bloody make it till supper time, never mind summer time.

Alice sensed his presence at the door before he'd even pushed it open. She'd been preparing herself for this. It had been inevitable that Gus, her knight in shining armour, would hot-foot it down to Surrey as soon as he heard about her change of plea. She'd managed to convince Nancy to keep him away in the aftermath of the attack, pleading fatigue and pain. Now she'd have to face the music and, somehow, she'd have to convince him to back off. She'd have to persuade the man she loved like a brother that she'd betrayed his trust. It was *that* single thought that pierced her heart. By the end of this visit, Gus would believe she was a dirty cop. Worse even than Knowles. She had no choice at all, so she hardened her heart and stripped her face of all emotion as she heard the door click shut behind him and his feet padding across the room.

He sounded pissed off when he spoke to the prison officer. 'Take a break.'

The gap between 'a' and 'break', she suspected, would have been filled by the 'f' word, had he not got his I'm-in-control voice on. *Oh Gus, what the hell am I doing to you?*

The officer, who'd sat in the chair at the end of the bed for the past two hours, picking her teeth and farting, got up without uttering a word and left the room, slamming the door behind her.

Gus' loudly uttered 'Tosser' almost brought a smile to her lips, but the stakes were too high.

'Stop pretending I'm not here, Alice. I saw your hand move when the door opened. You're such a crap actor. Look at me and tell me what the *fuck's* going on.'

Alice turned her head, her mouth curled in a snarl and said, 'No, 'how are yous?' Or 'Oh, Alice, what have they done to yous?" She clipped her words, making her tone harsh and waited for him to flinch at her abrasiveness. Instead, he snorted before grabbing one of the plastic chairs and flipping it round. Straddling it, he leant his arms across the back like she'd seen him do so often at The Fort.

She narrowed her eyes. '*So*, Gus has grown some balls, has he?' She'd expected him to be in bits. Easy to manipulate, easy to convince. But here he was, emotionless and looking at her as if she was a mutated specimen in a jar. If she wasn't careful he'd end up turning the tables on her and getting beneath *her* defences. She'd have to show no weakness. She cast her mind back to that night in the showers and Baby Jane's words. That memory was all she needed to keep her focused. Gus could throw what the hell he liked at her but she would hold her own. The alternative was too horrible to contemplate.

'Fuck's sake, Al. Give it a break, eh? What's with the 'Gus has found his balls' crap? You're not in prison now. No bloody red-haired Boudica in a hoodie to intimidate you, no damn dodgy prison officer to turn a blind eye.'

She turned her face away from him, raised her hand and mock yawned, 'Blah, blah, blah.'

Gus jumped up scraping the chair across the floor, 'Don't be an arse, Al. It's just you and me and I want to know why the fuck you've changed your damn plea. You know that idiot Kennedy's swanning about Brent like he's Nigel Farage in a brewery? *You're* letting him get away with it.'

This was so hard – so damn hard, yet it had to be done. She *had* to convince him. 'I'm doing fuck all Gus, that's what I'm doing.'

'Aw, come on Alice, you – if anyone – knows how many deaths he caused. How many weapons he put in the hands of kids in the borough. How many drugs he let filter through his fingers and up the noses of addicts. Where the hell is the Alice I know? The one Sampson looked up to, the one who kept us all together?'

Frowning, Alice bit her lip. *This was harder than she'd expected.* The monitor beside her beeped, showing her heart rate had increased. She took a deep breath and prepared her next blow. 'Ouch! That hurt!' She lifted her hands and, despite the oxygen monitor clipped to the middle finger of her right hand, gave a slow hand clap. 'Good try! Got the emotional lever in by mentioning Sampson.' She snorted. 'Truth is *he* was a stupid arse who should have had more sense than to go into a burning building. Glad I don't have to rely on him to watch my back anymore. Tosser, that's all he was.' As the words left her mouth, her soul shrivelled, each word a drop of salt on a slug's back.

Brow furrowed, Gus' eyes sparked that deep blue that told her he was only just holding onto his temper. 'Bitch! That was below the belt, Al.'

Good, she was getting to him! But all she wanted to do was to end it so she could curl up and weep. Ignoring the ice that encapsulated her heart, its deadly fronds gripping tighter and tighter, squashing it like an overripe peach, she forced a laugh. As she did so, the final piece of humanity left her. 'You don't fucking get it, do you? Sean's innocent. It wasn't him that was dealing with Big H and the others, it was me. Sean was *my* patsy, not the other way around. My only regret is that I didn't finish him off when I had the chance. Should have slit his throat there and then and I could've been off in the Bahamas sunning it instead of having to bide my time working with you. Now I'm banged up waiting for the next attack.'

Gus punched the wall, 'Stop it, Al – just fucking stop it.'

But she kept on – she had to. '*That's* why I've agreed to a plea bargain. Can't risk the next attack being fatal. Nah, this way I get eight years in a low security prison where *I* can be the big fish. A few years off for good behaviour and I'll soon be out. Meanwhile, poor innocent Sean has his life back. Win-win situation, what d'ya think?'

Alice's chest tightened as his eyes raked her face. If he continued for even one more second, she would explode. The struggle to keep her face screwed into a bitter gourd, was facilitated only by the thought that Sean Kennedy had, yet again, royally screwed her. Gus, razor sharp eyes ripping her to shreds, swivelled on one foot and without saying another word, walked out of the room.

Alice counted to one hundred in her head until, sure that he'd gone, relaxed her shoulders, dipped her head onto the pillow away from the door and wept. She was on her own.

Every conceivable bridge well and truly incinerated.

Chapter 6

'The Beast from the East is breezing in across the South, threatening major disruptions to our roads and transport systems. The Met Office has issued an amber weather alert throughout the country. With me is Reverend Charles Abernethy from St Augustine's Church in Woking. He and his parishioners are kitting out the church with camp beds and blankets in preparation for the storm. Tell me, how can our listeners help?'

'Well, this sort of weather is a real threat to the rough sleepers in our cities and St Augustine's is opening its doors. Any donations of tinned foods, blankets or warm clothes will be gratefully received.'

'If you've just tuned in, that was the Reverend Abernethy from St Augustine's in Woking, asking for...'

The one thing about looking the way Sean did was that nobody meddled with him. Even the taxi driver couldn't quite meet his eye. Probably thought he had some contagious disease or other.

'So, it looks like we're going to see worsening conditions over the weekend. Surrey Borough Council have sanctioned extra gritting and snowploughs to be on standby. Keep safe and don't travel unless you have to. This is Jake Reynolds signing out for BBC Radio Surrey.'

Sean paid the driver and stepped out onto a pavement that was becoming whiter as the snow flurries grew heavier. *Damn weather better not scupper my plans for the next few days.* He looked up at the posh, yet discreet, sign above the door of the solicitor's office and, taking a step forward, pushed the door open. Not ten minutes from his old stomping ground in Brent, Sean was all too aware that he was the last sort of visitor this solicitor's office was used to.

The receptionist was eating lunch at her desk when he entered. In a flash of varnished talons, she hurriedly shoved her sandwich down and looked up. Her smile faded as soon as she clocked him. Sean was amused to see her hand darting underneath the desk, presumably to hit the hidden panic button. Sauntering up to the heavy wooden desk, Sean leaned right over so he could get a fair old eyeful of her tits. Her warm breath, with a hint of garlic, filled the narrow space. He stared straight at her and employed his 'you better be scared of me, bitch' look, grinning when she rolled her chair back till it hit the wall. The pulse at her neck bounced into overdrive like a kitten's erratic heart beat seconds before you squash the life out of it. A wave of Dolce and Gabanna perfume wafted towards him. Swallowing, her eyes grew wide. He raised his index finger and reached over towards her face. Her pupils dilated even more and she swallowed again. He touched it to her face, right next to her lipsticked mouth – light and gentle. He removed it and, inserting it into his own mouth, he sucked, his gaze fixed on hers, 'Crumb… on your lip.' The woman flushed, her hand flying up to wipe her mouth and Sean grinned. 'Got an appointment with Russell Allison-Hinton. Give him a buzz, would you, darling?'

The receptionist blinked, mouth half-open. She flicked a glance, at the huge leather-bound appointment book and released an audible breath. Shoulders slumped, her voice held a slight tremor when she replied, 'Ah, you're Mr Kennedy?' Her eyes darted everywhere but at Sean. 'I'll just let Mr Allison-Hinton know you're here. Would you like a drink while you wait?'

Got you rattled, darling, haven't I? Sean stepped back from the desk, as he shook his head. 'No drink. I'll just wait over here.' He lowered himself into one of the huge mahogany-coloured leather chairs in the large waiting area. Allison-Hinton & Crouch were nothing if not ostentatious and *that* was exactly why Sean had chosen them... well, that and the fact that Allison-Hinton had a few secrets he'd rather Sean kept to himself. Poor bugger had sat pretty for the past year whilst Sean was in his coma. Probably rubbed his hands in glee when the prognosis came that he'd never wake. Well, he'd shown them all the power of Sean, hadn't he? Took more than a knock on the head from that little bitch to keep *him* down.

Every morning when he looked in the mirror he saw what the last year had done to him. What The Bitch had turned him into. His face held the unhealthy pallor of a corpse. He'd developed alopecia which meant his hair tufted out from his scalp in thin colourless clumps. He was working on building up his body strength, but he still had no meat on his bones, no muscle and even his new clothes hung on his emaciated frame. The worst thing though, was that he couldn't even manage a wank, never mind a shag, without a dose of Viagra. Even then, he could barely breathe. Not sure the momentary enjoyment was worth the toll it took on his body. Alice Cooper had a lot to answer for and *he* would make damn sure she'd pay.

He looked round the reception area, breathing in the wealth. Deep piled carpets, sturdy furniture, paintings no doubt done by the latest up-and-coming young artist. He knew Allison-Hinton's kids attended Harrow, ten minutes down the road from his gaff. The solicitor's boys spoke a different language with their pretentious straw boaters perched on their entitled little heads. Yes, Allison-Hinton, with his posh double-barrelled name, had done alright for himself. If he wanted it to stay that way, he'd toe the line and do *everything* Sean expected.

A door to the right opened and Russell Allison-Hinton appeared. A big man full of bonhomie and shit. He crossed the deep carpet, hand extended to greet Sean – a hearty smile on his face. 'Good to see you, Sean. Good to see you. You're looking well.'

At that moment Sean wished he had the strength to floor the man. Rubbing it in, ramming his virility down his throat – not literally of course. Allison-Hinton might like a bit of brawn, but not Sean. He couldn't stand poofs.

He followed the older man into his office, winking salaciously at the receptionist as he went. A smile fluttered around her mouth before scurrying away, like a mouse with a vulture on its case.

The solicitor's office was more of the same – magnolia walls and a cream carpet with heavy wood furniture and a faint tang of lemon hanging in the air. His desk was larger than the skivvy's one outside – *probably all about exerting his masculinity.* He might be a poof with dubious fetishes, but he was also a man to be reckoned with. That didn't matter to Sean, he couldn't care less what size the solicitor's desk was, as long as he could deliver the goods. And the goods, as far as Sean was concerned, were Alice Cooper's tits in a vice. Remembering *exactly* what had already happened to one of Alice's tits, he smiled and sat down on a large leather armchair with wings flying off either side. It was surprisingly comfy, and Sean was relieved. With little flesh padding his bones, he couldn't often settle into a seated position. The last thing he wanted to be doing during this meeting was fidget.

'Well?' Sean left the word hanging there, his eyes intent on the solicitor's face.

The other man's face broke into a wide smile. 'She agreed. Baby Jane's final bit of persuasion did the trick. She's signed the statement claiming responsibility for everything and exonerating you from all wrong doing. *That* combined with Big H's statement and the electronic trail we've laid, will let you off the hook and confine her to a long stay at Her Majesty's convenience.'

Sean grinned. He'd been expecting this, but it was good to have confirmation... and of course a signature. He leaned back and nodded. 'Now, we need to get her parents.'

Allison-Hinton frowned, 'What? But... I thought...?'

'Yeah, that's what Alice Cooper thought too. That's why she signed the statement. Stupid bitch! She should've known I'd go straight for the jugular. She has to suffer. And there's only one sure way to do that.'

Chapter 7

19:15 Marriners Drive

Gus was grateful that his flight back from Surrey had, despite the weather, been uneventful. He'd had more than enough to ponder. Seeing Alice so angry had shaken him. The exterior she'd cultivated, so hard and brittle, frightened him. This wasn't the Alice he knew. Her words were harsh and her demeanour even harsher. It was as if she'd crossed a barrier and there was no going back. Maybe she'd crossed it a long time ago. Maybe she'd crossed it in a cellar in Brent when Sean Kennedy got injured – or maybe even before that? Thrusting those thoughts to the back of his mind, he towel-dried his hair and walked out of the en suite into his bedroom.

What to wear? Opening his drawer, he settled for a crumpled looking Bob Marley T-shirt. The passing thought that he was becoming more and more like Compo as the days passed made him smile. Compo, the team's computer geek, had been wearing a Noddy Holder 'It's Christmas!' T-shirt this morning when Gus had left the office to head to Surrey. He hadn't the heart to point out that Christmas was long gone.

The smell of chicken tikka masala drifted towards him as he came downstairs. Patti, no doubt, was attempting to surpass him again in the cooking arena. *No damn chance!* She wasn't a bad cook, unlike his mum, but no way was she in *his* league in the curry department. Snatches of a weather report drifted through from the kitchen – *'batten down the hatches'* and *'Amber alert'* made him grimace. *When was this damn weather going to blow over?* Continuing through the living room, he whistled to his canary – Ringo – who puffed up her chest and whistled back, hopping from perch to perch as Gus took a moment to reposition her cuttlefish. *If only his life was as simple.*

Pasting on a smile, he walked into the kitchen and took a moment to watch Patti at work. He had much to be grateful to her for and he suspected she was, in the main, responsible for whatever sanity he still had. He smiled, conscious that she was aware of just how much the visit to Alice had taken out of him. On his return home, he'd had to shut the curtains and lie down for an hour to get rid of his headache.

She gave an exaggerated sigh, thrust out her hip and rested one hand on it. She pointed to the simmering pot on the cooker. 'This one's my best yet, McGuire. Jealous?'

Despite himself, Gus laughed, 'I know I've said it before and I'll probably say it again, but… in your dreams.'

The snort that left her mouth, like the stained butcher's apron she wore, was an inelegant contrast to her stylish tailored trousers and blouse and perfectly made up face. 'I reiterate – jealous! Now, are you going to tell me what happened today or not?'

Gus wound his arms round her middle and nuzzled her neck, breathing in the scent of the floral perfume she always wore. 'Not. I'll deal with this shit on my own.'

Patti tilted her head to one side to give him better access to her neck. 'I'd much rather deal with the Alice aspect of 'your shit' than the Gabriella/ Katie aspect. I actually like Alice and want to help if I can.'

She matched his height almost perfectly. She was beautiful, she was tough and *he* was scared to admit to himself – never mind her – that he was in danger of falling for her – big time. It pissed him off that his ex-wife was a bitch to her. Despite being in a relationship with his sister, Katie, Gabriella seemed to have taken on the role of Gus' protector and treated Patti like some sort of heartbreaker. Gus suspected that her antipathy was fuelled more by jealousy at how well Patti got on with Katie, than a desire to protect Gus' heart. After all, Gabriella had been quick to hot foot it off the sinking ship when he needed her most. He'd still been in trauma after being forced to kill his best friend in self-defence. *And* she hadn't been too bothered about his emotional state when she'd run off with his sister, had she? Anyway, now wasn't the time to think about his sister and his ex-wife.

Pulling away from him, Patti reached out a hand and ran her finger across the Bob Marley tattoo that adorned his bicep and nodded towards his matching T-shirt. 'You going with a theme tonight?'

Gus grinned. 'Mo, unlike some, will appreciate my sartorial efforts.'

Patti tutted and turned to stir the rice just as the doorbell rang, 'And you take *that* as a commendation from a man who spends most of his day in a pinny and the rest of the time in joggers and a sweatshirt? Sad… very sad.'

Humming, *every little thing's gonna be alright* under his breath – more in an effort to reassure himself than through any actual conviction – Gus walked out of the kitchen and through the living room into the hallway. Before opening the door, he took a deep breath to calm himself. Dr Mahmood would be proud of him, well, she would be if he didn't mention the tension headache tautening his forehead like self-inflicted Botox… or the sporadic galloping heartbeats… or the night sweats… or the insomnia. *Yeah, dead bloody proud!*

Forcing a smile to his lips, he flung the door open and ushered his best friend Mo and his wife Naila inside. Naila's face was flushed and she made a pretty picture with her long black hair escaping her woolly bobble hat. Muffled up in a bright red coat, with a matching scarf and with hiking boots on her feet, she was well prepared for The Beast from the East. Gus smiled when a quick glance at Mo confirmed Patti's point – Mo was indeed wearing jogging bottoms and a hoodie underneath a fisherman's jacket that matched the one that hung in Gus' under-stair-cupboard.

'We walked through the park. Snow's well and truly drifting now. When's this nightmare going to end?' Naila thrust a bottle of wine and a carton of Rubicon mango at Gus and began peeling off her coat.

Mo mumbled under his breath about wimpy Brits and how a little bit of snow brought everything to a standstill. The normality of the situation loosened the tightness in Gus' chest and his shoulders relaxed. He noticed the decided chill in the air that was nothing to do with external temperatures. 'Okay, you two... what's up? Mo been farting inappropriately again?'

Naila screwed up her mouth in a look that Gus was all too familiar with and jerked her thumb towards her husband. 'Ask *him*! He's the one that has to blow up *every* situation into a massive event. Mr Mountains and bloody Molehills, that's him.'

Gus looked at Mo, whose shoulders had slumped, and then back to Naila. It didn't take a genius to work out they'd had yet another falling out. 'Zarqa, I take it? What's my favourite oldest god-daughter done now?'

Zarqa was finding things tough at the minute and had started to ask difficult questions of her parents. Questions that Mo didn't want to address. The problem was, Mo and Naila had very different approaches to dealing with this particular issue. The strain of dealing with a hormonal teenager who was demanding they confront their pasts and reveal something they wanted to put behind them, was taking its toll on his friends. So it was no surprise when Mo's reply exploded from his mouth like projectile vomit.

'Tattoo!' and was accompanied by Naila's exaggerated sigh.

Patti, no doubt wondering what was taking them so long to come into the kitchen, sauntered through. As if sensing the atmosphere, she glanced at Gus, one eyebrow raised. Whatever greeting was on her lips stayed there as she took in the pugilistic stance of their friends.

'Tattoo?' Patti's tone was hesitant, yet curious.

Naila tutted and turned to Patti, hands outstretched, 'I told him to shut up about it tonight, but *no*. He can't keep his big mouth shut for a minute, can he?'

Mo turned to Gus, traces of the sulky schoolboy he'd once been, bringing a slight smile to Gus' lips despite the strained atmosphere. 'She's gone and got a bloody tattoo. Used fake ID and got a damn tattoo – on her wrist.'

Gus bit his lip. *Hadn't Mo done the exact same thing at sixteen?*

'Oh, good one Mo. That's right tell the copper that our daughter got an illegal tattoo.'

Mo turned and glared at her, 'What? You think Gus is going to hot foot it through the damn snow to drag his god-daughter off to The Fort for a major interrogation over a bloody fake ID, do you?'

Gus closed his eyes for a second. Tried to do the counting thing his psychiatrist had taught him, but gave up at five. By the time he reopened his eyes, the familiar gurgle of angry venom had wormed up from his stomach into his chest and erupted, 'For fuck's sake, you two need to sort this out. It's getting beyond a damn joke. It's been months since she first asked you and you're still behaving like a couple of school kids. She's in pain and she's confused and she needs you two to be honest with her.' He pointed his finger first at Naila and then at Mo. 'So man the fuck up and behave like parents.'

The only sound to be heard in the aftermath of Gus' words was the faint tinkle of Ringo's toy bell being pecked followed by her own answering cheep. Realising his hands were shaking, Gus shoved the wine and juice carton into Patti's hands and lowered his tone. 'I know this isn't easy for you, but you've had sixteen years to prepare for this day. It was always going to have to be addressed, you *knew* that.' He reached out his arms and put one round each of his friends and pulled them into his embrace, 'I love you, but you're tearing each other apart and that's *not* you. You need to sort this. Go and see the counsellor Dr Mahmood recommended.' He sighed, 'I know I'm not the best example, but even I get that letting things fester is destructive. You two mean too much to me to let that happen, so for God's sake, get yourselves an appointment and start the healing process.'

Tears glinting in her eyes, Naila hugged Gus and turned to her husband and hugged him too. 'He's right, Mo. We need to work out a way forward and we need to put Zarqa's needs first.'

Mo kissed her hair, and looking over her head as he held her, he nodded at Gus.

'Well, if we're not all hungry after that little scene, I'll be damned.' said Patti

Mo rubbed his hands together, 'Chicken tikka masala? Hope *you* cooked, Patti. Gus never gets the spices just right.'

Gus punched him on the arm and, just like that, the tension evaporated.

Hours later, stomachs full, the quartet retired to the living room for coffee. The wine had relaxed Gus and, in good company, he had managed to put all thoughts of Alice to the back of his mind. Mo had teased him about his Bob Marley tattoo and mimicked his gasps and 'wimpish' cries during the process, much to the enjoyment of Naila and Patti. Gus, despite his denials, took it all in good spirit and laid in with some bittersweet, shared stories from his, Mo and Greg's schooldays. The painting of Bob Marley done by Greg, in pride of place above the stove, made him feel close to his dead friend and he suspected Mo felt the same. Mind you, Mo didn't carry the baggage regarding Greg that Gus did. Mo hadn't been the one to see Greg kill his wife and son. Mo hadn't been the one who killed his best friend in order to save his own life. And Mo didn't carry that sense of failure with him every single day.

'So, Patti' asked Naila, 'Weren't you invited to the big hen do?'

Patti's face scrunched up. She was sitting on the sofa, opposite Gus. Gus grinned, eager to hear Patti's response. After their earlier conversation about Gabriella, he suspected her reply would be pithy, to say the least. He was right.

'That stupid, rude, jealous, conniving bitch didn't invite me.'

Naila flicked a glance at Gus as if to ask, 'Have I opened up a can of worms?' Gus responded with a wave of his hand, 'Just let Patti get it *all* off her chest.'

'Katie invited me, assuming, no doubt that her paranoid, possessive other half would share the details with me... and did she?' Patti's glare was poisonous. 'Did she heck as like? Stupid cow conveniently missed me off the email thread. Not that I was bothered. Last thing I wanted to do was head over to Dublin with Gabriella the Gross and her nervy sister-in-law-to-be for a weekend. Katie, I don't mind. She can be fun when she's not influenced by Gabriella.'

Nodding, Naila stoked the flames of Patti's ire, 'Don't know why Gabriella was organising it anyway. She's only just met the girl, hasn't she?'

'Exactly what I said.' Patti turned a triumphant pout in Gus' direction, 'Didn't I say that, Gus?' Not waiting to acknowledge Gus' nod, she continued, 'Truth is, Gabriella barely knows her. She's doing it for her brother and trying to rope us all in too. It's as if the fiancée doesn't have any friends of her own. Mind you, in fairness, she seems alright. Brainy too. Most of her friends are probably in Cyprus, so she won't know many people in the UK.'

Naila turned to Gus, 'You got Daniel's stag do all planned, have you?'

Gus had been putting it off for days now. Partly because he'd been so busy and partly because he couldn't be arsed. 'Eh – sort of.'

Patti laughed and punched him on the arm, 'Liar! You haven't even thought about it, have you? Come on admit it.'

Gus glanced at Mo for help, but Mo just raised an eyebrow and shook his head. It looked like he was on his own with this one.

'Isn't it tomorrow, Gus?' Naila looked at Mo, 'Didn't you tell me it was tomorrow?'

Mo, looking too bloody angelic to be believable, nodded, 'Yeah, I've been on at him for ages to sort it out, but...' he splayed his hands before him and shrugged. Gus glared at him. Flung to the damn lionesses. *Some friend you are.*

'Calm down, calm down,' said Gus improvising, 'I've got a venue lined up. Daniel will love it. It's right up his street'

Patti and Mo simultaneously looked at him, eyebrows raised, 'Oh, where?'

'Well, em.' Clutching at straws he blurted out, 'The Delius.'

Patti began to laugh, 'You're having Daniel's stag do at The Delius? Are you bloody mad? Gabriella will kill you? I *love* it!'

Naila frowned at Patti, 'Don't be mean Patti. We can't let him have it there. Not at the club belonging to a known gang leader.'

'Aw, come on Naila, Shahid's toned down his gangster lifestyle,' said Mo. 'He doesn't pimp anymore and I've heard he sold out his illegal trade to some thugs from Manchester. Think he only uses the club for money laundering now.'

'Oh, so that's okay, is it? Money laundering? Oh well, if *that's* all it is, then that's fine. Naila uncrossed her legs and pulled away from Mo, 'And because *he's* stopped exploiting women, the problem's gone away has it? Don't bloody think so. All he's done is move it elsewhere. Given some other tosser the power. Not bloody good enough. Gus, you shouldn't be supporting that sort of trash.' Naila's face was flushed, her fists clenched tight on her thighs.

'Hey wait a minute, Naila. I'm not supporting Shahid. He passed the Delius over to Imti and Imti doesn't stand for any of that shit. It's not being used for laundering – not any more. He and Serafina are making a go of it and it does a lot of good in the Thornbury community.'

Patti squeezed her friend's hand. 'He's right Naila. Imti's doing a great job. He's not crooked.'

Naila took a deep breath, cheeks pink, eyes flashing. 'I'm sorry Gus.'

Pouring her another soft drink, Gus squeezed her arm.

She smiled, 'Anyway, so who, apart from Mo, have you invited?'

Making a mental note to give Imti a ring in the morning, Gus shrugged. 'Just a few mates, you know?'

Patti's eyes narrowed. 'Which mates?'

'Well…'

'You've not invited anyone, have you? What sort of stag do will that be with you three standing about like a trio of lemons. God's sake Gus. The man deserves a decent stag do.'

Well, why doesn't he invite some friends of his own? 'I *have* invited folk…' Gus, despite being well aware that he was fooling no-one, refused to back down. Racking his brains, he came up with a solution, 'Compo and Taffy…'

Patti snorted in that inelegant way she did to show her disbelief.

He scratted around in his mental address book before plucking a final name from the air, 'Dad… he's coming too.'

Patti and Naila looked at each other before bursting out laughing. Holding her sides, Naila said, 'You've really pulled the stops out, Gus. You, Mo, Compo, Taffy and your Dad at The Delius… classy, very classy.'

'I didn't want to have to organise the damn thing in the first place, did I?' said Gus.

At the same time Mo, seemingly realising the implications of his wife's statement, folded his arms over his chest, 'Don't know what you're on about Nail, Daniel will be lucky to spend his stag do with us. Scintillating conversation, wit and humour. We'll take him for a curry too, won't we, Gus? What more could he want?'

Patti snorted, 'Something with a modicum of panache perhaps, rather than the quintet of farce. After all he's a bit more upmarket than you two.'

"Phew." Gus was indignant, "How can a guy who spends his time rummaging about in dirt be more upmarket than us?"

Patti and Naila exchanged glances and laughed. 'Shall we tell him?'

Acting like a pair of bloody schoolkids! Gus snorted, "Come on spit it out?

"He's hot, Gus. Really hot." Patti's eyes twinkled, "And he's all exotic."

"And he's an archaeologist – Indiana Jones and all that."

"What and Mo and I are just Northern parkins?"

Naila prodded Mo's stomach, "Well, maybe a bit more of a fat rascal than a parkin for one of you"

Realising they were beaten, Gus summoned Mo to the kitchen, ignoring the peals of laughter that followed him.

'How did it go with Alice today?' asked Mo. 'Is she bearing up?'

Gus studied his wine glass for a long time. Not raising his head, he shrugged. The words were difficult to say, but he'd no intention of lying to his friend. Mo knew him too well anyway. He'd spot deceit in an instant. 'She's not the Alice we knew, Mo. Prison has changed her.'

Saturday

Chapter 8

10:00 The Fort

Gus woke up to a six-inch-deep blanket of snow and a headache. He popped a pill and wished he could put his jogging kit on and run it off, but if the forecast was to be believed, he wouldn't be jogging for at least a few more days. He'd left Patti in bed nursing a slight hangover and walked through Lister Park to work. The lake was covered in ice topped by a layer of snow and he wondered how long it would be till someone tried to skate on it. The tracks round the park told him some dog-walkers had been out before him. Despite the chilly air, the park was busy – kids making snowmen or sledging or having snowball fights, but even so, Gus was distracted by his thoughts. Alice, and the way she'd behaved the previous day, haunted him. Had the things she'd claimed been true? Surely not. Could she have duped him like that for so long? It didn't seem likely, yet Gus had come across more than his fair share of corrupt coppers. The bottom line was, why would she lie? Her defence team was prepared to fight and they were still looking for evidence to exonerate her. It wasn't just her plea change or her big talk about Sean Kennedy being her patsy, it was what he'd seen in her eyes. Something was missing – like a piece of her soul had been ripped out and sold to the devil.

True, she'd been through the mill. The latest attack was by far the worst she'd suffered, but it wasn't the only one. Soon as they'd sussed she was a copper, some of the other women had targeted her. Not knowing when the next attack would happen would be enough to send most women loopy – but Alice? He wasn't looking forward to sharing this with Nancy and his team.

As soon as he walked into her office, DCI Nancy Chalmers got straight to the point. 'So, how did it go?'

The cinnamon and apple candle and the over-strong aroma of coffee made Gus want to fling open a window regardless of the blizzard that howled outside. Instead, he settled for walking over to the coffee table and blowing out the flame before settling himself on the leather armchair next to it. Nancy frowned, but said nothing. Instead, she stood up, walked from behind her desk and poured him a mug of treacly coffee that she deposited on a coaster beside him. Long legs outstretched, he slouched in the chair and watched as Nancy resumed her position behind her desk. He waited till she'd slipped off her slippers and pushed her chair out far enough to enable her to rest her ankles on her desk. He remembered a time, not so long ago, when he'd find the ladder in her stocking amusing. Life, however, had inured him to the amusing aspects of Nancy's idiosyncrasies and what was worse was that he didn't even care. Since Sampson's death and Alice's incarceration, he'd lost something... was it his humanity?

He put that thought away for another day over a large glass of whisky when he was alone in his living room with Greg's Bob Marley painting. Then, he could share his thoughts with his dead friend. It was the closest he ever got to feeling something... anything... these days. Well, except when he was with Patti. Not that he told her, though. No, that would be too dangerous.

'Gus?'

Nancy's tone was sharp and told Gus he'd delayed answering her earlier enquiry for too long. He shrugged. What was he supposed to tell her? That Alice had become a monster? A parody of one of those American actresses on '*Orange is the New Black*', all swearing and swagger?

'Gus!'

He sighed again and lifted his mug to his lips, knowing full well he was playing for time. Why had he agreed to come in today? He could have delayed it till Monday. It was his weekend off after all. *Should've put my foot down.* The truth was, he'd nowhere else to go. Patti was visiting friends later and his mum was too damn perceptive for her own good, so he'd vetoed a parental visit. If his mum hadn't dognapped Bingo for the weekend, he'd have gone up to the Cow and Calf rocks in the snow with him, spent the afternoon knackering himself hiking and rounding it off with a pint or two before heading home to a takeaway and The Voice. Bingo liked Will.I.Am.

Just as Nancy was about to repeat his name for the third time, he put his cup down and jumped to his feet, raking his fingers through his dreads as he did so. 'She's a damn mess, Nancy. Pale and weak as shit. If she was vertical, I could blow her over with one puff. She's hacked her hair into a buzzcut and she's clearly in pain.'

Nancy's lips tightened and she clasped her fingers together, tapping them lightly against her chin as she thought. Finally, 'And the rest?'

Gus paused in his pacing and shook his head. 'Still insistent. Hard as nails. Never seen her like this. Glad I didn't let Compo come with me. He's going to be devastated when I tell him.' He raked both hands in his dreads and groaned, 'Think we need to face it Nance. We've lost her.'

Chapter 9

DCI Mickey Swanson paced her office. The powers that be had decided to leave DCI Hawes in charge of the Rawsforth train wreck and she was furious. Her boss had hinted that it was to keep Hawes out of the hair of the 'real' anti-terrorist team, who had inherited him on job experience initiative for two months and considered him a liability. If there was one thing that pissed Mickey off more than any other, it was pandering to male incompetence. If Hawes wasn't able to pull his weight, then damn well tell him and confine him to a desk. Why should he take her job from her? Well, okay, the train crash wasn't strictly speaking *her* job either, but at least she was keen to look into it properly. Paddy Toner's family deserved that, didn't they? Besides, it was quiet in Vice at the minute. Her team were on top of everything and, if she was honest, she felt redundant. Not for the first time did she wish she'd stuck at DI. Desk jobs weren't really her thing. She craved the excitement of moving about, being on the street, responding to things with more than a click of her finger on the 'send' button of an email that more often than not bounced back anyway.

She had a feeling about the Rawsforth thing. Not some abstract Ouija board feeling – but one based on over twenty years of experience. The disappearing foreign woman, the idling car, the false name, they all pointed to a link to the vehicle on the level crossing, but DCI Hawes saw it differently. He'd told her she was letting her imagination run away with her. *Cheeky bastard!* She flung herself down on her seat and pressed the intercom, not for the first time that morning. 'Is that footage here yet?'

The paramedics had arrived within half an hour of the first phone call – a miracle really – but they'd been in the area. They took the names of the passengers, false ones included, yet by the time the officer had been free to take their initial on-scene-statements – a mere half hour later – Rose English AKA Izzie, had vanished. Mickey had access to the initial passenger statements and she had her own notes. What she needed now was access to the statements from other possible witnesses; passers-by, other drivers, cyclists. She needed to find out where that woman had gone.

A few things from the first statements had caught her attention. One was the false name, the other was the way the other passengers had said she kept looking around her. Little darting glances – definitely edgy. Macho man Mike had said she was rude to him, but both Jess – the teacher – and Jake – the blind man – had said he was annoying the girl. Mickey was curious to see what her demeanour had been like at Manchester Victoria station.

The door burst open and a uniformed officer strode into the office, face flushed, carrying a USB stick in one hand and with a file tucked under her other arm. 'Got the CCTV footage you wanted, Ma'am.' She slammed the door behind her and lowered her voice. 'Kept it on the QT like,' she said, tapping her index finger on the side of her nose.

Mickey sighed. *Why did everybody have to be so bloody melodramatic? You'd think they'd knock that out of them at training. Not like they were working on an episode of Line of Duty was it?* She pointed to her computer, 'Have at it.'

Within seconds, Mickey was looking at a nervous young woman in her late twenties, walking through Manchester

Victoria station to the ticket machines. 'She paid for that ticket by card. You've got the transaction time – get the details for me.'

The officer noted Mickey's instructions in a notebook and Mickey sighed, 'I mean *now*. Right now. Chop bloody chop. We've a missing woman to find.' *Where was the bloody melodrama when you needed it? That was the problem with today's PCs – they were inconsistent.* As the officer, red faced and tight-lipped, turned away to set the search in motion, Mickey paused the recording and zoomed in to the bridge overlooking the machines. Five people were lined up along it seemingly observing the concourse below. Were they looking for their missing woman? Maybe, maybe not, but it was certainly an option. One that needed following up. She waited till the PC, Afzal, if she remembered rightly, turned back to the screen before saying, 'See if you can ID any of them. Get IT to help you. I want their movements traced to see if they followed her.' When the PC got on her phone promptly, Mickey allowed herself a small smile. *Training, that's all that was needed, proper on the job training without pussyfooting around with all the time-wasting niceties. Afzal would make a good copper in the end.*

Mickey zoomed in to the concourse and to the people milling around. 'Get the tech team to do facial recognition too. I want to know if any of them followed her to the platform and got on the cross-country train. Also get them to backtrack as far as they can. I want to see where she came from. How did she get to the station? Did she get off a train? Which train? And when?' PC Afzal conveyed the instructions over the phone and all but stood to attention. Mickey nodded at the young woman and, when Afzal was nearly at the door, she said 'Good work, Afzal. We'll make a decent copper of you yet.'

Afzal paused hand on the door and turned back, grinning widely. When she spoke, it was in a firm voice, 'Anwar.'

Mickey frowned. 'Sorry?'

'My name is Anwar. Kaneez Anwar. I answer better to the correct name,' and before Mickey had a chance to respond, she left the room

Mickey grinned, 'Well, I'll be damned. That girl's got balls.' Still smiling she turned back to the screen and replayed the footage. Zeroing in on the woman's face, Mickey saw terror and nervousness. In slow motion, it was clear that her eyes were darting around as if assessing the danger around her. The sooner the techies got back to her the better.

Chapter 10

'*So, amid the chaos caused by The Beast from the East we have a local story that demonstrates one of the benefits of this inclement weather. Police in Keighley attribute the discovery of a major drug haul to the ferocity of the storm. Dense blizzards, freezing temperatures and high snow fall led them to discover a major marijuana production factory that would otherwise have remained hidden. How? – The intense heat from the factory's lights resulted in the snow melting from the roof, causing gutter damage to a neighbouring property. The homeowner fortunately saw the significance of this and contacted the police. As one officer quipped 'The Beast from the East has frozen marijuana distribution in the Bradford district. Beast from the East, One, Bradford drugs gangs, Zero. You're listening to Bradford City Broadcasting in the middle of the storm.'*

The call had come in as Gus and Compo were sharing a bacon butty in the incident room. Well, Gus had one bacon butty, whilst Compo had two – *both* of which were slathered in ketchup, *some* of which had made it onto his Kinks t-shirt and his right cheek. Gus had thought he could use the time since his meeting with Nancy to bring Compo up to date on the situation with Alice. However, every time he opened his mouth to begin, he visualised the look of utter devastation on Compo's face. He didn't want to replicate the despair that had crumpled the lad's face when he'd heard that, as well as losing Sampson, Alice had been imprisoned. The kid had been through enough and it was only in the past couple of weeks that he had seen a slight return to normality for Compo.

Gus could've kissed his mum, who regularly delivered the slightly over-done buns and cookies that Compo so loved. She took the time to talk to him and had invited him over for Sunday lunch with Taffy. Seemed that whether Gus liked it or not, his mum had adopted his team as part of the family. He loved her even more for that. She was a remarkable woman and right now, he wished she was here to soften the blow for Comps or at least to give him one of her comforting hugs.

After discarding many attempts, he'd finally managed to form an opening sentence in his mind. *Compo, we need to talk about Alice.* He tried not to see any similarities between that sentence and the title of a well-known book about a child psychopath, but failed abysmally. *This was shit.* None of those stupid leadership courses prepared you for this.

'You're quiet today.' Compo said, licking the ketchup off his fingers, 'Summat up?'

Just as he opened his mouth, determined to just get the first sentence out, a text came in. *Bloody hell! Why hadn't he switched the damn thing off?* He looked at it and grimaced – *Murder – in this weather – nice!* 'Come on Comps. Got ourselves a crime scene. Dead woman in Keighley.'

Gus mentally abraded himself for his relief at postponing the inevitable 'Alice' discussion with Compo and, to assuage his guilt, threw Compo the keys to his Landover. He steadfastly ignored the niggling voice in his head telling him he would live to regret that decision. 'You can drive.'

As Compo caught the keys in greasy hands, Gus squashed a groan. *Why hadn't he waited till he'd washed his hands?* Seeing the wide grin that lit up his face, Gus sighed. *Fuck's sake, he's like a damn two-year-old on the dodgems.* 'Don't forget your wellies and coat. It's brass monkey weather out there.'

Fifteen minutes later, Compo and Gus were driving – not in his spacious Land Rover – but in Alice's Mini, heading towards Keighley. The radio a gentle accompaniment in the background to Compo's tales about a computer game involving both dragons and aliens and, seemingly, plenty of sound effects – *lovely!*

'...*Blizzard conditions set to hit the North, Yorkshire grit sets in...*'

Gus' lanky frame was squashed into the seat and he thought his knees would seize up if they didn't reach the crime scene soon. Bloody practical jokers in The Fort had noticed his road tax was out of date. *Why the hell did they even bother to check? Yet another bloody thing to think about!*

'... *promise of worsening conditions over the weekend...*'

The buggers had clamped his wheels and ticketed his windscreen, and as a result he'd been forced to use Alice's Mini. She'd left it in his safe keeping when she got arrested before Christmas, but as things had come to light, Gus had deserted the vehicle in the nether regions of the staff car park. Out of sight, out of mind. Now, he'd had no choice but to use it as there had been no pool cars available.

'... *gritters at the ready with the army on standby...*'

What the hell was Compo doing? He's got the wipers on so bloody fast they're more of a hazard than the damn snow. But the lad was in heaven. Gus didn't know whether to be miffed or amused that he seemed to prefer the aubergine Mini with its conspicuous floral adornments to his masculine red Land Rover. 'This car's about as much use as a bloody Tonka Toy,' said Gus, well aware that he sounded petulant. 'We'll get stuck in the snow before we're halfway there. When I get my hands on the idiots that clamped my car, I'll kill them.'

Gus' phone rang – *Gabriella! Again!* Bloody Hell, this was the sixth time already today and he was getting sick of it. He'd get the damn stag party organised, didn't need her nagging him. He ignored the call, realising he'd pay for that decision later.

'*...keep travel to a minimum for...*'

Compo grinned, 'Always wanted to drive Alice's car. Can't believe I'm doing it.' He turned from Oak Lane onto Keighley Road, 'Hey Gus – it might be a Tonka Toy but it's got one significant advantage over the Land Rover.'

'Hmmph, what's that?'

'Valid road tax!' Compo laughed and clicking his fingers, repeated his statement, punctuating each word with a small pause. 'Valid. Bloody. Road. Tax.'

Gus threw him a dirty look and glared out the window, allowing the mesmerising snow to soothe his annoyance. It wasn't Compo's fault that he had been too preoccupied to renew his road tax, but to be honest he couldn't give a rat's arse. Compared to some officers, his transgression was mild.

'*... up to six inches of snowfall...*'

The Mini did surprisingly well, considering the atrocious weather conditions. The snowflakes were huge as Compo pulled off the road into a pub car park just down from the Worth Valley Railway station on Halifax Road. With meticulous care, he parked without mishap between a police car and a large blue Range Rover with a Scottish flag flying from the roof. Whether they'd be able to drive out again was another matter.

Gus took in the Range Rover and groaned, 'Just my luck. We've got my dad to contend with as well as a dead body. I was certain they'd find a different pathologist seeing as the body was located in Keighley.' Gus' dad – Fergus McGuire – insisted on viewing the crime scene and the body in situ if it was a suspected murder. Gus hoped against hope that Fergus would be on his best behaviour, at least he could be reasonably certain he wouldn't be in his kilt – Highland dancing classes were on a Friday!

Damn phone again! Gabriella – God, she really needs to get a life and stop bothering me!

Wishing he'd added an extra jumper under his fisherman's jacket, Gus got out of the car. An immediate chill hit his face and he regretted not picking up his gloves. *Bloody weather.* Just along the road where the Worth Valley Railway station stood, Gus could see the police cordons; fluttering yellow crime scene tape and police cars, all but merging into the snow drifts. On the opposite side of the road stood a neat line of four terraced houses, some of their occupants braving the cold to observe the police activity across the road, others watching from an upstairs window. Not that they could see much – the body was apparently right inside the station, on the concourse.

In his duffle coat, scarf wrapped round his neck in a python grip with a bobble hat replacing his beanie, Compo looked like a human version of Paddington Bear. Now that it was time to view the crime scene Gus became aware of the other man's nervousness. The lad's eyes kept flitting towards the group of officers hanging around near the tape and back to the car as if he'd like nothing better than to hop in it and drive off. 'You'll be right, Comps.'

Compo blinked, his gaze once more across the road. 'You think?'

'Look, it's part of the job, just like any other. Just try to bear that in mind. Come on, let's see what we've got.' Together they trudged through the three-inch snow, Gus conscious of Compo's slowing steps as they got nearer.

Who the hell had braved the Beast from the East in order to either kill someone or to dump a body? Gus grimaced as the icy breeze penetrated his jacket. Not ideal working conditions. Officers blew on their hands, gratefully accepting warm drinks from the owners of nearby houses. They were doing a grand job of keeping the gathering mob of thrill seekers under control and, hopefully, they'd be taking statements as they drank. Hissing

Sid, the head crime scene investigator, was always whinging on about the effects of adverse weather on the state of the crime scene. He wouldn't be a happy bunny. Not with the continuous flurries of snow and the forecast blizzards. It would be a race against time for his team.

Beyond the cordon at the far end of the railway station entrance, were a group of journalists huddled under huge multi-coloured brollies, all looking sorry for themselves. Gus grinned. *Served them right, bloody ghouls that they were!* A figure stepped away from the group and began waving. Gus could just about distinguish Jez Hopkins' way-too-handsome face. Last thing he needed right now was to chat with the damn journalist. Turning away without acknowledging him, he signalled to Compo to join him and the pair of them signed themselves through the outer cordon. Tosser would probably want an update on Alice, and Gus wasn't about to start chatting to him about *that* – no matter how jiggy Alice and he had been after the Weston case last year.

Grabbing a suit and bootees from the box at the side, Gus slipped under the crime scene tape, with Compo following. 'Ready?'

Compo nodded, but Gus could tell from his pallor and the way his eyes darted from side to side, that his officer was anything but fine. 'Look, this is your first crime scene involving a dead person. Be thankful that the weather conditions make it one of the easier scenes to view.'

On cue, Taffy, distinguishable by his walk from the other suited figures that worked the perimeter of the scene, appeared. 'The boss is right, Comps. Imagine if it had been a floater bloater, or a decomposed body in a house with the central heating turned right up or…'

Sure that Taffy was about to reference a fire victim and keen to avoid anything that would bring Sampson's death to mind, Gus interrupted. 'Aw, shut up Taffy. Show a bit of respect here.

We've got a victim who no longer breathes, no longer goes home to her family and no longer enjoys her life. We don't need to go into the nitty gritty of other crime scenes.'

Compo's face blanched even more and Gus cursed himself. Not only had he been too tough on Taffy, but he'd also made it worse for Compo. *Some damn role model he was.* He raked his fingers through his dreads once, sighed and turned away to get into his suit, all too aware of how inadequately he was supporting Compo. When he looked back the lad was ready. With his overall hood tight around his face he looked like a round-faced kid as he said, 'I'm ready, Boss.'

'Course you are.' Gus pulled his own hood up. 'Forget about the body for a minute. Instead, think about *why* we're here, what we're doing. Why we trawl into work. Why we pull all-nighters. Why we don't stop till we've done everything we possibly can.' He waited till Compo nodded before continuing. 'It's for them, isn't it?' He again waited for Compo's nod. 'So, when we go over into the tent, we'll hold it together because it's not about us. It's about them, those we represent. We owe it to *them.*'

Compo exhaled and his lips twitched in a fleeting smile. 'Don't worry Boss. I won't let you down.'

If Alice could see him, she'd be so damn proud of him.

Taffy, wrapped an arm round Compo, 'Course you bloody won't, Bruv. We got this.'

Gus looked at the two DCs and for the first time realised that despite everything they'd gone through before Christmas, his team *could* still hold itself together… even without Alice. He smiled. 'Don't want to interrupt the bromance, but we've got work to do.'

He'd only taken one step through the well-trampled snow, when a familiar ring-tone cut into the cold air.

'Shouldn't you get that, Gus? Might be important.'

Gus glowered at Compo. 'Bloody Gabriella! – mithering me about Daniel's stag do again.'

Compo nodded, 'Yeah, I know. Recognise the ring tone – *The Bitch Is Back* – good one.'

Gus sent it to voicemail. *She wouldn't give up – not when she had a fidget in her corset. There was no one more persistent than his ex-wife.*

Gus and his team made their way through the driving snow to the inner cordon which was down an incline made slippery by activity. He nodded at the young officer guarding entry, ducked beneath the tape and began to walk over the blocks distributed by the CSIs to make a walkway over the scene without damaging evidence.

His phone rang again. Gus took a deep breath and, ignoring Compo and Taffy's smirks, counted to three. 'You'd think she'd be too busy spa-ing or cocktailing or drinking Guinness or something to bother about Daniel's damn stag do.'

They walked towards the sandstone waiting room of the Ingrow, Worth Valley Railway station with its blood red doors contrasting sharply with the drifting snow. Gus had fond memories of journeys on the Worth Valley steam trains. He imagined many a child pictured themselves as Harry Potter as the train driver's papped their horns and let out blasts of steam before leaving the platform. *Shame this visit wasn't going to be as enjoyable.* Hissing Sid's team had erected a white tent to the right of the entrance. With the current weather, it rather resembled an igloo. Whilst the body would be protected from the on-going weather conditions, the surrounding crime scene was at risk of being obliterated with snow. Already Gus could see that many yellow markers had been all but covered in drifts. He only hoped the CSIs had been able to obtain something worthwhile, though he doubted it.

Poking his head through the tent flap, Gus waved to Sid who was working inside the tent. A loud Scottish voice boomed from inside making them jump, 'That you, Angus laddie?'

Gus scowled, *does he have to be so damn loud?* Turning to Taffy, he said, 'Go and check what the uniforms have for us...

oh and see if there's any hot drinks going, Compo will need one in a bit… lots of sugar.'

He swept the curtain aside and stepped into the confined space, wishing there was more air inside. His dad's massive frame was crouched, obscuring most of the body. Gus was pleased about that. Ease the lad in, so to speak. He hesitated by the tent flap, giving Compo time to adjust. From here, all they could see was a hand stretching out to one side and a head with long hair, darkened by the wet snow, facing away from them. 'When we approach focus on one part of the body at a time. Don't look at the face. Not till you've seen everything else. It'll be easier that way.'

Compo nodded, his eyes wide. Gus gave him a few more seconds, then stepped forward. The snow around the woman was stained red, as was the front of her coat. Her feet were bare. He raised a hand in greeting to his dad. 'Gun shot or stab wound?'

Dr McGuire hefted himself to his feet, breathing heavily with the effort, 'Stab wounds – lots of them, look.' He pulled the coat open, revealing that she was naked. Her body was a mass of stab wounds and, what looked like, cigarette burns. 'Won't know which wound actually killed her till the PM but my bet's on this one – straight to the heart.'

Gus risked another quick glance at Compo, who was breathing slow and deep, his eyes trained on the body. *Good for you Comps. Proud of you.*

'She's been beaten around the legs and feet too.' Dr McGuire pointed at the soles of her feet that also had multiple slashes over them. One toe nail was ripped completely off. She was of slim build, but not emaciated. Through her wounds, Gus couldn't see any tracks, so perhaps she wasn't a drug addict.

'Tortured.' It wasn't a question. Gus had seen these kinds of injuries before, but not usually on women. More often on men… usually gang members who'd broken the rules. Dr McGuire nodded.

'Her face?' asked Gus. Sometimes what had been done to the face was an indication of whether it was a personal motive or not.

Without speaking, Dr McGuire gently leaned over and, as if soothing a crying child, wiped the sodden hair from her bruised cheek. Gus lifted his gaze to her face. 'Jesus Christ!'

He stumbled backward and grabbed his father's arm. Dr McGuire took one look at his son's ashen face. 'What the bloody hell's wrong, Angus?'

Gus shook his head. 'Don't you recognise her?' His voice came out husky and weak so he swallowed, wishing he had a drink to get rid of the bitter taste in his mouth. 'We know her.'

The doc looked at the girl with a frown and shook his head. 'I've no idea who she is.'

Compo, pale but composed, put his hand on Gus' arm, 'Who is it, Gus?'

Gus jerked his arm away and took another step back. He couldn't get enough air in his lungs; the tent was too white... too hot... too stifling. A vice tightened on his rib cage, squashing his lungs, forcing his heart to thud. His breathing became shallow and rasped, raw against his throat. White flecks peppered his peripheral vision. Was it snowing in the damn tent? His ears filled with cotton wool. The sounds of the wind and people talking faded away. His cheeks were on fire and dizziness swarmed over him like angry bees, their buzzing magnified against the absence of other sounds. Ghostly faces floated above him, their mouths opening and shutting like marionettes. He began to pant. Just when his body began to slip to the ground, his Dad was there. He always was. Taking Gus' weight against his strong frame. Firm arms round his waist, his Scottish brogue familiar and comforting. The scent of pipe tobacco combined with soap and water, soothing.

'Breathe Angus, breathe. Slowly. That's it.'

Bit by bit, his breathing slowed and his chest loosened. He struggled upright and glanced round. The crime scene investigators who had stopped working, now turned away and a low hum of normality returned to the tent. *Shit!* Of all the places to have one of the worst panic attacks ever, he had to choose a damn crime scene with countless people around. He took a final deep breath and raised his voice. 'Sorry!'

Still shaking, Gus studied the young woman lying in the melting snow. There was no doubt in his mind, despite the bruising. 'It's Izzie Dimou.'

'Who?' Dr McGuire lumbered forward and peered at the woman's swollen face.

'Daniel's fiancée.'

As if willing it not to be true, Dr McGuire said. 'No? Are you sure? You're going to be best man at their wedding next weekend.'

'I'm sure.' With a pulse throbbing at his temple, he leaned over and closed her eyes just as *The Bitch is Back* started up.

Turning away from Izzie, his dad and Compo, he made his way out of the tent, welcoming the frigid air as he answered. Before he had a chance to say anything Gabriella was in full flow.

'I've been trying to get hold of you all day, Gus. Where the hell have you been?'

'Em…'

'My *delightful* sister-in-law-to-be hasn't turned up for the hen weekend that took me so long to plan. She's not even answering her phone or been in touch or anything. And the weather's crap. We can't even get out of the hotel.'

'Gabriella…'

'It's a damn cheek Gus and now I can't get in touch with Daniel either. And I bet you've not even organised the stag do. Bet you're hoping they've eloped so you can get out of writing the speech – I know you've been moaning to Katie about it…'

Gus visualised her hip thrust forward, one hand resting on it, long fingernails tapping the side of the phone and that impatient narrowing of the eyes that she had down to perfection. Someone was in trouble and he was glad that, for once, it didn't appear to be him. 'Will you just…'

'Inconsiderate. You'll need to—'

'Fucking shut up, Gabriella. Just shut the fuck right up.'

There was a moment of stunned silence. 'Don't you…'

'Will you let me fucking speak? Is Katie there?'

'No, she's gone for a sauna.'

Gus groaned. This wasn't ideal but he'd just have to do it. 'Look Gabriella. I'm at a crime scene.'

'Well, you can go after—'

'No, Gaby – it's Izzie… the body's Izzie's.'

Silence.

Fuck, he shouldn't have told her like this. Should've waited till he could speak to Katie first. 'You still there Gaby? You okay?'

There was the sound of talking in the background, weeping, before Katie's voice. 'I'm here now, Gus. I've got it. I'll look after her – you just do your job, okay?'

Still holding the phone to his ear, not feeling the cold or the snow settling on his dreads, Gus wanted to scream. Rage swelled in chest. Who the fuck would do this to Izzie? Clever, beautiful and about to become a member of his family. What had happened here? He remembered the last time he'd seen her alive. Sipping champagne with Daniel at the Paprika Lounge, teasing him about her husband-to-be for his shyness in her accented English and looking so happy… just like any bride.

His dad and Compo approached from the tent. 'Fucking hell, how am I going to tell Daniel? What am I going to tell him?'

He tipped his head back, savouring the icy softness of the snow against his cheeks. 'She shouldn't even be here. She was supposed to be in Dublin for her hen party weekend. Why the fuck is she lying dead in there, when she should be getting pissed in bloody Dublin?'

Life was too short and it was full of shit!

Chapter 11

13:30 Rubeus Pharmaceutical Headquarters, Manchester

'S-s-something's happened …'

The slight stammer on the first word, followed by the trailing away of the second, told Jordan Beaumont that something had, indeed, 'happened'. But what? Beaumont leaned back in his chair and swivelled towards the window, taking in the blight that was The Beast from the East. From his office, the only identifiable thing was an impenetrable barrier of snow, framed by zig-zag icicles hanging from the window frame. *Looks like he'd be stuck here for the night. On the upside, so would his delightful PA,* Mark. *Who knows what might happen?*

For a moment he allowed himself the pleasure of imagining breaking off one of the icicles and plunging it deep into the carotid artery of the idiot on the other end of the phone. He allowed the silence to continue, letting it stutter down the line like British Rail on a go slow, until the other man broke the tension with more inane words.

'S-s-something's gone wrong.'

Now, the stammer was worse. *My, my, it must be something bad.* Spinning back towards his desk, Jordan lifted his feet up and rested them on a pile of papers. Keeping his voice level, he instilled as much iciness into his reply as The Beast outside was inflicting on the traffic. 'Go on.'

The man on the end of the phone exhaled. Imagining the other man's foul breath, Jordan grimaced. *That's what you got with Romanians.* The foreigner really was a vile creature and

Jordan rued the day he'd enlisted him. *Full of melodrama, but lacking in finesse. The only positive thing he could say about him was that at least he and his mates had no aversion to getting their hands dirty – for a price.*

The answer came at last; a tissue thin whisper. 'She's dead. Well we think it's her. Must be her.'

Jordan removed his legs from his desk and stood up. This *wasn't* what he'd been expecting. Not what he'd been expecting at all. Sweat pooled under his armpits as he began to pace the room. He'd expected her to get hurt, of course he had. She wasn't about to give them the information they needed without putting up a bit of a fight, but they'd held a key card, so he'd been optimistic. He'd assumed he was going to be told that she was being difficult. Digging her heels in, not giving them what they wanted. He hadn't expected them to go and kill the bitch.

What was he going to do now? He needed to keep calm. Needed to work things out. Find out all the facts and go from there. He was good at this sort of thing, good at analysis. It was his job after all. Forcing himself to remain calm, he used the tone he would with his daughter when he wanted to placate her. 'Tell me.'

'We follow her – like you said. Thought she'd head straight to get whatever you wanted, but she ran. She must have seen us...'

Jordan wasn't surprised she'd clocked them – dirty looking thugs, all nicotine stained fingers, stubble and joggers. She'd have been hard pushed not to be able to work out *they* were the ones keeping tabs on her. *Should've paid a bit more and got some professionals – ones who'd blend in. Hell, shouldn't have told her I had eyes on her.*

'... but it wasn't us that killed her. Two Cypriot guys stole her – Turkish banditti – beat us up a bit too. *They* must've done it.'

Fuck's sake, this was worse than he'd thought. Turks snatching her? That was bad news. Jordan slid back onto his chair and glowered out the window. He had to get to the bottom of this – especially if the Turks were involved. 'Start at the beginning and *don't* miss anything out.'

Voice shaking, the caller continued. 'My uncle and friend pick up the other package and deliver it as planned.'

'What about the girl?'

'She left your building and went to Victoria station, just like you said. She dodged onto fucking stupid cross-country train instead of direct one to Bradford, so we lose her at Victoria. But that was alright. We had plan.'

Jordan shook his head. The trouble with idiots was that they *always* had a plan and inevitably their plans failed.

'We Googled train route and phoned Ivo's cousin.'

This was becoming more and more worrying. Too many people were involved and when you were dealing with illegals, loyalty went down the kazi. He sharpened his tone. 'Get to the damn point.'

'Ivo's cousin stole car from Bradford. He put car at level crossing to stop the train and my sister waited in car nearby…'

Fucking hell! They'd caused a train wreck!

'…when the train crashed Mariana told the girl her boyfriend sent her and the girl got into car – easy as shit. We met them in old mill Keighley… and that's when it all fucked up.'

You think?

'We tried to get her talk – but she not. Not even when we said we had boyfriend. The banditti stormed in with machetes.' The Romanian hesitated, 'They beat us up. Ivo has concussion and broken ribs. They made us leave. Told us keep schtum'. His voice became pleading, 'We couldn't stop them – they were mad and now she's dead. What if they trace her to us?'

The panic in the other man's voice resurrected Jordan's earlier image of the icicle and carotid arteries. He wasn't worried about Izzie Dimou being traced back to the Romanians – he just wanted to distance himself from them – make sure his own tracks were covered. But the Romanian wasn't finished. Sounding like he might burst into tears, he continued, 'And now Ivo's cousin and mate dead too.'

Fuck, could things get any worse? 'The Turks killed them?'

'No… drug dealers. The car they stole had grand of heroin in boot.'

Jordan laughed – halfwits went and stole a drug dealer's car! He'd instructed them to get the information at all costs – given them free reign… and *that's* what his monkeys had done. *Shame the organ grinder hadn't supervised them more closely.* Voice harsh, he said, all the while knowing a speedy escape was impossible for them in this weather. 'Ditch this phone and move onto number two burner. You're going to be busy. You need to find wherever Izzie Dimou was hiding. When you've delivered it to me, get on the first plane back to Romania.'

He took the battery out of his own burner phone. When the weather improved he'd dump it in the Tame. Depositing it in his bottom drawer and locking it, he sighed. What about the Turks? A chill settled in his stomach – their involvement did not bode well. Who were they working for and what exactly had Izzie Dimou told them? He needed to get ahead of the game. Find out what he could about possible competitors – but how?

With a tap on the door, Mark walked into the office, sashaying over like Bambi on ice, flashing his perfect smile and commenting on the weather. Jordan glared at him and sent him scurrying back out like a wounded deer. He sighed. *Looks like his romantic evening with Mark wouldn't be happening.* The boy was too prone to sulkiness. Too damn sensitive and *he* had other things on his mind. Much more important things. Like how the hell was he going to get out of this mess? Selling stuff to the Syrians was one thing. Being linked to a murdered woman was another and now the Turkish Cypriots.

What else linked him to the morons? His face paled. God! Of course, Daniel Farrier was in his old farmhouse on Saddleworth

Moor. He sank into the leather couch in the corner of his office and dropped his head onto his hands. Everything linked back to him… and with the weather set to get worse, who knew when he'd be able to get to the house? Who knew what state Daniel Farrier would be in when he reached him? On the other hand, perhaps Daniel could provide information. He'd just have to find someone who could extract it. Maybe the Turks would play ball – at a cost.

His other phone buzzed – his real one, not the burner. He glanced at it. It was his wife. Head ready to explode, he answered, pleased for once that she didn't allow him much time to speak. In the end, a mumbled acknowledgement that he was stranded and a confirmation that she and their daughter were okay, was enough. He hung up and sat gazing at the worsening weather outside, trying to work out how in the space of twenty-four hours he'd moved from being an industrial secrets thief to an accomplice to murder. There was no doubt in his mind – if Daniel Farrier survived however many days locked up in the upstairs back bedroom with no food and little heating, he'd have to kill him, eventually. He couldn't allow him to reveal that he'd been abducted and there was no way he'd keep quiet about it, not when he discovered his fiancée was dead.

No, he had to think of himself now. How could he leave Marcia and his daughter? Would he have to go on the run? Good job he always kept a bundle of cash stashed here *and* at home. There was nothing else for it, self-preservation must be top of his list. First Daniel Farrier, then the idiots he'd paid to do his dirty work. He'd just have to man up and make sure that from now on his dirty work was done properly.

Besides which, Daniel Farrier's wouldn't be the only body buried and forgotten on Saddleworth Moor… so why did the idea of what he had to do leave him nauseous?

Chapter 12

15:30 Bradford Mortuary

Gus' dad had fast tracked the post-mortem and slotted it in between that of a rough sleeper found under a bush in Undercliffe Cemetery and a drunk who'd fallen asleep under his car in the Old Bull pub carpark in Silsden. The Beast from the East was racking up its victims. Seeing Izzie Dimou spread out on his dad's slab was almost too much for Gus, so for once he opted to watch from behind the glass screen. This meant he was spared the dead body smells, enabling him to dispense with the Vicks under his nose.

However, he couldn't avoid the sight of blood and it was the blood that he really hated. The viewing room was sterile and it too had the formaldehyde smell he'd long associated with this environment. It was all white and bright. Gus could feel a headache prickling behind his eyes. There were blue plastic chairs dotted round the wall, but Gus chose to stand. Not because he wanted a bird's eye view – he really didn't – but out of respect. It was his thing. No matter how much these post mortems affected him physically, at least he was alive and he owed it to the victims to get justice.

It had been a long day, and he still hadn't spoken to Compo about Alice. Now he had this to investigate as well as hold his team together. Periodically, he'd been on the phone to Gabriella and was getting grief from her because they still hadn't located Daniel. *As if it was his damn fault if her brother had disappeared off the face of the earth in the middle of a damn snow storm.*

He'd got uniformed officers on the ground looking for him and interviewing his neighbours in Saltaire where Daniel was living – but so far, no joy. This bloody weather was making it difficult to conduct a proper investigation, especially with half their staff deployed in weather–related incidents. If Daniel's absence continued for much longer, his status would rise from 'person of interest' to 'suspect' and he didn't think that would go down too well with Gabriella. At least he didn't need to deal with her face to face for she and Katie were stranded in Dublin till the storm cleared.

Dr McGuire started his examination, talking into the microphone that linked up to the viewing room. Taffy, suited and booted with a mask covering his face, had elected to join Dr McGuire in the autopsy room. The bloodied coat that had been Izzie's only covering had been bagged in the hope that some forensic evidence remained. This could be fruitful in linking a suspect to the crime at a later date.

She looked frailer than Gus remembered. Maybe death did that to you. Her blonde hair was splayed out on the metal trolley, her eyes closed and her skin pale as Dr McGuire measured the length, depth and position of each stab wound. Now that the blood had been wiped away, the extent of her injuries were clear. Her face, torso and limbs were badly bruised and ligature marks round her wrists showed that she'd been restrained.

'Thirty-five stab wounds.' Dr McGuire glanced up at Gus and continued. 'The longest is eight centimetres, the shortest only a half centimetre. Some with serrated edges, some not. Their depth varies from one to eight centimetres, except the one to the heart. That was nine centimetres deep and certainly killed her.' He sighed and moved round the table, 'We've sent samples from under her nails to the lab – see what it turns up, eh?' Gus had seen worse – much worse. Yet, when it was someone you'd had a conversation with, laughed with, seen as a three-dimensional being, it hurt more. What the hell had led to Izzie Dimou being tortured so viciously? If he hadn't come across the darker side of human nature, Gus would have sworn that Daniel Farrier was incapable of such an act. However, he'd seen many things during his career and he was all too aware of how low some people could plummet. He couldn't dismiss him from the equation, especially not with his notable absence.

The thing was, Gus had no idea about Daniel and Izzie's life in Cyprus, beyond that they both worked in a University in the north of the Island. Izzie, he thought, worked in some science-based area and Daniel was in the archaeology department. Gus had visited Northern Cyprus a few years back with Gabriella and Daniel had taken them on a tour of various ruins. If Gus, remembered rightly, Daniel's bugbear was that there was little funding to preserve the various Roman monuments. Although it seemed that some European money had found its way into the pot more recently. At that time, Daniel had been single, so he and Gabriella hadn't met Izzie.

Moving to the bottom of the trolley, Dr McGuire lifted one of Izzie's feet and angled it so Gus could see the sole. 'These are slashes, rather than stab wounds. I think our torturer used a variety of weapons, Angus. I've counted, in addition to the stab sites, ten puncture wounds that resemble the size and shape of a meat prodder.'

Gus nodded to let his dad know he'd understood. No doubt Izzie's killer was a sadist. Did he carry a bag of tools with him? Gus leaned in and pulled the microphone closer to his lips, 'Any indication of how many perpetrators?'

His dad shrugged his huge shoulders. 'Perhaps only one, possibly two. Some of the more superficial stab wounds look hesitant. However, that could merely be our killer trying to extend the torture.'

'What about the cigarette burns?'

Taffy interjected, 'I've counted at least twenty of those too, Gus.'

Gus' dad nodded, his eyes twinkling, 'Good lad, Taffy. I'll count and mark them in a bit, but definitely in double figures. As well as that she's been beaten. I've got a couple of footprints here, which I'll photograph and send to the lab, but whoever did this also used their fists.'

'I presume she was killed elsewhere?' From his position, Gus could tell that lividity indicated she'd been moved.

'Yes, looks like she was killed and left for a while in a sitting position, before being moved. He lifted her slightly and pointed to a red stripe down one side of her back with a cross section stretching across at the small of her back and again about six inches higher. Some sort of dining chair I'd reckon.'

'Any forensics?'

'I'll bag up anything I find, Angus. Now, away ye go. I'm fine here wi' the laddie. Go catch Izzie's killer.'

All during the post mortem, Gus' phone had been vibrating in his pocket. *Gabriella!* And now as he left the hospital, intent on getting some exercise in by walking down to The Fort, it vibrated again. There was no way he could ignore it, so he answered, mentally preparing himself for a high-speed conversation on his way back to work. Gabriella was a pain, but right now she had every right to be.

Chapter 13

18:00 The Fort

The photo of Izzie Dimou that they'd pinned on the crime board was the only one they had access to. It didn't help that it was taken from her and Daniel's wedding invitation. The self-same image hung on Gus' fridge at home. After failing to make contact with Daniel, Gus had spent the better part of the afternoon talking, first to Gabriella, then to Katie. All flights to and from the northern airports were cancelled until further notice. Neither could shed any light on where Izzie had been prior to her missed flight to Dublin. She'd always been going to fly from Manchester because she had some meeting or other there, whereas Katie and Gabriella had chosen to fly from Leeds Bradford. Gabriella thought that Daniel was also supposed to be at the Manchester meeting but couldn't be certain. So, basically – a whole load of uncertainty.

Instead of heading straight back to The Fort, Gus had walked through Heaton Woods and on to Alice's house in Saltaire. Alice had given him the keys and when Daniel and Izzie had turned up, Gus had lent them the property. CSI's and uniformed officers were still there – but no trace of Daniel. Nor was there any evidence of an obvious crime scene, so it appeared Izzie had been killed elsewhere.

There was no indication of Daniel's whereabouts. The absence of any signs of a struggle cheered Gus a little. However, he couldn't avoid the elephant in the room. No matter how unlikely he thought it, their number one suspect – until otherwise proven – had to be his brother-in-law. So, the sooner they found him, the better. Gus had photographs of Daniel distributed, hopefully they'd get lucky and find him soon. Mind you, in this weather it was difficult to do anything. They'd concluded that Izzie had been tortured elsewhere and dumped at the railway station. Evidence was sparse and the weather had made it almost impossible. Still, Sid and his team had done their best. Gus could only hope that the post-mortem might throw up a lead.

His first job when he'd got back to The Fort was to pay his road tax and get the buggers to release his car. No way was he relying on Alice's Mini in these conditions and the pool cars weren't much better. Now that he had his Land Rover back, he could tackle most weather. In the meantime, the team were trying to trace Izzie's movements for the past couple of days, starting with CCTV footage from Bradford Interchange and Manchester Victoria train stations, to see if she'd commuted between the two. All he knew about her really, was what he'd gleaned in the two meetings they'd had, and – to be honest – he hadn't made much of an effort. Pissed off at having been guilt-tripped into being the best man, he'd allowed the conversation to flow around him and nurtured his annoyance in a silent rebellion.

He did know though that she was a Greek Cypriot living on the Turkish side of the island and that she and Daniel had met at the university. She seemed to be involved in some biochemistry research. He was waiting for a call back from the Turkish Cypriot authorities to see what information they had on Izzie Dimou. It may have been some sort of random attack, but the torture made that seem less likely. No, Gus was almost certain she'd been targeted and he needed to know a hell of a lot more about his ex-brother-in-law's fiancée than he knew right now.

Truth was, Gus didn't know much about Daniel. Despite him being Gabriella's brother, he'd rarely seen him when he and Gabriella were married. Gabriella wasn't going to be happy, but the lives of her now dead sister-in-law to be and her brother were going to be scrutinised under a microscope. They needed all the clues they could get right now.

Contemplating the limited information available to him, Gus was interrupted by the door swinging open and DCI Mickey Swanson entering. He hadn't seen Mickey since before Christmas when they'd raided a biker gang lair on Ilkley Moor and he was pleased to see her. He was even more pleased when she revealed the reason for her visit and explained about the level crossing crash the previous day and added that she'd just emailed him a link to all the CCTV footage she'd secured after. It seemed they had a lead on Izzie Dimou after all.

'Too much of a coincidence for my missing girl and your murdered one not to be connected.' She looked at the crime board and her face grim nodded, 'Yep that's the girl I found on the footage.' Pulling another chair up beside Gus, she continued, 'Now we've got the added problem of DCI Hawes to contend with too.' And she explained Hawes' behaviour at the crime scene.

Gus had heard of Hawes and suspected that Mickey was right that he would want to muscle in. Well, he'd be damn lucky. This was *his* case and he and *his* team would be the ones working it. He didn't think there was a terrorist link and would argue his corner. He dismissed the nagging thought that Nancy might try to take the case from him when she heard about his personal links to both the victim and the main suspect. He'd deal with that bridge when he came to it.

'And you're sure Izzie is the girl from the train wreck?'

Mickey glanced at the photo again and nodded. 'Four of the other passengers confirmed it.'

Gus got the footage up on his PC and Mickey talked him through it. 'That's her leaving the station concourse in Manchester. The bloke with her is the guy in the photo – fiancé?'

Despite the grainy image, Gus recognised him immediately, 'Yep, Daniel Farrier – he's AWOL. We've got a BOLO out for him, but no joy so far.' He didn't think Mickey needed to know his relation to Daniel. It was strange watching Daniel and Izzie leave the station with the knowledge at the back of his mind that she'd been murdered only a few hours later and Daniel was missing. They hugged and went their separate ways, with Izzie heading towards the Printworks. Gus called Compo over. 'We've got a sighting of Daniel Farrier in Manchester on Friday, can you follow up on that?'

Compo lumbered over, headphones in, head bopping to some rhythm or other. With a quick smile to Mickey, he scribbled down the time and camera details and went back to his workstation to do his magic, whilst Mickey continued. 'Managed to trace her to a company called Rubeus Pharmaceuticals near the Printworks in Manchester. Footage has her entering the building at three minutes past eight and picks her up leaving at seven minutes past nine, when she walked back to Victoria Station.'

Gus frowned. 'What the hell was she doing there?'

'Uniform phoned. Apparently, she had an appointment with a Jordan Beaumont, one of the chief execs.'

'Hmm, wonder what business Izzie had with a chief exec at Rubeus Pharmaceuticals?' Gus watched as Mickey fast-forwarded footage, thinking it made Izzie seem animated. He remembered how she'd looked on the slab in his dad's mortuary.

Mickey pointed at the screen. 'Look. This is interesting. D'you see when she comes out she's like a different person? Looking around her tracing and re-tracing her steps. Look, here she's on her phone, but still glancing around, like she's scared or something. Here, she's on her phone again and still looking round.'

'Looked like nobody answered or else maybe it was a very short conversation.'

'Maybe. You had any luck with her phone records?'

Gus snorted. Interactions with phone companies were the bane of his life. 'Request's been sent, but it's the weekend and they like to dick us around a bit. Compo's on it.'

Mickey turned back to the screen. 'What's *really* interesting is that if you watch the footage often enough you notice *these* two characters.' She paused the footage and zoomed in, first on a rugged looking man with unfashionably long hair, who walked about ten paces behind Izzie, and then to another man of similar appearance, but of slighter build, who was on the opposite side of the road seemingly keeping pace with her. 'We tracked these two, near Izzie all the way back to the station.'

Gus watched as Izzie walked towards the station, pausing three times to use her phone, darting glances around her as she did so. 'I think she clocked them. Look. Her eyes are skimming to each of them.' So, if the two guys were following Izzie that made her actions in hotfooting it off the wrecked train more understandable. The question was, why the hell would these two follow Izzie Dimou?

'They weren't in sight when she made her way to Rubeus Pharmaceuticals?'

'Nope. Looks like they picked her up as she left.'

Gus and Mickey continued to watch the footage through to when it cut out as Izzie went through the barriers to the platforms. 'I've put in a request for platform CCTV and will forward it to you when it comes through.'

Gus nodded his thanks He suspected the men following Izzie would have tried to follow her onto the platform, but it would be good to have it confirmed. Now they knew Izzie's movements up to around eleven am on Friday when she left the train wreck. His dad had put time of death at sometime between midnight on Friday evening and six am on Saturday morning. *God knew what Izzie had been subjected to in that time.* 'Hey Comps, see if you can tidy up the faces of these two men and get that sent out to uniforms.'

Gus sighed. 'This weather is making it difficult to conduct an efficient investigation. Ordinarily, I'd head to Manchester but looks like I'll need to contact this Jordan Beaumont via phone.'

He turned to Compo, who nodded. 'Yeah, yeah, I'm on it like a sonnet'

Gus shook his head, wondering how, at the same time, Compo could be so efficient and yet so gormless.

Compo's fingers flew over the keys. 'Here you are.'

Gus took the number, put his phone on speaker and dialled. Jordan Beaumont answered within three rings and Gus introduced himself. 'I'm investigating a murder in Bradford and would like to ask you a few questions about one of your Friday appointments.'

There was a pause. 'Well, I'm rather busy, couldn't this wait till normal office hours on Monday?'

Gus hated the affected tones of his put-on upper-middle-class accent which implied, 'I'm better than you, cos you're a public servant.' Gus allowed his displeasure to show in his clipped words. 'This isn't optional, Mr Beaumont. A murder investigation trumps your Saturday free time.'

He heard the other man inhale followed by the sound of him speaking to someone away from the phone. 'Okay, but can we make it quick please, my daughter needs me.'

'You had an appointment with an Izzie Dimou on Friday morning, could you tell me what it was about?'

Beaumont sighed, 'Izzie is one of the trust members of a university in Northern Cyprus which receives a research grant from the company. It was a routine meeting because she was in the UK. Nothing formal, just a bit of a catch-up, that's all. Very informal in fact.'

Gus raised his eyebrows and looked at Mickey, who returned his gaze. Beaumont was putting just a tad too much emphasis on the 'informal' element of his and Izzie's meeting. That didn't necessarily mean anything, most folk were a bit nervous when being interviewed by a police officer. 'Is it true to say the meeting was brief?'

'Well, yes. As I said, it was informal. We didn't have much to say – just a catch up.'

Something was off here. 'Bit of a trek from Bradford to Manchester on the day of her hen do just for a brief informal chat, don't you think?'

'Well, I don't know. She said she wanted to touch base, that's all. Nothing more than that.'

'What did you talk about?'

'The weather, a couple of mutual acquaintances in Cyprus and such like. I had to cut our meeting short as I had another appointment.'

Gus decided to let it go – for now. *With this weather, it wasn't as if Beaumont could do a runner.* 'How did she seem?'

'Sorry?'

'Her demeanour? How did she seem?'

'She was fine. Seemed happy. Looking forward to her wedding. I do hope nothing's happened to her.'

And there it was – at last. Gus had mentioned he was investigating a murder and yet it had taken Beaumont 'till now to enquire after Izzie's wellbeing.

Mickey shook her head, mumbling, 'pillock,' under her breath as she did so. Gus grinned and, keeping his tone icy, said, 'Actually, she's dead. Nice of you to ask at last. I'll be in touch.' And cutting the other man off, mid-bluster, he hung up.

'He sounds like a prat,' said Compo shoving a biscuit in his gob. 'Here Gus, I got that footage of Daniel. Bottom line is, he wanders along… goes into a Costa Coffee near the station… doesn't come out.'

'Eh?'

'Well, I ran my facial recognition programme for the following three hours and he didn't leave that Costa Coffee by the front door – no doubt about it.'

Gus walked over and looked at Daniel and Izzie's wedding invitation photo. A love heart encompassing their faces – smiling – not a care in the world. And now Izzie was dead and Daniel, by all accounts, had disappeared into the depths of a Costa Coffee in Manchester. *Not good, not good at all!*

Chapter 14

Jordan Beaumont threw his phone onto the coffee table and poured himself another large gin and tonic.

'Daddy, can we play my Frozen game again?'

Jordan downed his drink in one whole swallow. If he had to watch that stupid snowman slide down a snow covered hill even once more, he'd scream. 'Just a minute darling, Daddy's a bit busy.'

He began walking round the living room. He'd expected the police to make contact – course he had. Just not so fucking soon. *Damn Romanians and their stupidity.* He thought he'd have some time to organise things. He glanced over to the huge picture on the wall. The concealed safe behind it now contained his burner phone. The one he hadn't been able to ditch because of the damn weather. *Fuck!*

He'd been lucky to get home this morning. He'd got behind a plough that drove right past the end of his road. If Marc hadn't been such a wimp, he'd have stayed in the office and not risked the journey. It's not like Marcia noticed if he was home or not. Sometimes he thought she couldn't stand the sight of him. But, as it was, he'd been glad to get out of the office. Fucking Marc whimpering in the corner saying he'd been too rough with him. It was only a little bruise, for Christ's sake and a bit of tearing.

Mind you, he should have been a bit more careful, shouldn't have let the Romanian's phone call get to him. Now, he'd have to spend a grand making it up to the pussy or else it'd be sulks all-round on Monday at the office.

That detective had been a bastard. *Arrogant bugger with his snide tone.* Not sure he believed me, but thank God it was just over the phone. He'd need to get himself together though. If there's any blow-back from the Romanians he might need to meet with him face to face.

'Daddy, can we make a snowman now? I've got an orange for its nose.'

He groaned. Why the hell couldn't Marcia occupy their daughter for a bit? Melissa hadn't been off his case since he got back from work, 'Daddy this' and 'Daddy that'. Not that he minded – just he had other things to think about right now. Like what the hell was he going to do next? No doubt Marcia was in the gym. That seemed to be her default room any time he was at home. Poor Missy. Her mother never had any time for her. Everything else was always more of a priority for her than their daughter.

He sighed and placed his empty glass on the coffee table. *Smile.* 'All right, Missy. We'll go out in a bit, get your coat on – wrap up warm.'

He really needed to make sure those Romanians kept schtum! What a fucking mess!

Chapter 15

'Despite the storm blowing outside and the prospect of more to follow, we at Hospital Radio Epsom are in good spirits.'

Alice groaned, *glad someone fucking is. More damn snow!*

'... *if you're feeling lonely here's a Barry Manilow track to cheer you up...*'

Her groan deepened. *Barry fucking Manilow? Really?* The first time since she'd got here that she was alone and she had to listen to Barry sodding Manilow. Her guard had left to answer her phone – *not strictly protocol – but hey, what the hell – not like I can make an escape out the window in this condition.* Only the subdued lighting from the corridor outside, the whiteness of the snow from beyond the open curtains and the glow from her monitors, cast a glimmer round her room. She found the regular lines reassuring. She was *alive*! Things may be bad, but at least she was alive. *Morphine was a bloody godsend.*

The dull ache where they'd operated to remove her spleen was diminishing. She hadn't had the courage to look at her breast yet. The memory of Baby Jane chewing her nipple, the look of glee on her face when she swallowed it, brought bile to her throat. She'd had to have an HIV and Hepatitis test. The way her luck was going, fucking Baby Jane Inflictor of Pain would be a carrier. She laughed. Well, that would be one way out of this damn mess, wouldn't it? She was being stupid. She knew she was. Even if she had been infected, there were anti-viral drugs available. She'd be fine. Every time she moved, the raw area where her nipple had been, grazed against the gauze dressing.

A slight displacement of air and the faint smell of icy outdoors were the only indication that she was no longer alone. She hadn't heard the door open, nor footsteps approaching her bed. Yet, she knew someone was there and, what's more, she knew it wasn't the prison officer. *That explained the phone call.*

Her fists clenched. Her stomach contracted and screamed as if a vial of bleach had erupted, filling the cavity, paring the tender lining away like a vicious skin graft, layer by excruciating layer. Her rapid breaths punctuated the silence, but she refused to be the first to speak. It was the only defiance left for her and she was going to take it. Let *him* speak first. Let him put his sordid cards on the table. She would give him nothing.

It didn't surprise her that he'd managed to wangle his way past the guard. Why should it? He'd managed to have her attacked umpteen times from outside the prison walls and had succeeded in getting her so badly injured she'd ended up here. He wouldn't kill her. That wasn't his aim. No, Sean Kennedy wanted to intimidate her, show her how vulnerable she was, but he needed her alive. He needed her to exonerate him so he could go back to his old life.

His voice had changed – it had lost its rich timbre, its sexy laziness, its sardonic humour. Perhaps months with a breathing tube rammed down your throat would do that. Now, his words grated over her, making her skin crawl. It sounded faint and strained. 'Oh, poor little Alice. Look at you, so small and pathetic in a hospital bed. What's happened to you?'

She refused to respond. He could say what he needed to say and leave. However, she wanted to see what the man she'd put in a coma had become. She wanted to feed off his brokenness. Make herself stronger from his weakness. She turned her head and met his eyes. Christ it was worse, much worse, than she'd expected, yet she didn't flinch. If she hadn't known first-hand what this man was capable of, she'd feel sorry for him. Deep inside her heart a ribbon of hate unfurled. He deserved that. That and more. He deserved to rot and she made a silent promise to herself that when she could, she would make him suffer. More than that. She would kill him, with her bare hands. Unflinching, she met his gaze. He'd got skinny and wasted, as if he had a terminal disease. If she hadn't been hooked-up to the monitor, she'd be able to take him, even in her weakened condition.

He coughed, dry and rattley, as if he'd got something loose in his throat. When he settled, he grabbed a blue plastic chair from nearby and pulled it right up to the side of the bed. Reaching forward, finger extended, he stroked her face. Alice pressed her head against her pillow and gritting her teeth, wished she had the energy to punch him. Even if she thought someone would respond, she wouldn't call out for help. She wouldn't give him the satisfaction. He laughed and leaned in close, his breath foul against her cheek. 'I'm glad you kept your mouth shut, Alice.' His coarse lips rough against her cheek, peeling away another layer of innocence. *How had she managed not to shudder?*

'Mind you,' his laugh was bitter, cold as his heart. 'I'd rather you'd chosen to fight. For then, hurting your parents would have given me so much *more* satisfaction. Knowing your crippling guilt would plague you forever would be a more fitting punishment. However, unlike you, I'm civilised. I gave *you* a choice.'

His hand darted from where he'd rested it on the side of the bed and, with one vicious yank, he gripped her wounded breast in a pincer grip and twisted. A current surged through her body as if she was being electrocuted and a spark flashed in his eyes as she screeched. Spurred on by the sheer enjoyment on his face, she bit down on her lower lip, trying to staunch the sound of her pain, all too aware of the trickle of tears escaping her eyes. Her fists clenched into her palms, the sensation did nothing to detract from the pain around her nipple. She jerked her head up, trying to connect with his, but missed.

Grinning, he licked his lips and, before she could move her face away, he bent over and rasped his tongue over her tears. His saliva on her skin made her stomach heave. As he limped over to the door, she turned her head to the side and vomited.

Chapter 16

21:30 The Fort

There was nothing else Gus could do. The weather forecast was crap and there was a red alert out, so he felt he might as well head home. Compo was running things through his PC and was happy to do an all-nighter at The Fort; although Gus had told him he could have the spare room at his house if he wanted. He'd slipped the lad a spare key and told him to turn up any time. Taffy had just texted to say that he'd only just arrived home and would leave early to head back. Gus had his doubts that the lad would be able to make it back to The Fort from Bradford Three. Not if the weather forecast was accurate. *How the hell was he supposed to investigate a murder in these conditions?* The only saving grace was that they'd found Izzie Dimou's body before the weather got really bad.

Having elected to leave his vehicle in the station car park and hike home, Gus donned an extra jumper, slipped his jacket, hat, gloves and hiking boots on and with a last glance at Izzie's photo, he left through the front door. The skeleton staff they had on duty would keep things ticking over and he was local enough to return if necessary.

Leaving the building, Gus could barely see the glow of the street lights through the snow. The sky, dark and foreboding, seemed to be pressing down on the world. Its muffled silence was eerie and a shiver went down Gus' spine. It was like he was in a supernatural thriller and he half expected a ghost-like figure to appear before him. When he heard a cough coming from near his feet, he jumped, his heart skittering for a few beats before slowing to normal as he peered through the dark and saw a prone figure, half covered in snow, bundled up near the bottom of the steps. *What the hell?*

At least it was alive. Taking a deep breath Gus climbed down to the person and as he drew near, he saw that what he'd initially thought was one figure was actually two. Inadequately wrapped in a thin sleeping bag that had seen better days, were two shivering elderly figures looking up at him. He'd seen these rough sleepers before. They often walked around Lister Park and on occasion Gus had stopped for a chat and had even given them a drink and samosas from Mo's. 'Jerry, Dave, what the hell are you doing here? Couldn't you get into one of the centres?'

Jerry, the taller and skinnier of the two, shook his head, 'Didn't expect it to get so bad Gus. We're too late for any of the centres. Can't get there in this weather, can we?'

Dave coughed again. His eyes were rheumy and through the layers of grime etched into his face, he looked pale. Gus shook his head. 'Well, you can't stay here.'

Jerry nodded. 'Yeah, lad we know. We'll just rest for a minute and then we'll move on.'

Gus frowned. 'No, no. That's not what I meant. I mean you'll have to come inside. You can't stay out here in the cold. Let's get you inside and we'll find somewhere for you to keep warm till this has passed.'

Dave's eyes darted around as if he expected to see someone other than Gus and Jerry nearby. A tic played at the corner of one eye and he tried to press his prone body further under the pile of cardboard and sleeping bags that covered him and his friend. He began to flap his hands, and his voice was high and rushed, 'Can't go in a cell, Jerry, can't let them arrest us. We int done owt, you know?'

Gus knelt down. He recognised the symptoms, the flapping, the darting eye movements, the tic. He'd seen it with Greg often enough. 'He off his meds, Jerry?'

Jerry nodded. 'Ran out yesterday and couldn't get to the health centre. He's got flu or summat too.'

'Look, let's get him inside. We've got comfy rooms. We won't put you in a cell. You just can't stay here or you'll die. When you're settled I'll call Lynfield Mount and see if we can get some meds down here for him as soon as the weather breaks, okay?'

Jerry turned to his friend. 'You hear that, Dave? No cells. Just a nice comfy couch and a cup of tea. You're not arrested. You've done nowt wrong.'

With difficulty, Jerry and Gus managed to move Dave up the steps and through the doors into The Fort. It had taken all of Gus' patience and, he suspected, every iota of energy Jerry had, to reassure his friend. The smell of unwashed clothes and bodies was enough to make Gus' eyes water. Whatever had led these two old men to sleep rough was none of his business, but he was damn sure they would live to sleep rough again when the weather had cleared.

Hardeep, the duty officer, rushed round to open the doors for them. Gus mouthed the words 'Lynfield Mount' at the officer who nodded and picked up the phone. Gus guided them to the shower room, not because they smelled, but because he suspected it was the quickest way to get them warm. He led them through to the cubicles, told them to sit on a bench and put two of the showers on full heat. 'I'm going to wait outside. Here are towels, get stripped off and stand under there till you're warm.'

Dave, shaking his head profusely, backed into the lockers, his gaze fastened on the closed door. Gus looked at Jerry, 'You need to make him. We need to get him warm.'

'Don't like it here, Jerry. They'll lock me up.'

The harsh light bounced off Dave's skin emphasising its blueish hue. His entire body trembled – or maybe it was just his perpetual motion that gave that impression. Beads of sweat were visible across his unshaven upper lip and forehead.

Laying a reassuring hand on his friend's arm, Jerry lowered his voice to a whisper. 'No, they won't, Dave. Gus says he's going to get us a drink in a bit. Just need to get you warm.'

'They've locked that door, Jerry. Locked me in.'

Jerry looked at Gus, 'Can we leave the door open a bit? That'll calm him.'

Gus walked over and wedged the door open with a chair. 'That better Dave?'

Dave grunted but his hand movements became a little less frenzied.

'He's frozen – you both are. I'll see if I can find some warm clothes. No one else will disturb you – there's nobody here – weather's seen to that. Just get warm and we'll see about food and something for Dave's cold, okay?'

Jerry started to strip off, murmuring encouraging words to Dave who, head bowed, began to strip off his layers of mismatched garments. Gus breathed a sigh of relief as he left the shower room. *At least they weren't going to find these two frozen solid on a park bench in the morning.*

As he stood guard outside the door, Hardeep approached, his arms filled with a bundle of clothes. Gus grinned, 'Thanks Hardeep. They'll need something to put on.'

Hardeep nodded to the door, 'You know, her up top won't be right happy about this, don't you?'

From inside the room, Gus could hear Dave's yelps followed by Jerry's soothing tones.

'There, there Dave. That's it. Nice and warm, isn't it.'

Hardeep laid the pile of clothes on the chair that wedged the door open. 'She won't appreciate you bringing in waifs and strays off the street.'

Gus frowned. Detective Chief Superintendent Gazala Bashir was new to The Fort, having transferred from Birmingham in a sideways move. Gus hadn't had much to do with her to date, but word through the ranks had it that she was a stickler for protocol. Bringing two rough sleepers into The Fort to use the facilities would no doubt infringe upon umpteen of her risk assessments. 'It's all about how you sell it to the brass, Hardeep.' He patted him on the arm and winked. 'Doubt she'd appreciate the alternative newspaper headlines, *'Two rough sleepers freeze to death in front of Bradford's main police station'*. No, I'm certain she'll be happier with *'Bradford's coppers open their doors to the homeless'*.'

At Hardeep's barked laugh, Gus added, 'Try to get a hold of one of the Mental Health nurses who patrol with the uniforms. Might as well put one of Bradford Police's better policies to good use. They might be able to speed up an assessment of Dave's needs.'

Certain that Jerry and Dave were in safe hands, Gus headed for the door. *Might actually make it out of this place tonight.* He'd got to the reception area and was beeping himself out when Nancy called his name. He turned and saw her hurrying down the stairs, her face flushed by the exertion. *God, had the Chief Super found out about Dave and Jerry already? Well he was ready to fight his corner on this one.* But...

'Don't you have your phone on? Been trying to ring you.'

Shit! He'd put it on silent because he was fed up of the sound of *The Bitch is Back* every five minutes. *Gabriella was nothing if not persistent. Persistent* and *annoying!*

'Need to have a word before you head home.'

That sounds ominous. Gus nodded and followed her back to the lift and up to her office. *Bye bye whisky and a chance to think things through in peace.*

They'd barely sat down when Nancy launched into it, her annoyance obvious by the way she tapped her fingernails on the table. 'Had Her Nibs on the phone. *Seems* she got a call from some high up head honcho. *Seems* they gave her classified information. *Seems* she can only share some of it with me. *Seems* it's on a need-to-know basis and *I*,' she prodded herself in the chest, 'quite clearly don't need to chuffing know, unlike her High and Bloody Mighty.'

Gus frowned. *What did this shit have to do with him?* 'The Chief Super?'

Nancy snorted, 'What other Her Nibs do you know?'

Gus though it wise to keep quiet. Clearly Nancy was as enamoured by Chief Super Bashir as Hardeep.

'Seems to think she can tell me how to do my job. How to organise my staff. Cheeky cow.' She glared across her desk at him.

Taking a deep breath to stop himself from hurrying her along, Gus waited. Nancy would continue when she was good and ready and not a moment before.

'Thinks she's better than the rest of us. One of those women who get to the top against all odds and promptly shits on the rest of her sex.' Nancy slammed her palm on the table top and made a low growling sound in the back of her throat.

Hiding his smile, Gus tilted his head, in what he hoped was a mildly-interested fashion. 'And?'

'And?' Nancy raged, 'And? Don't you get it? Seems like I can barely be trusted with '*classified…*' she made the universal air quotes motion with agitated fingers. '*information*'. What does she think I'm going to do? Stand on the chuffing roof with a loud hailer and announce it to Bradford or something? Take an ad out in the T&A or the Chronicle? Tattoo it on my forehead? AWWW! Makes my stool ferment in a Demi John.'

Yeuch! Just the image he needed floating around in his head right now.

Gus got 'it'. *In fact,* he'd be surprised if the entire Fort, *including* the Chief Super herself, hadn't heard. But none of that solved the puzzle of why *he* was here, with a woman whose shit was turning to alcohol in a translucent container, as they spoke. Hell, he'd heard the term 'he'd drink whisky through a shitty cloot' – but this took home brewing to a whole new level.

'It's not funny, Gus.'

Gus, realising he'd allowed his amusement to make it to his mouth, wiped the smile off his face and replaced it with a serious expression. 'Look, I can see you're upset, Nance, but what's all this classified shit got to do with me? I'm up to my ears in this Izzie Dimou thing and we've yet to locate Daniel Farrier.'

Nancy exhaled, 'That's just it. The classified stuff is about your damn brother-in-law.' She folded her arms under her breasts, leaned back in her chair and grinned. 'Things for you, Gus, just got a whole lot more complicated.'

Chapter 17

22:00 North Park Road, Manningham

Mo stood in the dark and stared out the conservatory window. The steadily falling snow was mesmerising, yet Mo barely noticed it. His thoughts were elsewhere, in a different time and place. Sixteen years ago to be precise, in a time that he'd rather forget. *Who am I kidding? I'll never forget that. How can I?* It was a time that he wished with all his heart he could rewrite. A time before he and Naila had married.

Zarqa had been playing up again and it was only a matter of time before he and Naila would have to do something. It wasn't just the tattoo – it was other things. Her cheek, her sulkiness. The way she looked at them. The way she avoided them by hiding out in her room and when she did come out, she looked like she'd eaten rancid ghee. But the snide comments were the worst. The barely concealed implications that he and her mum were bad Muslims. That they had no morals.

Perhaps they would have been wiser to move away all those years ago. Perhaps, it would have been better for them to have left everything they knew behind. Maybe then he wouldn't be in this position now. He'd fought hard to hold his head high in the community. He and Naila, *together,* had fought hard. Some people had long memories, yet he'd hoped that the ones who'd mattered had relegated the past to the past. Seems like someone had leaked something, because how else would Zarqa know to start asking these awkward questions.

He glanced back as Naila approached and wrapped both her arms around him, enveloping him. He swivelled round and pulled her to his chest and, squeezing tight, dropped a kiss on her hair. The familiar smell of her shampoo soothed him.

'We'll have to tell her the truth, Mo. You do know that, don't you?'

Mo nodded. 'I know. I know. But not yet. Please, not yet. I can't bear to bring that into our home. Can't bear the thought of her knowing. Let's leave it till after the summer. Leave it till she's moved schools and is settled in sixth form.'

Naila sighed. 'We can't keep putting it off. She knows there's a secret and *that's* why she's acting out. You don't want her to hear it from someone else. She needs to feel she can trust us, Mo. Keeping secrets isn't the answer. You know that. Deep down you know that.'

'Please, Nail.' Give me a few more months to get used to it. Come to terms with it.' He rested his forehead on to her hair, aware that his tears would soak through to her scalp, yet unable to prevent them from falling. This was his worst nightmare. 'Promise me Naila, give me till after the summer. I swear we'll tell her then.'

Naila bit her lip. He hated that he was making her feel this way. Hated that he was forcing her, yet he couldn't see another way out of this. She was right. There had been too many truths left unspoken, left to fester. He held her at arm's length, his hands gentle on her shoulders. 'I need the time, Naila. I need to get my head in the right place. I'll work at it, I promise. I'll go to a counsellor. I'll work through all of it. We'll go together, but I need you to promise. I need you to help me be ready.'

Naila held his gaze for a long time and raised her hand to his cheek, 'I love you, Mo. So much.' Then, in a whisper, 'I promise. But only till after the summer, okay? – after her exams.'

Mo's shoulders felt lighter. He had a reprise. Now all he had to do was get himself sorted before September.

Chapter 18

21:45 Saddleworth Moor

D aniel came round slowly. He opened his eyes only to close them again, the corners of his eyeballs fighting against the pain that shot across from one temple to the other. He swallowed. His mouth was dry and chalky. Groaning, he tried to move his limbs, but they were numb with cold and his fingers protested when he moved them. He flexed them once or twice before stretching out his hand and clumsily patting the area around where he lay. Fabric – cold, damp, soft fabric. There were soft ridges in lines on the material and his mind went back to the cover he remembered that used to stretch over his grandma's bed. What was it she called it? – a candlewick? He'd not come across one since his gran had died. His head rested on a pillow that smelled of something old and stale. It was lumpy. He pulled the far end of the cover and flipped it over his body. It released a damp, musty smell, so he held his breath. When he finally breathed again, he could detect a faint lavender scent, moth balls and vile all-encompassing damp.

Where was this shit hole? As awareness of the environment around him penetrated his fuzzy head, he opened his eyes again – this time ignoring the pain. Dusky fluid shapes trembled before him, formless and indistinguishable. Where was he? Ignoring the pain behind his eyes, he kept them open and peered through darkness, looking for something to ground him. Something solid that would tell him where he was, because,

100

right now, he wasn't entirely sure. A fleeting thought crossed his mind. Had Gus done this to him? A stag do prank? But no sooner had the thought come, that he dismissed it. His stag do wasn't 'till tomorrow.

Certain that his head was about to explode, Daniel closed his eyes once more and tried to collect his thoughts. Okay, it wasn't his stag do, so what was this all about? If his mind wasn't so fuzzy, he'd be able to concentrate. He was sure that there was something on the periphery of his memory that he should be focussing on, but right now he could barely keep his eyes open, never mind formulate any thoughts. He cast his mind back, trying to do that thing Izzie told him to do, every time he lost his car keys; start with his last memory and work backwards. The thing was, after some thought, Daniel's last memory appeared to be of being in Manchester, waiting for Izzie. He'd been in that Costa near Victoria Station. *Shit! How the hell could that be his last memory?* That had been in the morning, the snow had barely started to fall… and now it was pitch black. What had happened to him since then? He swallowed the panic that rose in his chest and forced himself to concentrate.

He'd ordered a Chai Latte and sat with The Guardian in the corner, allowing the chatter from the other customers to flow over him. The coffee had tasted good. He'd taken a long draft and read an article about Donald Trump separating kids from their parents – *idiot!* He'd gone to the toilet and when he came back, he'd flicked through the rest of the newspaper, sipping his drink. It was after that things got hazy, no clear memories, just moving images, being helped out, a male voice 'He's taken a bit of a funny turn.' Low voices, stumbling along, a car ride… then nothing. Who the hell had taken him? A surge of anger made him forget his pain. He sat up, pulling the blanket around him and slid his bum up to the top of the bed. Quickly, he patted his hands over his pockets. *His phone? Wallet?* Nothing!

Pulling his legs up, he dislodged the part of the quilt that was underneath and pulled it over his legs. Sitting on the clumpy pillow, he leaned against a wooden headboard and tried to think. He'd been drugged, that much was clear. More than likely someone put something in his drink when he went to the toilet. *In a café?* A pub was in the realms of possibility – getting drugged in a café seemed unlikely, unless of course he was targeted – followed and targeted. Again, the question *who?* raised its ugly head. Someone from Cyprus, from the university or from the UK or someone else?

So, what did that mean? He thought about it. *Izzie!* Someone, somewhere knew what she was doing in Manchester. That was the only explanation. Who though? They'd been careful. They'd not told anyone. He'd convinced her not to. Unless, of course she hadn't listened. Who could she have told? He supposed she could have given Jordan Beaumont the heads up before they left Cyprus. None of this was in his plans. He needed to be out there keeping an eye on things. Was whoever had taken him planning to use him as leverage? Is *that* what this was all about? The more he thought about it the more convinced he was that that was the case.

He wondered if Izzie had spoken to her contact. If she had, it was just a matter of waiting out whoever had brought him here. If, on the other hand, she'd been intercepted *before* she'd shared her information then things had become a lot sinister. He needed to act now. He needed to assume the worst and get out of here. Wherever *here* was.

He flicked his hand over, looked at the time on his wristwatch. Fuck! It was Saturday. He'd been out of it for more than twenty-four hours, and God only knew what was happening to Izzie. He swung his legs out from under the blanket. It hadn't given him much warmth anyway and using the light facility on his watch he stood up and began to explore his surroundings.

As he moved, the shapes he'd noticed earlier became more solid. An old fashioned heavy wooden wardrobe in one corner to his left and a four-drawer chest of drawers against the same wall but in the other corner. Directly opposite the ancient double bed that he'd been lying on, was an empty fireplace with a grate and soot-blackened fire tools inside. To the right stood a heavy mahogany dressing table with a mirror attached to the top, similar to the one his parents had once owned. In between the wardrobe and the chest of drawers was the door. Daniel walked over the threadbare Axminster carpet and, suspecting he'd be unlucky, tried the door. It was locked. He kicked it and rattled the handle, but it was solid. He strode to the opposite wall where the curtained window was. The curtains were heavy and touched the floor. He pulled the cord, that hung from one side, and with a grinding noise they swished open. The window was covered in a mosaic of ice.

Daniel remembered his mother telling him that during the winter she sometimes woke up to panes covered in ice on the inside. He'd never expected to witness that for himself. His mum had told him and Gabriella how she'd breathed onto the pane to clear a space each morning to look out of. He put his face right up to the window, feeling the chill hit his cheeks and, his breath steaming before him, he directed it onto the pane until an imperfect circle of lighter ice appeared. Using the sleeve of his jumper he wiped it away, until he could see outside.

He groaned. When he'd been in the cafe there had been a sparse spattering of snow and although he'd been aware of the Beast from the East forecasts, he hadn't in his wildest dreams expected this. He could see little beyond the driving snow that swirled before the window. But what worried him most were the things he couldn't see. No street lights, or glow from neighbouring properties, no sound, except the blizzard. His torchlight illuminated the inches of snow that had drifted up the window, almost obliterating the bottom pane. He yanked the single glazed window, but it was sealed shut with what looked to be years' worth of paint. Anyway, even if he could open it, he had nowhere to go.

Shivering, he moved back to the bed and conscious that his bladder needed emptying, wrapped himself in the foul-smelling candlewick quilt. Despite the god-awful smell, he covered his head and ears and nose. The building he was in was old and unused, he was sure of that. Maybe an old farmhouse or something. Looking out the window had given him no clues to his actual whereabouts and he didn't even know if he was alone or not. He couldn't hear anything, but the walls of these old buildings were so thick that it didn't mean anything.

The only thing he could do for now was wait. In the morning light he'd be able to assess his external environment and perhaps by then, if anyone was here, they'd make themselves known to him. On the other hand, if he *was* alone, there was no chance of anyone getting here anytime soon. This both worried *and* pleased him. If no-one could get to him, how could he get out? And how long could he last without food? On the other hand, if he was on his own, he had time to work out a plan of action.

Chapter 19

22:00 Mariner's Drive

G us had ignored Gabriella's ever more frequent calls. All evening he'd allowed them to go to voicemail, but even he had to admit thirty texts and twelve voicemails were too many to disregard, especially in the circumstances. Curled up on the couch with Patti, Bingo snoring lightly beside them and a glass of malt in his hand, Gus was finally beginning to thaw after hiking home. The walk from The Fort had been strange. Oak Lane was deserted and yet the traffic lights kept changing colour, gleaming eerily through the sheets of snow. The streetlights gave the flakes a luminescent glow and it seemed that Bradford was coated in a curtain of silence. He would have liked to have jogged, but that was impossible. He could barely trudge through the drifts and he felt like a pioneer as he took the first step onto the virgin blanket that covered Lister Park.

The Bitch is Back trilled from his phone, and with a sigh, Gus mouthed 'sorry' to Patti and picked it up from the coffee table. 'Hi Gabriella.'

Her voice shrieked across the room, drowning out the quiet background music Patti had put on. Flinching, Gus held the phone away from his ear and allowed Gabriella's rant to run its course.

'Look, I know you've been trying to catch me, but I've been running a damn murder inquiry. You have to let me get on with it.'

'All I wanted to know was if you've found Daniel'

Gabriella's voice sounded thick, as if she'd been crying and Gus felt like a dick. He should have made the effort to at least text her. She'd lost her sister-in-law-to-be and her brother had disappeared, of course she was worried. What made it worse, no doubt, was that she was stuck in Dublin till the weather cleared, unable to do anything, and reliant on him for information. He made an effort to soften his tone, 'Look Gabriella. The weather here is crap, so we're limited till it clears. We've been to Daniel's house, but he's not there. Can you think of anywhere else he could be?' He'd have to ask her about the information Nancy had given him earlier, but he decided to lead up to that.

The sound of sniffling was abruptly replaced by his sister's voice 'Gus, she's in bits. Doesn't know what to do with herself. You *need* to keep her in the loop. She's going crazy here. We both are. You can't let personal stuff get in the way of you doing the right thing.'

Gus bristled. That was a low dig. How dare Katie infer that he hadn't contacted Gabriella because of personal history? Who the hell did she think she was, taking the moral high ground? *She* was the one in a relationship with *his* ex-wife. *She* was the one who had stabbed him in the back and now she was accusing him of not contacting Gabriella because of that. He glanced at Patti, who – clearly able to interpret the tone of the conversation – had moved closer placing a placating hand on his thigh. Taking a deep breath, but unable to keep the ice from his tone, he said, 'The weather conditions here are arctic, yet I've pushed myself and my team as hard as I can to find Daniel whilst trying to find out as much as I can about Izzie. Forgive me if updating Gabriella every two minutes isn't top of my list of priorities. Besides which, being the ex-wife, or my sister's partner, for that matter, does *not* give her special privileges.'

Katie started to speak, but he raised his voice and spoke over her. 'That said, Katie, I will do my best to keep her informed from now on. Now, if she's up to it, I'd like to ask her a few questions. Can she cope with that? She's the only one with any real knowledge about Daniel and Izzie.'

From the sounds of it, Katie had put her hand over her phone and Gus could hear little snippets of conversation, muffled over the line. Seconds later Gabriella came back on the phone. 'Ask what you want Gus, trouble is, I don't know that much. He was my brother but I hardly saw him. I hardly knew him.' And she started to sniffle again.

For fuck's sake, this is all I need. Gus gave her a moment before asking his questions. 'I know Izzie and Daniel met in Northern Cyprus, but how exactly did they meet?'

'They both worked for the University of Nicosia. He's an archaeologist and there are loads of archaeological ruins throughout the North. You know that though, Gus. Daniel was trying to get EU funding to work on some of the sites that were becoming more and more threatened. He was researching the Roman ruins at Salamis. As for Izzie, she worked at the Uni too, doing research of some sort. I've no idea what department, though.'

Gus thought about that, 'What prompted them to come to the UK to get married? Why not just get married there? It's not like either of them had a whole load of relatives scheduled to attend the wedding.'

Gus could almost hear Gabriella thinking, so he gave her time.

'Never thought of it like that. You're right though. To be honest, I got the impression that they were coming over here anyway.' She paused, 'Something to do with Izzie's research, I think – although I'm not certain. She was having a meeting in Manchester yesterday. That's why she was flying to Dublin from there. No idea what the meeting was about. Daniel was going to Manchester with her though. He was meeting up with some of his old cronies from the archaeology department at Manchester Uni.'

That tallied with the footage they'd obtained of Izzie and Daniel, although they still had to ascertain Daniel's movements after he entered Costa. Compo had reported a rear exit near the loos and so they were trying to access footage from the back of the building. Gus hesitated. 'Gaby. Did you know Daniel worked for MI6?'

A snort, followed by a silence that went on for longer than Gus thought necessary. 'Gaby?'

'Sorry, Gus – just a bit shocked. You telling me Daniel is a spy? Don't be daft. He's too geeky. You've heard him going on about ruins and stuff – bore the socks of you. You must be mistaken.'

Gus sighed, 'No Gabriella. I'm not mistaken.'

Sunday

Chapter 20

It was bitter sweet for Compo to be in The Fort in the dead of night on his own. He loved the solitude, loved the way the darkness surrounded the little halo of light that emanated from his computer area. What he didn't like so much were the ghosts that kept flitting around. Memories of him and Sampson jamming out their interpretation of *Bat Out Of Hell or* sharing a late night snack with Alice, distracted him. There was a huge gap in the team. A hollowness that he saw reflected in Gus' slumped shoulders and the dullness of his eyes. Gus carried all the guilt on his shoulders, and Compo could so nothing to assuage it.

The laughter Alice dispersed wherever she went had dissipated like a waft of smoke in a gale and Sampson's solidity, his calmness, his humour, was gone. Taffy was a good kid, a bit cocky, but still a good kid. Even he seemed less sure of himself now and Compo had no idea how he could redress the imbalance. If he could, he would. He'd do *anything* to bring a smile to Gus' lips, to lift his shoulders, to put the sparkle back in his eye. He'd had the feeling this morning that Gus was on the point of telling him something. He hoped it wasn't that he'd asked for a transfer. He couldn't bear it if Gus left too. Gus was the main man. He gave them direction, navigated them through the investigations. Without him at the helm, he couldn't see them solving half as many cases.

Peeling the wrapper off a Mars Bar, Compo pressed a button on his computer and looked to see if any other data had come up on either Izzie Dimou or Daniel Farrier. He'd had to probe deeper than he'd expected, because his initial search had raised a whole load of red flags. He wondered why the University of Nicosia in Northern Cyprus had such a high level of encryption on their data. What was so special about Izzie Dimou? And why had Daniel Farrier's file had a red alert on it? The programme he was running would be done in a couple of hours with any luck. Then he'd have the answers to his questions.

He picked up a can of Fanta and opened it, slurping up the fizz that landed on his hand. At this time of night, he was unlikely to be disturbed, so his fingers flashed across the keyboard, setting up encryptions, misdirecting any searches The Fort's IT security might start. Looping them to safe sites and deleting his activity history as he went, replacing it with innocuous search sites that wouldn't raise eyebrows. If he was caught doing this it would be instant dismissal. Compo wasn't worried. Nobody on the tech team had a hope in hell of picking up on things – *numpties*.

The site he wanted was one that heard chatter from around the world and might just have heard something about Izzie Dimou. He logged into the Justice Room using one of his hacker aliases – ReviAeternus – and drifted through, checking out who was active, who was passively watching and what topics were floating. Nothing that concerned him right now, but a few he'd keep an eye on in his own time. He typed in a query and floated it 'Izzie hit you?'

A few lights sparked down one side of the screen telling him his query had been noted. Jayray was the first to reply, 'Context?'

Compo, grinned. Typical JayRay response, always wanted more than he was prepared to give. 'Need to know.'

He waited… five seconds… ten seconds… fifteen seconds, then Pitbull Warrior chipped in, 'Aw give us a clue RevAe?'

'SN Dimou – that help?'

One by one the replies came back, 'Negative.'

'No'

'Nowser'

'Okay, alert and report – request active, ongoing, ciao.'

His friends would implement alerts deeper down the web. If there was anything out there, he knew they'd find it and get back to him. He minimised the screen. Now, maybe time for a shut eye for half an hour or so.

He positioned the back rest of his chair into the most reclined position he could, propped his legs up on another chair and pulled his beanie down over his eyes. The computer would ping when it was ready, so he set his playlist on shuffle and had just settled down when the door opened with a loud click. Assuming it was Gus, Compo said, 'Coffee's on boss, help yourself.'

Instead Nancy's voice had him wheeling backwards, nearly falling of his chair and struggling to his feet. 'Thanks, Compo, I will have some.'

Conscious that he'd taken his DM's off and that his toe was poking through his sock, Compo made his chair upright and shuffled his lower body under the desk. Nancy filled her mug and, skirting Compo's computer station, sat on a chair opposite. 'Did you get stranded, Compo?'

For a moment, he wondered what she was talking about. He got it. *The snow.* Truth was he hadn't got stranded – he was exactly where he wanted to be. The Fort was more of a home than the flat he had off Thornton Road near where the notorious Crossbow Cannibal had lived. Last thing he wanted was for Nancy to suss that out though. Much as she was approachable and all that, she was still his big boss. Well aware that he was blushing, he wanted to curl up and die. The fact that she had a coffee in her hand told him that he wasn't going to be let off the hook so quickly. Looked like Nancy was settled in for one of those cosy chats that always made him feel awkward. 'No, no – well, sort of, well what I mean is, Gus said I could go to his, but I thought I might as well crack on. Find out what I could about Izzie Dimou and Daniel Farrier, ready for briefing tomorrow.'

Nancy nodded, and blew on her coffee, seemingly focussed on whatever she was thinking. Compo took the opportunity to dart a glance at his screen and was reassured that although the dark web screen was active, it was his ongoing legal search for Izzie and Daniel that was on the monitor. Last thing he needed was Nancy seeing something she shouldn't. Not sure what to say, but uncomfortable with the silence, Compo rummaged in his drawer and brought out a packet of chocolate Hobnobs. He'd been saving them, but Nancy looked like she could do with cheering up. 'Hobnob?'

Nancy smiled, her eyes momentarily brightening and Compo's lips twitched in relief. He'd done something right, for once.

'Don't mind if I do. Haven't had one of these in years and the chocolate ones are my favourites.'

He opened the packet and placed two on a slightly stained napkin next to Nancy. She picked up the first one and began to munch with relish. Compo, still a little wary, began to munch on one too. Although Nancy sat half in the shadows, he could see that she was wearing her slippers. It made him relax somehow. If she was wearing slippers, she couldn't be an ogre. He knew she and Gus were close, but he'd hardly spoken to her. The silence, broken only by munching sounds continued, until Nancy, placing her coffee on his desk, reached over, helped herself to the packet and took out two more biscuits. Compo stifled his sigh as she placed the packet in her lap. They were *his* favourites too. *Oh well.*

Clearing his throat, he decided to man up, 'Gus looked worried this morning.' When Nancy responded with a nod, but said nothing, he continued, 'Before we got called out to the crime scene, I mean.'

Nancy placed her mug and the half-eaten packet of biscuits on the desk and pulled her chair a little closer. She picked up another biscuit and snapped it in half, studying it as if she'd never seen one before. A crawling sensation eased its way over Compo's chest. This was ominous. *What was she not telling him?* After what seemed like ages, she popped one half of the biscuit in her mouth and flicked the crumbs from her fingers, before repeating the process with the other half.

'Gus went to see Alice yesterday.'

Compo's face lit up, then seeing the worry etched across Nancy's forehead it shrivelled and died, lying in his stomach like festering roadkill.

Nancy sighed, 'There's no easy way to say this and Gus has got enough on his plate right now, so I'm just going to tell you. You need to be strong. For Gus.'

'I know she was attacked. Was it worse than Gus said? She's not in a coma or summat is she?'

Nancy waved her hand, 'She's fine. Well, when I say fine, I mean she's in hospital, which is why Gus could go to see her. However,' Nancy bit her lip, slammed her hand on the desk top, 'she's changed her plea.'

Compo frowned, 'What do you mean, changed her plea. How could she?'

'She's pleading guilty.'

The words didn't sink in for a moment and when they did, he jumped to his feet, 'I don't understand this. Why would she do that? Why would she plead guilty to something she never did?'

'That's just it. Alice said she *did* do it. She says *she* was the brains behind the entire drug and weapon running ring. Says Kennedy was onto her, so she tried to kill him. Big H the drug dealer confirms it all.'

Compo, fists clenched by his sides, glared at her. 'You can't trust a bloody drug dealer. They must be forcing her somehow.'

'If it was just that, I'd agree with you, Compo,' she shook her head, 'But it's not. They've found a money trail between Alice and a South American drug cartel that leads directly to an offshore bank account in her name. They've uncovered money transfers to and from that account supplying weapons to Syria and Afghanistan. She's in deep, son. She's fooled us all.'

The roadkill in Compo's stomach twitched, like a zombie coming back to life. Its long-nailed fingers extended and raked down his abdomen, scoring furrows of oozing acid in the lining. He picked up what was left of the packet of Hobnobs and squashed them in one hand, sending a flurry of crumbs onto the floor.

One word erupted from his throat in a screech, 'Nooooo!'

Chapter 21

Okay, it wasn't the Hilton, but at least it was warm and had a double bed. Sean Kennedy had been lucky to get this room at the last minute and he was relieved. He hadn't anticipated staying in Surrey overnight, but The Beast from the East had made mincemeat of his plans to return to Brent after his nocturnal visit to Alice in the hospital.

He'd paid for two nights just to be sure. Didn't look like the weather was going to ease anytime soon and the forecast was for worsening conditions for the rest of the weekend. In his physical condition, he couldn't risk being snowed-in in his car for any length of time. At least here he was safe and thankfully the wonders of modern technology meant he could just as easily implement his plans from here as from Brent.

He'd bought some toiletries from the small chemist next door and stocked up on a Domino's pizza, a four pack of lager and a selection of sweets and crisps. Once he'd eaten and downed two of his four cans, he washed his socks and boxers in the miniscule en suite sink, with the decidedly average smelling hotel-provided shower gel. If there was one thing Sean hated, it was wearing underwear two days running. You had to have standards after all.

Avoiding his reflection in the mirror above the sink as he scrubbed, Sean – for the umpteenth time – considered his options regarding his hair. He could shave it off completely. The only thing was, that made the angry alopecia patches more obvious and he was wary of using anything on his scalp to exacerbate his condition. So, he'd take the doctor's advice for now, and done nothing. So what if people thought he looked like a holocaust victim? He'd long since stopped caring what others thought. He hung his boxers and socks over the shower rail and padded back into the room, where the telly played quietly. Taking off his shirt and jumper he grimaced. Ideally he'd prefer to change those too, but he wasn't sure they'd dry in time. He hung up his shirt and sprayed it with aftershave, before folding his jumper and placing it on the desk, ready for the next day. He hated eating in the same area he was going to sleep in. Hated the thought of the food smells lingering in his clothes. It made his skin feel itchy and the last thing he needed to do was scratch. His skin was flaky enough as it was.

After tying a knot in the plastic bag that lined the hotel room bin, he placed it outside the door, before returning and lining up his two beer cans next to the kettle and coffee-making facilities. He slid the chair under the desk and positioned the armchair snug in the corner of the room adjacent to the window. Satisfied that things were in order, he walked naked over to the window and parted the curtains slightly. The snow had drifted against the glass and ice patterns meandered up from the snow in a hotchpotch collage. Cold caressed his bare skin making a flutter of goose bumps up and down his arms. He could see little beyond the small parking area beneath and the lights from the adjoining pub.

Everything felt deathly still and it reminded him of the hospital after he'd first come round from his coma. The first few nights afterwards had been the worst. Weak as a baby, he'd struggled to feed himself, hold a glass, sit upright in bed. He'd played it safe, took the time to formulate his plans. Used the quiet solitude of the nights to plot, while during the day he was amenable, yet frail and broken. As he gradually pieced together what had happened in the intervening months and what evidence was stacked against him, he put out feelers. First to the officers who came to take his initial statement. He pretended his memories were coming back and his doctors corroborated that that was the normal recovery from such an injury.

The truth was, he'd wakened with a memory as clear as a bell. Alice Cooper, nearly in his sights, spinning round and kicking the gun from his hand, following through with another kick and then… nothing. Not long after that he'd pieced together the preceding narrative. His dodgy deals, building up his network, moving drugs, recruiting officers with a little ambition, threatening the gangsters, getting control of the chess board and moving his pawns where he wanted. If he hadn't been careful, Alice Cooper's testimony could have taken that away from him. He'd pulled in favours and, lo and behold, Big H had recanted his testimony, citing intimidation from Alice Copper as his reason.

Sean had bided his time and waited 'till he had, with help from his solicitor, everything in place. Then he set the hounds on the bitch. Alice Cooper had nearly killed him, but he'd have the last laugh. She'd be the one with a life-time in prison ahead of her, whilst Sean was fully exonerated, looked up to by the force and vindicated – lauded even.

He pulled the curtains closed, making sure they met exactly in the middle. His skin was cool now, so he flopped on the bed, pulling the quilt over his legs. On the table beside the bed were four throwaway phones, all lined up perfectly. He picked one up and pressed speed dial. This phone contained only one number. As soon as it was answered, he spoke. 'The doctors say she'll be discharged on Monday, weather permitting. Make sure that when she returns, my girls still have access to her. Don't want her forgetting her obligations now, do we?'

The prison warden laughed, 'Copy.' and hung up.

He'd every right to laugh. His cooperation in this matter was earning him enough to put both his daughters through private school. Sean knew exactly *which* private school – just in case! He was nothing if not prepared.

Business taken care of, he leaned back against the headboard and flicked through the TV channels. Nothing that excited him. He wished he was in a better hotel where he could, for a fee, access some porn. Perhaps it was his little contretemps with Alice that had got him all horny. Perhaps it was the knowledge that all his plans were coming to fruition. He neither knew, nor cared. All he was aware of was that his hard-on needed sorting. Pronto!

He closed his eyes, curled onto his side and remembered the rush of power that had surged through him when he grabbed her bruised breast and twisted. The cow deserved it. With the vision of Alice's trembling lips and furious eyes, tears spilling down her pale cheeks, he orgasmed for only the second time since he'd come out of his coma.

Chapter 22

03:15 The Fort

Compo's eyes were blurry. He'd been at the computer all night, rarely leaving his seat. Nancy's words about Alice earlier had left him devastated. Alice was the glue that held the team together and it had been bad enough when she'd got arrested, but now? To have everything he held dear brought into question, Compo's world had crashed.

The team were his world. He could barely remember his parents – just a series of foster homes with bullies and perverts all ready to take it out on the wimpy kid – the weirdo. He was the one they laughed at and, after what seemed like millions of unsuccessful attempts to fit in, he'd given up trying. He was 'the geek', the one who was always slightly out of the loop. The one who ran away from everything – until he joined Gus' team that is. He hadn't run away from here. This team was his family and Gus' mum and dad were his extended family. He was part of something – a valued part of something and that was because of Al. She'd looked after him. Teasing him, not minding if he got ketchup on her paperwork, looking out for him – and now they were saying this crap about her.

It had taken him a long time, three Mars Bars, a gallon of Sprite and a lot of music to calm down, but he'd begun mulling things over. He plugged his ear buds in and resorted to The Doors for inspiration. If Jim Morrison couldn't inspire him no one could. He was half way through *Riders On The Storm* when he realised that if Gus and Nancy weren't going to weather 'The Storm' for Alice, he would have to.

He'd always looked up to Gus – thought he was infallible – but maybe he wasn't after all. Maybe he was too loved up or too worn down. Compo wasn't sure. But he *was* sure of one thing and that was that the ache in his belly and the hurt in his heart wouldn't go away unless he did something for Alice.

He thought long and hard about his friend and the one thing he did know was that she was nobody's fool. The second thing he knew was that she was as honest as he was. This *had* to be some sort of mistake. Alice – his humorous, bouncy friend – would never betray herself, never mind her team in that way. Never! No way was Al a bent copper. No fucking way! She was too good, too straight down the line to be bent.

So, no matter what Gus thought, *he* was going to sort this damn mess. Prove that he was as good a copper as the rest of them. That being the case, Compo set to work on jobs he could do only in the dead of night with no-one else around. At one point he considered trekking to his flat, but the thought of its cold atmosphere compared to the warmth of The Fort convinced him the hour-long hike through freezing blizzards just wasn't worth the effort. Besides it was like Alice was here beside him, watching over him. There was no way anyone would be able to trace what he was doing. However, just to be doubly sure, he got his personal laptop out of his rucksack and got cracking.

With the Izzie Dimou search still humming in the background, he dimmed the lights, plugged in his ear buds and set his music to *Dark Side of The Moon*, which, in the present circumstances, was quite apt. Oblivious to the snow drifting against the window, creating a barrier between him and the outside world, Compo set to work. He was going deeper than he had in years. Deeper than he was comfortable with but, with quiet determination he put all thoughts of what could happen to him out of his mind. Sometimes friendship was more important than a job – even a job he loved.

Chapter 23

04:05 Saddleworth Moor

The cold had seeped into Daniel's bones and he couldn't stop shivering, yet he was determined to either find a way out of this room or find a way to survive. That meant keeping warm, finding something to drink and making sure he could protect himself when the snow thawed and his captors returned. Food, he could do without for now. He was fairly sure he was on his own. If his captors were here they'd have made some noise by now, or he'd have seen even a faint light shining through the downstairs windows. Earlier, when the snowing had stopped for a short time, the moonlight reflected enough light for Daniel to see that there was no sign of a vehicle outside. He reckoned his room faced out over the front of the farmhouse because he could see, if he stood on tiptoe and craned his neck, the peak of a porch and snow-covered side buildings making a sort of half square round the building in which he was imprisoned.

Every so often a flutter of fear bubbled in his chest. Each time it did, Daniel swallowed it down and tried to focus on his own immediate needs. Worrying about Izzie and where she was, was pointless, he told himself. Yet it was too difficult not to worry. He'd sought her out in Nicosia. He'd inveigled himself into her life. He'd got her to confide what she'd discovered in her lab and he'd led her to Manchester.

The need to wee was getting progressively more desperate. He had to make a decision – designate a toilet area, because who knew how long he'd be trapped here, or wet himself. After weighing up his options, he whipped out one of the drawers from the old dressing table, tipped its contents in a pile on the floor, to be gone through later, and put it inside the wardrobe. Next, he'd grabbed the wardrobe's contents, a varied collection of mainly female clothing, and flung them on the bed. Aware that the wooden drawer was porous, he lined it with the old plastic sheet he'd found covering a chair near the window. Perhaps that might be enough to prevent any leakage. He used, with great relief, the makeshift loo shutting the wardrobe doors on it when he was done God only knew how he'd cope when he needed something more than a pee, however, he'd cross that bridge when he came to it.

Immediate needs taken care of, Daniel picked up some of the items of clothing. He didn't care how he looked, there was no heat in the farmhouse, so fashion was irrelevant. He picked up two misshapen, hand knitted jumpers and pulled them over his head. They were a bit tight, so he looked for a larger item of clothing he could put on top. When he found a slightly mouldy-smelling duffle coat, he put it on with no hesitation and feeling a bit like a Teletubby, he began to sift through the contents of the drawer he'd tipped out.

The previous farmhouse inhabitant had clearly been a woman, and judging by the clothes and trinkets, an elderly one who didn't get out much. His headache persisted, but that was a minor worry. He needed something to collect the ice he scraped off the window. Feeling dehydrated earlier, in a burst of stupidity, he'd tried to lick the ice off the window. His tongue had stuck to the ice and he'd had to rip it off, causing it to bleed slightly. As a result, he had a stinging tongue to add to his list of worries.

He picked up a jewellery box, opened the lid. Inside was a Wedgewood trinket box, its pigeon-egg blue with the trademark cameo on it, was of minor importance. Daniel had other plans for it. He took the ceramic container over to the window and, with the edge of an old black comb he'd lifted from the dressing table, he scraped a depressingly small amount of ice from the window into the container. It wasn't a lot, but he could repeat the process. Once it thawed he'd be able to drink it.

The thought that he was being proactive cheered him up, and he continued sifting through the contents of the room. When he found a box of matches, his heart nearly stopped. *Who would have thought anyone could ever be so excited about such a small thing?*

If the worst came to the worst, and he had to break the window pane to get snow to melt, he could at least light a fire to offset some of the cold. He looked at the heavy-duty old-fashioned furniture which looked so well cared for, as if it had been lovingly polished for generations and he imagined it had been in this family's possession for a very long time. Never mind. If it came to it, Daniel would cheerfully say '*bye, bye furniture*'.

Chapter 24

04:10 Titus Street, Saltaire

Not managing to fit in his usual jog had left Gus unsettled. Patti had long since gone to sleep, yet his legs were twitchy and his mind was like a rollercoaster, going up and down and roundabout. Patti, though he wouldn't tell her, snored just a little. Her chest rising and falling, her mouth open slightly. The temptation to lean over and kiss her was strong, but Gus would let her sleep. He eased himself out of the bed, and Bingo, asleep in his basket near the door, opened one eye, gave a half-hearted wag of his tail and joined in with Patti's snoring.

Grabbing his clothes as he went, Gus left the bedroom and shut the door firmly behind him. Sleep wasn't going to come. Not with images of Alice's sunken cheeks and emotionless eyes, like two dank caverns, haunting him. Of course, there was Izzie. She had been tortured. Gus' dad confirmed that it looked like professionals had inflicted the wounds on her body, so Gus couldn't stop wondering what she'd gotten mixed up in. Then there was Daniel. Where had he gone? None of this looked good and Gus was itching to get on and do things. The interviews in the local neighbourhood had ground to a halt as the weather deteriorated. He couldn't get to Manchester or to the scene of the train crash. If Daniel was implicated in Izzie's death then he needed to be out there catching him. If – on the other hand – he was also a victim, he needed to be out there looking for him. Truth was, the only investigating going on was whatever Compo could do digitally. All other avenues were closed. Even the lab, bar a skeleton staff, had shut down.

After sneaking downstairs, Gus scribbled a quick note for Patti and got his outdoor clothes on. It was madness, but he needed to be doing something. Needed to work off this excess energy that was keeping him awake. He shoved a hat over his dreads, wrapped a scarf round his neck and left the house.

For now, the snow had stopped. More was forecast, but Gus wasn't bothered by that. He set off down the drive to the snicket beside the Sainsbury's on Keighley Road and began to trudge towards Saltaire. It was only a couple of miles, but in this weather, it would take him the best part of an hour if not more. The snow was at least five inches deep and trudging through it made Gus' calves ache. Still he kept on, enjoying his accelerated heart rate and the slight sweat that formed under his outer clothes, despite the cold.

The walk had an ethereal feel to it. It was almost otherworldly, like he was the only person on the planet and he relished it. Relished the time to think. The snowing, when it began, offered a rhythmic calmness that was soothing. The occasional car headlight swept over his solitary figure as he traipsed along the pavement. Mostly, his were the only foot prints in the snow, but occasionally he saw an animal print and once, from under a bush in a garden, he was caught off guard by a fox staring at him. *Poor sod, he'd have a hard time finding food in this weather.* By the time he reached Alice's house, the one where Daniel and Izzie had been living for the past few weeks, Gus hesitated.

When he'd been earlier, he was accompanied by other officers and a CSI team. Now, he was on his own, and for the first time since he'd left Mariner's drive he questioned his actions. He wasn't even sure if he was here to find some evidence about Alice or about Daniel and Izzie. Alice's house had always been a place of joy and laughter. She'd been like an over-excited kid when she'd first moved in, insisting everyone come for afternoon tea. It had been her sanctuary, her solace, or so Gus had thought, from the trauma of her involvement with Sean Kennedy. Now Gus wasn't so sure. Now it seemed that Kennedy had been the innocent one. *Is she really bent?* If she was, her belongings certainly didn't reflect hidden wealth. How could he have got things so wrong? It was with that thought that Gus realised he was here to try to find something, anything to put lie to what Alice was admitting to. However, whilst he was here he'd keep an eye open for something that might shed some light on where Daniel was.

The gate was wedged shut by the snow, so Gus climbed over it, landing in a drift up to his thigh. He cursed and climbed his way out of it, before walking up the small path and inserting his key in the lock. A welcome blast of heat hit him as he pushed the door open, allowing a shower of snow to clump on the welcome mat inside. Gus kicked as much as he could of the drift back outside and shut the door. He stood for a minute in the dark, searching for a trace of Alice's familiar scent. All he could smell was a lemony air freshener and a faint tinge of bleach. It was as if Alice had never been here. Pinching himself for being fanciful, he reached out and flicked the light on, blinking rapidly at the sudden glare. He was immediately transported back to when Alice still lived there.

Above a round table, adorned by a neglected looking plant, perched a framed photo of her with her parents taken last summer in Cyprus. Her parents, so serious, looked fondly at Alice who sported the widest grin. She'd often told Gus that she felt like a changeling; like she wasn't really her parents' daughter, but some imposter. On closer inspection, Gus saw that she shared her mother's dark eyes and her father's hair. She was no changeling, so why had she done a complete turnaround with her plea? He moved further along the hallway. Looking at photos wasn't going to help him discover something to help Alice. If there were any clues they would be in her office. He put his hand on the bannister and began to climb the stairs.

He knew this house as well as he knew his own. He'd helped Alice move in, had spent hours here with her over the last couple of years. She'd confided in him, he'd confided in her. Now it seemed all of that had been a lie. She'd certainly played him. And not just him, but his parents and the team too. Hell, he doubted Compo would get over this, not so soon after losing Sampson.

Reaching the landing he looked round. The house felt displaced. The absence of Alice taunted him, laughed at him. Daniel and Izzie hadn't put much of a mark on the house, but nonetheless their presence had edged Alice out. It had been a mistake to let them live here, but – faced with the combined pressure of Katie and Gabriella – he'd relented. Better to have the place lived-in than lying empty, stagnating in Alice's absence.

He couldn't put his finger on what in particular made him like this. Probably just a reaction to how Alice had been when he saw her – her betrayal. Ignoring the main bedroom, which had been given the once over by Hissing Sid and his team earlier, he headed to the small room at the end of the corridor. The door was shut and although the CSIs had gone over it too, they'd found little evidence that Daniel or Izzie had used it much. In fact, judging by the scatter of paperwork on the dining table it looked like they'd used the dining area in the corner of the living room as an office.

From Gus' point of view this made his job easier. Chances were, anything he found in here would belong to Alice. He rested his hand on the door knob for a fraction of a second. Did he really want to do this? What if he found something that incriminated Alice even more than she already was? Could he betray her like she'd betrayed him? Would he be able to hand over evidence that would land her in further trouble? He exhaled and depressed the handle. Who was he kidding? The London police had been all over the entire house when they first arrested Alice. If there was anything incriminating to be found, it would've been found already. He knew he wasn't really looking for evidence against her. He was looking for that faint glimmer of hope her words at the hospital had denied him. Dammit, he was looking for her innocence. *What a damn fool I am!*

The door slid over the wooden floor and jammed. Gus pushed harder but it wouldn't budge. It didn't matter, it was wide enough for him to enter, so he stepped into Alice's home office and glanced behind the door to see what the obstruction was. A wedge- shaped door stop had jammed under the door preventing it opening fully. Gus kicked it out of the way and the door slid shut, blocking out the light from the hallway. Stretching out his hand to the light switch, Gus froze. Was that a noise from downstairs?

Instead of putting the light on, he opened the door and listened. There it was again. It could be snow falling off the roof. The thought flashed into his mind and straight back out again. The noise was nothing like snow sliding down the roof and crashing to the ground. He knew exactly what that noise was. Hell, he'd heard it often enough – made it often enough.

After glancing round the office, he grabbed the lamp from the desk and made his way downstairs. Whoever was trying to pick the lock on the kitchen door was not very proficient or they'd have had the door open by now. He'd been on at Alice for ages to upgrade her security and he could probably pick her back-door lock in a jiffy. Maybe the intruder's fingers were frozen – no way you could pick a lock with proper gloves on – thin nitrile ones at a push, but even leather ones made it hard to manipulate the tools. Whoever this was, it had to do with Izzie's murder. Perhaps it was Daniel. No, he'd have a key – unless he'd lost it. But wouldn't he just phone Gus for a spare? Besides which, even if it was Daniel, he wasn't convinced of the man's innocence. He'd need to prove himself to Gus.

Thankful that the hallway light was dim and presumably hadn't penetrated to the rear of the property, Gus reached the bottom of the stairs and flicked it off. No point in advertising his presence. Whoever was coming in from the back alley had clearly not bothered to check out the front of the house. *More fool them.* For now, Gus was waiting for them. He paused outside the closed kitchen door. If he waited till they cracked the lock, he'd have more chance of catching them. If he disturbed them too early, they'd head off into the night and after his trek through the snow, Gus wasn't sure he'd be able to keep up with them. Closing his eyes, he did a mental walk through of Alice's kitchen – hoping that Daniel and Izzie hadn't seen fit to rearrange things during their short occupancy. It wasn't a big kitchen; a breakfast bar at the end of a freestanding unit, a huge fridge, once filled with ready meals and beer, and a variety of bobbing head toys dotted across the windowsill, next to an aloe vera plant.

He cracked the kitchen door open and slid into the dark room, skirted the table and stood beside the fridge where he couldn't be seen from the door. The sounds were clearer now. The scratch of metal on metal. Jiggling, Gus could visualise each of the movements – a slide, a juggle, a twist, a slide – and, if you were lucky, or skilled enough, the lock would give. When he heard – above the scraping – a muffled curse followed by a kick on the door, Gus grinned. *Not as easy as you think, matey!* The scraping recommenced and then a grunt that Gus recognised as satisfaction. Standing on the balls of his feet, heart racing, he waited. A gust of freezing air signalled the door being pushed open, followed by the sound of someone kicking snow from their feet. Gus edged forward. Anticipation hitching his breath in his chest. *Come on Daniel or whoever you are, let's be having you.*

He waited till he heard the intruder move into the kitchen, closing the door behind them, before leaving his hiding place. As if sensing his presence, the intruder swung towards Gus. He was tall and skinny, dressed in black. A balaclava covered his head. It was clear that he wasn't Daniel. Daniel was more stooped and carried more weight. Well, whoever it was, Gus was about to find out what this guy wanted breaking into Alice's house. Gus fancied his chances. However, he hadn't anticipated the speed of the other man's reactions.

As he moved forward, the other man lifted his hand to waist level and swung the bag he was carrying at Gus' knees. Caught by surprise, Gus' legs collapsed and he fell to the ground, landing on one knee. Pushing himself upright, the intruder grabbed his dreads and pulled his head forward, before kicking him in the face. The taste of blood was immediate as his nose burst, sending a gush down the back of his throat. As the intruder retracted his foot, Gus grabbed it and twisted, pushing upwards as he did so. The other man hopped twice before crashing to the floor, his arms catching the table and knocking a plant pot to the floor as he fell.

Gus drew his sleeve across his bloody nose and propelled himself to his feet. Leaning over, he grabbed the intruder by the collar and, pulling back one arm, fingers fisted, he paused, breath heaving in his chest, heart pounding. With deliberate effort he relaxed his fingers and released his grip, allowing the other man to fall back to the floor, his head cracking on the tiles. Jaw tense, Gus released a slow breath and counted to five. 'Get that fucking mask off your face and tell me what the hell you're doing here.'

The intruder pushed himself up on his elbows. When he spoke, it was in accented English. 'Fuck you.'

Gus stepped closer and leaned over the prone figure, wishing he'd slammed his fist into his face earlier when he had the chance. He reached out to the mask and grabbed it. It slipped off the man's head at the same time as he raised a knee and connected with Gus' testicles.

'Fuuuck!' The pain shot through him, his scrotum shrivelling into his belly. As Gus stumbled backwards, his hands cupped the aching area, barely able to control the nausea. The intruder, jumped to his feet, grabbed his tool box and dived towards the door. Wrenching it open, he ran outside into the blizzard, casting a backwards glance at Gus. In that moment, Gus saw that beneath his stubble, it was clear the man's skin was tanned. His attacker looked like someone more used to Mediterranean climes than the snow they were having now.

The blast of air, brought Gus round and he staggered out in pursuit, trying to push the pain to the back of his mind. His legs wobbled yet, despite the sweat on his brow, shivers wracked his body. Straining his eyes through the blizzard, Gus saw a shadowy figure disappearing through Alice's back gate. He followed, knowing that any footprints would soon disappear in the blizzard. The snow sucked at his feet, and his legs, leaden, struggled to pull each foot from the snowy quagmire.

He followed the figure through the gate and looked both ways. Barely discernible footprints furrowed the snow in both directions along the back alley. Looked like the fucker had the presence of mind to leave in the opposite direction from which he'd arrived, leaving Gus with a fifty-fifty chance of following the right route.

Taking pot luck, Gus headed to the right, hoping that the masked intruder would double back towards Victoria Road. However, he'd barely rounded the bend when a growling engine heading up towards Bingley Road told him he was too late.

Trudging back to Alice's house, he thought over what had happened. The intruder was definitely not Daniel and from his accent he was not Bradford born. Which made him wonder exactly what was so important that he had to stage a break-in in the middle of the worst snowstorm Bradford had seen for years. He was convinced that the attempted burglary was about Izzie's murder rather than Alice's current position. When he reached the door, he scooped up a handful of snow, carried it indoors and grabbing a nearby tea towel, wrapped the snow in it. After securing the door, he headed back upstairs to Alice's office, phoned for a CSI team and sat down welcoming the cool ice pack on his groin as he went over the evening's events. *What exactly had Izzie been up to?*

Chapter 25

It wasn't the dull but insistent throb in her breast that kept Alice awake. It was fear. Fear and worry, and anger and disappointment. Despite her best efforts to convince Gus of her complicity – her duplicity, the sadness in his eyes had curdled her heart. She'd never seen him look so disappointed, so betrayed. How she'd held it together, she would never know. The later visit from Sean Kennedy had been traumatic and painful, yet it hadn't affected her like Gus' had. Where Gus' visit had torn her soul from her, Sean's had lit a fire in her gut. If she ever got out of this mess, Sean Kennedy would be dead. Her fingers clutched the bed sheets and her lips tightened. Sean Kennedy better stick to his word and leave her parents alone. If he didn't, she'd kill him. Hell, either way, she'd kill him. He'd pushed her over a precipice and there was no going back for her. Not now. Her sole aim was to get revenge. No matter how long she had to wait, that slimy bastard would pay.

The only thing was getting through this. Till now she'd sworn Gus to secrecy, to keep her parents out of the loop. Now that she'd admitted blame, all bets would be off. Too many truths left unspoken. Would he phone her parents and let them know what she'd done? The thought of her mother's frown as she tried to make sense of what her changeling baby had become broke her heart. Her father would try to be stoical in that tentative way he had. His specs would be taken off and put back on again repeatedly. They'd be ashamed of her. Their little

Alice. The child they hadn't expected to ever have. The child that, despite not fully understanding her, they loved so much. Would their love shrivel and die? Would they hate her?

The trouble was she didn't trust Sean Kennedy an inch and she had been forced to alienate the one person she could have trusted to help her. Now, she was on her own and her enemies were everywhere – Sean Kennedy had made sure of that.

The door opened and Alice tensed. She could tell from the heavy footsteps that it was a different prison officer. Change of shift apparently. She recognised him. He was the one who'd turned a blind eye when Hairy Mary and her crew had got her in the showers, the one who'd stood back and let Baby Jane do her worst, so she knew he was in Sean Kennedy's pocket. Gripping the plastic fork, she'd managed to swipe and hide under the blanket after Sean's visit, she kept her hand under the sheet. It wasn't much, but it was better than nothing. She'd only be able to use it if he came close enough and she'd only use it if he was a threat.

The footsteps paused and Alice held her breath, releasing it only when she heard him turn retreat. *Thank God. He was only checking on her. Probably just getting a rise out of panicking her up, no doubt on Kennedy's orders.*

Seconds later she heard the turning of the slats of the blinds that covered the small window on the door. She jerked round and saw that he'd closed them and had now turned towards her, a purposeful look on his face. Hoarfrost rushed through her veins as she saw him moving towards her pulling on his belt, a grin on his face. The final shred of humanity faded and her mind went into survival mode. Meeting his gaze, she used the freezing shock coursing through her body to focus. An image of a brittle icy superhero flitted into her mind and she smiled recognising the figure as herself.

'You ready for me, bitch?'

A wave of Millions aftershave drifted to her – her favourite – until now. Two steps closer, she could see his cock pushing against his boxers, smell the underlying musk of excitement. He was like a feral animal – the expensive scent not covering his skunk's stench. With one hand in his boxers, releasing his erection, he slipped on a condom and flipped the sheet up from the bottom of the bed, revealing Alice's tiny frame in her faded green hospital gown.

Alice gripped the fork tighter. She was in no position to move. Wires sprung from her arms attaching her to the machine by her side. *Should she yell? No point.* Bastard would have cleared it with his mate outside the door. As he climbed onto the bed, knees forcing her legs open, Alice tensed her lower limbs and made to raise her arm, but he gripped her arms, pressing his bulk onto her, making her immobile. Her entire body was on fire and under his weight she could barely breathe, never mind move.

When he was done he collapsed onto her chest, breath coming in hard gasps, musk filling the air around her and released his grip on her arms. Alice, able to move now, lifted her arm and with a strength she hadn't realised she still had, grabbed his hair with one hand. Before he had a chance to react she pulled her left arm from beneath the sheet and sunk the fork into his neck. He yelped and tried to grab her hand. She used her adrenalin to raise her head and fastening her teeth around his nose, she bit as hard as she could, all the while remembering Baby Jane's triumphant look, when she'd bitten off her nipple. Alice fed on her anger and kept biting, ignoring his scrabbling arms and the iron taste in her mouth. She stretched her other hand to her side and pressed the emergency button, before releasing her jaws. Using the last of her strength, she tipped him, still whimpering, onto the floor.

Within seconds the door burst open and Alice's nurse rushed through. She stopped dead, looking at the prison guard, trousers round his ankle, flaccid penis still with a condom on, nose gushing blood and plastic fork stuck in his neck. Moving to stand beside Alice, she took her phone from her pocket and dialled.

Chapter 26

As he hobbled upstairs, Gus' testicles throbbed like he'd been kicked by a shire horse. Going back into Alice's office, he jammed the door wedge under the door with a force born of pain and frustration. The intruder had gone – he was sure of that – but no point in taking chances. At least if the door was open he'd hear any further break-in attempts. More importantly though, he'd be able to hear when the crime scene team arrived and head downstairs to meet them. He didn't want them guessing he'd been searching through Alice's stuff.

His groin pain hadn't diminished and the ice in the tea towel had no effect other than to leave a wet patch on the front of his jeans, as if he'd pissed himself. *Just what he needed with the CSIs en route. Knowing his damn luck, it'd be Hissing Sid too.* He could imagine the senior crime scene investigator spreading the word far and wide. Every crime scene from now on in would be a bloody fiasco. Tena Lady's would be planted on his desk alongside portable urinals and men pads – *Joy!*

Pulling himself to his feet, Gus vacated Alice's office chair and wandered into what had been her bedroom. Surely Izzie would have a hairdryer or something he could use to dry his trousers. No way was he stripping off downstairs and putting them in the tumble dryer – that would be even more ammunition for Hissing Sid. Spotting a hairdryer, covered in fingerprint dusting powder, he plugged it in and tried to dry off his jeans, praying that Sid wouldn't arrive till the patch was less obvious. Five minutes of heat to his balls did nothing to alleviate the pain and little to dry the patch, so he gave up and went back into Alice's office. There on her desk was the Matchbox Mini he'd given her the Christmas before last. He'd had it custom built with a little blue light on the roof. When you pressed it, it played Alice Cooper's – the real one, as Alice called him – *No More Mr Nice Guy*. Turns out that Alice Cooper rock star was probably more genuine than his Alice. He picked up the car and pressed the light, remembering Alice's gleeful grin when she'd opened it. A lot had happened since then. A lot of shared memories, a lot of sadness, some joy, plenty of laughs. But above all a deep and, or so he'd thought, lasting friendship. One he would miss every day. He put the car back on the desk and hardened his heart. No more sentimentality. He'd had his fill of dirty coppers and if Alice was one, then he'd had his fill of her too.

The thing was, Gus was honest enough to admit, if only to himself, it was personal to him. Her betrayal gutted him just when he was beginning to have faith in humanity again. Just when he needed her to be real, to be true. So, he did the only thing he could do and opened her drawers and began to search for something to either confirm or refute what she'd admitted to. Surely, she couldn't have lived a lie like that for so long without leaving some evidence dotted around. He pulled each drawer out and slid his hand inside the gap, searching for concealed envelopes or any indication that Alice was hiding things, but it was to no avail.

Truth was, deep down inside he was aware that it was a pointless exercise. If Alice had pulled the wool over his eyes for so long she'd be smart enough not to leave anything incriminating behind. Besides, her house had been searched before. At the back of his mind was the thought that Alice may have outsmarted them all and hidden something so well, it would be impossible for them to find.

Giving up, he sat down and swivelled back and forth on the chair trying to take his mind off both Alice and the pain. *Where the hell were the crime scene team?* A tingle at his temple told him he was due one of his headaches. The ones that often signalled a series of palpitations and sometimes a major panic attack. He wasn't surprised. After everything that had happened over the last few days, his worries over Alice and the rest of the team and now the kick to his balls, he'd been through the mill. He was only just holding it together. Since Sampson's death before Christmas, a ball of spiky anger had settled in his chest, niggling him constantly. Getting sharper for no reason at the most inconsequential of things. He'd even yelled at his mother and that, in Gus' book, was a cardinal sin. She, under no circumstances, deserved to be on the receiving end of his anger. It had made him edgy. He'd been cutting corners a bit, being less sympathetic at interview, keener to take on the bad guy role and somehow been more effective that he used to be. Nancy had told him that he was cloaked in coldness sometimes – he grinned, he was certainly cold now. Alice's central heating was less than efficient.

The doorbell rang and Gus jumped to his feet. That'd be Sid and his team no doubt. He walked to the door and tried to dislodge the wedge – no point in risking any questions about why he was there rather than downstairs in the relative comfort of the living room. The wedge wouldn't budge. *Fuck's sake.* In his temper earlier, he'd rammed it under the door so hard, that now the damn thing was stuck. He kicked it again, but still it wouldn't move. The doorbell rang again, so he bent down and tried to prise it out with his fingers. As he squeezed it, it collapsed a little at the broad end. Cursing again, he yanked it harder and when it came out he saw that the back part had come loose. He frowned and lifted it up. There was something inside.

The doorbell rang – an elongated ring now. *Sid was getting impatient.* Tipping up the wedge, Gus inserted two fingers and gripped the contents. For a second he looked at what he'd discovered and grinned. *Gottya Alice!* He popped it in his pocket and went downstairs and opened the door. 'For God's sake Sid, I was in the loo. Can't you even wait for a couple of minutes?'

Chapter 27

Mickey – glad that she'd invested in a four by four with snow tyres – had managed to get home in one piece. She'd had a few near misses and had crawled along at a snail's pace. It had taken her nearly two hours by the time she'd abandoned her vehicle on the main street and trekked up to her home with its welcoming lights that had been set to timer. Since her husband had gone off with her best friend and her son had gone to uni, there was no one to make sure she came home to a welcoming glow behind the curtains. No, that was just another one of the many tasks she'd taken upon herself to ensure she didn't feel she was rattling about in a mausoleum.

Every bone in her body ached with the cold and her toes and fingers had taken ages to thaw. She'd poured herself a large gin and tonic and flung herself on the couch, wondering if perhaps she should have taken on the cat her neighbour had tried to force on her. At least a cat wouldn't desert her for her best friend, or the appeal of a university so far away that she was limited to the occasional Skype call and the odd Whatsapp message. She pulled the fleece blanket over her legs and settled down for the night. The living room was cosy and the thought of warming up a huge king-size bed on her own fell far short of her hopes for her home life when she'd turned fifty. She would sleep on the couch like she'd done most nights for the past few months.

She allowed her mind to wander, the soporific benefits of the gin and tonic making her drowsy. It wasn't that she was lonely exactly. Her job kept her too busy for that, it was just that she felt betrayed by the men in her life. Whilst she'd focussed on her career to make sure they could afford a house in the country and private education for Freddie, her husband had been planning his grand escape with affair after affair. The thing is, she'd been too busy to notice and, truth be told, too much in love with her job to care. Now, here she was rattling about in a big house without even a cat for company. *Who am I kidding? I'd forget to feed the cat and I'm never home anyway. No, a cat's a bad idea – a very bad idea.*

When she woke it was still dark outside, although it was morning. She had an uncomfortable crick in her neck, a bitter gin aftertaste in her mouth and a faint sweaty smell filtered up to her nose as she flicked off the fleece. Barefoot she padded over to the window and pulled the string to open the curtains. Overnight the blizzard had obliterated her footprints and it looked like no one bar, judging from the prints, a three-legged fox had ventured out overnight. Cursing herself for making the journey home, Mickey wished she'd just bedded down at The Fort overnight. Now she was stranded. No way would Sandy Lane, between Oxenhope and Bradford, be passable in this weather. She turned over, flicked on the TV in search of the weather forecast, the results of which upset her even more. Calendar News.

'Homes in the Dales cut off, leaving communities isolated and vulnerable as fresh blizzards sweep the region. Severe weather warnings. Motorists advised not to travel unless absolutely necessary.'
Bollocks!

Mickey flung the remote down and headed into the kitchen. Peering into the fridge, her fears were confirmed. Apart from a random slice of dry rye bread and a bottle of prosecco, the fridge was empty. Feeling less than hopeful, she tugged at the freezer door and was pleased to see a loaf of frozen bread. Well, she could have toast at least. Perhaps there'd even be some jam in the cupboard.

The faint ring of her mobile in the living room had her padding back through. *Gus!* 'Hello?'

'You at The Fort?'

Mickey snorted, 'No, bloody trapped here in Oxenhope. No hope of getting in till the bastards deign to grit The Tops. Us leafy suburbs residents are, according to that twat Piers Morgan, meant to take to't slopes on our damn snowboards wearing nowt but shorts cos we're tough in't North.' This was said in an exaggerated Yorkshire accent, 'Bloody tosser, taking the piss out of Northerners, wish one of them serial killers he interviews would boil him up and eat him with some Chianti and fava beans.'

Gus' laugh drifted down the line, his voice became serious. 'Someone tried to knacker my knackers last night, Mickey.'

Mickey's eyebrows rose. She sank onto the couch, pulling the fleece around her shoulders and made a mental note to check the central heating before tuning back in to Gus' description of the intruders at Daniel Farrier and Izzie Dimou's rented house – the one that Alice had only recently bought.

'So, what were they after?' she asked when he'd finished. She'd been going to ask why he'd been there in the middle of the night but something in his voice told her that his motivation had been more Alice than Izzie.

'That's just it – I think I found what they were looking for. As I was sitting in Alice's office waiting for the CSIs I used this door stop thing to hold the door open so I could hear if the bastard came back.'

Again, Mickey stopped herself from asking the obvious question which was 'why had he gone upstairs rather than wait in comfort in the living room?' Instead, she patiently waited for him to continue. As he spoke, she imagined him shrugging, his blue eyes dark, murderous, like they'd been on the moors when he thought Alice was going to be hurt. His dreads would be awry where he would have raked his fingers through them and his shoulders stooped with the burden he always seemed to carry. He cared too much and *that* was why he was an excellent officer. Mickey's only worry was that one of these days it would all be too much for the lad.

'When I heard the CSIs I yanked the stop out from under the door, but I'd wedged it too tight. I pulled again and it came out, but the casing broke and inside was a USB stick.'

'Christ, Gus – I wish I was there. I'm cursing myself for coming home last night. Should've stayed in The Fort really, but I didn't want Dale to worry.' As she uttered the lie, her cheeks flushed. *For God's sake, she'd have to tell everybody soon.* Last thing she needed was them finding out she'd been lying about Dale ditching her. That would make her pathetic and that was the last thing she wanted to be. She didn't need their pity. She was *not* that person. Later. She'd spill the beans later.

'I've just handed it over to Compo, so we'll know more in a short while. I think that's what they were looking for. I only saw one of them, but there was someone waiting for him. The car sped off too quickly for there not to have been someone inside just ready to go. I'm going to look at mug shots – and maybe we'll get some CCTV of the car on some of the main roads. That's one benefit of this fucking snow, traffic is light.'

Mickey snorted, 'Yes but visibility is crap.' She thought for a minute. 'Look, I'm not there and I know your team is diminished but – don't know how you feel about this – what about Lewis Gore?'

'Eh… Lewis Gore? What about him?'

'He's back at work now. His psych evaluation after The Tattoo Killer came back and he's signed fit for work. Clearly, with the new baby and his physical limitations, he's not going undercover just yet, but he's been assigned to my team and – well he's good. In my forced absence he could be my deputy.'

Sensing Gus' hesitation, Mickey added, 'And he can keep his mouth shut too.'

As if he'd made up his mind, Gus said 'Yeah. You're right. I could work with Lewis. He's a good copper and I'd welcome his help. I need someone more senior than Taffy by my side. Let him know I'll expect him at The Fort ASAP. And… thanks.'

Chapter 28

Jordan Beaumont paced the floor, appreciative of the underfloor heating that soothed his feet as he moved. He'd cracked the curtain open a little and didn't know whether to be reassured or panicked by the storm's continued ferocity. He was sweating. Marcia kept the house too damn warm and at the first hint of snow she'd cranked the heating up an extra few notches. He'd known even when he married her that she was a frigid bitch and this just served to confirm her reptilian status.

He was well in the doghouse; his wife hadn't spoken to him since he got back from the office. Her 'I'm sure if you'd made the effort, Jordan, you could have got home earlier,' grated on him. *Like to see her driving through Manchester to Staleybridge in the midst of The Beast from the East. Dozy cow.* She was always so distrustful these days. Since she'd discovered his little dalliance with his previous secretary, she'd acted like she had something on him. She'd been the one to insist he change PA. *Little did she know just how much he welcomed the change. Mark was truly delicious. Aw well, what she didn't know couldn't hurt her.*

It wasn't Marcia and her damn huffiness that bothered him now though. It was this damn storm. If he'd been able to get through Snake Pass, he would have gone to the farmhouse before he came home. *Or would he? Perhaps not.* His gut felt raw at the very notion of what might be awaiting him there. But worse was the fear that, somehow or other, Daniel Farrier had escaped. If that happened there was no doubt at all that he'd link Izzie Dimou's murder to his abduction and fuck knows how much that bitch had told him. Things were not looking good right now. Flashing pound signs were fading by the second and if he didn't sort things out, it wouldn't be long before they disappeared altogether.

Checking that the door was shut, he flung himself onto the couch and extracted the phone from his dressing gown pocket. Things were getting out of control and he'd had no contact from the Romanians. It was like the snow was closing things down, suffocating him, freezing his assets. *Why the hell hadn't they been in touch?* He dialled the only number the phone contained. He was taking a risk phoning from the house, but he was desperate – besides, he hadn't used this phone before and it was doubtful that anybody would triangulate this call. He needed to know if they'd found *it*. If they had, they could get up to the moors and finish what they'd started. If not – well, Daniel Farrier was dispensable. *As long as there are no leads back to me – no worries.* But first he needed the USB and the bitch hadn't given that up.

The phone rang and clicked straight to voicemail. Jordan wanted to tear his hair out by the roots. Idiots were being paid to be on the end of the phone. He imagined them, greasy little men, with their nicotine stained fingers and brown teeth, laughing when they saw this number flash up. He wouldn't put it past them to yank his chain. He dialled again and was gratified to hear the sound of the call being answered, followed by the rattley sound of whichever one of them had answered clearing their tobacco ridden lungs. The sound had his stomach churning. 'Well?'

Another rattling cough was followed by the unmistakeable sound of someone spitting. 'Yes?'

Jordan didn't recognise the voice and his heart sank a little. He couldn't have dialled the wrong number. 'Who's this?'

'You thought you had trouble, Mr Beaumont – but believe me you have no idea. None at all.'

The accent was strong, but not Romanian. This man seemed more educated, had a better command of English. *The Turks? – Who else could it be?* Well, if *they* thought they could get the once over on Jordan Beaumont they were sadly mistaken. 'What do you want? How do you have this phone?'

The laugh was hard. 'Well, let's just say your little Romanian thugs have been dealt with. Hope they've left nothing on them to incriminate you.'

A prickle ran up Jordan's spine. Who the hell was this man and what had he done to the Romanians? He wasn't actually bothered about their welfare and by the sounds of it that was just as well as – whatever their fate – it didn't seem to be good. No, Jordan was more concerned about what they may have left behind. What could be traced to him. All the more reason to get rid of the damn phone. The thug on the line was still speaking.

'We know who you are. We know where you live *and* who you live with. Your daughter is rather cute – your wife, meh… not so much.'

The prickle became sharp, like claws tearing at his back. They knew his wife? His daughter, Missy? He had an almost uncontrollable urge to run up the stairs to her room, check she was okay, cuddled up to her My Little Pony. Sanity prevailed. If they'd dealt with the Romanians, then they must be in Bradford. He exhaled, using the breath to calm himself. 'What do you want?'

Again, the laugh. 'Make no mistake, we are more than able to make sure the police officer who was waiting for your friends at the Dimou girl's house knows all about you. We need to know where Daniel Farrier is.'

So that was it. These men wanted Farrier for the same reason he did. 'I can't help you. Why do you think the Romanians were there? I want to find Farrier too.'

'I don't like to be messed about.'

Jordan's breath caught in his throat. 'I'm not messing you about. I don't know where Farrier is any more than you do. The Romanian's couldn't find him.' He glanced round the overly warm living room as if expecting his tormentor to appear. It was time to placate them. If he could convince them he had no idea where Farrier was, then perhaps he still had a shot at the big bucks. Farrier must know what his fiancée had done with the formula she'd stolen. All Jordan needed to do was bide his time till the storm passed over, convince the archaeologist to share the info with him and he'd be quids in. How hard would it be to convince a weedy archaeologist to share his information? Especially if he told him it was the only way to save Izzie. 'Look, I don't know where he is. I'm not messing you about. But I'm out now. All I care about is my family. I'm not going to look for Farrier anymore. You can have him.'

The Turk gave a low barking laugh.

Jordan paused and removed the phone from his ear, head tilted to one side he listened. Was that Marcia? Or Missy?

The living room door was flung open and a giant of a man with stubble, long hair and a three-inch pink scar down his cheek, walked in, 'Just what we were thinking.'

He pushed Missy into the room in front of him. One massive hand was slapped over her mouth, tears streamed down her cheeks. Her eyes flitted from her dad and around the room. The bigger man held the phone away from his ear and grinned as he shoved it into his pocket. The emptiness of his eyes sent a chill over Jordan as he stepped forward, desperate to reach his child.

'Stay put.' The Turk lifted Missy's hair with his other hand and yanked her head back, exposing her throat. The pulse in her neck fluttered like a fledgling bird's chest. He moved the hand from her mouth, thrust his jacket back and, eyes trained on Jordan, removed a machete from his waistband.

Jordan stopped, swallowing hard, his eyes moved from the machete to his daughter. He willed her not to struggle, not to move, not to do anything. She was trembling, her eyes frantic, her arms rigid by her side. He saw her pyjama bottoms darken – a puddle of urine formed on the carpet by her bare feet and his heart broke.

The man laughed and yanked her hair again, making her lip tremble, 'Scared little girl?'

Jordan dropped his phone to the carpet. *Where the hell was Marcia? Maybe she'd heard them and managed to escape or phone for help*. He wanted to go to his daughter, but the machete pricking into her neck, stopped him. Instead, he stretched out his hands, 'It's okay, Missy. It's okay. Daddy's here.'

The thug pressed the tip of the knife further into her throat causing a droplet of blood to form at the tip. He mimicked Jordan's voice, 'Daddy's here… Daddy's here.' He laughed again, 'Lot of fucking good he is to you, Missy.'

Jordan stumbled forward, but was again stopped.

'Stay where you are.' The thug dragged Missy further into the room and flung her onto the couch. 'Don't move. No noise.' When he turned to Jordan, his smile was lazy. 'You got a nice family, but…' he shrugged, 'not for much longer.'

It was then that Jordan became aware of a keening sound from behind the closed door. It opened and another man, shorter and slighter, with more hair and less stubble, entered. He dragged Marcia behind him. His wife struggled and despite having something stuffed in her mouth was managing to make a racket. Jordan wanted to hit her himself. Couldn't she be quiet for once? The last thing they needed to do was to antagonise these two. He reckoned they'd killed Izzie Dimou and, if they were to be believed, the two Romanians too. Marcia needed to shut up damn quick if they were going to get out of this in one piece.

Her hands were tied behind her back with her dressing gown cord. Despite the terror in her eyes, her botoxed face remained tight and expressionless. The smaller man thrust her toward Jordan. She stumbled and landed against him, knocking him backwards as he tried to stabilise her. He was relieved that she was gagged, the venom in her eyes was enough to bring tears to his.

On closer inspection Jordan was sure the two men were related – brothers probably. The younger one kept glancing at the giant one, his eyes darting round. It was clear that the bigger man was the boss. Marching forward, machete dangling loosely from one hand, the larger man kicked at Jordan's legs and indicated with the knife that Marcia should sit next to their daughter. Jordan saw the look she darted at Missy when she stood on the wet carpet and he could have struck her himself. *What the hell!* This was their daughter and she was turning her nose up at her. What sort of mother was she?

'We thought Izzie Dimou would roll over and give us the information we wanted. However, she was more resistant than we anticipated.' He flicked the machete tip under Marcia's chin, forcing it upward. 'That though, is neither here nor there. What is relevant is the fact that we need Daniel Farrier.' He moved the machete from Marcia to Missy, 'So, how can we convince you to give him up?'

Jordan, hands splayed before him, blinked rapidly. The fear in his daughter's eyes sent his pulse shuddering and sweat dappled his forehead. He tried an experimental smile, seeing the tip of the machete press into her neck again, he swallowed. What could he do? Daniel Farrier was his only bargaining chip. If he gave him up, they'd kill all three of them.

Missy, seemingly finding her tongue uttered a hoarse, 'Daddy.'

Jordan's breathing became shallower. What the hell was he supposed to do? He had a gun, but it was hidden in a cupboard in his own office. *No damn good to him there, was it?* Missy's face was red, her small body trembling. If anything happened to her, how could he live with himself? Words tumbling out in an incoherent babble, he said 'Look, you can have money. No problem. I can go to the bank. Do a transfer first thing. Just don't hurt my baby. I can give you some now. I have some. Then more tomorrow.'

The older brother grinned and shook his head, 'Oh no. You misunderstand. We don't want payment from you – we have our heart set on greater things. We want Daniel Farrier and the formula.'

Jordan's heart hammered, his palms sweated as he thought frantically for a solution to this situation. What could he do to convince them? 'No wait, I have money in an offshore bank account.' He ignored Marcia's glare. He'd kept that hidden from her. He'd made sure to have an exit plan that she knew nothing about. One that would allow him to settle in Thailand or a country where things were less rigid. 'You can have it... you can have it all.'

Giant man's grin widened, his nicotine stained teeth, bared in a grimace of joy. 'Oh, I think you'll tell us all about that account anyway. But first...'

The tip of the knife dug deeper under Missy's chin. The girl was sobbing, her skinny arms like matchsticks against his beefy ones. Her breath hitched in her throat. Marcia, eyes wide and glazed, watched on – her struggles stilled.

Everything rested on his shoulders now. What could he do to stop this nightmare?

Without thinking, he dived across the floor and flung himself at the larger man. The younger brother, as if galvanised by Jordan's activity moved to grab him, but he was too late. The larger man tipped Jordan onto the floor as if he was shrugging off an unwelcome comment. He laughed, 'You will suffer for this.'

Chapter 29

One more cup of coffee would make him even more jittery than he already was, but Gus didn't care. Despite his walk through the snow to Saltaire and the subsequent fight followed by the equally arduous walk back, he was tense. The snow played havoc with his jogging routine and even though his balls still ached, he wanted the release that only jogging could bring. The rhythm of his feet pounding concrete allowed him to exercise his demons – think through whatever case he was on at the minute. Instead, he contented himself with pacing the incident room, circling the tables, coffee cup in hand.

The USB stick he'd found hidden in the door wedge opened up a shed load of questions. Did it belong to Alice? If it did, Gus dreaded to think what would be found on it. An entire raft of evidence that would see her locked up forever? On the other hand, if it belonged to Izzie or Daniel, then maybe he'd find the answers to a whole host of questions surrounding Izzie's death and Daniel's disappearance. This brought his thoughts straight to Daniel's MI6 connections. He'd been told in no uncertain terms to leave that well alone – that the spooks were on it. There was no way in hell Gus could do that though. For one, Gabriella would never let it go if he did, but more importantly, Gus wasn't going to let some invisible government agency stop him from doing the job he was paid to do.

He had a Skype call set up with the University of Nicosia and was looking forward to finding out exactly what Izzie had been working on. He'd been warned not to break Daniel's cover when he spoke to his university employers and that rankled. *Did they really think he was so unprofessional?* But what *really* annoyed him was them keeping him out of the loop. The information they were sitting on could help him track Izzie's murderers and help him to find Daniel. The man had disappeared for Christ's sake – and the agency he worked for had no idea where he was, yet still, they were playing games. Gus was sure they knew a whole load more than they were letting on and it pissed him off. So much for inter-agency cooperation.

He sat down at his PC and waited for the call to connect. Seconds later two men in lab coats and a woman with her hair pulled back in a severe bun sat in a semi-circle staring at the screen. Introducing himself, Gus hoped that their English would be good enough for a serious conversation. He was relieved when the woman, in near perfect, if a little accented, English introduced herself as Daniel's boss Ariadne Chronis and the other two men as the lead researcher, Sevket Abaci and senior lab technician in Izzie's department, Giannis Doukus. They'd already been informed of both Izzie's death and Daniel's disappearance and were keen to express their sadness.

It wasn't the ideal way to conduct an interview, yet Gus had no option. 'I wondered if you could tell me a little bit about the work that Izzie was doing at the university.'

Before Abaci – a tall balding man with small eyes – could open his mouth, Ariadne interrupted, speaking in rapid Greek. Abaci responded with a wave of his hand, before turning back to the screen smiling. 'My colleague begs me not to blind you with science, DI McGuire.'

Gus smiled, 'Yes, perhaps a lay person's explanation would be best – science was never my best subject at school.'

Abaci thought for a moment and began, 'You understand what bio-weaponry is?'

Gus nodded.

'Well, a major research project has been funded, partly by Rubeus Pharmaceuticals in Manchester and partly by various European countries. The thrust has been to create vaccines against some of the bio-weapons that are being illegally developed in countries like Syria or Russia. The formulas for these weapons are so secret that their exact composition is known to only a few of the world's topmost scientists.'

So far Abaci's explanation made sense to Gus. With the recent attacks using novichok on British soil, this was fairly topical and, Gus was aware, had wide-reaching repercussions.

'In our labs we try to deconstruct the various viruses in order to develop counter vaccines. That is the sort of thing Izzie was working on. I cannot be more specific as the work we do here is top secret.'

To Gus, 'top secret' and 'bio-weapons' screamed volatile situations and scope for abuse. 'Any idea why Izzie would make an appointment to see Jordan Beaumont, chief executive of Rubeus Pharmaceuticals, whilst in the UK?'

Abaci looked at Doukus and they both shrugged. 'No idea. Izzie would have no need to talk with our sponsors in the UK. She wasn't high enough up the chain.'

'Could she have discovered something that she wanted to report to the UK?'

Laughing, Abaci leaned forward, eyes twinkling and waved a dismissive hand at the screen. However, what Gus was more interested in was Doukus' body language. At Gus' words, Doukus had crossed his legs and folded his arms across his chest, his gaze focussed on the floor.

Abaci said, 'We are in the business of researching antidotes, not doing illicit things. We have all been vetted to the highest degree. Our references are impeccable. I think you are, what do you English say, snivelling at the wrong tree?'

Gus smiled, 'Barking up the wrong tree, is what you're after Professor Abaci. What about you, Dr Doukus? Have you anything to add? Did Izzie seem distracted? Have you noticed anything odd?'

Doukus leaned forward, his hands clenched so tightly on his knee that Gus could see the blood leave his knuckles. 'I don't know anything much. Isabella and I work together, that's all. We colleagues. She seem fine.'

Ariadne leaned over and placed a hand on top of Doukus' and squeezed. *Odd... There was something more to Doukus' unease than met the eye.* Gus made a mental note to pass that information onto Interpol – *Nobody could accuse him of not being a team player.*

'You're talking vaccines and counter vaccines. Can you tell me what the consequences of such a bio-weaponry attack would be – especially if there wasn't enough vaccine to go around?'

Abaci, rubbed his fingers over his stubble. 'Any one of the many bio-weapons we work with could wipe out entire cities. The human casualties would be phenomenal and the chances of their effects spreading to neighbouring cities, and in some cases neighbouring countries, would be certain. These are highly developed and highly dangerous weapons. We are continually striving to take counter measures against the development of ever more lethal strains. The isolated instances involving novichok in your country are small fry. Our day to day work is all about keeping the threat 'small fry'.'

Gus thought about that. 'So, in terms of bio-weaponry espionage, we'd be looking at millions, billions of dollars?'

'At least. There are many countries who are desperate to have a bio-weapon of mass destruction in their arsenal. They would pay very big bucks for it. However, not to burst your, is it, balloon? Detective, Izzie Dimou had no access to such formulas and so, I think your train of thought redundant.'

'Which countries would be most interested in your work?'

'Ah, I think you know the answer to that already. Syria for sure. Russia almost certainly, North Korea perhaps, if they haven't developed their own, and any number of despot countries throughout the world. Right now bio-weaponry is on everyone's radar for one reason or another.'

Gus wanted to press harder, but judging by the implacability on the three faces before him, it would be a waste of time. He'd just have to leave it there for now. 'Ariadne, before I go, what can you tell me about Daniel? What was he working on? Anything that would make him a target?'

Ariadne laughed, 'Not unless the European Commission is interested in targeting a stuffy doctor obsessed with excavating and protecting the Roman site at Salamaris in Northern Cyprus.' She waved her hand and with slender fingers, pushed her hair behind her ear, 'Daniel was an archaeologist, Detective. He spent his time applying for funding to excavate and restore a beautiful site – nothing more and nothing less. As far as we knew, he was going home to show off his beautiful fiancée to his sister and to get married.' It is a tragedy that Izzie is dead. They seemed to be quite happy together.'

Hmph – well that was a load of rubbish. Daniel Farrier was very much the opposite of what Ariadne had just described. But how far did his subterfuge go? Did Izzie know he was MI6? Also, Gus found her use of the word 'quite' a little strange. He shrugged. Probably an idiosyncrasy that got lost in translation. There was little more to be gained by extending the conversation. Interpol, Gus had been told, were following up on Izzie's and Daniel's lives in much more detail and with the weather here being what it was, he'd no chance of getting over there to grill them much more. To Gus the whole bio-weapon thing seemed more than a little dangerous. Perhaps

Daniel was investigating Izzie Dimou because MI6 suspected her of bio-weaponry espionage? Perhaps she'd tangled with the wrong country? Maybe she'd set off a bidding war between two countries that had gone wrong with her in the middle. Interpol would check the validity of Abaci's claims that his lab was secure. If there was one thing Gus was sure of, it was that nothing was entirely secure. He'd seen people do bad things for a bag of crisps, never mind for the millions that a virus or a formula for a bio-weapon could pull in.

Chapter 30

08:25 Epsom General Hospital, Surrey

Never had Alice felt so alone, so bereft. Not when she'd first learned about Sean Kennedy's betrayal or even when she'd sliced Gus from her life two days earlier. It wasn't the violation – this was just another one in a long succession of attacks. When it was happening, it was as if it was another person's body being penetrated. Someone else's dignity being exploited. The pain didn't even register, the trickle of blood trickling down her inner thigh belonged to someone else. Not her. Not her body, not her soul and definitely not her heart. It couldn't be her heart because it had long since shrivelled up like an autumn leaf; brittle, dead.

So, if it wasn't the violation, the assault itself, what was it? Something deeper than that? Something much more visceral? Cancerous? Something she couldn't slice from her like a rotten tumour. She wanted to sigh, but she didn't have the energy. All she wanted to do was sleep for a million years. She'd read Life of Pi. Seen the film and, for good measure, had even seen a theatre production and never had she managed to work out why Pi would be happy to drift off on a raft, co-dependant with a tiger. What optimistic stupidity would make him think he could survive the sea *and* the tiger? *She* wasn't so foolhardy. She'd reconciled herself to death as soon as Hairy Mary and Co had delivered their ultimatum in that shower room. She wouldn't survive the prison journey with her predators circling.

No, that wasn't strictly true. She'd reconciled herself to death as soon as Sean Kennedy came out of his coma. In that moment, the tenuous hold on a life she was beginning to love in Bradford, slipped through her fingers. As soon as his far-reaching venomous tentacles slipped round the throat of her witnesses and squeezed the lies from Big H's throat, Alice's fate had been sealed. The damage she'd done to the rapist officer gave her little satisfaction. It wasn't enough. He deserved more and had she had the energy, she wouldn't have been able to stop herself from pummelling him to a pile of mush on the ward floor. Her mind kept going back to the plastic fork sticking out of his neck and she wished she'd been able to stab it further in – deeper. The faint tang of blood in her mouth didn't disgust her. Its acrid taste gave her some power back. She'd mangled his nose and she wished him a long and painful reconstruction. The scars would always be there on his face branding him the rapist he was.

There was no pain – just an over-arching dull throb that pinioned her head to the pillow, her limbs to the mattress. Inside, she was raw, like someone had scooped her innards out and rinsed her out with vinegar. It wasn't physical though, it was inside her soul – in her mind, her being. This was how it would be for her for the rest of her life now. Just as well that wouldn't be for very much longer.

The nurse who'd found her had taken photos of the scene she'd walked in on. She – her name was Amreen – had kicked the guard twice, hard in the ribs. She reminded Alice of herself before Sean Kennedy, before this. And she'd wanted to reach out and cradle the girl – protect her from the bastards who would want nothing more than to break her spirit, her strength – but Alice had nothing left to offer.

She hadn't said anything. Turned out, she didn't need to. Amreen's testimony would be enough – well, that and the physical evidence. Alice had been too much in shock to speak, but Amreen had bent the truth a little. She'd said she'd witnessed the end of the rape and Alice's subsequent defence. She'd been like a guardian angel – ferociously protective. Insistent, even when her shift ended, on staying with her patient. It had been Amreen who'd performed the rape kit. Talking softly all the time, not sugar-coating it, just being there – warm, reassuring, calm. Alice wanted to thank her, but she couldn't. Her mouth wouldn't move. The words wouldn't come. Neither would the tears. Not when the doctor came. Not when her breast wound was redressed, not when her rapist cursed her as he was dragged handcuffed from her room. When they'd asked if they could call someone, she'd turned her head away. She had no one. She'd made sure of that – *no*, Sean Kennedy had made sure of that.

At some point during the early morning, she was wakened by low voices talking by her bed. Instant panic jerked her upper body upright. Her hands clenched into fists and her heart beat a staccato rhythm that she imagined the world could hear, filling the dark void of the room. Through the semi-dark, Amreen smiled down at her. She reached out and rested her hand on Alice's forehead for a moment, – seemingly satisfied – she returned to the shadowy figure that stood behind her, 'She's all yours. Don't tire her out though. She's been through a lot.'

With a smile to Alice, she left the room – leaving her alone with her solicitor. The one Nancy had got for her. This time Alice managed a sigh. All those people wasting their time and money and energy on her. She wasn't worth it. *Couldn't they just leave her alone?*

Bernadette Crossan pulled out a chair and sat down. For long moments she sat in silence. Her perfectly made-up face a stark contrast to Amreen's fresh-faced look. Her business suit perfectly matched to her high-necked blouse. The slight frown pulling her brows together was the only indication that she was concerned. 'Dispensed with the prison officer in your room, Alice. They couldn't really refuse after what you've been through.'

Alice held her gaze but said nothing – she couldn't care less if they positioned a platoon of walruses in her room with her – it was all too little, too late.

Alice's unblinking stare seemed to unsettle the solicitor, for she gave a nervous laugh and leaned forward, 'You okay, Al?'

She held Alice's gaze and seemingly realising the other woman wasn't going to respond, said, 'Look, I have to feed back to DCI Chalmers. She needs to know how you are. That you're coping.'

Moving her head to the right, Alice refocused on the curtained window, Nancy didn't *need* anything from her. Alice didn't *need* to give anyone anything. She'd taken herself off the playing field.

Bernadette tried again. 'They're going to push to prosecute the prison officer, Al. It'll play in your favour. You'll be given protection when you go back to prison. No-one will be able to get to you there.'

Alice almost wished she had the energy to laugh. She'd ended up here because of an attack in prison. Didn't anyone get that? She wouldn't be safe anywhere. But that wasn't what mattered to her now anyway. Only one thing mattered. 'Does Nancy have my parents?'

The words came out harsh, like each one skated over broken glass, splitting open on their journey from her lips.

The solicitor shook her head.

Alice turned her head away and closed her eyes. 'We're done here.'

Chapter 31

When Gus had handed the USB stick over to Compo earlier, the lad had been monosyllabic. His only words, a few minutes later were, 'It's encrypted. I'll let you know when I've decoded it.' And he promptly turned his back on Gus.

At first, Gus put it down to a combination of two things; lack of sleep – as testified by the bags under his eyes and his unhealthy pallor, and a lack of sugar. For some reason, Compo appeared to have squished a packet of Chocolate Hobnobs to smithereens and left them scattered on the floor. *Perhaps he'd had a rough night.* Gus would wait till he was in a better mood before directing him to clean it up. Shame about the Hobnobs though. Gus quite fancied one with his coffee.

Just as he had that thought, the door opened and his mum's head appeared. 'Knew you'd be here, Angus. Thought I'd do a detour with the dogs and bring you these to cheer you up in this bad weather. They're a new recipe. Bran muffins, ultra-healthy.'

A kerfuffle by the door had Gus closing his eyes for a moment, 'Please say you didn't bring Heather and Meggie into the station, Mum.'

Looking indignant, Corrine McGuire flung a dirty look at her son, 'Have you seen the weather out there? Do you really want me to leave them outside? Have a heart, Angus, have a heart.' She stepped into the room with her two dogs following, tails wagging as they recognised Gus and began to tug at their leash to reach him. Corrine let them go and they made a beeline for Gus who – despite his tuts – ruffled their ears. *For God's sake does no one in my family possess an ounce of professionalism?*

Corrine, carrying a bulging bag in her gloved hands, descended on Compo, her face flushed with the cold. Sitting at his computer station, Compo, shoulders slumped and elbows bent, looked like he'd been the only kid not invited to the party. 'Compo, my love, you'll have some of my muffins, won't you?'

Compo looked up and offered a half-hearted smile. 'Aw, great Mrs M. Love your baking.' Looking as if his body was weighted down, he got up and took the bag from Gus' mum.

Frowning at Gus in a 'what have you done to the poor lad' sort of way, Corrine, whipped off one of her gloves and held her hand to his forehead, 'Are you poorly Compo? You look pale.'

Compo glared at Gus and shook his head.

What the hell was that all about? Gus racked his brains for something he'd done or perhaps not done. Had he spoken too harshly to Compo, or missed his birthday? His musings were interrupted when the door opened again and in walked the Detective Chief Superintendent, a surly teenager trailing behind. Since their previous chief had committed suicide, there had been a bit of a reshuffle and now they'd inherited the rather stern-faced Gazala Bashir who had transferred from Birmingham recently. Presumably, the girl was her daughter.

Gus exhaled. He didn't know who to curse; his mother for bringing the dogs here in the first place or DCS Bashir for choosing this precise minute to visit when he'd barely seen her since she started.

The DCS's eyes moved from the dogs to Gus then back again. They drifted to his mother who, bundled up in her outdoor things, looked a little like a Pillsbury doughboy and from there to Compo who had opened the bag, extracted the tin and stuffed a whole muffin in his mouth with a trail of crumbs dotting his Kinks t-shirt.

This was bad, very bad. Gus had barely spoken two words to the woman and now, here she was in a room that was beginning to smell of rather fragrant steamy dogs and burnt muffins. He opened his mouth to explain, when Heather dragged away from him and seeing someone new to slobber over, raised a still damp paw to his boss' light green skirt. For a moment he closed his eyes, hoping that when he opened them again, the scene would be *sans* his mother and two wet dogs, but no. His eyes moved from the damp patch on DCS Bashir's skirt up to her face and he braced himself for the onslaught that no doubt was to follow. But the teenage girl had smiled and extended her hand to Meggie, who wagged her tail furiously and licked the girl's hand.

Bashir opened her mouth, her eyes flashing as she pushed the dog away, but before she had a chance to utter a word, Corrine had rushed over, hand extended, warm smile on her face. 'Oh hello. You must be my Angus' boss. He thinks *so* highly of you. The Fort's in such capable hands, or so he tells me.'

Looking a little overwhelmed by the whirlwind that was Gus' mum, DCS Bashir extended her own hand and shook Corrine's. Still smiling, Corrine glanced at her son and gave an almost imperceptible wink before turning back. 'I know I shouldn't have brought the dogs in, but I thought I'd drop off some sustenance for these two as they've been hard at it all night and I know they won't have bothered with breakfast. Ordinarily, I'd leave Heather and Meggie outside.' She picked up the dropped leash and said in a voice reserved for babies and pets, 'Wouldn't I, my sweet angels,' before turning back to Bashir, 'But, what with the weather the way it is, I just couldn't risk anyone seeing them and taking a snap of them outside The Fort.'

She gave, what Gus recognised as an affected laugh, 'Wouldn't want news headlines *Abandoned dogs left to freeze outside Bradford's biggest police station*' or some such dross. You know what the press are like, don't you? Anyway, lovely to meet you. Come on Heather, come on Meggie.' and she was off, leaving Gus to face the music.

He opened his mouth to speak, but Bashir, seeming almost as bemused as he was, raised a hand, 'Don't bother. I don't want to hear it. It's exceptional circumstances, so we'll turn a blind eye – this time.' She glanced at Compo, and shook her head slightly before continuing, 'I only came to tell you that we've okayed Lewis Gore's temporary transfer to your team until such time as we can make permanent replacements. I've been told he's on his way in.'

She looked once more at Compo as if wondering what his role was. Meeting her gaze, Compo offered the open tin. 'Muffin?'

Gus could've crowned him. The muffins were misshapen, with evidence of being overdone on the top and no two were the same size. *Why did his mother insist on doing this? When would she realise she just couldn't bake?*

Gazala Bashir, moved her head a mere fraction and looked at Gus, 'Are you sure your team is up to this current investigation?'

Looking at Compo, who had stuffed another bun in his mouth and was now chewing noisily, Gus straightened and met her gaze. 'My team is very efficient at what they do. I wouldn't replace any of them, but I do welcome Lewis Gore as a temporary member. His skills will be invaluable.'

Bashir pressed her lips together and nodded, 'Okay, but I want regular updates. Investigating this murder with the weather like this is fraught with difficulty. Come on Moona, let's get you something useful to do, since schools closed.'

As the DCS left the room, her surly daughter trailing behind again, Gus turned to Compo. The lad was huddled over his keyboard casting the occasional glance at his monitor, his back pointedly angled away from Gus. What was it with the lad? Compo was usually so buoyant, so upbeat. It took a lot to bring him down. It occurred to him – Alice. *Has Nancy spilled the beans to Compo before Gus had the chance to?* Catching an admonishing glance from Compo, Gus sighed. He really didn't want to have to deal with Compo's sensitivities right now. That was something Alice usually did. But Alice was gone, so, he'd just have to get used to it. He walked over and placed a hand on Compo's shoulder. Like a truculent three-year old, Compo shrugged it off, keeping his eyes firmly on the screen of flashing images.

Gus, having been caught out before, scanned Compo's desk for drops of ketchup or other sticky substances before resting his bum on it, long legs stretched out before him, arms folded. Angling backwards, he was able to see Compo's face as he worked. A crumb dangled from his lower lip, emphasizing the ferocity of his concentration.

'Take it Nancy's spoken to you about Alice?'

Compo responded with an abrupt nod.

Shit, I'm really going to have my work cut out at this rate. 'Come on Comp's, give me a break. I'm finding this as hard as you are, you know?'

Compo's fingers stilled on the keyboard and he swivelled his chair a little and glared at Gus. 'Should've been *you* who told me, Gus. Not Nancy. Don't hardly know her, do I?' He shook his head and mouth trembling, crumb dangling precariously, he shrugged, 'Should've been *you.*'

The lad was right. It should've been Gus that told him. Nancy would've been sensitive – of course she would, but *he* was Compo's friend. *He* was the team leader. He *should* have made the time. Truth was, he was putting it off. Making excuses, prevaricating. He splayed his hands in front of him. 'You're right, Comps. I've no excuse. I should've told you. I was being a knob. Thinking about myself, not sure how to break it to you.'

He raked his fingers through his dreads and sighed, 'I made excuses to put it off, but being honest with you Comp's, I just didn't want to say it out loud. This is Alice we're talking about. Our Alice. I'm gutted. Gutted and fucking mad as hell.'

Compo, reached out and squeezed Gus' arm. 'It's okay, Gus. It's okay. I get it.'

Gus shook his head, 'No Compo. I was a dick. Left you dangling.'

They sat in silence for a while. 'Maybe she didn't do it Gus? After all, you said it yourself, this *is* Al we're talking about.'

Gus pushed himself up from the desk, lips tight. 'She did it Comps. She told me so. The evidence is there and everything adds up. She's more of a dirty cop than Knowles was. She deserves to be locked up. The Alice we knew doesn't exist. You've got to accept that. It was all an act. That woman made a fool of us. I'll not forgive her for that – not ever. Now I need to know what's on that USB, so get cracking, eh?'

Chapter 32

10:15 Saddleworth Moor

When Daniel woke up, the first thing he noticed was the biting numbness in his limbs and extremities. Flexing his fingers and toes sent shooting pains up his arms and legs, so he lay there cocooned in musty fabric, bones heavy. Little by little, he tried to circulate blood round his body. He hadn't intended to sleep. He'd curled up on the bed to keep warm with the aim of working out a plan of action that would aid his escape from this place and to find Izzie. As the tingling in his fingers and toes receded, he realised he was lucky to have woken up at all. He could just as easily have drifted from slumber to death – hypothermia was that easy to give in to.

The windows had frosted up again, but through them he could see the glimmer of light that only sunshine on a winter's day could provide. He hoped the blizzard had worn itself out, and now that it was daylight, he'd be able to get his bearings. Perhaps a passing farmer or some kids out sledding would be within shouting distance. Failing that, he'd have to find his own way back to civilisation – and he'd have to do it before his captors returned.

Still wrapped in his layers of mould, he rolled to the edge of the bed, got unsteadily to his feet and made his way to the window, dizziness making him stagger. The circle he'd made earlier had disappeared. He scraped it clear once more, aware of the dull gnawing hunger in his stomach and hoped the bright light of day would reveal an escape route. With every hour that passed, the likelihood of his captors returning increased. On the plus side, Gabriella would by now be aware that something was up. When Izzie didn't turn up for her hen do and he didn't turn up to the stag do – that's if Gus had actually bothered to arrange it – she'd do something. He didn't know Gus very well, but he seemed like a decent enough chap. Not many men would take it on the chin if their wife went off with their sister.

He peered out through the gap. The world was white. Outbuildings were nearly covered with drifting snow, their ridged roofs standing proud, liked iced ridges on a cake. The front part of a tractor was outlined peeking out from the side of the biggest building – *a barn?*

The snow was pristine. It seemed too cold for even wild animals to explore, if the lack of footprints was anything to go by. Through the sun, snow clouds were visible with the promise of more snow. However, as Daniel watched, the wind picked up and from nowhere, whirls of snow gusted up, making it nearly impossible to see more than a few feet ahead of him.

Gritting his teeth, Daniel realised he would have to bite the bullet and make his escape any way he could. He might not be used to these conditions but he was trained. Pressing his forehead to the window, he peered downwards to see what was beneath him. It was difficult to distinguish individual shapes, and he couldn't be sure, but it looked like snow-covered bushes. It was a risk he was prepared to take – but first to prepare.

Okay, so the clothes in the wardrobe were old, stinking and female. *Who cared?* He needed layers if he was to survive a trek over unchartered territory. He began to add layers of socks, baggy nylon trousers with elasticated waists – the owner had clearly been a large woman – and humungous home knitted jumpers in shades of greys and insipid turquoise. Feeling a little like one of those Disney characters in their oversized suits he waddled to the window. He'd found two stretchy woollen hats and had pulled them on his head, glad that they covered his ears which felt icy to the touch. Unable to find gloves, he pulled the sleeves of the cardigans down to cover his hands.

Picking up a large ugly lamp, its frayed electric cord dangling, he approached the window and smashed it against the glass. The lamp broke into a pile of brittle ceramic dust and the window remained intact. Daniel looked round again. What else could he use? He'd expected the glass to be easier to break than this. He picked up one of the chairs. It was heavier than it looked and he was weak. It would be difficult to get a good swing at the pane, but he was determined to break it. He dragged it to the window, hefted it by the back and braced himself to swing it. He hit the window once – it shuddered but didn't break. He groaned and dropped the chair to the floor. Breathing heavy with the effort, he picked it up again and, summoning every ounce of determination, he took another swing. It hit the glass, the cross frames protested then split, making the glass shatter, sending splinters flying into the snow.

Cold air buffeted into the room bringing with it swirls of icy snow. Ignoring the cold, Daniel used his well-padded elbow to clear the rest of the glass from the frame. For a moment he considered using the bedding to make a makeshift rope, then realised that none of the bedding was strong enough to hold his weight. The sheets were worn and as he tried to tie them together, they separated and stretched. *Not sure I can trust them. Have to risk the long drop.* He climbed onto the sill and swung his legs over. The drop looked higher now he was actually going to do it. He hoped none of the bushes were thorny. Taking a deep breath, he counted to three and jumped, aiming for the bundle that seemed to be the largest bush.

It wasn't till he landed that he discovered the 'bush' was actually a bricked barbecue. Through the snow, his head hit the bricks and before he had the chance to lift his head, a blossom of scarlet had melted the snow around his head, making the area look like an outdoor abattoir. Using a handful of snow, he tried to freeze the cut into submission. It took him longer than expected to settle his vision and catch his breath. The outside ambient temperature wasn't much different from the temperature in the bedroom. However, lying in the drifting snow was sending chills right through his bones. When, at last, he tried to push himself upright, he realised he'd twisted his ankle. Tentatively, he rotated it. *Thank God it's not broken.*

He got on to his feet and with hesitant steps, dragging his throbbing ankle across the snow, he headed to the nearest downstairs window. Peering through the part-frozen pane, he saw a huge wooden table dominating the centre of the room, with an over-sized cooker behind and an old-fashioned fridge looming out from the corner of the room. Directly beneath the window was a massive sink. Brilliant. The prospect of food and the possibility of weapons cheered him up immensely.

Bracing himself, he brushed the drifted snow off the window sill along with a concealed window box and pushed against the window. It shook and seemed loosely fitted into the rotten frame. Using his good foot, he kicked the wooden window box and when it fell apart, he grabbed the largest piece of wood, weighed it in his hands and using all his upper body strength he hit the window pane with it. Expecting it to take a few swipes to have effect, Daniel was surprised when the glass shattered leaving an uneven star shaped hole.

Using his earlier trick of elbowing out the loose glass, he cleared a space and hoiked himself up onto the sill and, with some effort, managed to half fall into the sink, leaving a smear of blood from his head on the ceramic. Lack of food and the cold made his movements clumsy and by the time he'd extricated himself from the sink, his breath came in rapid pants. Pulling out a chair from the table he slumped into it and glanced round the room. The pantry door stood half open, revealing shelves of tins that made Daniel's heart sing. Beans, soups, tuna – he didn't care. He could eat a scabby horse with no qualms whatsoever, but beans and soup would do the trick too – after he'd caught his breath.

A few minutes later – tin of tomato soup in hand – Daniel opened drawers, searching for a tin opener, trying to quash the thought that perhaps he'd die of hypothermia and starvation here in this lonely old farmhouse for want of a tin opener. No, he wouldn't let his thoughts go there. When in the second to last drawer he found one, nestled next to a gas lighter he was almost delirious. Shuffling over to the gas cooker he felt like he was pushing his luck, but still – with crossed fingers – he fiddled with the unfamiliar knobs and when he heard the welcoming sound of gas he lit all the burners before looking for a pan to heat his soup in.

The pain in his fingers and toes as blood began to circulate was excruciating yet Daniel knew he had to bear with it. His toes were already painfully blue. The last thing he wanted was for them to get frostbitten. Welding his hands round the now cooling mug of soup, he felt his teeth chatter as his body began to warm up.

Chapter 33

10:30 The Fort

'Rough sleepers in Bradford and Leeds have struggled to cope with the extreme temperatures brought about by Storm Emma and The Beast from the East. Bradford's many faiths have come together, opening the doors of their Mosques, Gurudwaras, Temples, Churches and Synagogues to rough sleepers throughout the city. Imam Khalil Majid from the Jamul ul Masjid Mosque on Leeds Road says 'It is at times like this that our different faiths unite us in helping those less fortunate than ourselves'. Whilst Rabbi Meir Raben from Bradford Synagogue says, 'The multi- faiths of Bradford always work together behind the scenes so that in a crisis we are ready to step up to the mark together as a unified force.'

'From Bradford Cathedral in the city centre to St Pio Friary on Sedgewick Place and the Hindu Cultural Society on Leeds Road, doors are open, food and drinks are being served and warm clothes distributed.

This is Nakeem Hafis from Look North'

Lewis Gore banged the door open and shuffled in – a huge yeti of a man with an equally large smile. Gus wondered how Lewis could be in such good humour after the trauma he'd been through a year ago. Mind you, his new daughter must have been of as much therapeutic benefit to him as his sessions with Dr Mahmood – maybe even more.

Gus got up from his seat to give the man a hug and was enveloped in a bear-like hug that left him gasping for breath. He was glad that Mickey had thought to have him temporarily seconded to the team. Mickey was out of action and they were already down two officers with Sampson and Alice being out of the picture. Since the Tattoo Killer last summer, Gore's face had been splashed all over the papers, making it near impossible for him to resume his undercover role. Not that he was quite fit enough yet anyway. Not after what had been done to him. Gus was glad to see him looking so well though, he was well aware that scars were only skin deep. Sometimes it was the scars you couldn't see, the ones in your brain that were the worst to deal with.

'Good to see you again, Gus. Even better to be working with you. Sandra sends her love.'

Gus remembered the quiet dignity and strength of Lewis' heavily pregnant wife when her husband had been abducted and smiled. 'How is she? Coping alright with the new arrival?'

After getting his phone out Lewis swiped the screen, his eyes lighting up as he showed Gus a photo of his wife and baby – 'Kayleigh's eight months old now.'

The baby had looked more squished and wrinkled than beautiful when Lewis and Sandra had brought her to the station as a new-born to show off to his colleagues. Gus smiled and flicked the screen to the right, pleased to see that the months had ironed out Lewis' baby's creases and that she was now a grinning, smiling, toothy bundle of chubbiness that he could genuinely coo over. Gus loved kids and had always had his heart set on a huge family like Mo's. Maybe he could have all boys to balance things out a bit – but in reality, he wouldn't care what sex his kids were – he'd just love them in the same way his parents had always loved him and Katie.

Compo too had risen to greet the man and was subjected to a bear hug that knocked his beanie hat right off his head, revealing flattened dark curls. 'Hey, it's the Compster,' said Lewis, mock sparring with Compo, bouncing on his toes and ducking like a professional boxer. *Well, the man did have the Mike Tyson build.*

'How you doing man?'

Gus marvelled at the fact that Compo could so easily turn on a smile for Lewis, whilst simultaneously frowning at him. He really had to find the space to put things right with the lad, but right now wasn't the time. Right now, he had to bring Gore up to speed. Before he had the chance to start, Gore turned to him, a grin lighting up his dark features, taking the sting out of his words, 'So, you got it in the nuts last night and in the process probably let our killer go – nice one Gus. Glad you were more on the ball – if you'll excuse the pun – with the Tattoo Killer last year.' The big man's chortle rumbled up from the soles of his feet and ricocheted round the room.

Compo would normally have laughed and attempted one of his high fives or at the very least a finger click – but no. Instead, he harrumphed and turned back to his computer station, his shoulders hunched and tense. Wishing he could shake his nerdy officer, Gus instead shrugged and turned to get Lewis some coffee. 'Ha bloody ha. Very funny. I'm still recovering from that. However, my enforced wait at Alice's house paid some dividends.' He explained to Lewis about the USB stick that Compo was in the process of trying to decode.

Handing Lewis his coffee, Gus continued, 'This damn weather has played havoc with the investigation though. No-one's been out and about, so the house to house enquiries brought zilch. No sightings of Izzie being dumped, no sightings of her being snatched. The last sighting we have of her is at that train wreck in Rawsforth on Friday.'

Lewis hefted his large frame on top of one of the desks and cradled his coffee cup as he studied the crime boards. 'Daniel Farrier showed up yet?'

'No not yet. Mickey brought you up to speed?'

'Mostly. Give me a quick recap.'

'CCTV at Bradford Interchange showed them boarding a train to Manchester Victoria. Body language looked relaxed and normal. They both alighted in Manchester and CCTV showed them parting company at the exit. She went towards the city and he went in the opposite direction. Chance CCTV at Costa's along from Victoria caught him entering there, but no sign of him exiting. Officers on the ground said there was a back exit that leads to a small carpark where deliveries are made. Unfortunately, there is a distinct lack of CCTV there. We trawled the CCTV in the surrounding area hoping to pick him up on foot, but no such luck. Perhaps he got a lift from the back exit and unless we know the make of the vehicle that's a dead end.'

'So what are we thinking, Gus? Someone snatched Farrier?'

Gus shrugged, 'What I've not added to the wall is the fact that Daniel Farrier is MI6. That's only being disseminated on a need to know basis.'

'That adds a different slant to things. Are the spooks being arsey with you?'

'That's about right. They've taken the Farrier enquiry out of my hands but of course, that's not gonna happen. Izzie's murder and his disappearance are linked. We just need to work out why. Hopefully, Compo will find something on that USB that'll clarify things.' Gus looked at Compo and received only a 'Humph' for his trouble.

Chapter 34

10:55 Saddleworth Moor

Despite the blackness that encompassed him and the pounding that started somewhere at his temples – and travelled right across his skull to the throbbing bump at the back of his head – Jordan Beaumont couldn't close his eyes. Every time he did so, images of his daughter came alive before him – tears streaming down her face, her breath catching in her throat, screaming as her mother was tortured with slow and extreme precision. She'd railed against the man who'd held her, forcing her to watch whilst their tormentor – soaking up her anguish, feeding off it, breathing it in – grinned and continued his work with enjoyment.

Gulping and shivering, rivers of snot rolled down Missy's face whilst the younger brother gazed into the distance as if zoning out the butchery that was unfolding before him. The giant Turk must have raided Jordan's sex toys, the ones he kept hidden in his office. With glee, he turned his attention to Jordan. Stuffing a ball gag in his mouth and securing it with a silk tie, he yanked Jordan's head backwards and using another silk scarf, he tied his hands together and attached them to his feet, effectively hog-tying him.

Jordan attempted to hold eye contact with the Missy. He had to keep her as still and quiet and compliant as he could. His only thought was for her to survive this nightmare. Willing her to look at him, not at what the monster had done to her mother, he made ineffectual noises behind his gag. There was no way out of this for him, he understood that. He'd seen the mania in the older brother's eyes. How could *he*, ineffectual Jordan Beaumont, out-manoeuvre and control these animals? He wished his heart hadn't been filled with greed. Wished he'd never thought he could make a quick buck. He wasn't bothered about Marcia. He didn't care about her. She was dispensable – she deserved this in a way, but Missy? No, they could do what they liked to Marcia as long as they left Missy alone, as long as they let her go. He'd give anything to ensure that she came out of this in one piece – damaged emotionally for sure – but hell, she could get over this.

The giant had stripped down to the waist now. His torso and face splattered with Marcia's blood. His sneer wide and feral. Jordan looked at her. She'd stopped moving. Maybe she was dead. Jordan saw a red drip fall from the index finger of her left hand. It twitched once as if to flick the blood away and it stopped. A gush of air escaped her mouth and her head lolled forward.

Jordan's heart pounded. What the hell would the monster do now that Marcia was unresponsive? He didn't have long to wait for an answer. Turning to Jordan, the giant grinned. A Celtic warrior about to spare his foe? Jordan didn't think so. His shoulders ached – maybe if one of them popped out of the socket he'd be able to do something. His hip joints raged against the pull of the restraint. Who was he kidding? He'd never be able to take on the brothers. Adrenalin had control of the older one and his brother was too cowed to make a stand against him. Tears seeped from Jordan's eyes as he looked at his daughter. She looked so small and beautiful. Her long hair, sleep-tussled, fell around her shoulders. A few stray strands stuck to her face with snot. Rope wrapped around her chest, immobilising her, keeping her upright in the chair. Her nightie rode up her legs as she squirmed in the chair and Jordan strained against the ties as he saw the Turk unbuckle his belt.

It was what followed that pierced Jordan's eyes through the darkness. Those were the images that would be forever seared into his retinas – the ones that stopped him from closing his eyes.

He was in the boot of some big vehicle and it was moving, he was shaking from the cold. They'd dumped him in the back, thumped the lid down and within moments had taken off. Initially, the ride had been smooth, or as smooth as could be expected in the current conditions. Now though, they were moving more slowly. The car had skidded on a number of occasions and he'd felt the ABS kick in. He sensed they'd driven off the beaten track, which wasn't good for him. He had no way of knowing where his daughter and wife were. Had they slung them into the back seat in order to get rid of the evidence or had they been stupid enough to have left them back at home? Either way, nobody would be alerted 'till later on today when their cleaner was due. That's if she even made it through the snow.

The ride was bumpier now. Where the hell had they taken him? He had no doubt this was his last journey and he had no idea what he could do about it. Any fight had left him back at his house. All he wanted now was to get it over with.

The vehicle stopped and, judging from the movement of the chassis, the brothers descended into the snow. He braced himself, waiting for the boot to open but it remained closed. Straining his ears for any indication of what was going on outside, Jordan held his breath. Nothing. It was like being in a tomb – a freezing, soundproofed tomb. His feet and hands were so numb that he felt almost complete sensory deprivation. No sight, sound, feeling. The only sensation grounding him in reality was the smell of new leather and the visions that tormented him.

He must have drifted off, for the next thing he was aware of was a blinding light in his eyes and hands grabbing him. For a second, he thought it was some other-worldly experience – God's hands grabbing him. It came back to him in a second. The smell of blood, combined with fresh air and the guttural sneers of the Turks brought him right back to earth. He blinked against the light, trying to see through it, to what was beyond.

He was out of the boot, rough hands under his armpits, hauling him along. He couldn't feel his feet, was aware only of the dull sensation of them thudding along behind him as he was dragged. If he split in two right then, he doubted he would feel a thing. He must have been crying because the taste of salt and the pain in the cracks at either side of his mouth were welcome sensations to him.

They stopped and with a final upward hoist, he was flying through the air, only to land on his front on something hard. Again, they yanked his arms. Excruciating pain surged through his hips and shoulders. Had they amputated his limbs? He yelled behind his gag, more pain as he was turned over onto his back. It was then that he realised they'd released his restraints. A glance to the side informed him his arms were still attached to his body, but lay uselessly at his side, pain surging through them as blood tried to reach his extremities. He couldn't focus. He wanted to move, to rail, to scream, but he was as immobile as he'd been before they released him. The younger brother lowered the light and Jordan became aware that he was lying in some sort of trough looking up at the brothers. To either side, piles of snow lay haphazardly as if they'd just been thrown there. Two spades protruded from the pile nearest his captors. Jordan realised that his 'trough' was actually a man-made hole in the snow – an igloo in reverse. What was worse was the look on the monster's face as he grabbed one of the shovels, scooped up spadesful of snow and began to shovel it over Jordan's body.

Jordan attempted to move, ignoring the agonising pain that scorched his limbs as he tried to gain enough power to pull himself up from his tomb. Snow, hard and cold splatted on his face and Jordan could see that the monster had joined his brother – two sinister gravediggers happy in their work. As the snow layered up, weighing down, first his arms and then his legs, warmth suffused his groin area as urine soaked his pyjama bottoms. Almost immediately it turned cold and claggy as the snow fell around his head. Spluttering he tried to spit it out as it covered his mouth, his head shook from side to side as he tried to clear the ice from his nostrils and all the while the brothers laughed at his antics, slowly shovelling more and more snow until his head was trapped, leaden and still as the last shovelfuls forced his eyes closed. Slowly pinioned under the snow, his body was pushed deeper and deeper into his snowy grave. The last image burned into his vision was the terrorised and uncomprehending look on his broken daughter's face and how gradually the light in her eyes faded and eventually died. It would haunt him throughout eternity.

Chapter 35

13:30 The Fort

As soon as he saw Nancy's face, Gus jumped to his feet and strode across the office to meet her. 'What is it? Is it my mum? Dad?'

At his words, Compo's head jerked up and he too made his way towards Nancy, a half-eaten Mars Bar in his hand.

Nancy, ashen faced, placed her hand on Gus' arm and shook her head. 'Not your mum or your dad. It's Alice.'

Gus' heart skipped a beat. *Alice?* Even after everything he'd recently found out, the thought of something happening to her still had the power to make his legs shake – and judging by Nancy's expression something bad *had* happened. From the corner of his eye he saw Compo halt, eyes huge, flicking between Gus and Nancy.

Gus swallowed, 'Go on. Tell us.'

Nancy moved past him and pulled out a seat from the table and lowered herself into it, her palms pressed onto the table, bracing herself as she lowered her frame onto the chair like someone twenty years older than she was.

'She's been raped.'

The word 'raped' hung in the air – alien and toxic.

'Raped?' Compo said the word as if he'd never heard it before.

In that moment, that single word had succeeded in sweeping away all of Gus' anger and disappointment and frustration with Alice. Everything she'd been through over the past months hit

Gus like machine-gun fire, one at a time – each making their mark, each piercing the wall he'd erected around his heart. Flashes of her grinning, laughing, teasing rolled through his mind. This was Alice – his Alice, and no matter what she'd done, surely she didn't deserve this. 'How? Who?'

Nancy passed a hand over her face, 'Fucking prison guard.'

Shocked by Nancy's profanity, Gus exhaled. 'In the hospital?'

Nancy nodded, seemingly the ability to speak too difficult as she struggled with the news. Gus dragged his hands through his dreads and began to stride to and fro across the room, his breath coming in short pants. What the fuck was going on? How many more wardens, guards or officers were going to abuse their power before it was too many? Memories of Knowles having a heart attack on the floor outside this very office flashed before him. Bastard had avoided being punished for abusing his power. He'd died quick and easy before leaving his wife and family as well as Bradford police to face the consequences of his treachery. Sean Kennedy was another one. Gus had no doubt that even if Alice had set him up, Gus was sure Kennedy was no angel. He'd read the various reports, studied his record, gone over his arrests and – reading between the lines – Kennedy was bent. Even more bent than Alice?

He pulled his arm back and pummelled his fist into the plasterboard wall near the door. From the dent, plasterboard fell in little clouds of dust, but Gus wasn't finished. Not by a long chalk. He drew his hand back, uncaring of the blood smears across his knuckles and was about to drive it into the wall again when he was grabbed from behind. Strong arms circled his chest, pulling him back – Lewis Gore. Gus struggled for a few moments and relaxed his body, allowing Gore to bear his weight for a few moments longer. Brushing Gore's arms away, he took a deep breath and was just about to ask Nancy for more details when Compo – face flushed, fists clenched by his side, chin thrust out – spoke in a low voice. 'This is down to you, Gus.' Compo faced Nancy, '… And you.' He turned and kicked the nearest desk leg. 'Fucking let her down when she needed you the most. You make me sick, the pair of you.' He spun on his heel and strode over to Gus, getting right in his face. 'She always had your back. Even when you were being a twat. Oh yeah, we all bent over backwards for you, didn't we? Took care of you.'

His voice had escalated as he spoke, drops of saliva splattered on Gus' face but Gus, mesmerised, just stared at Compo. Nancy made to intervene, but Gus shook his head and she backed off. Gore looked from Compo, to Gus to Nancy and back again. He stood on the balls of his feet, bouncing slightly as if ready to swerve towards any of the three of them should he deem it necessary.

'We all ignored your moods and your temper and your fucking downright fucking bastarding shittiness. But you? What do you do? The minute there's a bit of trouble you roll over and leave Alice to get on with it on her own.'

Breathing heavily, Compo took a step back and lifted his fists up, turning his hands this way and that, as if amazed that they were clenched before unclenching them. His shoulders slumped, head tucked down, he continued in a whisper. 'This is Alice. *Alice*!' he shook his head, 'We know her for fucking fuck's sake. We *know* her. She's not done owt wrong and now this has happened.' He looked up, his eyes flashing. 'You've let her down…' his voice hitched 'We've all let her down – every fucking one of us. She's worth ten of all of us and we've left her on her own to be violated and abused. Hope you're proud of yourself Gus. Hope you're fucking proud.' And he turned back to his computers, rammed his headphones on and pointedly turned his chair away from them.

Nancy sighed and closed her eyes. Gore patted Gus on the shoulder and went back to the desk he'd taken over. Gus stood there, hands loose at his sides, head full of conflicting thoughts. Reeling from the news of yet more trauma for Alice, compounded by Compo's uncharacteristic response, a sudden heaviness settled in Gus' limbs. He'd completely underestimated how badly Alice's absence had affected Compo. Not only that, Compo's words had hit his jugular. It hadn't taken much for him to assume the worst regarding Alice. He'd been quick to accept that his Alice – his sister Alice – was worse than Knowles and Kennedy put together. How the hell had that happened?

A month ago, he'd been convinced of her innocence, now a few weeks later he'd been easily convinced of her guilt. He hadn't stood in her corner, fighting tenaciously for her till every shred of proof was either dispelled or proven. Alice, small though she may be, had never ever wavered in her support of him and his family; not when he killed Greg, not when Gabriella left him for Katie, not when he withdrew into himself, not when he was too selfish, too wrapped up in his own guilt to visit her when she was near death, and not when he went off grid to protect his mum. Now he'd let her down, not once, but twice. What sort of friend was he? What sort of boss? Every word Compo had uttered was true. He looked at Nancy and her slow nod and slight smile told him that she understood.

She raised her voice. 'Compo get on it,'

Compo tensed at her tone, and as her words registered, he turned, a tentative half smile playing about his lips.

Nancy smiled and continued, 'If there's evidence to refute the case against Alice, you're our secret weapon… Find it. Don't quote me but just find it – do what you need to.'

Before she'd finished speaking, Compo was out of his chair, and hugging Nancy. Turning to Gus, he shuffled his feet, hands stuffed in the pockets of his cargo pants and opened his mouth to speak.

Gus grabbed him and hugged him to his chest, 'Don't you dare apologise Compo. You shouldn't have needed to say what you said, but I'm glad you did.'

Taffy walked in at that minute, bundled up in a winter coat, hat, scarf and gloves. Snowdrops melted on the surface, as he entered the central-heated office, pulling his gloves from his fingers. He looked round at the tableau before him and frowned, 'What's going on?'

Compo, clicking his fingers, gangsta style moved over to his computers and began pressing buttons and packing stuff into his rucksack, 'Fucking justice is going on. That's what, Taffy my boy. You're with me, come on, we're relocating to my flat to do some 007 stuff.'

A short laugh escaped Nancy's lips and Gus shook his head, 'Christ, Compo. Don't go all *Die Hard* on me. I'm still in shock with the amount of cursing you just did. Don't let it become a habit, eh?'

Compo grinned and saluted. As Taffy moaned about having already walked three miles to get to work in a blizzard, he pulled his gloves on again, seemingly reconciled to going with Compo.

The dynamic duo were nearly out of the door when Gus called after them. 'Comps? Just do your best eh? That's all you can do.'

Chapter 36

13:45 Premier Inn, Epsom Surrey

'*S torm Emma is wreaking havoc throughout the UK with Scotland and the north of the country being the worst hit. Here in Surrey, the met office has released a red alert. Clive Jones is on the ground with reports of road closures and freezing conditions. What can you tell us, Clive?*'

Sean Kennedy pressed mute on the remote control and flung it onto the floor beside the bed where he lay sprawled in his boxers. 'Fucking storm Emma.' He parodied the over-excited tones of the BBC weather reporter. He'd been stuck in the room for hours – trapped in a stench of his own making with only the fucking BBC to keep him company. Or, at a push, one of the equally mundane TV channels, all of which spouted drivel about the weather at every opportunity. As if the UK population were incapable of looking out their damn windows and seeing the snow for themselves – idiots!

Limbs heavy, he lay in the overheated room, aware of the smell of sweat his body was producing. He was rotting from the inside out and, despite the free availability of hot water and toiletries, Sean couldn't bring himself to move. Alternating between numbness, cramps and taser shots of pain, his body ached. His throat hurt when he swallowed – slivers of glass stuck at the back of his tongue. Immune system shot, there was nothing he could do but hope that it didn't get any worse. Bet that fucking bitch had given him some germ or other – dirty bitch! Even at her lowest, the cunt was causing him grief. A hacking cough took him by surprise. It went on and on, slicing his throat – making his eyes water, forming droplets of sweat on his forehead.

Fuck, this was shite. Giving himself a minute to recover, he lay on his back, looking at the patchy paint on the ceiling through glazed eyes before he began to breathe slowly and shallowly from his chest. He could taste blood – sickly and thick which made him want to cough again – to get it out of his mouth. He closed his eyes and slowed his breathing further – wishing he hadn't knocked the water bottle off the bedside table onto the floor. In a moment he'd try to reach it, but not right now. Not till his chest loosened.

Taking care to move his hands only a little in case he provoked another coughing attack, he ran his fingers along the rumpled sheet. At last, just within his reach, he touched the familiar plastic of his inhaler. He wasn't supposed to use it so often and it hurt like hell when it hit his windpipe, but he needed to ease his chest. Bracing himself, he stuck it in his mouth and took as deep a breath as he could whilst pressing the button releasing the dose into his shattered lungs. It stung like hell as it went down, and the blood taste increased, making his salivary glands fill his mouth with turgid spit. The taste was strong. He let the inhaler fall to the side and waited. *How much fucking longer before the bastards found something that worked for him – something that boosted his immune system and helped his lungs?* Of course, it was all Alice fucking Cooper's fault. Right now, the fact that she was perhaps in as bad – if not worse – state than he, gave him no pleasure. She was a cunt who deserved everything he'd made happen to her and more.

His phone rang and he sighed. Time to attempt a change in position. He picked his phone up from the wooden surface next to the bed and smiled when he saw the name flashing on the screen.

Pulling himself into a sitting position, he took a deeper breath, pleased to note that his chest seemed looser and answered, 'Hi Mum. You alright?'

'I'm fine Sean, me and your dad were just concerned about you. Are you keeping warm in this cold weather? You know what the doctors said about you looking after yourself. Last thing you need is a chill getting into your chest.'

Sean recognised the worry in her voice. She'd been fussing around him since the moment he'd woken up. Apparently, she'd visited him every day when he'd been in his coma; talking to him, reading aloud, playing music. His dad had confided that she'd tried everything to reach him. At one point she'd played every recording they'd ever made of him growing up. Days on end of her talking him through what was on the screen, his dad sitting beside her. The only thing she hadn't done was turn to religion. Even in her darkest hour his mum – a firm atheist – had not been tempted by the hospital chaplain.

One night, after Sean had come around, but before he'd been discharged, they'd managed to convince her to go home and rest. It had just been Sean and his dad sitting in the half-lit room, trying to think of something to say that wouldn't send the other into deep introspection. Finally, his dad – always the quiet one of the couple – had started to laugh. Sean at first hadn't known what to say. He'd no idea why his dad was feeling joyful. As his laughter became louder, Sean was torn between pressing the emergency button for help, convinced that the pressure of his illness had sent his dad loopy and trying not to be drawn into the compelling hysteria himself. The latter option won out and Sean gave in to his own laughter.

His entire body had ached as the laughter jiggled his shoulders and bubbled up his throat, making him gasp for breath. Tears, only partly of laughter, seeped from his eyes and rolled down his cheeks. He pulled his arms round his chest, cushioning himself against the paroxysms that shook his body. After what seemed like hours, the father and son had wiped their eyes and allowed their hearts to slow and their breathing to deepen.

Sean took longer than his dad to recover, his sparse frame too weak to bounce back. Every breath hitched painfully at the back of his throat and his wheeze was more pronounced. Without saying anything, his dad squeezed his shoulder and helped his son into a more upright position before fitting the nebuliser over his face.

After he sat back down, he giggled once more and wiped his hand over his face before catching Sean's curious gaze. 'She never gave up on you Sean, not for one bloody second. Not when the nurses tried to prepare her for the worst, not even when your sister said it might be for the best to let you slip away and *definitely* not when that bloody pious git from the chapel came in all bloody '*God's will*' and '*Welcome places in heaven.*' He paused and shook his head slightly. The love and admiration for Sean's mum shone in his eyes as he spoke, 'She was like a warrior. A five-foot one ball of warrior-ness. She turned to him and raised her head – you know, like she does.'

Sean grinned behind the mask. He knew exactly which look his dad was referring to. – he'd been on the receiving end of it too many times as a kid not to have an exact visual of it etched in his mind.

'Her chin jutted out and, I must admit, I was tempted to give the priest a head's up to what was to come. But he smiled and said 'there, there' to your mum. Right then I decided that I'd leave the patronising git to his fate.' He laughed again, and slapped his thigh, 'Oh it was brilliant. She turned to him and said in her quietest, most polite tone, '*If you don't remove yourself from the vicinity of my child, I will stick that piece of fiction you're holding up your arse… sideways*'.'

Sean had laughed. He could well imagine his mother saying something like that. She was valiant in defence of her children – more so for him, he had to admit. Sean's sister had always rubbed mum up the wrong way. Probably why she'd been keen to turn the bloody machines off.

Back in the present, he tuned into what his mother was saying, making a mental note to work out some small punishment for his sister; *that dog of hers was a whinging little yappy thing – worth thinking about.*

'You don't have to worry about me, Mum. I'm good.' He was reluctant to speak too much in case his mother's acute ears picked up on the thickness of his voice or the shallowness of his breathing. He was glad she couldn't see him, because one look at him would have her phoning an ambulance and the last thing he needed was for his presence in Epsom to be logged anywhere. She had some sort of inbuilt calculator that seemed to scan his entire frame every time she saw him, calculating loss of muscle, increased pallor and pain indicators.

'You got enough food in, Sean? You don't know when you'll be able to get out. You need to wait till the ice has completely gone. Your bones are fragile, you know? Can't have you falling over and fracturing something now, can we?'

Sean rolled his eyes, she'd got that right. He could feel how fucking fragile they were right now. Throbbing they were. 'I've no intentions of going out. You know me, Mum. I'm a hothouse plant – more your sauna man than your snowman.'

She laughed. A tinkle of laughter down the phone that made him smile, 'Love you son.'

Sean's smile widened and his shoulders relaxed, 'Love you too, Mum. Don't worry about me. I'm great. Last time you came, you filled up the freezer, I've got plenty to eat and the house is warm as toast – amazing what central heating will do.'

He heard the smile in his mum's voice as she replied and imagined her petite frame untensing, 'Oh you, Sean. Always teasing your old mum. Now, I don't know when your dad and I will get up to see you, what with the storm and the snow and all that. But as long as we know you're okay.'

A pang of guilt contracted Sean's chest. Lying to his mother wasn't one of his favourite pastimes, but needs must. No need for her to know he was three streets away from their family home right now. No need to worry her. The least she and his dad knew about his plans for Alice Cooper, the better. Some secrets were best kept to himself. It was best for all concerned that she thought he was safely tucked up in his flat in Brent.

His phone beeped a signal to say he had another call waiting, and after a quick glance he frowned, 'Hey Mum, got another call waiting. Best take it. I'll phone you back later.'

His chest tight, he answered the call. 'What's up?'

'Bad news, I'm afraid Sean old boy.' It was Russell Allison-Hinton, his tone full of bonhomie and patronising bluff.

Sean closed his eyes and counted to three. When he reopened them there was yet another weather report involving swirling snow lines and red alert symbols on the telly. *How fucking apt!* Seemed like the story of his life. He moved his head side-to-side, relieved when his neck cricked, removing a little of the stiffness that plagued him on a daily basis. 'Go on.' He was aware his tone was abrupt but he didn't care. Bloody tosser, Allison-Hinton had let him down before, so he shouldn't be surprised at Sean's tone.

'Well, em... it's a shame really. Totally outside my control, you understand?'

Sean growled down the phone. 'Just spit it out, will you?'

'Yes, yes, of course... of course. It's just well, I want to...'

'Just tell me, right now.' The tension was seeping back into his neck as he enunciated each word with a pause that spoke volumes in between.

'Yes, well... one of the prison officers got a bit frisky and raped Alice Copper during the night.'

For a moment, Sean was confused. How the hell was that bad news? Anything that punished that bitch was a cause for a celebration, surely? The implications sunk in. The fucking prison officer had fucked things up for them. Sean pushed himself to his feet only to fall back onto the bed as his legs buckled beneath him, his breathing shallow in his chest. Fucking sneaky cow! Now, she'd get preferential treatment in the prison. Officers wouldn't dare let Sean's colleagues have free access to her now. All eyes would be on them and Sean's plans to ratchet things up for Alice would be on hold. Smarmy bitch had dodged a bullet. 'Fuck sake, couldn't the tosser keep it in his pants?'

'Apparently not. He's been arrested and will no doubt be suspended. Not that any of that helps us.'

Sean sighed. The TV was now showing footage of rosy cheeked kids on sledges, whirling down hills at a rate of knots, their parents supervising from a distance, travel mugs of coffee in gloved hands. Oh, how the middle classes lived, thought Sean. In the distance an old fella was shuffling along, head bowed against the wind, carrying armfuls of newspapers, yet the reporters only had eyes for the wholesome families. That poor old fucker was most certainly *not* having fun.

Sean was aware of the tension down the phone. He could hear the other man's breathing. It was louder and quicker – raspier. Sean, the expert in breathing, grinned. If Allison- Hinton wasn't careful he'd be having a full-blown panic attack.

'This is *your* problem – fix it. Make sure there's no let-up for her in prison,' he paused, eyes narrowed, thinking, 'And make sure you have eyes on her parents at all times. They're our biggest bargaining tool.'

Chapter 37

14:20 Holmfield Court, Bradford

The sense of relief that had flooded through Compo after he'd yelled at Gus was tempered with guilt. There was no doubt in his mind that it had needed saying, but Compo wasn't comfortable with challenging Gus like that – and especially not in front of Nancy and Lewis. He'd done it for Alice though and that was the one thing that had stopped him from backing down. In Alice, Compo recognised a kindred spirit – someone flawed and vulnerable, yet someone, who at the same time dug their heels in and, against the odds, survived. Only this time, he wasn't so sure Alice *would* survive. He was determined to do his best to bring her back to the team.

Now that they were brought round to his way of thinking, Nancy and Gus had been happy to turn a blind eye to his investigation. They'd told him to work from home for now and Compo interpreted that as 'go as deep and as dark as you need to without implicating West Yorkshire Police in anything untoward'. He'd been assigned Taffy to interface with Gus and follow up on any leads on the Izzie Dimou/Daniel Farrier investigation.

The two officers had left the station, with Taffy mumbling about only just having some feeling back in his toes. There was no point in attempting to drive, the gritters were mostly engaged around the motorways and the streets outside, Bradford city centre had remained ungritted since the previous night. In truth, the grit was useless against such heavy blizzards. So they'd set off, cutting through the side streets, wading through piles of snow, heading down to Thornton Road. Compo had been in The Fort since his return from the crime scene at Keighley station and had been largely oblivious of how bad the snow had got. After hefting his rucksack on his back, wishing he'd thought to grab a pair of wellies from the boot of Gus' car before setting off, he trudged head down against the wind, Taffy leading the way.

Damp was gradually seeping up his cargo pants, making them cling to his shins and thighs. His parka offered little resistance to the driving snow or the cold. Huddled over, furry hood drawn tight round his face, Compo thought about the tasks ahead. Apart from having to delve deeper into Izzie Dimou's and Daniel Farrier's pasts, which was already running away gently on his work's PC system with alerts set up to link to his home system, he was liaising with Manchester police who were securing CCTV for more sightings of either Daniel or Izzie. Then there was the USB that Gus had found in Saltaire. It was encrypted, and Compo was – bit by bit – breaking through the encryption. Again, alerts would be sent to his home system when the programme had finished.

His main concern now was Alice. Nancy had sent him all the information Alice's lawyer had obtained from the prosecution team. Whoever had set Alice up had done a great job. The layers went deep and Compo had a few ideas of how to ferret out the origins of the trail Sean Kennedy and his crew had used to implicate Alice. Despite Nancy's final warning that they might be wrong and Alice may have got herself into something really bad, Compo was convinced of her innocence. He'd use all of his contacts, all of his skills and he'd go as dark as was necessary to prove Alice's innocence.

His thoughts were interrupted by a snowball hitting his face. It disintegrated on impact and slithered down his cheeks to drip off his chin. His head jerked up and shaking the last of the ice off his face, he glared at Taffy. 'What the…?'

Taffy, grinning, had already scooped up another handful of snow and was compacting it between his gloved hands. 'Come on, not scared of a bit of snow are you? Show me what you've got, lad!'

Compo wiped the wet from his face, hoiked his rucksack further up his back and, eyes narrowed, bent over and scooped up a pile of pristine snow. 'You better start running I've a good aim!'

Firing off a snowball which hit his friend in the chest, Taffy began running down Hollings Road past Jasmin Terrace with Compo in hot pursuit whooping and laughing. Another snowball hit Taffy in the back of his head making him shake his head like a friendly dog after a dip in the River Aire. Spinning round, he grabbed some snow and all the while running backwards sang, "Catch me if you can! Catch me if you can!".

Compo, snowball at the ready, gained on his adversary, grinning like a child visiting Santa. Taffy inadvertently veered towards a deep drift of snow and was taken unawares when Compo let loose an icy missile. Failing to catch it, Taffy stepped back. His feet went from under him and he pedalled the air briefly, before ending up in the middle of the drift. Taking full advantage Compo grabbed some snow, moulded it and fired it, before repeating the action twice more in quick succession. 'Submit, Taff,' he yelled, 'Submit.'

Raising his arms up over his face, Taffy laughed. 'Okay, Okay. I give up – stop it.'

Compo did a quick victory circle on the spot then reached down to pull Taffy from the pile of snow. As soon as Taffy gripped his hand, Compo realised his mistake and seconds later he was lying beside Taffy in the snow, the pair of them laughing uncontrollably.

By the time they arrived at Thornton Road five minutes later, the snow had become a blizzard and the wind had sped up. Storm Emma had arrived in Bradford.

Wet and shivering, yet laughing, Compo took a left into Holmfield Court with Taffy following. As they climbed the stairs to Compo's flat Taffy said, 'Hey Comp's I didn't know you lived—'

'Yeah, yeah' said Compo, trying to find his keys – his tone flat. 'I know I'm right in the heart of the red-light district. Dun't mean I use the facilities does it?'

Taffy frowned, 'Hell Comps. Wasn't gonna say that, I was going to say that the Crossbow Cannibal live in these flats, didn't he?'

'Don't call him that – that's what he gets off on.'

Taffy blushed and shuffled his feet. Modifying his tone, Compo continued, 'Gus hates it when the press gives them a title. Says it glorifies them when all they deserve is to rot quietly in prison with their boring old name.'

Taffy, head on one side, seemed to think for a minute, then nodded. 'Stephen Griffiths that was his name wasn't it. Did you meet him?'

Compo shook his head. 'He was arrested before I moved in. That's how I can afford the rent. They were desperate to get folk in.'

'So – this flat of yours it's…?'

Realising what Taffy thought, Compo laughed and shook his head. 'Don't be daft. I might have wanted a cheap flat, didn't want it that cheap though! Griffiths' was upstairs. Nobody lives in it for long.' He rubbed his chin with his fingers, 'Nobody stays in any of these flats for long – except me that is. I don't mind it here. It does me.'

He slotted his key in the lock and faced Taffy. 'I've never had a visitor here before, Taff.' He turned the key and pushed the door open a fraction. 'Actually, I've never had anybody visit me in any of the places I lived in before either. Reckon it's because folk think I'm weird. Never really had a friend 'till I joined Gus' team.' He stepped through the door and stopped. 'Now I've lost two of them in the space of a few months. We've got to get Alice back. Can't bear to lose her as well as Sampson.'

Taffy wasn't sure what to expect when he stepped through the door after Compo. It wasn't so much Compo's words that made Taffy realise just how lonely he was – how badly he'd been affected by Sampson's death and Alice's subsequent arrest. It was the haunted look in his eyes. His nervous, almost pleading tone as he avoided Taffy's gaze. The slump of his shoulders and, worse than any of those other things, the momentary blankness in his eyes that echoed his words. In that instant, Taffy realised that all of Compo's life was invested in the team. He could have kicked himself for never asking him about his family, his life outside The Fort. He suspected that Compo had a story that would be completely different to his own happy home life with devoted, supportive parents.

Taffy had an almost uncontrollable urge to wrap his arms round Compo and tell him everything would be alright. But he stopped himself – he couldn't be the one to give Compo hope that could so easily be stripped away again. He'd much rather be honest with his friend – prepare him for the worst and hope for the best. 'We can only do our best, Comps. But, no matter what happens with Alice, I'll still be here. I'll still be your friend and so will Gus. We're a team – family, yeah?'

Compo shuffled his feet and gesturing with his head, invited Taffy to move into the cramped hallway. It was dark and Compo – seemingly comfortable with the dim light – took his coat off and hung it on one of three hooks next to a radiator by the door before untying his sodden shoelaces and kicking off his boots by the radiator. He gestured to his friend to do the same and as Taffy shrugging his coat off, took a step closer to the radiator, its heat rose to his face and with the light shining through the door pane, he could already see steam rising from

Compo's coat. Compo might not be at home much, but he certainly kept his flat warm.

Compo moved down the narrow hallway, flicked on a light switch. There were four doors leading off the corridor and Compo headed for the one facing them at the end. As Taffy walked behind Comps, he was aware of his damp socks leaving footprints on the brown carpet, so he tried to step on the existing ones left by Compo. Curious, he looked at the posters that lined the walls. Each one was framed in a simple black frame. The Doors at Winterland, featuring a long-haired bare-chested dude. *No idea who they are.* A psychedelic poster of Jimi Hendrix dated 1968 – vague idea who he was. Another psychedelic poster of a woman, this time Janis Joplin at Avalon Ballroom dated 1967. A poster with an effeminate lad in a purple shirt open to the navel with 'Born To Boogie' emblazoned across the top – again no idea. Until, at last, one that Taffy recognised – a poster of John Lennon with the quote *'Possession isn't nine tenths of the law. It's nine tenths of the problem.'*

'I know him – John Lennon. He's dead in't he?'

Compo moved to stand beside Taffy, looking up at the poster. He reached out his hand and touched the glass. 'They're all dead' His tone was flat. 'They all died young. John Lennon in '80, shot aged forty.'

Taffy looked back at the row of frames and back to Compo. There was something about his friend that worried him. The sadness in his eyes as he too looked at the row of dead rock stars. Compo walked back along the corridor, stopping at each frame in turn and touching the face of the artist. 'Marc Bolan – car crash September '77 – age twenty-nine. Janis Joplin, '70, heroin overdose, age twenty-seven. Jimi Hendrix, '70, choked on his own vomit – age twenty-seven. Jim Morrison, '71, possible heart attack, suspected drug overdose – also aged twenty-seven.'

Every one of the artists was one of Compo's heroes. Taffy had seen him wearing t-shirts with their faces or names on them. Presumably the music he listened to on his headphones was that of his dead heroes.

Compo turned and walked back along the corridor. 'The seventies was a bad time. Seems like this decade is too.' He thrust open the door that opened into a living room. What first drew Taffy's eyes were the framed posters that lined these walls too. These people he recognised: Amy Winehouse, Prince, David Bowie, George Michael, Dolores O'Riordan – and the one thing they all had in common was that, they too, were dead.

Speechless, Taffy allowed his eyes to drift over each of the posters. Squirming maggots of unease turned his stomach. Compo's flat was like a photo mausoleum – a shrine to the dead artists Compo worshipped. He was sure this wasn't healthy, but he had no idea what to say.

Fortunately, he was distracted by the expanse of equipment that stretched along the back wall of Compo's living room. Holy shit! This was impressive. Taffy hesitated in the doorway, taking in the rest of the space in a stunned silence.

Whilst Compo's work area back at The Fort was at best 'lived in' and at worst 'downright unhygienic', this was the complete opposite. The entire living room was almost spartan apart from the pictures on the walls and the elongated workstation on which sat an impressive amount of PC screens, docks and towers with wires erupting like spaghettis from a series of sockets attached to the back wall. The only other furniture in the room was a single chair that looked like it had barely been used, two computer chairs and a massive TV that hung from the opposite wall and appeared to be linked to the sea of PC equipment.

Taffy started when a sudden burst of music erupted from the TV. He recognised it as a George Michael track, but wasn't sure of the title. Compo lowered the volume and stood, biting his lip in the middle of the room. Before Taffy could speak, he raised one finger in the air. 'Oops nearly forgot.' And he skirted the armchair and went over to a small table nestled in the corner of the room that Taffy hadn't noticed. He picked up a box of matches, struck one and lit the large green pine Yankee Candle that stood in the centre. 'Mrs McGuire gave me this,' he said blowing out the match.

Taffy grinned, 'Bloody hell Comps, how do you manage to keep your flat so bloody tidy?'

Blushing, Compo shrugged, 'Never here, Taff. Prefer it at The Fort. Got everything I need there.'

Taffy moved over and flung himself onto one of the computer chairs. 'Looks like you've got all you need here too, Comps.'

Compo shrugged and sat down, shaking the mouse which activated four of the five screens. 'Not quite. I don't usually have the team here.' And he began to check the programmes he had running.

Chapter 38

'The Beast from the East has paid some unexpected dividends for West Yorkshire Police. In the midst of the storm, police detected unusual heat sources in a property in Keighley causing the snow to melt as soon as it landed on the roof. On closer inspection, West Yorkshire Police were able to seize and disband one of the largest cannabis farms in the district, preventing tens of thousands of pounds worth of cannabis from hitting the streets. Meanwhile in other news, across the region emergency services are being stretched to breaking point with burst pipes and electrical faults playing havoc. This is Capital Radio News...'

Gus and Lewis Gore had spent the last hour following a snow plough along Keighley Road and still had to hike the last mile through Keighley town centre to the cenotaph where the bodies had been found. Gus had taken the call from Hissing Sid, saying that some of the wounds were similar to those found on Izzie Dimou's body and had elected to face the weather to see for himself. Keighley town centre was usually alive with a bustling community making full use of its quaint shops and cafes. Today – apart from the two lads who'd had the misfortune to uncover one of the two bodies whilst enjoying a snowball fight and the crime scene teams – the square was deserted.

A large tent had been erected over the corpses and Gus could see a uniformed officer with two young lads over the road, no doubt escorting them home. Gus was happy to let the lads go home. The officer would have taken their details and Gus could catch up with him later. He doubted the lads had much to offer and they'd be better off at home playing video games and drinking hot chocolate. Gus and Gore signed themselves into the inner cordon and approached the tent, walking on the slabs that had been set out for this purpose. Hissing Sid turned to greet them. 'Bloody hate this sort of crime scene. Most of what we get is ruined.' He sighed and released a fart that sounded like a gunshot which ricocheted off every building on the square, exhaling its noxious fumes over Gus and Gore.

'Fuck's sake,' Gus spoke under his breath. Experience had told him that the less fuss he made about Sid's unsociable behaviour, the less Sid did it.

With an angelic smile, Sid swept open the tent flap and ushered them in, 'Least I did it outside, Gus.'

Yeah, very sociably conscious of you, I'm sure. Gus stepped through and saw that two male bodies lay side by side, their clothes slashed and covered in bloody knife wounds.

'Once we'd swept the snow off, we saw that they'd been left like this. Bar their shoes, they're still dressed – unlike Izzie – but even so, you can see the cuts are different sizes. And..,' Sid pointed to their bare feet, 'their soles have been slashed.'

Gus bent over. Sid was right, there were definite similarities to Izzie Dimou's wounds, but that wasn't what caught his attention. He pointed to the smaller of the two men, 'That's the guy who broke into Izzie's house last night and kneed me in the balls.'

Gore looked at the dead man, 'I'm assuming that not all of the damage to his face is down to you, Gus.'

'Nope, you got that right. I managed a couple of punches, but whoever did this really let go.'

'Looks like they thought he'd got something important from Izzie's house doesn't it?'

Gus turned and walked towards the exit. 'Yep, which means we really need Compo to get to the bottom of what's on that USB stick pronto.'

What was going on? How many men were implicated in Izzie Dimou's death? These two were very similar to the thugs who'd followed Izzie on leaving Rubeus Pharmaceuticals. When they got the CCTV footage cleaned up, he was sure their faces would match. So who had killed them? This didn't lead him very much closer to finding Daniel either, which clearly wasn't going to please Gabriella. Right on cue, *The Bitch is Back* resonated from his phone. With an exaggerated sigh, Gus sent it straight to voicemail. Seeing Gore's questioning look he shrugged, 'Gabriella. Can't just let me do my job, got to keep micromanaging.' He was slipping his phone back into his pocket when it rang again, this time just a normal ring tone. 'McGuire here.'

'Oh, so you are able to answer?'

Gus cursed under his breath and turned away from Gore who was grinning like he'd won the damn lottery. 'Hi Gabriella, phone went to voicemail before I could answer,' Straightening his shoulders, he added, 'I am at a crime scene right now, you know. Can't be speaking to you on the phone every five minutes.'

There was silence on the end of the phone and a muffled sniff followed by Katie's voice, 'Is it Daniel?'

Fuck! 'No, no it's not Daniel. We're still trying to locate him.'

Katie said something to Gabriella and then she was back talking to him, 'Look Gus, all she needs is to be kept in the loop – that's all. It's hard for her not being there.'

Gus' momentary pang of guilt was replaced by relief. Gabriella, in person, was infinitely worse than Gabriella with the buffer of a phone between them. 'Look Katie, I can't be dealing with her all the time. You need to stop her phoning. It's distracting. I need to focus. Tell her she'll be the first to know when we find him.' And before Katie could agree or disagree, he hung up only to have the phone burst back into life in his hand straight away. This time he checked the number before answering.

Mickey's voice came across the line loud and clear. 'Bloody carnage at Jordan Beaumont's house. Manchester CID's just been on the phone. Cleaner found the wife's body and the daughter near dead and Beaumont nowhere to be seen. You need to get there, they're expecting you.'

Gus glanced up at the sky, heavy with snow clouds, and grimaced. 'Got a helicopter for us, have you Mickey?' Her answering snort told him all he needed to know. Bloody typical. She couldn't get from Oxenhope to Bradford, but he was expected to drive to damn Staleybridge. Looked like he and Gore were on their own for this one.

An hour later, Gus and Gore were still in Gore's car. 'Can't you go any faster?' Gus leaned forward in the front passenger seat of Lewis Gore's Volvo XC90, peering out the windscreen at the blizzard outside. He was being unreasonable, but the intel they'd just received from Mickey was the first clear lead or hint of a lead they'd had since finding Izzie Dimou's body – other than the USB stick that Compo was working on, of course. When he'd taken the call about Jordan Beaumont's family from Mickey, he'd thanked God that the constable in Manchester Met had had his wits about him and had linked the CCTV footage of Izzie going into his offices with the house in Stalybridge which was now a crime scene.

'The current red alert in the face of Storm Emma looks to be staying in place for the foreseeable future. Drivers are advised to avoid driving where possible.'

The radio crackled and went dead before bursting into a crackly Ed Sheeran number and finally going silent again. Thank God for that. Gus wasn't an Ed Sheeran fan and right now the last thing he wanted to listen to was the ginger pop prince droning on about perfect love or whatever.

Having judged Gore's car to be the best chance they had of getting to Stalybridge in the current conditions, Gus was on the edge of his seat. The M62 was closed so they'd decided to take the A58. Gus was beginning to wonder if they'd make it; the snow was blinding and what would normally take an hour and a half from Bradford, promised to take a hell of a lot longer.

Ignoring Gore's muttered curses, Gus mulled over what had happened. He suspected that the chap he'd had his encounter with the previous night had something to do with the goings on at Beaumont's house. He'd spent hours poring over the database. The guy had been foreign, but Gus wasn't much of a linguist so had been unable to identify his accent with any certainty. He'd spent a bit of time with the e-fit guy and was desperate to get the image he'd generated out to as many forces as he could. Now that he'd turned up dead in Keighley, Gus was even more determined to get an ID on him and his friend. Maybe that way they'd get a clue to who'd done this to them and to Beaumont's family. It seemed too coincidental for the two incidents not to be linked. The only trouble was, in the current weather conditions, most police work was being done at local levels with the emphasis on making sure the rough sleepers and the vulnerable were taken care of and that drivers weren't stranded in their cars. He doubted many officers were keeping up with BOLOs right now.

Fiddling with the radio dial he managed to get a burst of noise, which turned into a staticky weather report.

'The A636 and A616 are blocked completely by an overturned lorry. Gritters are attempting to clear the A62 after record amounts of drifting snow have led to

*abandoned vehicles… **static**… but Gemma has been reunited with her puppy in a news story to warm your hearts in these freezing blustery conditions.'*

'Fuck's sake!' Gore's expletive powered out of his mouth in a snarl of rage as the car in front skidded right across the lane into oncoming traffic. Had it been a moment earlier it would have been alright as the roads had been deserted apart from their vehicle and the one in front. Gore pulled the steering wheel to the left to avoid slamming into the car's rear end. The oncoming vehicle was a Morrison's lorry with an image of a giant courgette with the immortal words *'No courgettes kept in this vehicle overnight'* emblazoned across its side.

Its horn blared long and loud, as the two vehicles narrowly avoided a collision. Lewis Gore's Volvo bumped over some piles of packed-up ice that had been sluiced to the side of the road by a gritter at some point. His tyres lost their purchase on the road and Gore tested his brakes, but the car was in full skid now and picked up momentum before slamming hard into a snow drift. The seatbelt cut across Gus' chest, ricocheting him back, moments before his air bag erupted, trapping him against the seat. Almost immediately, a warm gush spurted from his nose and his ears began ringing. The pressure of the airbag against his chest evoked memories of his last panic attack when they'd found Izzie Dimou's body. Blood trickled down the back of his throat and he could do nothing but swallow it.

Wondering how Lewis had fared, Gus ignored the metallic taste. 'Gore, You alright?' As he spoke, his hands moved to find the release catch for his seatbelt. If he didn't get out from under the airbag soon, he'd asphyxiate. With each shallow breath his chest became tighter. His fingers scrabbled under the nylon fabric. Already the temperature in the car was falling and the adrenalin push made his body shiver. At last his fingers touched the metal casing and he pressed the button. 'Gore?' He tried again. Still silence.

Pulling the strap away from his body, he pushed the fabric from the door, hoping to be able to access the handle, flick it and fall out into the snow. His chest was becoming tighter with every passing second and he tried to block the thought that he was being entombed in a vehicle that was becoming buried in snow. He could hear moaning from his right and was relieved. At least Gore was alive. Pressing all his weight to the left, Gus found the handle and, releasing the catch, the door sprung open a few inches before being embedded in the drifting pile of snow they'd crashed into. Pushing the airbag to his right, Gus gained some leverage and pressed all his weight against the door. It gave, but only another couple of inches. Blood still trickled down his swollen, throbbing face. The skin was tight over his cheeks and the tingling numbness was increasing by the second.

He twisted his body, pulling his legs to the side and again applied pressure to the door. If he didn't manage to get out soon, the continuing snowfall would make it even more difficult. Gore's laboured breathing was a welcome distraction to his right. He needed to get out of the car in order to help his friend. Bending over, he used his fingernails to dig a small trough round the door frame that was stuck in the snow at the bottom. One more push. Another few inches, but if he slipped off his coat he reckoned it would be enough. He wriggled out of his fisherman's jacket and leaving it on the seat behind him he edged his way into the snow, scraping his shoulders against the door as he did so. By the time he'd extracted his entire body, he was sweating and panting.

What the hell had just happened? Lewis had been closer than he should have to the car in front that was for sure. Gus had the grace to realise that he was partly to blame for that as he'd kept urging his friend to drive faster. The other reason though had been Gore's desire to make use of the path the car was carving out of the heavy snow as it fell, obscuring the wheel ruts almost as soon as they were made.

Pulling himself onto his knees – aware now of the cold seeping through his body and the snow before him turning red – he dragged himself over to the car and grabbing his coat, he thrust his arms into the sleeves, leaving it open as his fingers were too cold to pull the zip up. Sticking close to the car, he edged round it looking for Gore, 'Lewis. You there?'

A muffled groan came from the other side of the car and Gus made his way towards it. Lewis Gore lay on his back in the snow, having clearly completed a similar manoeuvre to Gus. His eyes flicked open when Gus touched his forehead. 'Hope the car's okay. Sandra will fucking kill me otherwise.'

Gus laughed, the relief that the big man was okay made him forget his own pain until Gore spoke. 'You look a damn mess Gus. Patti will ditch you now, for sure. You look like Quasimodo on a bad day, lad. Might as well face up to it, you're as ditched as my damn car.' And he released a guffaw that made Gus want to punch him in the face. Bloody idiot, this was no laughing matter. It was only then that Gus realised that Gore was bleeding from an elongated gash across his forehead. *Shit!* Collapsing onto the snow beside Gore, Gus lay down with the arbitrary memory of himself and Katie making snow angels in their back garden when they were five or six years old. *Fuck sake, get a grip, Gus.* He sighed and closed his eyes, enjoying the soft touch of the flakes as they landed on his lids.

Despite Mickey urging them to get to Staleybridge ASAP, Nancy had told them to wait till the weather had cleared a bit. However, Gus – impatient as ever – had convinced Gore to risk the drive to Stalybridge. Now he realised just how foolhardy they'd been. Gore needed medical help and he himself could probably do with a couple of painkillers to see him through the rest of the day. He turned to survey the surrounding scene. He'd expected to see the Morrison's truck idling at the side of the road and a Discovery with its front end smashed. But the road was empty. The vehicles' tracks disappearing under the snow as he watched. He grabbed his phone – no signal. *Fucking typical!* His jaw tightened, making the ache across his nose throb even more.

'Bastards!' Shouted Gus shaking his fist first in the direction of the long gone Morrisons van and then in the direction of the Discovery. Then, once more for good measure, 'Bastards!'

Deep laughter rumbled across the blizzard and he turned to see that Gore had managed to struggle to his feet and was leaning against the car, a handful of snow held to his cut. Gus exhaled, thinking back to how he'd made a cold pack in the early hours to ease his pain. *The many medicinal qualities of snow!*

'Hey Gus, there's a shovel in the boot,' said Gore, laughing once more.

Chapter 39

Daniel's ankle had swollen to the size of a damn tree trunk; fortunately, it felt numb. It was so good to feel warm again – and full. Two tins of tomato soup had done the trick. Okay, it wasn't a steak or even a McDonald's but it was warm and flavoursome and it filled a hole. He'd even found some tea bags – so what if they were Better Buy ones? They added colour to the hot water and had a vague – alright a *very* vague – resemblance to the real deal. At the back of the pantry had been a discarded packet of digestives. Who cared that they were a few months past their sell by date – not Daniel. Dunking biscuits in tea made him feel almost normal.

Invigorated, he put his mind to his current predicament. He didn't know what had happened to Izzie, so he refused to dwell on her. He'd think about that when he had to. The main thing right now was to get himself out of here and to safety. He still had no memory of who had brought him here, so that didn't help. The house was neglected. Damp ran down the living room wall, unravelling brown water stained wallpaper 'till it hung like a slurry of snakes on the sodden carpet. A thick layer of dust covered the heavy wooden furniture and an overwhelming mustiness permeated the air. Further exploration had uncovered various useful bits and pieces. A couple of sharp kitchen knives in sheaves were now slotted down the back of the belt he'd found in the upstairs wardrobe. He'd slipped a further pocket knife – unfortunately not a Swiss Army one, but

213

nonetheless it could potentially be the difference between life and death for him – into his pocket. Perhaps the most useful acquisition had been the pair of crutches he'd found at the back of the musty smelling cloakroom.

The only footwear available that would go over his oversized ankle was a pair of size twelve wellies that stood by the back door as if awaiting the return of their giant-sized owner. His sprained foot was cumbersome – alien to him; an appendage over which he had no control. It was like a lump of beef on the end of his leg and his toes were puffy and pale as a lump of lard. Not a good sign, Daniel was sure. Still, at last he managed to stuff it into the wellie, although it was a tight fit. It was strange trying to manoeuvre it around, even with the crutch. The other wellie was too big for him, so he stuck old bits of newspaper into the toe and it seemed to do the trick. As long as he could move, he had a chance to escape – the questions were *when* should he make his move and in which direction?

Visibility was non-existent and, peering through the window at the blizzard, Daniel wished he had a radio or TV so he could get weather updates. Not that it would do him much good; he had no idea where he was. It looked like there was nothing else for it. He'd have to brave the weather, make his choice of direction and hope for the best. He dragged himself back into the kitchen and checked the supplies he'd crammed into the mouldy old army rucksack he'd found. A few tins, a spoon, some dry clothes, a kid's cricket bat, matches, some old newspaper and a tin opener. Before slipping the rucksack on, he layered up in all the clothes he'd found upstairs. He'd had trouble with the stairs but had managed to drag himself up on his bottom so he could explore the rest of the rooms. The only things of interest he'd found were a couple of kids' drawings pinned to the wall in one of the bedrooms. One of them had the name Missy Beaumont scrawled across the bottom in large childish writing. Too much of a coincidence for it not to be Jordan Beaumont's daughter. At least that explained whose property he had been held in and, presumably, who had ordered his abduction. He wondered what the hell the bastard had done to Izzie. He could only hope that she'd escaped his clutches and was with friends.

Now that it was time for him to leave mild panic fluttered in his chest as he pulled a motley collection of hats, scarves and gloves on. He decided to do a quick reconnoitre round the periphery of the farmhouse. Upon opening the farmhouse door, a gust of wind sent him stumbling backwards. A gale had picked up and was whirling up bucketsful of snow and spinning them like a whirlpool. That, combined with the driving blizzard, covered Daniel in snow within seconds. A furious gale whirled up bucketsful of snow and in no time was it crawling down Daniel's neck, biting at his face. Keeping as close to the walls of the house as he could, Daniel braced himself and began to skirt the building with the wind at his back offering him welcome momentum.

It was impossible to guess the time. The sky was oppressively low, filled with dark pregnant clouds. Hampered by the dead weight of his foot, progress was slow. Despite the cold, sweat pooled under his armpits and speckled across his forehead – or maybe that was just the snow landing. He laughed, the sound loud and echoey against the howling wind. Cold caught in his chest making him cough as his breath hitched in his throat. It was as if he was in the middle of an apocalyptic experience. He half expected to be surrounded by figures dressed in furs and escorted back to his room in the farmhouse and served dry toast and water.

Leaning on his crutch, he rested for a moment; eyes streaming as freezing tears nipped his raw cheeks. This was harder than he'd expected. Each time he placed his good foot on the ground it sank a full foot into a snowdrift. And pulling it out each time took unimaginable effort. That, combined with dragging his other foot through the snow, was rapidly depleting his reserves. He hadn't travelled far and there was no way he could possibly see far enough in front of him to determine the best direction to travel in. On the other hand, there was no way he could stay here. As soon as the snow cleared enough, his captors would come back for him and who knew what they'd do. He had to leave. If they did come, he needed to be prepared. He stopped and, leaning his crutch against the wall, pulled his various outer layers up and extracted the knives from inside his belt; one he tucked down the inside of the boot with his good leg, the other slotted into a side pocket in his rucksack.

Gripping his crutch once more, he pushed himself away from the wall and – instead of following the contour of the building – set off diagonally. The absence of any sort of delineation made his sense of isolation complete. There was nothing out here other than the farmhouse and the snow – plenty of damn snow. Almost at once, the full force of the storm thumped him on the back, making him stumble. He righted himself and continued. He had to keep moving if he was to survive the temperatures. *Keep moving, one step at a time.* From nowhere the lyrics of *One Step Beyond* boomed in his mind. Madness. He loved Madness. *Do do doooo… do do do do do doooo! Love that track. Keep moving, one step at a time. Come on Danny boy, you can do this.*

Chapter 40

Taffy had never watched Compo at work before – well, not in such close proximity or for such a length of time. He was still reeling at the contrast between Compo's home and his workstation.

Compo had looked uneasy until Taffy had said, 'Look Compo, why don't you do what you're good at and I'll do what I'm good at?'

Compo had nodded and wandered into his tiny kitchen, returning moments later with cans of fizzy pop, huge bags of crisps, packets of biscuits and chocolate bars. Taffy had thought they were to share until Compo stacked them at one end of his workstation – the end furthest away from Taffy before nodding in the direction of the kitchen and mumbling 'help yourself, there's loads there'.

Curious, Taffy had wandered through and was again surprised by how pristine Compo's kitchen was. When he opened the drawers, he found one set of cutlery and one set of crockery, a bowl, a side plate and a dinner plate. After opening the fridge, he saw that Compo's staples consisted of chocolate – mainly Mars Bars, and full sugar soft drinks ranging from Fanta to Coke to Irn Bru. The single cupboard had multi bags of crisps; Hula Hoops, Seabrook's Prawn Cocktail and salt and vinegar, big bags of Tortilla chips; cheese flavour, Sensations; sweet chili flavour and sour cream and chive flavour Pringles. Biscuits consisted of digestives, custard creams bourbons and there was also a variety of muffins. *Compo was all set to survive the Zombie apocalypse!*

Taffy grabbed a packet of crisps, a can of coke and a Wispa and resigned himself to developing both diabetes and a heart condition as well as chronic obesity by the time they could re-locate back to The Fort. When he got back into the room, Compo was already lost in his quest to find something on Alice, his focus aided by his headphones. Taffy watched the screen, fascinated with the conversations this new Compo was having.

Warrier Queencess:	ReviAeternus, you make my eyes bleed with all your demands. Cease with all your orders.
ReviAeternus:	Don't be such a drama Queencess. You revel in this. Cut back when you got something for me.
JayRay:	I got stuff rolling on the Mini girl. IGNORE The Queenster, she's outta her depth – Her warriorness is depleted.

Taffy watched fascinated as Compo conducted conversations and, bit-by-bit, decoded the encryption on the USB with the help of his Dark Web friends. At last, he settled down to his own job which was the monotonous task of checking all the Manchester CCTV footage for Daniel Farrier and going through the pile of reports that MI6 had so kindly sent over. When Gus had seen how much they'd sent, Taffy had thought he'd be pleased – but Gus had cursed. Turns out most of this would be irrelevant stuff, designed to keep them occupied and out of their hair, which – Taffy sighed – was why he'd been tasked with it. Good job Compo had set a programme up on Taffy's PC to cut through the crap and search only for key words.

Chapter 41

B y the time Gus and Gore arrived at Jordan Beaumont's home, the crime scene investigators had almost finished processing the scene. Walking along the street that was lined with various law enforcement and CSI vans, Gus was aware – despite the freezing conditions – that this was an affluent area. The snow was no disguise for well-manicured lawns and privet hedges coiffed to within an inch of their lives by the look of their silhouettes. It was near impossible to catch sight of any of the houses as they passed, so well hidden from the road were they. However, evidence of drives cleared of snow spoke of pride in their properties and enough money to pay for the service. Gus doubted that many of the inhabitants of these houses would be prepared to do the work themselves. As if to prove his thoughts wrong, he saw a family of four working together to clear their long drive. The children's shrieks of laughter contrasting with what he'd heard about the fate of Jordan Beaumont's daughter.

The house he was looking for was halfway along the lane, the gate guarded by two ruddy-faced officers, one of whom kept stamping his feet as if his goal in life was to compact the snow as much as possible, whilst the other periodically blew on her hands before shoving them back inside the pockets of her bulky police-issue coat. Unruly police tape fought against the wind and was becoming increasingly elongated as it threatened to tear itself loose from the gate posts that held it in place. The combination of wind and plastic created that burring sound that Gus found so annoying. It reminded him of the disappointment of broken kites, tangled in spiky trees on windy days.

Gus and Gore flashed their ID at the outer cordon, smiled as the officers attempted to enter their names onto the log with their frozen fingers and dipped under the tape. As Gus had suspected, the drive leading up to the house was as long as the lane itself. Foot traffic had trampled the snow except for where an area with tyre tracks had been covered by plastic sheeting to protect it from the wind and snow. Trouble was, it looked as if the tracks had been covered before the CSIs had arrived. He hoped they'd be able to find identifiers in the data base. The house at the end of the curved lane was half the size of The Fort, but in red brick. Following the metal blocks put down to protect the scene, Gus and Gore moved towards the front door which stood open, bright lights spewing out casting shadows amidst the cacophony of movement that typified a heavy crime scene.

Approaching an officer in a high-vis jacket with a cup of something steaming in her hands who was barking orders at other officers, Gus hoped his instincts in risking the drive to Staleybridge would be proved right. They needed something to drive this investigation forward. 'Inspector Estefan? We're DIs McGuire and Gore from Bradford.'

The officer's voice was deep and raspy – perhaps the result of a lifetime of whisky and cigarettes – when she responded. 'Fucking shite weather, eh? You got here? Thought for a while we'd have to send a crew to dig you out.' She paused and raked their bruised faces with narrowed eyes, 'Looks like you two might have had a run-in with our killer. You okay?'

Gus, conscious of his swollen nose and the dribbles of blood down the front of his jacket, glanced at Gore. Lewis' forehead had developed a contour rivalling Bradford's Cow and Calf rocks, but at least the bleeding had stopped. 'Was a close thing, but we're here now. What can you tell us?'

'Fucking disgrace, that's what it is.' She shook her head and kicked a bundle of ice. 'Whoever's done this was a sicko.'

Gus waited, allowing her the time to process her thoughts. Crime scenes were always
difficult and those involving children were the worst.

She flashed a quick grin at Gus, 'Sorry about that. They've just taken the daughter away. I'm still reeling from that, I suppose.' She sniffed and Gus suspected it wasn't from the cold.

'Take your time.'

Thrusting her hands in her pockets, Estefan spun on her heel and, with a perfunctory gesture, indicated they should follow her into the house.

In spite of the open doors and the driving wind and snow outside, heat blasted Gus in the face as he entered Jordan Beaumont's home. His immediate thought was that he'd entered a house influenced by the current external environment; it was clinically white – sterile. Well, that was apart from the blood spatter that trailed down the stairs into the hallway and drifted along the white carpet to a door half way along to the left. Dotted over each of the spatters were yellow number tags. Sticking to the blocks, Gus followed Estefan towards the door with its bloody welcome sign.

'We reckon they got in by scaling the small shed at the back of the house and entering through the daughter's bedroom. Seems like the alarm system was off.' She tutted. 'Why the hell do they bother with state-of-the-art technology and then not bloody use it? That alarm system could have given them enough of a warning to save their lives.' Hesitating by the door, she turned and pointed up the glass walled staircase, 'Reckon they… and we know there were two of them from the footprints in here…' She hitched a thumb into the room, 'sneaked past and entered the master bedroom, subdued the wife and then one of them went back for the daughter. There are marks on the stairs to indicate they were dragged down and along the hallway into this room, where, we believe, Jordan Beaumont was. How he didn't hear anything is beyond me – but I'm assuming he didn't, because there is no sign that he tried to leave the room or, for that matter, phone for help.'

She stepped onto the block beyond the door and indicated they should enter. 'Prepare yourselves.'

Gus took the lead and stepped forward first. As was his habit, he stood in the doorway for long minutes, with Lewis peering over his shoulder. Neither man spoke. Gus allowed his eyes to drift slowly around the periphery of the room, taking in everything. The dishevelled settees, cushions on the floor; pictures and paintings scattered broken on the floor amidst ornaments and glasses. Besides the smell of blood, which always made his stomach heave, he could smell alcohol – *whisky*? Someone had been having a drink and spilled it, perhaps when the intruders arrived. On the oversized glass coffee table, a phone with headphones still attached lay, discarded in a pool of amber liquid – the whisky? For now, he ignored the dead woman sprawled on the couch and focussed on the upright chair that stood opposite her. Cable ties lay discarded on the once white carpet. This, he'd been told, was where Missy Beaumont was forced to watch her mother be tortured to death.

His jaw clenched. Anger at the destruction, anger at the stench of violence that hung like poison in the air. That little girl would never un-see what she'd witnessed that night. When other children were out building snowmen and sledging or having snow fights, she would be struggling with flashbacks of what had happened this snowy night. It made Gus wonder just who The Beast from the East really was.

'Any idea where the dad is?' Asked Gus, eyes still on Marcia Beaumont's corpse.

Estefan shook her head. 'Nope. The daughter's not speaking – too traumatised. Bad enough seeing what happened to her mother, but to be raped too – why would they do that?'

Gus moved closer to the dead woman. 'This – all of this – was done to punish Beaumont and for no other reason. Lewis, get Compo on the phone and get him digging deeper into Beaumont's history. He's been up to no good.'

Lewis pulled his phone from his pocket. 'How can you be so sure there's a link between this and Dimou? Surely her visiting his offices that day could be co-incidental.'

Gus nodded, 'True… But…' he knelt down and studied the slashes on the soles of Marcia Beaumont's feet. 'These look familiar to you?'

Gore leaned over, and nodded, 'the two men today…'

'And Izzie Dimou too.'

Gore took a look and dialled Compo and Gus studied other wounds on the body. Although no expert, he could detect many more wounds that were too similar to Izzie Dimou's to be anything other than a definite link. He turned to Estefan, 'Can you get me any ANPR footage starting from the camera nearest to this location? '

Estefan nodded, 'Sure, but we don't have a vehicle make yet.'

Gus grinned, 'Get the prints of those tyre tracks sent to my techie geek.'

'There's one at either end of this lane – posh folks don't like speeding in their neighbourhood.'

Gus was aware that ANPR footage was often heavier in richer areas and it riled him. What about the folk on poor council estates, did they not deserve this sort of protection? 'Get any ANPR you have sent over too. If there's anything to be found Compo will find it.'

Estefan snorted, 'Visibility is so crap today he'll not be able to see a number plate.'

'I'm not bothered about the number plate. There can't have been too many vehicles out on a night like this, I'm hoping that the track will give us an idea of the sort of vehicle we're looking for. If Compo uses the time parameters we have, he may have a chance of isolating the perpetrators' vehicle.'

Estefan snorted, 'Yeah right. No chance.'

'I'm willing to take a punt on my expert. Get the stuff to him and he may surprise you.'

Still looking doubtful, Estefan turned and yelled an abrupt instruction to one of her officers, who all but ran out the door in their haste to carry it out.

Lewis held his phone out to Gus with a single word. 'Compo.'

Gus took the phone, and turning away from Estefan, said, 'Hi Comps, two things. First of all, you'll be receiving some images of tyre tracks. They're a bit obscured by the snow but they're the best we've got. See if you can ID the sort of vehicle they belong to. Next get on to the ANPR footage starting with the nearest to Blundering Lane. Focus on traffic between three a.m. and eight a.m. We're looking for a large enough vehicle to have travelled from Bradford to Manchester with ease in the current weather conditions and probably with at least two occupants. If you can see it approaching Blundering Lane and then leaving again a couple of hours later, all the better.'

Compo's voice became muffled and Gus visualised him with his phone tucked into his beanie and pressed against his cheek as he typed instructions into his network of computers. A wave of affection for Compo washed over him. The lad had been right to call him out over Alice. His voice became clearer again, 'What've they done boss?'

Gus considered his words. 'They've robbed a little girl of her enjoyment of snow for the rest of her life – that's what the bastards have done.'

There was silence as Compo digested Gus' words, then, 'I'm on it.'

Gus smiled, he had no doubt that if Compo couldn't find those bastards then no one could. 'Comps,' he hesitated, unsure how to continue and half scared of what the reply might be, 'You got anywhere with Alice?'

'Nah, I'd call you straight away, Gus. You know that.'

'Yeah, right. Sure,' he paused, unused to being so tentative with Compo. 'Izzie Dimou's USB?'

'Not yet. Still running. Getting there though. Maybe another hour.'

'Ok, Thanks Comps.'

The sound of Compo hanging up as soon as he'd stopped speaking told Gus he still hadn't been forgiven – not entirely. And who could blame the lad.

Chapter 42

16:15 Saddleworth Moor

This wasn't right. With no idea of how much time had elapsed since he'd left the safety of the farmhouse walls to strike out through the blizzard, Daniel was becoming more and more disorientated. It was almost dark now. By accident he'd stumbled across an old barbed wire fence and, once he'd realised that the barbs came every hand width or so, he was able to use it to guide himself along. He reckoned that a fence meant a field and a field meant either crops or cattle, either of which meant access routes, possible vehicles and most importantly some form of civilisation.

He pushed the gnawing worry that farmers had tractors and were therefore not obliged to live in the vicinity of their fields to the back of his mind. If he just kept plodding along – well hirpling along – then he'd be okay. With his crutch under his left arm and the barbed wire fence loosely circled by his right hand, he just about managed to keep upright. All sensation in his twisted leg had gone and it was only the pull in his thigh that told him he was still dragging it along behind him. Progress was slow. Twice he'd fallen and twice he'd taken what seemed like forever to get back to his feet. His cheeks had stopped stinging as the drifting snow swirled around them. The mishmash of clothes that served to keep him warm, also dragged him down.

As he reached a broken part of the fence, he paused to look round him. Snow patterns swirled but the snowfall seemed to be lessening in intensity. Straining his eyes against the icy wind he scoured the landscape as best he could. In one direction the snow undulated for eternity before him. Gentle inclines followed by gradual slopes ad infinitum. In the other direction the scene was more interesting. Trees, branches weighted down by the predictable white stuff, were dwarfed by the drifts that stretched up their trunks to meet the overladen branches. Unidentifiable shapes with sharp edges and smooth surfaces dotted the space before him, unmoving and oddly alone. In Daniel's mind they became sentries watching out for him. Beyond the smallest copse of trees, the sharp edge of a roof jutted out. Wondering if snowy conditions played the same tricks on the mind as desert ones, he was reluctant to believe his eyes.

He squeezed his eyes tight shut and, when he opened them again, leaned forward, shifting his body weight onto his crutch. No. His eyes were not paying tricks on him. There was some sort of building in the distance. Thank God. Even if it was uninhabited, it would at the very least offer him shelter and the chance to get out of the relentless wind – a chance to regroup and consider his options. More importantly, he'd created some distance between himself and his captors.

With renewed effort, Daniel released the barbed wire and, feeling ever so slightly bereft, headed towards the distant building. It couldn't be that far away. Ignoring the throb in his groin, caused by having to pull his leg behind him, he battled on. The sky was darkening and he was aware of how easy it would be to become disorientated, so with added effort he ploughed through the snow. Once or twice, he struggled with drifts that reached the top of his thigh, but on the whole, knee-high drifts were all he had to contend with.

Do do doooo … do do do do do doooo! One Step Beyond! Keep moving, one step at a time. Come on Danny boy, you can do it. With every step becoming increasingly more difficult, he fought to continue. He was so warm that he couldn't distinguish between the snow landing on his brow and sweat bubbling up. Laughing, he imagined the snow sizzling and boiling as it landed on his forehead – steam clouds rising into the freezing air creating a bubble of mist around him. That would be one way to hide himself from his attackers. He'd be like a superhero, his superpower being the ability to boil water on his forehead – he laughed again.

The building was close now. If he stopped to make a snowball, be thought he could probably hit the wall. He needed to get shelter and boy was he tired. If the building wasn't so close, he'd just snuggle down into the snow and have a rest. Innuits lived in ice homes, didn't they? Igloos. He used to love making igloos in the back garden with Gabriella. Even then she was a bossy cow, ordering him about as if she knew better than him how to genuinely make an igloo. He'd got his own back on her one year though. He'd helped her build it and when it was done she wouldn't let him in, she said he hadn't pulled his weight and there was only room for one. He grinned. She'd got a bloody shock when he'd pushed the whole lot down on top of her. She'd cried like the baby she was and pretended she'd been frightened. He'd only left her there for a few minutes – bloody drama queen even at that age.

The long and short of it was that their parents wouldn't let them make igloos anymore – said it was too dangerous and they – meaning Daniel – were too silly and irresponsible. So, they bought Gabriella a play house for in the garden and he was only allowed in when Gabriella said so. Of course, *that* was only when she wanted him to do something for her.

He looked up again, measuring the distance now – not far at all – then…

Fucking hell! Daniel fell to his knees, his crutch sinking into the snow. *Noooo! How the hell had this happened?*

The building shimmered as he watched. For a second he thought it was going to disappear, but he realised it was the tears in his eyes that were causing the shimmer. He blinked once… then again… This was too much – too damn much. There was the distorted pile of snow where he'd landed on the barbecue. The broken kitchen window, with the curtain wafting out through the gap – the door he'd exited earlier. How the hell had he managed to walk for so long only to end up right back where he'd started?

From nowhere, lethargy tugged at his limbs. The shivers had gone and the numbness in his extremities had become welcome friends. With difficulty, he slipped the rucksack off his back, positioned it in front of him in the snow and bent forward, resting his head on it and curled up in a foetal position, except for one leg which protruded at an awkward angle from his body. He closed his eyes and was at peace.

Chapter 43

'What the fuck are you doing back here already?'

Lulu shambled into the cell and did a double take that, if Alice hadn't been so shattered, would have made her smile. Alice was sprawled on the bunk she'd vacated a few days earlier and had no intentions of moving for the foreseeable future. The medical examination, followed by a list of intensive questions – all of which she'd refused to answer – and the journey back to the prison had been interminable. Her entire body hurt. Her breast throbbed, her nipple was raw and the dressing lay heavy over it. Her arms were marked where she'd struggled against her attacker to pull herself up and launch herself at her rapist.

As for the rest – well rough, tender and achy just about summed it up. Still, there was an upside to it all and in her current situation. Alice was happy to take any positives. The fact that she'd been raped by a prison officer meant that *she* was in a position to make certain demands – or rather – her solicitor was. So, instead of being moved from her old cell into an area of the prison where she'd be vulnerable to Hairy Mary and her posse or – worse still – Baby Jane Enforcer of Pain, she'd been allowed to move back in with Lulu. All of which meant that Sean Kennedy's stranglehold over her, via his tame guards, was loosened. Now all she needed to know was that her parents were safe and she'd be, if not exactly happy, resigned to her fate.

When Alice didn't answer, Lulu sharpened her tone, 'Well, Lady. You gonna answer me or what?'

Or what? Now *that* nearly brought a smile to Alice's lips. If only Lulu knew what had happened to her –she'd know that her feeble 'or what?' threat was a waste of time. Alice shrugged, wishing her shoulders would move without sending jolts of pain through her body, 'You know me, Luls? Couldn't wait to get home.'

Lulu cackled – phlegm rattling in her throat – and threw her Marlboros onto the small desk that occupied one corner of the cell. 'Cheeky Mare!' She moved over and plonked her sizeable arse on one of the two plastic chairs, making it skid across the floor. The sound made Alice wince. Her head pounded and she was probably dehydrated but she couldn't work up the energy to pull herself off her bunk, leave the cell and traverse the corridor to the water fountain. She'd leave it for now.

Lulu turned and picked something up off the desk. 'Here.' She threw the item to Alice, who winced as she raised both hands to grab it.

It was a packet of painkillers.

'You look like you need these.' Lulu, leaned back in the chair making it groan in protest. She raised one leg and rested her calf on the opposite knee. 'You gonna tell me what happened? Fucking Hairy Mary said Jane bit off your nipple. That right?'

Alice nodded once – abrupt.

'… And swallowed it?'

Alice couldn't suppress her shudder. Since it happened, she'd tried not to think about it. Tried to shut it out of her mind, to push to the recesses of her mind, the memory of Jane's chin dripping with her blood, her nipple between her teeth. Now, Lulu's words made her gag in reflex and acid flooded her throat.

'Hell Alice, didn't mean to upset you, love. Wouldn't do that for all the world. You just lie there and I'll get you some water for your pills.' Hauling herself to her feet, Lulu shuffled over and laid her gnarled, arthritic hand on Alice's forehead. Alice closed her eyes and turned her face to the wall. The sound of Lulu shuffling towards the door was a relief. Her fists unclenched by her side and with effort Alice swallowed down the bile that stung the back of her throat.

Lulu's words, just before she exited the cell, were the final straw for Alice.

'I got your back, Alice. Nobody touches you on my watch and gets away with it. Not Hairy Mary, or Baby Jane, okay? I got this.'

A tear snuck out the corner of Alice's eye. Before all this, she'd held Lulu in check. Told her she was fine, could handle it herself. Now though, she was done protecting folk. Done with being the police officer. As far as she was concerned, Lulu could do her worst. Hairy Mary had known she was under Lulu's protection, yet whatever Kennedy had paid her, had made the other woman greedy and she'd taken the risk. Now she'd pay for it.

Alice raised her hand and wiped away her tears. They deserved it, the lot of them. They were all well aware of the reach that Lulu had. The contacts she had inside *and* outside the prison. Hell, they'd seen her have other inmates dealt with in the past – shivs in the shower, glass in their meals, overdoses of heroin. Whatever Lulu wanted, Lulu got. Her notoriety as a gang leader in Brixton was well-documented. For Alice, the fact that she saw Sean Kennedy as a competitor, had meant Lulu had protected her as much as she could.

Alice had refused to enlist Lulu's help. Until now, she'd been determined not to go down that road. All her instincts had told her that if she succumbed to that, the road back would be full of potholes and obstacles. Once you've dabbled with the dark side, it wouldn't be easy to come back.

As Lulu shuffled back in, Alice turned to her and watched the older woman slosh water over the floor as she approached with a plastic cup, now half empty. Alice smiled, her mind made up. 'Sit down, Lulu. I need your help. Let me tell you exactly what's been going on…'

By the time Alice had finished her story a good hour later, she was exhausted. Lulu on the other hand was alive and alert. Firing questions at Alice, clarifying details and at last making her promise. 'I'll keep your folks safe Alice. But in return, you're going to have to help me with something!'

Alice sighed. She'd half expected this. Nothing in prison came without cost.

She nodded once and lay down on her bunk, her eyes closed immediately and as she drifted off to sleep she heard Lulu making arrangements on the illegal phone she somehow or other managed to keep hidden from the guard.

Monday

Chapter 44

Lewis Gore snored like a volcano about to erupt. For long seconds at a time he'd stop, lulling Gus into a false sense of security, only to start up again with a crescendo of rumbles that seemed to start in his toes and bounce off every one of his bones on the way up to his snout. By which time the snores had built in volume until they rattled in Gus' head, sending any thought of sleep out the window.

Gus turned over in the narrow single bed and pulled a pillow round his ears, determined to drown out the noise once and for all, only to nudge his nose, which, of course, just *had* to start bleeding again. *Fuck's sake!* While hopping out of bed, he cupped his hands under his nostrils, cursing Gore as he moved towards the bathroom, drips of blood making his hand sticky. Gore had spent a sizeable portion of their journey from Bradford to Stalybridge moaning about sleep deprivation on account of his baby. Having spent a mere few hours with Gore, Gus suspected that the only person getting any sleep in the Gore household must be the big man himself, for how anyone – baby included – could sleep through that racket, he'd no idea.

Allowing the blood to drip into the ceramic sink, Gus put on the cold tap and – eyes glazed – stared mesmerised at the patterns made by the spatters. As if he hadn't seen enough blood spatters today to last him a lifetime. His thoughts drifted to Jordan Beaumont's daughter. No matter what her dad had done, the kid didn't deserve this. If there was one kind of criminal Gus detested above all others, it was the kind who took their revenge by hurting the loved ones of their targets. Sheer cowardice as far as Gus was concerned – but the crime scene at the Beaumont's home showed something worse than cowardice. It stank of evil enjoyment.

The men who'd tortured Marcia Beaumont and exacted further revenge on the child had done it to get off on it. Beaumont would have caved – Gus was sure of it. The photos on the man's phone showed that, whether or not his relationship with his wife was strong, he loved his daughter. Photo after photo after photo showed that; Beaumont and his daughter eating ice-cream each with a dab of raspberry on their noses and round their lips, pictures of them making googly eyes at animals at Knowsley Safari Park, photos with silly animal ears and tongues superimposed on top. Mo's kids were always sending him Snap Chats like that. These were all indications of a man who loved his daughter. Beaumont, Gus was sure, would have done anything to save Missy from her fate. The purpose in torturing Marcia Beaumont had been beyond revenge or manipulation – it had been purely for fun, for enjoyment, for sexual gratification. But what they'd done to Missy had been beyond even that. Gus couldn't forget what they'd done to that little girl. When he found them, they'd pay for that.

Gus switched off the tap, rolled a length of loo roll round his hand and pushed it under his dripping nose. With the fingers of his other hand he nipped the bridge of his nose. Rumbles followed by muffled murmurs drifted in from the bedroom. *Oh Hell, now he's sleep-talking too.* Gus raised his head and looked at his reflection in the mirror above the sink. His nose was still swollen and had started to turn a delightful purple colour – *aubergine?* He had a flashback of Alice laughing at him one time when a drunk witness had given him a black eye. He'd moaned about it being purple and she'd punched him, none too gently, on the arm – as was her way – and said 'idiot, that's not purple, its aubergine.'

What the hell had happened to them? Here he was in a pokey little room in a Travelodge with a rumbling volcano and Alice was in a pokey room in Stanton sharing a cell with God only knew who. He still thought she'd have been safer in hospital, but Nancy said she'd demanded to be returned to the prison. Alice had said that's what she wanted. How the hell could she think she was safer there? Not after what had happened to her a few weeks ago. Maybe they'd put her in solitary – keep her away from Sean Kennedy's cronies. He really hoped Compo would come up with something – anything to throw doubt on her admission.

From the bedroom he could hear his phone ringing. *Compo?* He threw the bloody tissue in the loo, grabbed some fresh loo roll and flushed, before rushing to get his phone, stubbing his toe on the way. Bloody Gore hadn't even flinched. He was still there murmuring to himself between snores whilst Gus hopped about like an idiot and all because he'd not wanted the ringing to wake up his companion. After throwing himself onto the bed and flicking on the bedside light, Gus answered, 'Compo, what've we got?'

As soon as Compo spoke Gus could tell he was excited – that he'd caught something good. He visualised the lad pacing back and forth, an item of food in one of his hands, the phone in the other; various empty cans dotted around his work station. He remembered he'd sent him home to do dark deeds on the darknet.

'Boss, we've cracked it. Me and Taffy.'

The sound of two over-excited lads high-fiving sounded down the line, and Gus nearly cracked a smile. Taffy and Compo were a good combination. Maybe as good as Compo and Sampson had been – before Sampson played the damn hero and ended up dead, that is.

'It's singin' pure and sweet,' said Compo, elongating the 'a' in 'and'.

Gus glanced at Gore and wished he could say the same about him. 'Any chance of sharing the song then, Comps?'

'Eh? What song?'

Gus sighed, and as Gore's 'singing' reached an all-time high, he reached over and prodded his sleeping companion in the arm, which served to make his yodelling soften to a splutter of puffs, for the time being. God, sometimes being the boss was hard work. He squeezed his eyes tightly together and then opened them as wide as they would go in the hope it would wake him up a bit. Sensing a dribble at his nose again, he dabbed at it, got to his feet, padded over to the kettle and flicked it on. A coffee might make him focus and it didn't look like he was in any danger of getting any more sleep anyway. 'I just meant tell me what you've got.'

He listened to Compo chomping on something as he ripped the sachet of coffee open and tipped it into the mug. His stomach rumbled. When was the last time he'd eaten? Yesterday morning? He grabbed two sugar sachets and tipped their contents into the mug too. Maybe the sugar rush would see him through the next few hours. A slurp from Compo as he took a drink and – at last, he spoke. 'She was a whistle blower.' He paused, presumably for effect.

Gus poured the water into his mug, gave it a few stirs with a teaspoon and sat down on the plastic chair, wincing at the coldness on his bare legs. It was going to be a long night. 'A whistle blower?'

'Yep. Don't get all the science or owt, but the university Izzie Dimou was employed at in Northern Cyprus, as we know, has some sort of reciprocal agreement with Rubeus Pharmaceuticals who are a government-backed company. Reckon that means they're all official secrets and that. They're looking at developing effective treatments for biological diseases that fall under the Category A classification.'

'Category A?'

'Stuff like smallpox, anthrax and that.'

Shit, that was some serious stuff. Abaci and Doukus had said as much, but they'd categorically denied that Izzie could have access to anything critical. *Makes you wonder why her colleagues at the university had chosen to be so vague.*

Compo continued. 'Well, all this stuff in the wrong hands can be used as bio-weapons.'

'Yeah, I got that from my Skye interview yesterday. Still don't see how any of that indicates Izzie is a whistle-blower.'

'Well… seems that Izzie came across some tests and experiments that were flying under the radar. Seems like one of the scientists was developing something he shouldn't and Izzie – who was a senior researcher – stumbled across it.'

Gus frowned, 'You telling me that one of the scientists at Izzie's University in Cyprus was developing some sort of biological weapon and Izzie found out?'

'Yep. That's how it looks. One of Izzie's colleagues was developing a vaccine to counter a new bio-weapon developed in Syria – something by the name of AX22. However… according to Izzie's data, it seems that this scientist was simultaneously using AX22 to develop a deadlier, more complex, more resistant strain – AX23.'

'Fuck!'

'But do you want the punchline?'

Gus rolled his eyes *bloody punchline!* 'Just tell me, Comps.'

'If I'm reading this right, the AX22 vaccine actually included some sort of accelerant – they called it ACC22. From Izzie's notes the two compounds were to be used as part of a two-pronged weaponry by whichever country gained access to it.'

Shit! That little USB stick held a lot of extremely sensitive information. Gus shuddered. It didn't bear thinking about what could have happened if the Romanians had found it. Their dead bodies in Keighley indicated that all of this information would have fallen into the wrong hands – but who's? This was a lot to take in. 'Not sure I get the two-pronged bit.'

Compo crunched on something, swallowed and said, 'Well, looks like whoever had the AX22 could use it to attack a target – maybe a city hosting a summit or summat. The AX22 vaccine *with* the accelerant ACC22 would be administered. This, instead of protecting the vaccinated population, would actually weaken them. The bastards would follow up with the even deadlier AX22EX – BOOM! AN-IA-FUCKING-LATION!'

Gus was speechless. This was huge. No wonder MI6 were keeping things so tightly under their belt. It made everything so much clearer. It also brought Daniel's well-being into question. Izzie had been killed for access to this USB. Gus could only hope that Daniel's MI6 training would kick in and he'd be able to hang on till they located him. That, of course, was assuming he wasn't already dead. 'Anything else?'

'Well, our Izzie was a bit of a techie geek – not as good as me, but good. She'd managed to clone the scientist's lap top and mobile phone and downloaded everything she found to this USB, and – if I'm right – to a protected location on the cloud.'

Gus slapped the palm of his hand against his forehead. What was he thinking? Lack of sleep was making him unfocussed. 'Is it Doukus? Is that who's behind all of this? I thought he was hiding something yesterday.'

'No, not Doukus. This scientist wasn't one of the two you interviewed yesterday. This one is third in line in terms of seniority at the university. Name's Dr Young. If Izzie's data is right, he was out to sell the AX22 vaccine and the AX23 bio weapon. He was in talks with Syria, Russia, and Pakistan.

'Shit, Comps. You need to get Nancy onto Interpol. We need to pick him up.'

'Too late, Boss. I ran him and he's dead – hit and run four days ago apparently. His flat had been ransacked – who knows who's behind the attack, or for that matter whether they got the formulas. The thing is, we've got everything Izzie downloaded, but there's some code that I've not managed to decipher yet, so whether that's everything there is or not, I don't know. We don't have the final chemical compound, so nobody can start working on a cure for this until we get the rest of the information.'

'Right Compo, I'll get onto Nancy, anything else?'

'Anything else? Izzie's death and his disappearance are linked. How do you think Daniel's disappearance fits in?'

Gus' hopes for Daniel's safe return had been diminishing over the past hours. Now he was sure that Gabriella's brother was dead. Whoever had tortured and killed Izzie, the Romanians and Jordan Beaumont's family wouldn't hesitate to kill Daniel when he'd given them all he had. When the snow cleared, he fully expected that some dog walker or other would come across both Jordan Beaumont's and Daniel Farrier's bodies in due course. 'Reckon they took Daniel as leverage to encourage Izzie to hand over the USB. They don't have it yet and they clearly don't have Young's data either, that's why they came to Alice's place in the night – they were still looking for it.'

'Yes, but was that Izzie's only copy?'

'No, I don't think it was. Izzie would have kept a backup which, I suspect, is the one you're working on. I suspect she was going to disseminate the intelligence she had collected with the pharmaceutical company – after all they are government funded. She probably thought Beaumont would be an ally. Perhaps she going to share her findings with him? Or, perhaps she was going to confront him. MI6 know a lot more than they're letting on, that's for sure.'

'Maybe she handed the evidence to him and that's why he was abducted.'

That didn't sit right with Gus, but he let it lie for now. He had the idea that Izzie being followed after her meeting with Beaumont somehow linked up. 'Keep trying to identify those two dead bodies in Keighley. I want as much information on them as possible.'

Gus phoned Nancy and brought her up to date all the while Gore remained asleep, giving a mostly rhythmic – though still irritating – accompaniment to the proceedings. No way would Gore wake up if his baby cried during the night. *Fat lot of good he'd be!* Taking great pleasure in it, Gus – in perfect synchronicity with the snoring – whipped the duvet off Gore's snoring frame, flicked the lights to full power and put the telly on full boom.

'Whilst Storm Emma is heading north, leaving a trail of destruction behind her throughout the Manchester district, we aren't out of the woods yet. The forecast indicates more blizzards and snow storms with estimated lows of minus ten degrees. Snake Pass is still unpassable and the Met Office's Red Alert is set to remain in place for the foreseeable future. School closures throughout the North of England look likely, meaning another day of sledging – but don't forget to wrap up warm. That's it for now from Manchester News. Next update at six am.'

Gore, like a slumbering bear awakened in mid hibernation, growled and extended his massive arms in a stretch that threatened to knock Gus' cooling drink off the bedside table. 'What's up, Gus? Had a good sleep?'

Gus grimaced and ignored the question, choosing instead to dive straight into the information Compo had found. He'd just reached the end when his phone rang again.

'What's up, Comps?'

'Two things. First is we've managed – or rather Taffy has managed – to isolate a likely vehicle for the Beaumont abduction. Caught it leaving the end of Blundering Lane and managed to follow it through to the edge of Saddleworth Moor. Looks like a Discovery. Big fucker with snow chains – probably wouldn't have made it otherwise. It disappeared for a good three hours and we thought we'd lost it – maybe it got jammed in the snow or summat. Anyway, we caught up with it again and it continued on for another couple of miles. We lost track of it again for another few hours. The weather's playing havoc on the roads. We've not seen it since one o'clock this morning. Still waiting for it to reappear.'

'Great' said Gus, 'Send me the last sighting co-ordinates, Comps. We'll check it out.'

'Can probably do better than that Gus. Thing is, when I ran a background check on Beaumont's properties a farmhouse came up – it seems he inherited it from his grandparents – it's just two miles from our last sighting of the Discovery. Coincidence?'

'You know what I think about coincidences, Compo, don't you?'

Compo laughed, and Gus was surprised at how much lighter his heart felt on hearing his friend's laugh.

'No such fucking thing,' said Compo

'Exactly.'

Chapter 45

'*M*anchester in complete whiteout…. continuing blizzards.*'

'Tell me about it.' Gus was freezing. His fingers were numb, his toes almost as bad. Gore's state-of-the-art car seemed to have taken its heating system and replaced it with an American-sized fridge. Hell, even Alice's damn temperamental Mini offered more insulation from the elements than this bloody monstrosity. Waste of damn money. Soon as Compo's intel had come in, Gus had contacted DI Estefan who'd run it past her Super. The upshot was Gus and Gore were ordered to wait for them to assemble their SCO19 team. Gus took one look at Gore, who snorted and shook his head. Gus couldn't have agreed more. Within minutes the pair of them were out the door and heading for Gore's Volvo.

'Many schools over the region will be closed due to the adverse weather.'

Gus sunk his chin down to his chest and hitched his jacket up over his mouth in an attempt to preserve some heat. Okay, so it wasn't just the weather that was causing him grief. It was the lack of sleep, hunger and lack of caffeine. Also, Gore's ebullience was really pissing him off. Gore was the one with the new-born baby, yet it was Gus who was sleep deprived. *Was he jealous?* He'd always wanted kids, Gabriella had been reticent. Never mind, with the way things had worked out it was probably for the best. How would you explain that whole Gabriella-Katie thing? Talk about complicated.

Gus watched the windscreen wipers push the steady fall of snowflakes to either side of the glass. He hoped the armed team arrived before he and Gore did. Judging by what had been done to Jordon Beaumont's family, an extendable baton, pepper spray and a stab vest wouldn't be of much use, although the vest might warm him up a bit. He hoped Gore had a couple of tasers rolling about in the back of the car, but having seen the baby seat in the rear of the car, he doubted it. Gore wouldn't be the first officer to clear out any weaponry after starting a family. He couldn't blame him. Last thing you wanted was for your kids to taser themselves. How could you live with the guilt?

'One man knocked out by falling icicle has been rushed to North Manchester General with a suspected skull fracture. Whilst on a more positive note, volunteers have been handing out blankets to Manchester's rough sleepers and...'

Gus reached over and switched off the car radio. He'd had more than enough depressing weather news for one day. Besides, who the hell knew what they'd find when they reached Jordan Beaumont's farmhouse? Weather or not, Gus suspected his day may be about to get worse.

His phone rang and after a quick check to eliminate the possibility of yet another call from Gabriella, he answered. The line was crackly and it took him a moment or two to place the voice. Giannis Doukus had seemed on edge during their Skype conversation and now he seemed outright nervous. His accent was heavy and combined with the bad line, Gus found it difficult to concentrate, so it was a relief when a woman's voice came over the line. *Thank God!* He flipped the phone to speaker so Gore could listen in. 'Yes, I remember you, Ariadne. Lovely to speak to you again, although I am concerned we may get cut off. The weather conditions here are appalling.'

'Well Detective, that being the case, I will get to the point. Giannis has come to me with some notable information and although we have passed this information to both Interpol and your MI6, we got the impression that perhaps it wouldn't be shared with you.'

Gus grimaced and Gore made the universal hand movement attributed to sexual self-gratification, which made Gus smile.

'Giannis isn't concerned with the wider implications. His motives are all about Isabella. You see, he and Izzie were once a couple – until Daniel came along and swept her off her feet.'

Gus frowned, *Daniel? Really?* Gus hadn't had Daniel down as the sweeping-off-feet kind of guy. However, that nugget of intel explained Doukus' nervous appearance during their Skype call. 'I'm listening, Ariadne.'

'Professor Young, one of our senior researchers was killed in a car accident recently. Giannis suspects it is because Izzie confided her suspicions regarding Abaci. You see, Izzie told both Young and Doukus that there were programmes running underneath the ongoing research programme that monitored the research statistics. It concerned her.'

So, Dr Young wasn't the scientist who'd been developing the AX23 formula or the ACC22 one. It wasn't Young whom Izzie had been concerned about, it was Abaci. Doukus' voice in the background, speaking in Greek, interrupted the conversation for a moment and then Ariadne was back. 'Giannis wishes he'd paid more attention. He should have listened to Isabella, but he was upset and hurt.'

As the talking continued, Gus just silently wished Doukus would shut up. He wasn't concerned with the other man's emotional state – he just needed the information regarding Abaci. The information MI6 had chosen not to share with him.

'The upshot of all of this detective, is that Giannis – after your interview – went back to the lab and he retraced Izzie's footsteps; her digital ones that is.'

Struggling to maintain an even tone, Gus forced his lips into a smile and said, 'Yes? What did he find?' The line crackled and Gus glared at Gore as if he was to blame. Gore braked and pulled to the side of the road, 'If I drive in any further you may lose your signal. Finish this conversation first.'

'Abaci, has been running counter experiments which deconstruct the existing bio-chemistry and remodel it...'

Adriane consulted with Doukus in Greek and Gus remembered that this wasn't her area of expertise either. When she came on the phone again she said, 'As near as I can understand from Doukus, Abaci has used his research to create a vaccine that, rather than provide an antidote, will instead mutate into an existing bio-weapon. If a government held this doctored vaccine they would be lulled into a false sense of security and when confronted with a bio-weaponry attack, they will exacerbate the spread of the virus by administering the false vaccine.' She took a breather before continuing, 'Alongside this, the deployment of the more sophisticated virus – a deadlier strain of the virus, would cause international panic and death in the millions. Whichever country holds these two formulas could hold the rest of the world to ransom.'

Compo's earlier 'AN-IA-FUCKING-LATION,' sprung from Gus's lips in a stunned, whisper, earning him a frown from Gore. Ariadne was still talking. 'Izzie captured this information and, according to Doukus, she has altered some of the statistics, hopefully rendering Abaci's findings inaccurate. She appears to have stolen the correct formula leaving Abaci with a dud. Interpol are in pursuit of Abaci as we speak, however it seems they don't know who he is working for. I can't believe I have worked with this man for so long. He is a traitor... and I considered him a friend.'

Gus could empathise. His feelings – when he thought Alice had betrayed him – had been so intense he'd been unable to function. But Alice wasn't responsible for the potential devastation of the world. He could hear the grief in the woman's tone.

'Thank you for sharing this, Ariadne. Please pass my condolences to Giannis for his loss and thank him. He was right – this information wasn't shared to us. However, tell him that as we speak we have experts working on retrieving information that Izzie left behind.'

Ariadne spoke again in Greek. 'Detective, Doukus says be very careful. This information is very valuable and in the wrong hands could do untold damage. Too many people have died already, he hopes that you will be able to prevent any more casualties. Goodbye.'

Gus looked at his colleague as Gore re-started the engine. 'The plot gets thicker and thicker.'

'And uglier and uglier.'

Gus couldn't disagree.

Chapter 46

He hadn't eaten for hours. The hotel had settled down for the night and apart from the flickering images coming from the TV that he'd left on silent for the company and the occasional creak or cough from the next room, Sean Kennedy could have thought he was the only man alive. Not that he considered himself particularly alive – not right now. His temperature had flared up again and every time he swallowed it felt as if someone was using his throat as a cheese grater. So, when the call came, it was almost a relief from the stench of his own body and the increasingly maudlin thoughts that filtered through his mind.

'Yeah.' The single word was about all he could manage, but that was fine. It would no doubt serve to knock that idiot Allison-Hinton off balance. Whatever his solicitor was phoning with at this time of the morning, Sean was under no illusion that it would be good news. The man was annoyingly proper. The only thing that would prompt him to ring a client so early in the morning would be a catastrophe. Sean could only hope that whatever catastrophe it was, it would be manageable.

'Eh, Sean. Sorry to wake you so early. Wouldn't have bothered you if it hadn't been quite so urgent.'

Sean sighed, wincing as even the exhalation of warm air was enough to ignite a fire from the base of his tongue down his gullet, ending in a ball of flames in his belly. *What the fuck was wrong with him?* He tried to focus, but the flashing lights from the telly were making his eyes go funny, and the pain in his gut was superseded by a searing pain behind his eyes.

'Gimme a minute, okay?' His words came out slurred and he hoped Allison-Hinton would assume he'd downed a few beers. Last thing he wanted was for him to think he was under par – never show the enemy your weakness, that was his motto – well one of them anyway.

Allison-Hinton, mumbled an arse licky sort of apology, sounding like one of Sean's mum's wittering old friends. As he continued to waffle on, Sean took a moment to rest the back of his crown on the headboard and take a few shallow calming breaths. *That was better.* Stretching out one hand, whilst trying not to move his head too much, Sean switched off the telly – plunging the room into near darkness. The streetlights outside cast gentle orange shadows through the half-drawn curtains, landing on the sparse fittings of the lonely hotel room. Sean closed his eyes for a second and massaged his temple. The pressure relieved the pain and when he reopened his eyes, the flecks of colour that had haunted his peripheral vision were gone.

He pressed the speaker phone button and prepared himself for whatever news was

heading his way. 'Get to the point.'

The solicitor, interrupted in mid flow, paused, breathed in, exhaled and began. 'We, well, em… we appear to have lost Alice Cooper's parents.'

Sean clenched his fists, *Bastard!* His throat, thick and slime-filled tightened. He

swallowed, willing himself to ignore the pain.

'You've done what?'

Allison-Hinton's tone took on the erratic stutter of a machine gun with no ammunition left. 'Don't know how it happened. They were being tailed. Our men in Greece had them under observation at all times and then… well…'

Over the line the solicitor's breath came fast and heavy and Gus pictured him

shrinking behind his huge desk, like the coward he was. How he hated that man.

'No excuses! I warned you.' Sweat soaked through his T-shirt, making him clammy.

Was it a reaction to this phone call or something worse – much worse? His limbs were shaky, as if he'd run a marathon. He coughed. Long gone were the days when he could run a hundred metres, never mind a damn marathon. It was all that bitch's fault and now this pillock was telling him they'd lost her parents – *his leverage* – gone!

'Sean. There's more.'

'More?' If he could have summoned up the energy he'd have rolled his eyes. What more could there be? Losing her parents was bad enough. How the hell could two trained ex SAS soldiers manage to lose two middle aged, eccentric and oblivious scientists who barely focused on anything other than their damn animal observations?

'They're dead.'

For a minute Sean thought he meant the Coopers, then he replayed the conversation.

No Allison-Hinton had clearly said they'd lost them– meaning they'd gone AWOL. Not dead. Surely not dead.

'The Coopers?'

'No... not them. Abdul and Kieran. Garrotted outside the Cooper's apartment. A professional job – a hit.'

A hit? Who the hell would have realised they were keeping tabs on the Coopers, never mind organise a hit to snatch them? Only one image came to his mind. The image of a small dark-haired woman glaring defiantly at him from her hospital bed – Alice Cooper. How the hell had she managed to outwit him?

'You. Have. Fucked. Up. Big. Time.' He disconnected the call, before sagging back onto the bed.

Chapter 47

'Wake up, Alice. Got something to tell you.' Seconds earlier, Lulu's phone – the illegal one that somehow or other she never got caught with – had vibrated. Yet, despite being woken from a deep sleep, she sounded as alert as ever. Her gravelly voice strong, her eyes bright as she popped her head over the side of the bunk and peered down at Alice.

Alice, on the contrary hadn't been asleep. All night she'd been lying on her back, her head resting on her bent arm, her dark eyes open, just waiting for lights-on so she could get up and live through yet another interminable day. For hours, she'd stared up at the bulging mattress of the bunk above her. Every move Lulu made was accompanied by creaking springs and the threat of the whole bunk giving up the ghost and collapsing on top of Alice. Considering her current stream of bad luck, Alice considered the chances of that quite high. At least she'd be dead and there would be no reason for Sean Kennedy to hurt her parents. The only thing was, she knew only too well just what Kennedy was capable of and her death wouldn't guarantee her parent's safety. No, that would be too easy.

Lulu had a variety of dealings in the outside world – a huge network of operations to keep up with, so Alice was well used to hearing that noise off and on throughout the night. Lulu's business seemed to flourish between the hours of ten pm and six am and – according to Lulu – the main reason for her trusting

Alice, a copper, to keep schtum was that she had first-hand dealings with Sean and anyone who'd got the once over on *that little weasel'* had earned a favour or two from Lulu.

'I'm not sleeping, Lul. What's up?'

Lulu smiled, her upside-down face looking strange, 'They're safe. We got them.'

Alice closed her eyes and exhaled. From nowhere tears welled in her eyes. She brushed them roughly away, conscious that Lulu had averted her gaze so as not to embarrass her. She sniffed and wiped her nose with the back of her hand. 'Brilliant. Thanks, Lul. Where are they?'

'Where we arranged for them to be. They'll be fine there.'

Alice smiled – they'd be more than fine there. They'd be looked after and no questions would be asked. Realising there was more to the story than a straight rescue – after all Sean Kennedy had almost as wide a reach as Lulu and was equally invested in keeping a hold of her parents – she looked straight at the other woman. 'Casualties?'

Lulu shrugged, 'Not on our side.'

Alice let that settle in her mind for a moment. *Did she care if someone had got hurt- someone who'd been threatening her innocent parents?* It took her all of two seconds to find her answer. She looked at Lulu and nodded once. The matter was closed. 'Thanks, Lul.'

But Lulu wasn't content to leave it there, 'You're not forgetting our deal, are you?'

Alice shook her head, 'No, Lulu. I've not forgotten.'

Chapter 48

05:55 Saddleworth Moor

Daniel was disorientated when he opened his eyes. He was lying in a soft bed – warm and cosy. So why did it hurt so much to open his eyes? He tried to reach out for the light switch, but his hand wouldn't move. It was so dark and he didn't really want to move, but he wanted the light. Needed to rub his eyes. A strange humming buzzed from somewhere nearby. *His alarm clock? The smoke alarm? Aw, for goodness sake shut up!* He wanted to yell, but his voice refused to co-operate and then there was light. Blinding light. He scrunched his eyes shut. *Put the damn light out, Izzie!* Seconds, or was it minutes or even hours, later he opened his eyes. There were voices. *Put the radio off Izzie! Trying to sleep here. Why are they shouting?*

He snuggled down further, his cheek resting on something very cold. He opened his eyes. What the hell was the white stuff falling around him? His head lifted. It was everywhere. It was then that he saw the two dark figures in the distance. They were looking for something, torches flashing, calling a name... his name. Why did he think they were a threat? Weren't they there to help him?

His heart began to pound. Something wasn't right, but he couldn't focus. Couldn't get his brain to form a coherent thought. It kept jumping around – a farmhouse? Musty clothes and eiderdown? He tried to move his hands and dislodged a layer of snow from his arm. Just how long had he been out of it, lying here in the snow? He moved his leg and realised that if he was going to move away from the men, he'd have to crawl.

Still not sure why or even *if* they were a threat to him, he lifted his head again. They'd moved to his right, their torches casting shadows in his peripheral vision. Their voices seemed fainter and he thought now was the time. Bracing his forearms in front of him, he began to pull himself forward. Only one leg worked so it was difficult to move. He dug his elbows in and his good knee and tried to propel himself onward. His shoulders ached, his breath froze as he exhaled. Managing mere inches at a time, he collapsed in the snow. It was too cold and he was chittering and yet he had an overwhelming urge to strip off his coat.

Maybe if he did he'd be able to move more freely. He paused... thought. The two men were still to his right, a little further away now. Perhaps if he just stayed still they'd miss him and go back to wherever they'd come from. Perhaps they weren't even looking for him. No that wasn't right – they'd called his name. Or had they? Maybe he was confused, maybe they'd lost their dog. Maybe... maybe nothing. He'd been frightened earlier and had made his escape – from the farmhouse he remembered that now. What else could he remember? A knife? Yes, he had a knife – two knives, one in his rucksack, which he'd left behind him in the snow, where was the other? He moved his arm and scrabbled around near his leg. He touched something hard, stuck inside his wellie boot, but couldn't quite reach it. It was reassuring though to have it there. He peered to his left and saw some trees. If he could get there he'd be able to take off his boot *and* get the knife.

Sighing, he changed his trajectory, pulling his weight, using his arms. Every half foot he stopped for a rest. The voices faded in his mind. Like dull echoes against the snow, he moved on. The wind whistled around, storming up great flurries of snow. That was good, they wouldn't be able to see him. He could barely see the trees now, just great outlines, barely visible. Never had Daniel been so vulnerable. Never had he been so exhausted, so drained.

He kept going, dogged, determined. His leg was like a dead tree trunk behind him and all he wanted to do was speed up. He flashed to that film he'd seen with Izzie. The one where the guy fell into a ravine and in order to save himself he'd gnawed off his arm. Could he do that? Was it necessary? If he could get to the trees and get some shelter, even just for a short time he could recoup and think. He stopped for another rest and took the chance to look at the trees again.

Brilliant! They were closer than he thought. Why were they moving though? Was he hallucinating?

They were really close now, what the heck – they were yelling at him – but how could trees yell? The two hulking shapes moved through the snow, directly towards him.

'Daniel? Daniel Farrier?'

Chapter 49

Storm Emma had played havoc with Gus and Lewis Gore's journey. Every route they took placed an obstacle of some description in front of them. And when they got closer to the farmhouse the roads became smaller and harder to navigate. They'd spent forever in Manchester attaching snow chains to Gore's car. Gus' fingers were still complaining at the cold that still lurked in his joints. It had been hell, but judging by the number of abandoned cars they'd passed en route, it had been time well spent. Gus hadn't wanted a repeat of yesterday's scary journey from Bradford. Sometimes Gus was sure they were only on a minor farm track. The car heating kicked in sporadically, resulting in them alternating between sweating buckets and shivering uncontrollably. The sheer cold had made them have to stop on more than one occasion to relieve their bladders and, each time, Gus was sure the wind would whip his penis off or freeze the urine as it left his body.

The headlights barely pierced the gloom despite Gore having his fog lights on and Gus wondered whether the SCO19s would have any better luck in getting to the farmhouse. He'd pinned everything on finding Daniel here. It was logical. The men who'd taken Jordan Beaumont had been caught within minutes of the farmhouse he'd inherited. Well, on a good day it would be minutes, on a bad day – like today – it had taken Gus and Lewis hours. He was glad to have Lewis with him. The big man, despite his snoring, was solid and dependable.

259

He was completely on-board with the logic of Gus' thinking. What they'd find when they finally reached the farmhouse was anyone's guess – nothing good, if the carnage they'd left at Beaumont's house was any indication. Was Beaumont still alive, or had he got something stashed away at the cottage that those two wanted?

His phone rang, startling him from his thoughts – Compo! He flicked it to speaker phone and answered. 'Y'all.'

'Hey boss. Did a bit more digging and guess what?'

Gus hated this tendency of Compo's to make him guess what he'd discovered. There was absolutely no way he could begin to guess what he'd discovered – he was in awe of Compo's talents, but he really wished the lad would just spit it out.

'What?' He sensed Gore looking at him. And realised his tone had been sharp. He adjusted his appraoch, 'Sorry Compo, bad time here. Driving in this bloody weather's like swimming through my mum's gravy. Have you got something for me?'

'Damn right I have Gus, damn right I have.'

Gus heard the distinctive sound of Compo clicking his fingers.

'I put a trail on the movements of that vehicle over the past week and guess what?'

Gus sighed, 'Just tell me Compo. I'm all out of guesses.'

'Well, turns out on Thursday, before the storm got really bad, it was caught on the exact same camera near Saddleworth Moor. Bit of a coincidence eh? *And* an hour before that it was caught around the Manchester Victoria area.'

Gus grinned. This information made it even more likely that there was a link between Jordan Beaumont's abductors and possibly Daniel and Izzie. He frowned, it didn't add up though, that Beaumont had arranged for his wife and child to become victims – obviously Izzie was a different kettle of fish. He didn't know her and folk would do a hell of a lot for money. It remained to be seen whether Jordan Beaumont was an innocent victim or if he was complicit.

'That's not all though,' continued Compo, his words running together, 'It was also caught twice on the camera nearest to the Worth Valley Railway in Keighley – the one right near Dalton Mill – and,' he paused in a *ta da* sort of way, took a deep breath and continued, 'it's been hanging around Alice's house for a couple of weeks – well since Daniel and Izzie moved in anyway.'

That was interesting. Gave them a concrete link between Jordan Beaumont and Izzie and the car. The sound of Compo taking a bite of something made Gus' stomach rumble. He was in danger of collapsing like an old Victorian drama queen. He couldn't imagine Gore being gallant enough to whip out the smelling salts to revive him. On the upside, Compo's intelligence was great. He was dotting the I's and the T's would hopefully be crossed when he and Gore reached their destination. Hell, it was a great feeling when hard work began to pay dividends.

Through a mouthful of something, Compo began speaking again. 'Thing is Gus. Taffy suggested cross referencing the number plates and times to see if they were working in a group and… guess what?'

Here we go again! Gus glanced at Gore who was smirking and shaking his head. If they hadn't been at risk of getting trapped in the snow, Gus would've thumped him on the arm. Instead, he contented himself with glowering at him. Gore responded by briefly raising the middle finger of one hand.

'Go on, Comps. I'm listening.'

Gore's grin widened, probably because the expression on Gus' face belied his placid tone. Gus winked, his face softening. He could well imagine Compo whizzing between screens on his office chair like a demented dervish, music blaring in his headphones – *wonder what he's listening to for this case?* – crumbs flying unnoticed, Taffy, in the background, pulling together all of the paperwork. Compo was back.

'We hit Bingo! Well – when I say Bingo, I don't mean your Bingo. Nobody, least of all *me* would hit your *Bingo. No…*'

Well used to Compo's digressions, and sensing he was about to go around the houses in order to clarify what Gus already knew, he cut in, ignoring the snort of laughter from Gore. 'I know exactly what you mean. What did your protégé's brainwave reveal?'

'Eh?'

Another snort from Gore as he manoeuvred round a snow covered bump in the road managing to right the vehicle from a very slight skid.

'What did Taffy's suggestion tell us?'

'Oh, yeah, right, get it. Might be summat or nowt, but we discovered another car that was at Rawsforth when the train Izzie Dimou was on crashed and it was caught on the same cameras as the other car near the mill in Keighley, though significantly not near the railway station. We got a list of all the places this vehicle had been and, gue—?'

Determined not to offset the question, Gus interrupted, 'Did the sightings correspond to our other vehicle, by any chance?'

'Brilliant Gus, well done.'

Gus let that go, amid more snorts from Gore, 'Lewis got a cold, Gus? Is he well wrapped up – it's cold out.'

At these words Gore's smiling face turned in to a frown, 'What the fuck do you think I'm wearing Compo? We're in the middle of Saddleworth Moor in the worst storm in my memory and you ask if we're wrapped up?'

Gus, now laughing, raised his hand, 'We're a bit cold. Heater's not working very well and Gore's a tad grumpy. Just ignore him.'

Gore again shared his raised middle finger with Gus, who returned the gesture. 'Go on Comps.'

'Well, they're not always exactly in the same vicinity, but enough of the time to make it suspicious. Thing is, we've linked the car plates to those two dead blokes yesterday in Keighley. Turns out they're Romanian – from Manchester – but the car caught in Rawsforth belongs to their cousin. Nancy's got them in for questioning. Strange thing is, another one of their relatives was killed on Friday – looked like a drug hit. Their prints were matched to what was left of the car that caused the train wreck.'

'Good work Comps. Any news about Alice, or anymore from the USB?'

'Making progress, will update later, Gus. See ya.'

'Eh, Comps?'

'Yeah'

'What's your song for this case?

'*Unspoken Truth* by Shakra.'

How bloody apt. Too many truths had been left unspoken recently. Something Gus intended to rectify when he could.

Chapter 50

T affy couldn't take his eyes off Compo. He was a completely different person when behind the computer. Taffy had never had the time to study Compo in action, but he was glad he had the opportunity now. Compo had made him swear a *'what happens at Compo's stays at Compo's'* sort of oath and now he was certainly seeing a whole load of stuff he never in a million years thought he would. He sat at Compo's side watching conversations play across the screen – conversations on the deep web, conversations that made only partial sense to him. After the first few hours, he'd got used to the darkness in the room. Compo had insisted they shut the curtains and dimmed the lights; claiming it got him in the zone. To be honest it was a relief for Taffy not to have to see the worsening weather conditions outside.

One screen had interactions from the Justice Room, another had ones from Beyond the Pale and a third was running an ongoing data analysis programme Compo had whipped up to isolate the CCTV images that may have a view of both cars' occupants.

Compo let out a sudden whoop and wheeled himself over to the Justice Room screen. A message had flashed up

JayRay:	Been sniffing. Followed scent and got goods. You on?
ReviAeternus:	Which hit?
JayRay	AC

264

Taffy had picked up that AC was Alice. Looked like JayRay had come up with the goods.

ReviAeternus:	How many bitcoins?
JayRay:	It's hot – flaming – on fire.
ReviAeternus:	Again, how many?
JayRay:	Enough. More than enough.

Compo laced his fingers together and pushed his hands away from him, palms out, creating a cracking sound that made Taffy shiver. His face set, Compo tucked his chair right under the table, took a glug of Coke, rammed a handful of Tortilla chips into his mouth and set to work.

ReviAeternus:	Trade?
JayRay:	What you got?
ReviAeternus:	This piece takes backdoor access to next level – better than Sham door or RoofTop
JayRay:	Proof?

Compo laughed out loud, grabbed more Tortillas followed by a large bite of a Mars Bar and pressed a few keys. Turning to Taffy, he raised his hand for a high five. 'Already breached his back door – had it set up, just in case. He'll give us what we want for this technology.' Puzzled, Taffy frowned, 'Won't he be pissed off with you for hacking him?'

'Nah, he asked for proof. Had all his protection in place and I still got through. He'll be begging for this.'

JayRay:	Jammie. Give me 5

The conversation went silent and Compo turned to Taffy, his grin wide. Like a kid whose eaten all the red smarties. 'Hey

Taff, he's going to try to outdo me but he won't be able to. Give it three minutes and he'll give in.'

Intrigued, Taffy glanced at his watch and began the countdown. 'What've you done Comps.'

Compo shrugged, 'Nowt much. Just created a programme that can get through his backdoor undetected. He's trying right now to close the doors and lock me out.'

'And you'll sell that to him.'

'Nah, not sell. I'll exchange it for real info about Alice.'

Taffy wasn't sure how he felt about that. Last thing he wanted was for some hacker to have access to a programme that could effectively access all sorts of businesses and governments. 'Eh, Comps, is that a good idea? I mean will Gus be okay with it?'

'You heard, Gus. He said '*do what it takes*'. You heard him, right?'

Taffy nodded, reluctant, 'Well, yeah, but not sure he meant this sort of thing. I mean, you're leaving systems wide open with that.'

Compo raised his chin, opened his mouth and shook in the last of the tortillas, seemingly unconcerned that half of the crumbs landed on his t-shirt.

'Nah. Don't be daft. I wouldn't do that. JayRay is a White Hat hacker. He'll put it to good use. I'd probably have exchanged it over the weekend for intel on an original retro poster, anyway.'

'So why not just give him it?'

'Protocol Taff. Exchanges are fine, but we don't like to owe each other too much.'

The Justice Room PC pinged and Taffy jumped to his feet as Compo whirled his chair round to face the monitor.

JayRay: Dude, you're tops. Lulz!

For a minute Taffy was disconcerted, then he remembered Compo had told him Lulz was Internet speak for 'lol'. Seemed like JayRay was happy. *Now, let's hope he's got something convincing to help Alice.*

Compo: Need to see the goods first
JayRay: Taster coming your way.

A window pinged open next to their conversation. It was a video. Compo enlarged the screen and they saw an image of Sean Kennedy in an office – all magnolia and cream with heavy wood furniture. He sat opposite an older, much smarter man, who kept playing with the things on the desk that separated them. It was date stamped Friday. This had the potential to be good. Compo's fingers flew across the keyboard.

ReviAeternus: Need more – Sound?
JayRay: Solicitor Allison-Hinton. Harrow. Got
                sound. Also, RAT'd solicitors PC. You
                need deeper sniff, let me know.

As Taffy and Compo watched they saw Sean Kennedy smile. Not a pleasant sight. The man had deteriorated since his pre-coma photos – emaciated, straggly hair and, if that smile was owt to go by, a nasty streak. He certainly made the solicitor look nervous. The larger man couldn't seem to hold Kennedy's gaze. His eyes flitting anywhere but directly at his visitor. All the while they talked, his hands rearranged the pens, pencils and the executive toy on his desk.

The sound kicked in, making Taffy jump. It was as clear as if the conversation was happening right there.

'Well?' Sean Kennedy glared at the solicitor. The word a bullet shot in the quiet room.

The other man's face broke into a wide smile and for a moment he suspended his fidgeting. 'She agreed. Baby Jane's final bit of persuasion did the trick. She's signed the statement claiming responsibility for everything and exonerating you from all wrong doing.'

Baby Jane? That was the bitch that had landed Al in the hospital. Taffy grinned and risked a glance at Compo. Compo's head was going up and down like one of those nodding car toys, his smile wide. They'd got a definite link between Kennedy, Kennedy's solicitor and the bitch that had attacked Alice.

The solicitor continued. '*That* combined with Big H's statement and the electronic trail we've laid, will let you off the hook and confine her to a long stay at Her Majesty's convenience.'

Compo's face darkened as the import of the man on the screen's words sank in. 'Fucker,' he murmured under his breath

Now Kennedy was grinning, like he'd been expecting this. He leaned back and nodded. 'Now, we need to get her parents.'

'Fuck!' The word was out before he could stop it. Taffy glanced at Compo. 'The bastards are going after Alice's mum and dad.' Taffy had only met the Coopers briefly, but he'd liked them. Now, looking at Compo, he saw a side to his friend he'd never seen before. His fingers were flying over the keys, his face unsmiling, a frown dragging his eyebrows together into one elongated angry-looking caterpillar. Taffy could just about decipher the words he whispered under his breath; 'bastards' and 'not on my watch.'

Taffy turned back to the screen. Allison-Hinton was frowning now and his hands were all over his desk ornaments again – not a happy man.

'What? But... I thought...?' Allison-Hinton's voice trembled.

Kennedy laughed. 'Yeah, that's what Alice Cooper thought too. That's why she signed the statement. Stupid bitch! She should've known I'd go straight for the jugular. She has to suffer. And there's only one sure way to do that.'

They had the evidence. Now all they had to do was work out a way to get it to the people that could use it without incriminating themselves. Taffy had faith that Compo would work it out.

Chapter 51

06:50 Saddleworth Moor

'About bloody time too.' Gus was beginning to think they'd never arrive, but when he'd thought they could force Gore's Volvo no further, the Satnav had chimed up: '*You have reached your destination.*'

Peering through the window, Gus shuddered. If this was their destination he couldn't see a damn thing and certainly no farmhouse. Nothing. The landscape was an undulating, unrelenting wave of white – stark and primal in the pre-dawn glow. The blizzard had blown itself into a breeze, but Gus worried about being able to drive out again. The snow chains had been a godsend, but Gus wasn't prepared to rely solely on them – a bit of logic was in order. 'Reckon you should turn the car round so we're facing the right way.'

Gore complied, accelerating carefully over snow mounds, leaving a mishmash of tyre tracks in the otherwise pristine snow until, at last, the car was pointing back the way they'd come. Gus took out his phone and checked for a signal so he could contact the team but there was none. Oh well, they'd just have to manage on their own.

'Now we walk' said Gus, wishing he had another layer of clothes to add under his fisherman's jacket. He patted his pockets and discovered a bottle of Wee Bru lurking in their depths. After pulling it out he tossed it onto the back seat with a shudder. A caffeine loaded coffee was what he craved. The very thought of the cold drink in the present conditions made his stomach shrivel in protest. They got out and, with no need to consult with each other, they trudged round to the boot and took out two extendable batons, pepper spray, a crow bar and a heavy-duty spanner.

Gore looked at Gus and grinned, 'Toss you for the crow bar.'

Gus laughed, 'You have it. I'll stick with the spanner. Always wanted to play Cluedo in a deserted farmhouse on Saddleworth Moor.' He peered through the gloom, wondering exactly what direction to go. 'Can't see any sign of a building far less a farmhouse.'

Gore had trudged a few feet to one side and was bending over in the snow. 'Look at this.'

Gus waded through inches of snow till he could see what Gore was so interested in.

'Mostly covered, but think it looks like tyre marks – big fucking tyre marks.' And he blew lightly on the snow, displacing the topmost layer.

Gus grinned. Gore was right. At least now they had a direction to go in – although, on the downside, it seemed that they also had some company. And most likely not of the friendly sort.

'Hope back-up arrives soon,' Gus said, moving in the direction of the nearly covered tracks. The wind, although gentler than it had been, still made progress slow and Gus was unsure whether snow was still falling or just being dislodged from the sparse trees that were dotted around. They walked on for minutes in silence, conserving their energy and focussing on making sure they didn't veer off the trail. Every breath was an effort as the frosty air caught in their throats, making the simple act of simultaneous walking and breathing excruciatingly difficult.

'How far do you reckon we'll have to walk?' said Gore, panting slightly.

'No idea, but hopefully not much further. When we get the lay of the land, we'll have to come up with a plan.'

Fifteen minutes later they came across a dilapidated fence and just beyond it a series of buildings. 'The tracks veer to the right here, but I reckon we could cut across the field and approach the farmhouse from that side.'

'Let's try to keep as much under cover as possible. We'll stick to the tree lines where we can. It'll take a bit longer but we don't actually know what to expect when we get there.'

Gus could see the sense of Gore's proposal. Cutting across the field would speed things up, but they'd also be exposed. Looked like they'd have to take the long route and hope that the element of surprise would pay dividends when they neared the house. At the back of Gus' mind was the hope that they'd find Daniel, although he tried to keep that quashed. Logistically, the chances of finding a dead body were much higher and judging by the scene at Jordan Beaumont's house, their adversaries didn't appear to possess much in the way of compassion.

As they struggled through the snow, occasionally toppling over when their feet caught an unsuspecting obstacle hidden beneath the white blanket, Gus wondered what condition they'd find Jordan Beaumont in – if indeed they'd find him at all! When they were yards away from the nearest building they paused under a tree, partly to catch their breath and partly to consider a plan of action. Just visible between two buildings was a car. The roof and bonnet were covered with a few inches of snow indicating it had been there for a while. He listened, but apart from the wind and trees, Gus could hear nothing else.

Gore grabbed Gus' arm and nodded to the right. 'Someone smoking.'

Gus strained his eyes. He could just about see the faint glow of a lit cigarette. *Someone was about.* They waited till they saw a sputter of flame as the cigarette flew through the air. As the smoker moved, Gus was aware of the stranger's bulk. *He would be one tricky fucker to take down.* Pointing to the next tree, Gus indicated they should move closer. Step by step – keeping an eye on the buildings – Gus and Gore crept through the snow. When they reached the next tree, Gus realised that the wall of what looked like a shed that stood a bit away from the main two-storied building was their next source of cover. He was now near enough to study the farmhouse. Its roof was decked with snow and Gus reckoned that the walls were made of sandstone, similar to his parents' house. According to Compo's information, it had been lying empty for a couple of years, ever since Beaumont's mother had died.

He looked around. It was such a bleak place and Gus couldn't imagine living here. He suspected there would be no phone line and his phone had no signal, so he hoped that whatever was about to go down – they wouldn't need an ambulance. His mind flashed to the last time Gore had needed an ambulance. It was after nearly dying at the hands of a tattooing serial killer. He remembered speaking with Gore's wife and he was determined that no matter what happened today, Gore would go home to his wife and baby. That family had been through too much already.

'The shed.' Gus nodded towards the building and when Gore nodded back he took off. Half way to the building his foot caught in something. He stopped and looked down. The snow was hollowed, as if something had been lying there and then been moved. But what was really interesting was the item he'd tripped over. It was a rucksack. He picked it up and taking off his gloves, wrestled with the buckles. Inside were tins of soup and a kitchen knife. He looked at Gore who nodded. 'Take it. We might need it,' so he pocketed the knife, swung the rucksack on his back and put his gloves back on.

'Look at this. 'Gore pointed to two sets of boot prints, with unmistakable drag marks in the snow between the prints, leading towards the farmhouse. *A dead body being dragged?*

It didn't seem likely that the rucksack and its contents could belong to Beaumont, so maybe, just maybe – if they were lucky – they'd belong to Daniel and maybe – just maybe – if they had a little bit of extra luck, he'd be still alive. Any alternative to that would be awful. Gabriella was on his case enough, but if he failed to bring her brother back to her in one piece, who knew what she'd do.

With renewed energy they set off, keeping an eye out for any movement from the farmhouse. As they neared, a light was visible from a front window sending an eerie amber glow over the snow. Reaching the side of the building – with Gus in the lead – they sidled along, careful to hug the walls. Snowdrifts had built up beside the wall, making it more difficult to walk, but at least it offered a welcome relief from the unrelenting breeze and offered some cover. As they reached the corner, the light seemed brighter. Gus poked his head round and waited, listening for any sounds from nearby – nothing that sounded human. He skirted the corner and approached the window from which the light shone. It had one of those high sills typical of solid farmhouses, meant to withstand all sorts of conditions. He reached the side of the window, Gore just behind him – so close he could hear his breathing. Taking a chance, Gus popped his head up and had a quick peek inside.

He glimpsed a spacious old-fashioned living room with the sort of furniture he remembered from his grandparents' house. From the light of the single unshaded light bulb he saw one man sitting on a saggy looking chair. Another stood, shoulders hunched, leaning against the wall next to the fire, warming his hands. Standing up against the chair, within arm's reach of either man, were two machetes. *Not good.* Bundled on the sofa was another person. The sound of coughing drifted out. They'd lit a fire in the grate and as the coughing got worse, the man who was sitting down stood up and threw another blanket over the prone man. Was that Jordan Beaumont? Didn't seem likely they'd be so kind to him. Perhaps it was Daniel? They'd want to keep him alive if they needed information about the USB stick from him.

Gus ducked down and turned to Gore. 'Two men with machetes and one in a poor condition lying on the sofa.'

'Shit!'

'Best bet is to head round to the back of the house and see if we can make an entry there. We want to surprise them if at all possible.'

'Yeah, the only good thing is that, unless they also have a firearm, machetes' are an up-close sort of weapon. Hmm, machetes against our extendable batons, what do you think? Fancy our chances?

Gus shook his head, 'We have to assume they'll have guns too. Although it looks like the machete is the weapon of choice.'

'Well you know what they say about men and their machetes?'

Gus looked at Gore with a frown, 'Em, no?'

'Small dicks.' And he wiggled his gloved small finger and shook his head, his

expression woeful.

Gus snorted. Gore had a habit of using his humour to diffuse tension and, right now,

Gus needed to get rid of some. Leading the way, he circled back to the house. When Gus glanced back he saw that Gore was attempting to smooth their tracks as best he could by using the crowbar to fill their footsteps. No point in leaving anything to alert them if they came out for a smoke.

'So, what do you want to do?'

Gus weighed up the odds. Whoever was on the couch in there was in a bad way and who knew how long he'd last if the other two decided to get nasty. They'd no way of ascertaining the ETA of their backup. Weapons were an issue. 'Let's see what's round the back. Maybe something will pop up. Maybe the farmer's left a conveniently loaded shotgun by the back door, maybe back-up will arrive by the time we get there.'

Gore snorted, 'Your optimism never ceases to amaze me.'

Heavy snow clouds obscured the moonlight, making visibility poor as they rounded the corner. Approaching what turned out to be the kitchen's window, a breeze caught the curtains, wafting them outwards. Gus jolted backwards, assuming it was one of the men from the living room and berated himself for being such a wuss. *Looks like someone's done our job for us.* Getting closer, Gus saw that the window was broken and the glass cleared from round the rotten wooden frames. Gore tugged his sleeve and pointed to a deep furrow that was half filled by the recent snowfall. Gus studied it for a minute, understood its implication and looked upwards. Someone had jumped from an upper window Looks like they'd had an uncomfortable landing as, when Gore swept some of the snow away, a brick-built barbecue was revealed. Did these tracks belong to the same person who'd left the rucksack in the field and been dragged towards the farmhouse?

There was no light coming from inside, so Gus used his phone torch to see inside, shielding the light with his hand. The kitchen was empty except for an array of dated furniture dotted around the walls with a central table covered with a variety of open cans and used dishes. The old gas cooker in the corner was slathered with food, beans or tomato soup by the looks of it and Gus' desire to climb in, rush over and turn on the gas burners to warm his entire body, was almost irresistible.

Gore nudged him and, bent from the knees, linked his gloved fingers together indicating that he'd give Gus a foot-up. Gus placed his hands on the sill, balanced one foot on Gore's proffered hands and hoisted himself upwards. He got one leg up and over the sill and froze. A voice speaking in another language was coming closer. He propelled himself backwards and fell, landing on Gore who let out a great whoof of air. Before Gore had a chance to speak, Gus placed his hand over the other man's mouth. For long minutes, the two of them lay there in the snow beneath the window. Tuneless humming drifted out to them, accompanied by the occasional sound of furniture being moved and stuff being banged around. Gus' heart pounded against his chest and he hoped Gore couldn't feel it through his layers. Last thing he needed was to be teased.

A cramp developed in Gus' leg where it was wedged under one of Gore's, but he'd no intention of moving in case they made a noise. At one point he was sure he'd seen a shadow pass the window and he held his breath, imagining the machete man looking out. As long as he didn't look downwards they'd be okay. As his leg became more numb, Gus cursed, *Fuck's sake! Come on, come on. What the hell are you doing in there, preparing a fucking banquet?*

Finally, all went quiet. They waited another couple of minutes, ears straining for any tell-tale noises from indoors. Nothing. Gus began to extricate his leg from Gore's, cursing again as waves of pain shot up it as the blood began to circulate. He rolled off the other man who lay there for a few seconds, said 'Fuck – you're heavier than I thought, man.'

Dusting himself off, Gus shook his leg and did a couple of preparatory stomps to see if full sensation had returned. 'Try again?'

Gore snorted, 'Right, but don't expect a cushioned landing this time if you fall. Soon as you've got your grip, I'm backing off.'

Grinning, Gus repeated his earlier manoeuvre, swung both legs over the sill and into the large sink. As quietly as he could, he climbed from the sink, padded over to the solid wood door that their earlier visitor had left ajar and with care closed it. By the time he'd turned round Gore's upper body was through the window, but when Gore tried to pull his lower body through, he did a sort of slippery forward motion and landed on the floor with a bang.

Startled, they both held their positions for a minute, then, hearing nothing from beyond the door, Gus helped Gore to his feet and said right in his ear, 'talk about making a fucking entrance, Gore.'

'Got a plan?'

Gus shrugged. He had no answer to the question. Seeing a door to the side, an idea came to him. He walked over, pulled gently at the handle and grinned. Now here was a way to even the odds a little.

Chapter 52

06:50 North Park Road

Mo, hunched over, sat in a well-used armchair next to a wood stove with only a few glowing embers left in the grate. He glared at it, and then at the single log left in the basket next to the fireplace. This was not the damn weather to be traipsing out to their garden shed. Naila had told him to bring in extra wood – nag, nag, nag – and, as usual, he'd put it off and, as usual, she'd been right. Picking up the log, he opened the stove door, flicked the vent half open and bunged it in.

Naila, bundled under a blanket on the chair opposite him, yawned and said, 'So, you going down to the shed?'

Mo glowered at her, wondering if he could get away with just shoving a jumper and his big coat over his pyjamas and dressing gown before going out. Sodding neighbours had eagle eyes and last thing he needed was for it to be broadcast at the mosque that he was roaming about in his pyjamas in the early hours. A quick glance at the clock told him it wasn't actually the early hours, but that didn't matter – they'd still find summat to criticise. They'd had it in for Mo ever since he'd chopped down the part of their Buddleia tree that was infiltrating his garden. For about the fiftieth time he glared at his phone and then at his wife, 'No reply. Where the hell is he, Naila? Why's he not picking up?'

Naila yawned again, her tangled hair loose around her face and a frown etched across her brow. 'I don't know, love. He's

278

in the middle of it though, in't he? Izzie's murder and Daniel's disappearance must be his top priority. He'll get back to us when he can.'

Mo jumped to his feet and paced the room, 'Yeah, and when's that going to be? What the hell are we supposed to do in the meantime, huh?'

Naila rose and walked over to her husband, placing a hand on his arm and turning him towards her, 'We'll do what we've been asked to do, okay?'

He wrapped his arms around her and squeezed, taking strength from her warm body. 'It's not okay though, is it? I've got you and the kids to think about. Last thing we need, with Zarqa the way she is, is more hassle, more upset — and what if it's dangerous?'

Calm as ever, Naila gave a small laugh, 'It'll be fine. Gus'll phone back in a bit and everything will be sorted.' She pulled away from him and pushed him towards the door, 'Go. Get. The. Wood.'

Mo pouted and she made a shooing motion with her hands. 'Go on. I'll put some chai and toast on.'

Halfway to the door, Mo turned back and hugged her, 'Love you, Naila.'

She wound her arms round his neck and kissed him, 'Love you too.'

Flinging on his old jumper and his coat over his PJ's, Mo peeked out the kitchen window. Shit, Nosy Nazir's kitchen light was on. He walked over to the switches by the back door and disabled the motion sensor on their external lights. *No sense in advertising his pre-dawn, half-dressed trek to the shed.*

Wellies on, he cracked open the back door, shuddering when a blast of cold hit his face. *Effing Beast from the effing East.* He stepped out and immediately his feet went from under him and he landed on his backside. The earlier activity from his nocturnal visitors had compacted the snow and, with a new layer on top, it was lethal. Using the wall to help him, he scrambled back onto his feet, with a quick glance over to see if his antics had been spotted by next door. *All quiet on the Western Front.* Placing his feet with care, he picked his way towards the shed, trying to use the half-filled tracks left earlier. *God it was cold.* He tugged at the hasp, his fingers sticking to the frozen metal as he tried to flick it open. *Effing Storm effing Emma.* He'd just released it when a voice penetrated the darkness causing him to slip, ending up, once more, on his arse in the snow.

'Late night visitors, Mo? Having a snow party, were we?'

A familiar head topped with a prayer hat appeared above the fence, near the offending bush. Mo cursed under his breath. *Nosy effing bastard. Can't mind his own effing business even in this weather.* Getting to his feet and brushing the snow off his coat, Mo reigned in his initial retort which went something along the lines of *sod off, you nosy prick* and instead shook his head, 'Just kids throwing snowballs, that's all.'

Looking unconvinced, his neighbour stared pointedly at the compacted snow tracks and sniffed. 'Didn't seem much like kids to me. Inshallah this isn't something I need to alert neighbourhood watch about?'

Neighbourhood bloody watch! Pompous prick! Mo kicked the pile of drifting snow away from the front of the shed and squashed the sudden urge to pick up a handful, make a snowball and fire it straight into his neighbour's supercilious face. *Jackass!*

'We have standards to uphold. Especially with the dross that's flooding the area from Poland and the like – dragging us into the gutter they are. We need to be vigilant.'

Mo stopped, fists clenched by his sides. It was exactly this sort of narrow-minded shit that got his dander up. Wasn't only the Eastern Europeans to blame, the Pakistani community needed to own its failings too. Turning, Mo stepped towards the fence and, past caring how this was reported at mosque, said, 'Why don't you, for once, mind your own damn business?'

He would have turned away at that point, but a flashback from sixteen years ago of this very man barring Naila's entry to the mosque surfaced. Tears had streamed down her face, as she cast anxious glances around her, only for the community – led by this man – to turn away; to disown her. Anger that he'd swallowed down for years, surged up from the soles of his feet, into his chest. He placed his hands on the top of the fence and almost spat the next words at his neighbour, like a machine gun firing ice balls instead of bullets. 'Or, better still, instead of being the pious prick you are, maybe – Inshallah – you can stop your son sitting in his car on Scotchman Road selling weed to twelve-year olds. Or beating up his Pakistani wife before screwing his Gora one or laundering his filthy drug money through one of the restaurants he's set up on Barkerend Road.' Mo was breathing heavily now, his chest heaving, his eyes flashing. He prodded his neighbour on the shoulder, 'And if you ever, ever say one bad word about myself or my family you will have *me* to answer to, and believe me – your drug dealing son won't rush to your defence. You got me?'

There was silence between the men for long seconds, then Nazir stepped back. Without another word, the head disappeared from atop the fence and Mo was left wondering exactly what repercussions he would face for his outspokenness.

Mo was glad to get back indoors with a pile of wood in one arm, the other dragging the biggest sack of wood he could manage. His mind still drifted to the words he'd uttered outside. The combination of years of biting his tongue for Naila's sake, concern over their nocturnal visitors and worry about the row he'd had with Zarqa before bedtime had all conspired to make him lose it, big-time. He wasn't concerned for himself. It was Naila he worried about. Naila and the kids. His words would have some sort of blowback, but right now, he couldn't care less. They were a team and his temper outside had broken his agreement with his wife. Head down, he sat at the kitchen table, with a steaming hot spicy chai and a plate of buttered toast before him while he tried to put his row to the back of his mind. He picked up his phone again and hit speed dial. It rang out and eventually kicked onto voicemail. *Shit, Gus, pick up!* It wasn't like he could leave a message: '*Hey Gus, just so's you know, Alice's mum and dad were shoved through my back door by two masked thugs in the early hours of this morning. Their only words were 'don't tell anyone they're here, or else.'*

Naila, chai in hand, pulled up a chair on the opposite side of the table and grabbed a piece of toast, 'No joy?'

'Nope.'

'I've just been in to check on them. They're sleeping like babies.'

Mo nodded, 'And the kids?'

'I left them to sleep in – there's no school today, so I thought I'd give them a long lie until we decide what to tell them about our visitors.'

With his index finger, Mo skimmed the skin off the top of his tea and put it in his mouth, 'Poor things were petrified.'

Naila sighed, 'They sure were.'

He stretched his arm across the table and linked fingers with his wife. 'What the hell's going on? Why would someone snatch Alice's parents from their home in Greece, fly them in some sort of illicit private jet to a landing strip outside Leeds Bradford Airport in the middle of the worst storm in decades and deposit them with us? It makes no sense.'

Naila squeezed his fingers. 'Gus'll know what to do.'

'Yeah when he bloody gets in touch, that is. Meanwhile, how do we keep their presence here secret? Mr Nosy Nazir from next door's already been quizzing me.' He bit his lip.

Naila frowned and leaning over, prodded his arm with one finger 'Spit it out, Mo. What have you done?'

When he told her, Naila laughed.

Mo shook his head, 'You're not pissed off at me?' *Women! He'd never get them – never in a million years.*

'Hell no, why should I be? This whole Zarqa thing has made me realise that we should have stood up to him years ago. We've done nothing wrong – he is the one who should be doing the soul searching – not us.' She entwined her fingers with Mo's 'As for the other.' She shrugged, 'We need to start sending out messages that this drug dealing on our streets is unacceptable. We should hold our community up to scrutiny, not turn a blind eye. For we all know what happens when we don't address what's under our noses.'

Mo, bit his lip. Naila was right. They should have been preparing for the day they had to tell Zarqa the truth. He should have been addressing what was under his nose. Preparing the way. Looking out for his family.

As if sensing his introspection, Naila tugged his hand, 'No, Mo. I'm proud of you. The Young Jihadists have been highlighting these issues for ages. Maybe you *should* bring it up at the mosque? Make a stance.'

'I just want an easy life, Naila. Don't want the hassle. We've got enough on our plate right now.'

Naila tilted her head to one side. 'Maybe this is exactly the time to do it. Maybe this could be what bonds you and Zarqa. If you supported the Young Jihadists on this issue perhaps it will help resolve some of the differences between you and your daughter.'

'Ah, if only. But we both know that our differences are much closer to home.' He looked at Naila, hating the way her face flushed. Even after all these years, the shame was still there. Didn't matter that the shame wasn't hers to bear. It still lived inside her, like a gremlin she could never get rid of.

Her tremulous smile and sad eyes broke his heart – yet still she lifted her head, chin raised, 'Do you fancy a fry-up?'

Distraction tactic. Mo sighed. He was used to that. Naila's go-to response when under pressure was to cook. 'Eggy bread?'

Mo grinned when Naila nodded; he loved Naila's fry-ups and eggy bread was his favourite. If it calmed her down, he'd eat eggy bread for any meal of the day and twice on a Friday.

His sadness lifted a little when she smiled. The uneasy flush left her cheeks as she said. 'I'll go and wake the *other* kids.'

Whilst she went upstairs Mo busied himself adding wood to the stove. Maybe he'd shut the cafe for the day and they could have a family day with Alice's parents. His girls loved them and they could play board games and drink hot choc... The sound of Naila's frantic whispered shout down the stairs had him running. *Had something happened to Alice's parents?* Reaching the bottom step, he glanced up. Naila, ashen faced, was heading down. Her voice, though quiet, was anxious. 'It's Zarqa, she's not in her room – not upstairs.'

'Bathroom?'

Her response was sharp, 'No, I checked. She's gone.'

Blood thundered in Mo's ears. *His baby. Where the hell was she? This was all his fault.* He ran upstairs, pushing passed Naila and entered her room. The bed was made, everything in its place – her stupid One Direction poster with Zayn's face encapsulated in a big red love heart, her lap top open on the desk, yesterday's jeans thrown in the corner.

He whirled round and went to the bathroom – the door was ajar so he knew she wouldn't be in there. Still he looked, whipping aside the shower curtain, just in case. Downstairs again, grabbing his still dripping coat from the radiator in the hallway, he unlocked the front door and yanked it open. Shoving his feet into his walking boots, he peered outside into the blizzard. On the path he could see the rapidly fading steps where Zarqa had walked. If he was quick he could track her. His Rocky ringtone filled the air behind him. He slammed the door shut, rushed past Naila who stood, arms folded around her middle, tears streaming down her face, and on into the kitchen. With his breath coming in ragged pants, he grabbed his phone. 'Zarqa?'

Naila, pulled his arm, mouthing, 'Is it her?'

He shook his head, 'Hi Patti, what can I do for you?' He frowned and took a deep breath, exhaling it slowly and turned and spoke to Naila, 'She's okay.'

He began pacing the kitchen. 'She did *what*?'

He continued listening until finally, he said, 'Okay, yes she can stay for now, but I want her home this afternoon. We need to talk.'

With a huge sigh he tossed his phone on the table and cradled his head in his hands, his fingers digging into his skull. Naila went to him, 'What is it, Mo? Where is she?'

He enveloped her in a hug, savouring the scent of her coconut shampoo and wondered what the hell he was going to do. 'Zarqa's at Gus'.'

'Gus'?'

'She arrived there an hour ago. Thankfully, Patti was there looking after Bingo otherwise who knows what she'd have done. Told Patti she'd run away from home.'

'Fuck!'

The expletive from his wife's lips echoed round the room. Naila rarely swore. Her eyes filled with tears and Mo pulled her to him, 'I'm sorry Naila, really sorry. I just don't know what to do.' And thinking his legs wouldn't hold him up for a moment longer, he lowered himself into the chair.'

Nail pulled out a chair and sat beside him. 'We've got to deal with this Mo. *You've* got to deal with it. She deserves to know.'

'I told you, after her exams, ok?'

'Hell Mo, have you ever thought that this not knowing, asking questions and getting no answers might make her mess up her exams?'

Mo closed his eyes. 'She'll have to wait. This isn't just about her is it? It's about *us* and the community and about *everything*. We need time. We need time to set things up, to prepare.' He patted her arm. 'After her exams, okay?'

Chapter 53

06:55 Saddleworth Moor

Gus flicked a series of switches and the farmhouse was plunged into darkness. It wasn't pitch black, but Gus hoped it was dark enough to give him and Gore a bit of an advantage. As soon as the lights went off, they positioned themselves at either side of the door. Within seconds, the living room door opened and they could hear the two men talking in raised voices – *Turkish?* Presumably they were arguing over who should check out the light situation. Gus hoped that whichever one of them came through, they'd be without their machete.

Footsteps along the hallway followed by a bang and a clatter as something got knocked over. A single staccato word – *an expletive?* And the footsteps continued. As the door opened, Gore pressed himself against the wall, ready to pounce, whilst Gus – concealed by the door – waited, crowbar in hand. He hoped he wouldn't need to use it as the noise of a scuffle would no doubt alert the other man.

As soon as their prey walked in Gore moved behind him, wrapped one arm round his chest and the other over his mouth and propelled him into the middle of the kitchen, allowing the door to swing shut. A stream of Greek flooded the room as the man struggled. Gore slapped his massive hand over his opponent's mouth temporarily quelling the angry words until Gus came from behind the door and shoved a ball of food bags into the struggling man's mouth. Gore pushed their

286

prisoner onto one of the pine chairs and rapped the length of rope they'd found in the electricity cupboard round his chest, arms and chair. With his adversary largely immobilised now, Gus took the time to study him. Body odour, sharp and piercing, hung round him like a shroud. A spattering of acne scars dotted his cheeks, stubble covered his chin. He was the smaller of the two men, still Gus guessed he weighed more than him.

All he and Gore had to do was secure his limbs to the chair and move him onto the pantry. That done, they looked at each other and grinned. They waited for the other man to grow suspicious and come looking for his partner. They moved back to the door and opened it a crack, listening for any activity from the other room.

When the initial burst of adrenalin finally dissipated, Gus shivered. Despite the warmth generated by the AGA, the broken window rendered the room cold – almost freezing. Trying to keep warm, he rubbed his hands up and down his arms and shook his legs. Gore, suffering from the cold too, copied him. At last, after about ten minutes, they heard stirring from the living room. The heavy tread of a bigger man made its way along the hallway and Gore and Gus resumed their earlier positions.

The man flung the door open, yelling at the top of his voice in his mother tongue. The door ricocheted off Gus' head, stunning him for a moment. Meanwhile Gore, who was a big man himself, launched himself at the other man. However, the foreigner was larger and, as if he sensed Gore coming from behind, pivoted round, trunk-like arms raised, and smashed one into Gore's face. An explosion of blood splattered over the floor and Gore yelled. Gus dived from behind the still juddering door and launched himself at their opponent, but he too was floored by a swipe from a muscular arm. Breathing heavily, the giant Greek towered over them as they tried to regain their composure, then with an inhuman roar he raised a massive booted foot and kicked each of them in the head.

When Gus came round, his head drooped forward, his chin resting on his chest, saliva dribbling from his mouth. In contrast to the numbing cold that had encompassed him for most of the day, he was cocooned in warmth. The sort of warmth that made you question your luck. The sort of warmth that made Gus realise he was probably in deep shit right now. *Fuck, was his head sore.* When he moved, pressure exerted itself against his chest and his heart began to race. *Not now, get a grip, Gus.* He realised the pressure was external, not the inner tightness that accompanied his panic attacks. Breathing through his mouth, willing himself to be calm, he flicked his eyes open – just for a second. A thick rope was wound twice round his chest. He wiggled a little, but it was taut. *Not good.* Taking a moment to ground himself, Gus replayed the sequence of events that had led him here. *Big fucking tosser, built like a bloody mountain – even bigger than Gore.* A frisson of fear shot up his spine. He didn't want to die – not like this. He thought of Patti and his parents... and his team. They needed him, so there was nothing else for it – he had to get out of here.

Keeping his eyes closed, he strained his listening, trying to work out who else was in the room with him. A grunting half snore seemed to be coming from somewhere in front of him, *Gore?* He listened again – *Yep, definitely Gore.* A wave of relief swept over him. *That evened up the odds a little – well, if you didn't count the fact he was tied up with a sodding headache from hell.* The spit of the fire was faint and the occasional sound of chair springs protesting told Gus that at least one of his attackers was in the room – probably sitting in one of the armchairs near the fire. *Wonder where the machetes are?*

The mustiness of neglect and damp tickled his nostrils. He was still in Jordan Beaumont's farmhouse. Keeping his head bowed, Gus risked a longer look. The fire sent amber and gold shadows flitting across the floor and an eerie daylight was beginning to penetrate the dark farmhouse. He was sitting in one of the kitchen chairs, tied in the same way he'd secured the smaller man earlier. When he tilted his head up just a fraction, he saw that Gore was sitting directly opposite him, trussed up just like him. Gore was still unconscious, his head lolling onto his chest, blood covering his top. Angling his eyes to the right, Gus saw the old sofa with the bundled-up form on it that they'd seen through the window earlier. He strained to see who it was. *Daniel? Beaumont?*

To his left, as he'd guessed, sat their attackers. Both slouching, like they were on holiday – maybe this did constitute a holiday pastime for them. Blinking a few times to clear his vision, Gus noted a mental inventory. Despite their size difference, they were too alike not to be related – brothers probably. They each sprawled awkwardly in the chairs, legs splayed, a loosely held machete balanced over their knees. Stubble dotted each of their faces, their hair greasy, their jeans filthy. *Blood stains?*

Gus studied them. The larger man dwarfed the chair, his tree-sized limbs sticking out, his head tilted to one side resting on his shoulder. His knuckles where he held the machete were covered in blood – *Gore's?* Gus' eyes drifted to the smaller man and saw that his face was battered and bloody. He frowned. He and Gore hadn't done that. His gaze drifted back to the other guy's bloody knuckles. *Ah ha – friction in the camp – maybe he and Gore could play on that?*

He glanced back at Gore and saw that he was awake and watching him.

'You okay?' Gus mouthed the words.

Nodding, Gore mouthed back 'Sort of,' before glancing down at his restraints.

Gus grinned. It was good that Gore still had his sense of humour. *'Any ideas?'*

Before Gore had a chance to respond there was movement from the side and a large foot kicked his chair, sending it flying backward. It toppled and Gore's head cracked onto the floor with a sickening crash, blood soaking into the carpet immediately.

'Salak Piçler!'

That doesn't sound good.

Eyes glinting, the larger man turned to Gus, machete raised above his head.

Chapter 54

07:45 Premier Inn, Epsom

Getting dressed had been a struggle. Every movement released a wave of body odour that smelled like decomposing fish. Sean wondered if his body was rotting from the inside out and releasing its putrid stench through his pores. His limbs refused to co-operate with the messages his brain was sending to them, but he had no choice other than continue. Never before had a sweaty stinky bed in a lonely hotel seemed as palatable. Rumpled clothes and disengaged limbs were the least of his worries. The fuzz in his head pressed down on his eyes, he could barely open them without flinching. His throat was so raw he could taste blood with each painful swallow. Much as he would like to take a shower, bask in the warmth, sooth his aching bones – he had no strength left for that.

When he'd taken the phone call, Sean had realised there was nothing else for it. He had to make his way back to Harrow and pronto. He dressed quickly, then headed down to reception, his wallet in his hand. If he wanted a ride he'd have to be prepared to pay over the odds for it.

The lass behind the desk was on the phone. She was young and foreign – probably Eastern European, which as far as Sean was concerned was good news. She'd be on minimum wage and could probably do with a few extra quid. Leaning against the counter, wishing he could sit down, Sean allowed the ebb and flow of her phone conversation to merge with the radio that played softly in the background.

'Yes sir, we are still open…'

'And here, at Box Hill in Surrey, we have Jamie and his friend Gurpreet. 'What are you going to do today boys? I see you have your sledges with you.'

'If you wish to cancel you will have to contact our head office.'

'We're going sledging and then my mum says we can have hot chocolate'

'I am aware of the weather conditions, sir, I am being asked to direct all calls to head office. They will be able to help you.'

'Well, these two kids seem to be making the most of the snowy weather. They don't seem to be bothered by the The Beast from the East. It's not yet 10am and the area is busying up. Now I'm off for a well-deserved hot chocolate, this is Melissa Sowerby in the snow at Box Hill, Surrey.'

By the time she'd ended the call, Sean was only just able to speak. His forehead clammy and covered in sweat.

'Are you ok, sir? Shall I call a doctor?'

Sean could tell by the way she wrinkled her nose that his body odour had reached her. He tried to raise his lips into a reassuring smile, but judging by the girl's expression, he had only succeeded in frightening her. He lifted his wallet up and leaned his arm on the counter before attempting to speak. 'Need to get to Harrow right now.'

He struggled to get the words out and the girl frowned, 'Sorry?'

'Harrow, need to get to Harrow. Right now.'

'Oh, sir. The taxis aren't running. The weather is too bad.' She gestured to the door at the flurrying snow outside.

Sean exhaled. As his breath reached her, she jerked her head back, her mouth turned down at the sides. Sean wanted to smash her in the face. Who the hell was she to flinch at him, bloody immigrant – probably illegal too. He leaned further over the counter, a thin strand of hair flopping onto his forehead and took a wad of twenties out of his wallet, 'You find me someone to drive me to Harrow in the next hour and this is yours, okay? There's another two hundred pounds for the driver.'

The girl's eyes dropped to the notes in his hand and then lifted back up to his face. She nodded and pointed to a chair in the corner. 'Sit down before you fall over. I will see what I can do.'

Sean stumbled over to the chair and all but fell onto it, his gaze focused aimlessly on the blizzard outside. A snowplough, spitting salt onto the road, drove past – its engine thrumming in protest while its wheels gouged great mucky ruts into the snow. Behind it, a car crawled, lights on against the overcast skies, skidding every few yards. Its bumper was already bashed, it looked like a fresh bump too. When it pulled to a halt outside the hotel, Sean's heart sank. It sank even more when a young man got out and, after three failed attempts at slamming the driver's door shut, kicked the nearest tyre. *Surely this wasn't his ride to Harrow?*

The youngster lit up a cig and, puffing heavily, waded through the snow to the automatic doors. A waft of freezing air as they opened made Sean huddle deeper into his coat. The lad remained near the sensor, keeping the doors open as he took a few quick drags. *Inconsiderate git!* Sean wished he had the energy to get up and slap the lad across the back of his head, but hell, he couldn't even muster the energy to shout at him.

Tossing his cig into the snow, the lad walked through the doors, with an 'a'right?' to Sean that carried all the swagger of a Geordie Shore character.

Definitely want to thump him. He watched him roll over to the counter, bang his palm down repeatedly on the small bell and when the girl appeared from the back, he pressed both hands on the surface, propelled himself upwards and kissed her on the lips.

'You a'right, Felka? That the tosser want's a lift to Harrow?'

Felka, cheeks flushed, flapped her hands ineffectually at him, her coy smile belying her annoyance, 'Ssh, he can hear you Wasyl!'

Yes, I fucking can – tosser!

The lad leaned closer and, laughing, lowered his voice a little. 'Looks half dead to me – better get the readies up front.'

Fucking little prick – he might get a surprise.

Felka shushed him again. Coming from behind the counter, she smoothed down her uniform skirt and approached. 'I have your driver. He will take you to Harrow.' She looked around herself and stepped to the side. 'Can I have my money, now?'

Sean grinned. *Bloody mare was wise enough to keep their little transaction out of sight of the security cameras!* Well, at least she'd done what he'd asked – and well within the timescale he'd specified. He held out the roll of notes, his grin widening when she grabbed it quickly with another surreptitious glance at the cameras. *A five-minute phone call cost him more than a quick screw and a fumble with a well-used crack head whore – ah well that's life.*

He turned to the lad. 'Hope your heater's working.'

Chapter 55

Heart hammering, Gus stared up at the raised machete. Its blade glinted in the firelight, sharp and stained russet in bits. *This was the end.* The smaller man, wakened no doubt by the racket, had jumped to his feet, shouting something in Turkish. He threw Gus and Gore's IDs on the floor in front of Gus' chair. The only word Gus recognised was 'police'.

Eyes frantic, grin wide, the larger brother took a step closer to Gus and, machete still raised, spat in Gus' face. Gus, ignoring the saliva trickling down his cheek, didn't flinch, refusing to give him the satisfaction of revealing just how scared he was. The man laughed – loud and hollow, and with a heavy accent said, 'Who cares. Police or not police, who cares Vulcan?'

So that's the smaller brother's name.

Vulcan, machete held loosely by his side, glanced at Gore. The pool of blood growing. He kicked Gore lightly with the toe of his boot. 'Fuck's sake Furkan! If *he* dies,' he pointed to Gus 'that one won't give us anything.' His accent was heavy, but his vocabulary seemed better than his brother's.

Furkan grimaced, 'Don't need anything from them.'

Vulcan sighed, and averting his gaze said, 'How do you expect to get *him* out of the country without help?' And he pointed his machete at the prone figure on the couch.

Spluttering from the body on the sofa diverted Furkan's attention away from Gus. 'Get him drink – water – now. Go.'

As Vulcan scurried from the room, Gus tried to ignore his heart plummeting to the soles of his feet. Vulcan, it seemed, exerted a little control over his brother. Furkan lowered his machete, and Gus exhaled a long slow breath as the other man approached the couch, dropped the machete on the floor and, placing his arms around the prone figure, pulled it onto its back and up into a sitting position.

Daniel! Gus tried to keep his face expressionless. His stomach lurched, his heart pounded. *Now all I have to do is keep the three of us alive! But how?* Daniel was shivering, his pallor – with its bluish tinge – frightening. Gone was the well-put-together, slightly standoffish professor. Daniel looked in a bad way, but for some reason, these two brothers seemed to need him. *Did they know he was MI6?* Right now, he looked anything but a spy. Mind you, he'd never really had the 007 suavity about him. God, he wished he was privy to the classified shit the Chief Super had kept from Nancy. It may have provided him with a bargaining tool right now. 'He needs a doctor.' Gus kept his gaze lowered as he uttered the words.

'Kahretsin!' Furkan lifted the machete and approached Gus, his eyes full of venom, making Gus wish he had kept quiet.

Vulcan scurried into the room, spilling water over the rim of the glass he carried. He knelt beside Daniel and held the glass to his lips. 'Drink,' the 'r' of the word had the extra burr Europeans use when speaking English. The giant turned back to the couch where Daniel lay.

Daniel sipped and his coughing abated a little. His voice was hoarse when he spoke, 'Cold.'

Vulcan draped a blanket round Daniel's shoulders and Daniel immediately tried to clasp it under his chin. It was then that Gus realised that two of his fingers were black and his hand was shaking almost uncontrollably. *Frostbite?* He needed to get him out of here and soon – before he died of hypothermia or gangrene or something.

'Daniel, it's me, Gus. We'll get you out of here.'

Daniel started, his head moved towards Gus. His eyes took a while to focus, but when they did, he started to laugh – long and loud and hysterically until a paroxysm of coughing wracked his body. When he finally stopped, he looked at Gus and said, 'Good luck with that, mate.' He leaned back and, resting his head on the lumpy pillow, closed his eyes.

Furkan turned back to Gus, his face split in a grin that Gus could only describe as threatening. He stepped forward, grin widening, his pupils dilated as if he was on something and Gus' heart thumped against his ribs. He'd seen that look too many times before not to recognise it for the madness it was. The huge man stopped, feet apart in front of Gus. Holding the machete in one hand he patted the palm of the other with the blade as if considering which part of Gus to slice.

Vulcan stepped forward, slightly to the side of his brother. 'Let's have a cigarette,' From a packet that bore the logo 'Omar Turkish Cigarettes', he extracted two cigs. 'We can plan. Come on, leave him for now. He's not worth it.' And Vulcan swung away towards the door.

Furkan glared at his brother, his lips twisted in displeasure. 'Wait!'

The younger brother stopped, half turned, his fingers touching his bruised face. 'Come on, cigarette. The police pig can wait.'

Furkan threw back his head and laughed. Gus flinched as a wave of halitosis mixed with pungent stale cigarettes hit him. 'Okay.' He punched Gus in the ribs, shrugged and walked towards the door.

Gus' shoulders slumped, and he retched. A tickle of bile dripped to the carpet, yet his stomach unknotted. *Thank God!* Maybe he'd be able to think straight without the threat of the machete in front of him. Furkan had almost reached the door when he turned, his eyes flashing and – with his rotten teeth bared in a mawkish snarl – he lunged towards Gus, machete raised.

The pain when it sliced his thigh rocketed through his body. Gus yelled and strained against his ties, trying to staunch the blood that spurted from the wound. His chest tightened when he looked down and saw blood everywhere. The hammering started against his ribs. *What if the bastard had nicked an artery?* There was nothing he could do except slow down. He looked up at his attacker and cursed. The other man laughed and the next thing Gus saw was a massive foot hooking under his chair, clattering him onto the floor. Still, blood poured from his wound, but slower now. Gus inhaled, trying to stop himself from passing out whilst the brothers conversed in rapid Turkish near the door. He wished he could understand what they were saying. He needed to have some sense of their motivations. He studied their body language, his heart sinking.

The older brother, Furkan, gesticulated with his blood-soaked machete, his movements over expressive and uncontrolled. Vulcan on the other hand kept his head down, casting furtive glances at Gore and Gus. When his brother drew close to him, he backed away. His tone seemed placatory and when at last Furkan grinned and slapped his brother on the back, the younger man's shoulders relaxed.

After the pair left the room, it took Gus a few moments to collect his thoughts. He'd landed on his shoulder which throbbed madly. However, he'd avoided his head crashing onto the concrete floor which was barely covered by the worn carpet. His back was towards the couch and he faced Gore, who lay ominously still, his black skin now grey coloured. The bleeding on his thigh had slowed to a trickle and Gus grimaced, Furkan had been toying with him. No way would he have risked hitting an artery and having Gus bleed out. No, he'd want to take the time to enjoy his hobby. This was only part of the torture that Gus was certain would follow. For a split second he envied Gore's unconscious state.

Someone was behind him, touching his back. 'Stay still, I'll try and loosen this.'

Daniel! Thank God!

'Be quick, they've only gone for a fag.'

Daniel snorted, 'They're Turkish Cypriots – they won't stop at one cig. I've been timing their cigarette breaks – ten minutes on average – sometimes twelve.' All the while he spoke, his fingers worked at Gus' back. 'Damn fingers are useless. Frostbite. Gone black.'

Daniel's breath was catching in his throat, and the heat radiating from his body was obvious to Gus as he worked. 'Right, that's as loose as I can get them. Wait a minute. I'll get you a weapon.'

Gus heard Daniel shuffle across the floor, his breathing becoming more laboured by the second. He broke into another paroxysm and Gus thought he'd never get back to the couch before the Turks returned. 'Just get back to the couch. Don't let them catch you.'

But Daniel was back now, pressing something long and pointed into Gus' hand.

'Got it from his 'torture kit.' Slot it up your sleeve. You might get the chance to use it.'

Torture kit? The thought that he held the implement used to puncture holes into Izzie Dimou made him a little nauseous. His mind flicked back to the post mortem – her pale body dotted by puncture wounds. *Sick fuckers!* He slotted it, handle first, up his sleeve. The rope was not quite as tight around his chest. And it gave a little as he wiggled it. *Was it loose enough to slip up over his shoulders?*

As Daniel – wheezing like a knackered steam train – crawled back to the couch, Gus heard the front door open. 'Quick.' But there was no time. Daniel was lying next to the couch when the living room door swung open.

Fuck!

Daniel's voice, reedy thin, called out. 'Help, help. I've fallen.'

The brothers rushed to Daniel and together lifted him back onto the couch. Vulcan had just leaned over to mop Daniel's brow when Furkan lifted his machete and whacked his brother across the shoulder with the blunt edge 'Salak! I told you to take care of him.' The brothers faced off against each other, Vulcan holding his injured shoulder, his eyes flashing, whilst his brother threw back his head and whooped like a rabid hyena.

Gus didn't stop to think, he just strained against the rope, and wiggled it up to his neck, freeing his arms. Still attached to the chair by his calves, he slipped the meat prod down his sleeve, and grabbed the handle. 'Hoi you, big boy. You're a piece of fucking shit aren't you, attacking your brother like that?'

Furkan turned, smile wide, eyes flashing. 'Oh, the English think he brave.' He sauntered over, tapping the blade of his knife against his left hand as he neared. Gus could feel a balloon filled with sharp rocks expand, filling his chest, jabbing and piercing his skin from the inside out. It egged him on. He lifted his chin, filled his mouth with saliva and aimed it at the Turk's feet. 'Prick!' *Come on, come on, you psycho bastard, come closer!*

Laughing again, Furkan stopped right in front of Gus. He lifted his foot and Gus, seeing what was coming his way, brought his arm with the meat prod round to the front and jabbed as hard as he could at the Turk's thigh – as near to the groin as he could. *With any luck, he'd hit a major artery!*

Off balance with his attempted kick, Furkan stumbled a little before righting himself, yowling. Gus kept stabbing, blood splattering over his arm and face, yet still he kept jabbing and jabbing, each thrust a little weaker than the one before. As if in slow motion. Furkan lifted his machete and growling like the animal he was, he raised it two-handed above his head and started to bring it down. Gus tried to wriggle backwards, but with his legs still attached to the chair it was futile. He saw what was coming and braced himself to receive it…

A mountain landed on top of him, splattering the chair and releasing Gus from its shackles only to replace them with a dead weight across his lower body. His injured leg screamed. More blood, warm and metallic, soaked into his trousers and spread over the carpet. It took a moment for Gus to realise that the blood wasn't his. Heart thundering, he stared at Furkan who lay across his lower body, machete handle sticking out of his back. Behind him, Vulcan stood, face pale, shivering. 'He deserved that.'

Before Gus could respond, he noticed a red laser dot on Vulcan's forehead. The front door clattered open and yells of 'Don't Move!' exploded through the house. Footsteps thudded down the hallway accompanied by shouts of 'clear' as they approached.

At fucking last! Gus lowered his head on the floor and waited for them.

Chapter 56

Breakfast in prison was the time of day Alice hated the most. Mealtimes in general were bad, but breakfast was the worst. The women had had the night for petty animosities to fester, for the stir-crazy to blow things out of proportion, for homesickness to settle in their guts like rancid cheese. Alice had come to expect some sort of disagreement in the morning and if she was lucky, if she kept her head down and stuck with Lulu, she'd usually manage to avoid being part of it. So, when the alarm sounded just as she was about to make the first decision of the day – brown or white bread for her toast, she wasn't entirely surprised. She turned round half expecting to see a fight erupting in the corner.

Instead, the officers ran to the back of the dining hall and something was slipped into Alice's hand. She glanced down. *A shiv*. Looking up, she met Lulu's eyes. The older woman nodded and Alice got it. This was all for her – the alarm, the skirmish at the back of the dining hall, everything.

She stepped forward and found herself engulfed by a sea of bodies, forming a large circle around her. Someone was pushed into the centre of the circle – someone huge and rabid – Baby Jane Inflictor of Pain. She saw Alice and her face broke into a gap-toothed smile. She stepped closer to Alice, her arms splayed by her sides, her fingers beckoning Alice towards her, 'Come on then, Come *on*.' Her voice was guttural.

Alice circled the edge of the group of women. Her mouth broke into a smile. Lulu had set this up. Lulu had given her this chance and the last thing Alice was going to do was give up on it. Baby Jane had taken too much from her already. Now it was pay day. Payback time. This time the odds would be even.

Alice looked round and saw that Baby Jane's enforcer's arms were yanked behind her back by two of Lulu's bitches. Hairy Mary and her crew were likewise restrained. Alice took a step forward. Her body was aching, but she didn't care. This was *her* chance. This was her opportunity to exact revenge. The thurrump of adrenalin soaring into her limbs, propelled her forward. Despite her injuries, she had agility on her side. Baby Jane was like a buffalo, too big and cumbersome to negotiate any artistic moves.

Alice jolted forward jabbing the shank at Baby Jane and diving back before it had a chance to connect. Baby Jane stumbled while trying to grab Alice's wrist. Alice laughed. The bigger woman was too predictable – too damn easy to trick. Repeating the movement twice in quick succession, Alice sniggered as Jane stumbled to one side and then the other trying to keep up with her.

God I could do this forever!

Lulu's voice came from the edge of the circle, 'Get it done Al. You've not got long. The girls can only keep the officers busy for so long. Just do it.

Grinning, enjoying the power seep through her body as Baby Jane flailed around the circle, the jeers from the spectators egged Alice on. This was the first time that Alice had been in control for a long time. She was desperate to savour it, but on the other hand she was aware of how many favours Lulu had cashed in in order to make this happen. Time to get it done.

Alice dived forward and Baby Jane, anticipating a repeat of Alice's earlier move, over extended her arm. Alice kept going and dived up close to her, her body hammering into the bigger woman. Jane, momentarily wrong footed, spun round but Alice was on her. She grabbed her, spun her round and yanked her arm up her back till the woman was yelping in rage as much as pain.

'Guess what bitch? Your time has come.'

Alice sliced the home-made knife down Jane's sweaty T-shirt, uncaring whether she nicked the flab that was concealed beneath or not. The woman's breasts swung heavy and pendulous in the air and Alice grabbed one. Holding it in one hand, her small hand unable to circle it fully, she pulled the shiv up.

Jane roared, and as Alice let her crash onto the floor, she grabbed her bloody breast. But Alice wasn't done. She stood over the woman, straddling her body and with the Shiv pressed under Jane's chin, she said,

'Open. Fucking open.'

Baby Jane shook her head, and Alice pressed harder. 'Open.

Baby Jane hesitated, her gaze fixed on Alice. For ten seconds they locked eyes until, as Alice increased the pressure on the shiv, Jane looked away and opened her mouth. Alice rammed the nipple in. Her eyes flashing, sweat dotting her forehead, Alice pressed the shiv a little harder, under the other woman's chin. 'Fucking swallow.'

Gipping, Baby Jane shook her head, but Alice held her nose with one hand the other over her mouth. It was only then that Alice became aware that some of the other women were holding Jane's limbs down. Jane threw her head from side to side, making mewling noises, like a trapped cat.

Alice leaned down and spoke in her ear. 'Do it. Just do it. I *know* you can – you've done it before.'

Jane went limp beneath her and under her hand, Alice felt the big woman chew, then swallow, gipping as she did so. Alice kept her hand planted firmly on her mouth till she was sure it was done.

Tears sprung from Jane's eyes and rolled down her cheek. Alice didn't care. She removed her hand and, her voice cold, said, 'Open.'

She checked Jane's mouth before pushing herself off the heap of flab that lay whimpering beneath her. She looked around for the shiv, but it was gone. She stuck her hand in Jane's jogger trousers pocket and frisked her. Happy with her find she kicked Jane in the side and turned away.

'Quick.' The sound was an urgent hiss. Alice stood up and walked back to her table. Lulu pushed an oversized sweatshirt at her. 'Cover up.'

By the time the prison officers came over, Baby Jane was beginning to sit up, pulling her ruined T-shirt around her bloodied breast and claiming to have seen nothing.

One of the officers stared at Alice as she escorted a weeping Baby Jane from the dining hall, but Alice kept chewing her toast chatting to Lulu as if she hadn't even noticed the skirmish in the corner. She'd done the necessary and that was that.

Chapter 57

The next hour was a blur to Gus. The SCO19s stormed the farmhouse, and within half an hour an air ambulance was landing in the field at the back. Lewis Gore had a very faint pulse and Gus hoped he'd survive this. Daniel had fallen into a fitful doze and kept mumbling Izzie's name. Gus sighed. He'd be the one to tell the man he'd lost his fiancée and he wasn't looking forward to this. However, on the plus side, at least Gabriella would be relieved to have her brother back. The two injured men were stretchered out into the cold daylight air, making use of the temporary reprieve in the blizzard.

The younger brother stood quietly as he was cautioned and cuffed. After Gus had been extricated from under Furkan's body, Vulcan had all but collapsed into one of the armchairs, his right leg jiggling up and down. He'd alternated between casting furtive glances at his brother's corpse and wiping his fingers across his eyes and down his face. Gus understood how he felt. Killing someone you love is not easy to come to terms with – Gus had first-hand experience of that.

One of the SCO19 team had applied a tourniquet around Gus' leg, but still he'd lost a lot of blood – *another pair of jeans lost!* Movement around the farmhouse kept coming in and out of focus and the faint nausea every time he moved his head made him stay still. He was relieved when a paramedic appeared in the living room and got to work cleaning his wound and administering morphine.

Next time Gus looked up, it was to see Nancy enter the room bundled up in her winter coat with a scarf wrapped round her neck. 'How the hell did you get here?'

'Helicopter.' Nancy's tone was muffled behind her scarf. 'The blizzard's abated a bit, so I hitched a lift with the paramedics. They'll airlift you out in a bit.'

Gus had never been so pleased to see a familiar face, 'Gore?'

Nancy shrugged. 'Not sure. They've taken him and Daniel Farrier to Manchester General. Doesn't look good though.'

Gus winced as the paramedic rolled him onto a stretcher. 'Daniel?'

'Oh, he'll probably live. Might lose a couple of fingers in the process though. Paramedics say they only just got to him in time.' She leaned closer to Gus and spoke in a quiet voice. 'You messed up here. You shouldn't have blundered in on your own with Gore. Totally unacceptable and irresponsible *and*, if my memory serves me right, you ignored a direct order.' She glared at him and it was as if her disappointment sparked off a chain reaction that increased the pain generated by each of his wounds. Having been on the receiving end of Nancy's wrath before now, Gus took the path of least resistance and only nodded. What else could he do? She was right. All of this was his fault.

Gus couldn't quite decipher if her humph was of disgust or acceptance of his unspoken apology, so he waited – trying not to focus on the army of ants that seemed to be nipping and pulling at every injury he'd obtained.

'I've kept this as low key as I can – although, make no mistake, there will be a full and rigorous official investigation,' she lowered her voice to a whisper and spoke in his ear. 'The substance of your defence will no doubt be the extreme time pressure to rescue Daniel Farrier, the extraordinary weather conditions and your belief that the SCO19s would – being an elite organisation with access to state-of-the-art technology as opposed to a crappy Volvo – be on site before you. Am I clear?'

'Yes Ma'am.' Gus was under no illusions that anything short of professional formality would not be tolerated at this point.

'Right,' Nancy cleared her throat and continued. 'I want to give you the chance to talk to Daniel Farrier before MI6 butt in. Can't stand the thought of those arrogant suits strutting all over our investigation. We've done the ground work, we should see it through. Think you'll be up for it or should I step in?'

Gus smiled. 'What do you think? Both Farrier and the Turk are mine. Do whatever you do to keep the spooks away from them. I want first dibs. Just need to get this scratch stitched and I'll be right.' He glanced down at his leg and, as the morphine began to kick in, realised just how much pain he'd been in.

'Good job you're being taken to Manchester General too. Nothing more natural than you wanting to visit your brother-in-law.'

Gus choked down the word 'ex' and just smiled. Nancy was right, he had a ready-made excuse to be near Daniel when he was fit to speak. He just hoped the spooks didn't descend before he was cleared and ready to go.

'What about Vulcan?'

Nancy winked, 'I pulled in a few favours after expressing my disappointment with the SCO19s about you and Gore being left on your own in the cold. We've taken him to a station in Ashton-Under-Lyne, but for some reason the paperwork has been delayed. You need to get sorted and out of the hospital ASAP.'

What the hell? So much for her concern over his injuries and his well-being. Clearly this was his punishment for fucking up. On the other hand, he was damn lucky Nancy was still prepared to back him after his huge cock-up.

As Nancy turned to speak to the paramedics, he grabbed her arm, 'Keep me updated on Gore.'

Nancy patted his hand. 'I will, but you need to own your mistakes, Gus. I understand that Gore would have been as gung-ho as you, but *you* are the senior officer and *you* need to put the safety of your team first.'

Nancy was right, he'd been an arse and if Gore died he'd never forgive himself. What was wrong with him? He couldn't make a good decision if his life depended on it. First Alice and now this travesty. He needed to pull it back. Get his butt in gear and tie this case up tight.

Chapter 58

'Ace bloody space man.' His PC had pinged and within ten second Compo had jumped to his feet, wiggling his arse in a parody of a constipated chicken, then raised his hand in front of Taffy's face in expectation of a high five.

Taffy slouched in Compo's armchair, his coat covering him like a blanket, his legs propped up on the coffee table was awakened by Compo's racket. He blinked a couple of times to get his bearings and jumped to his feet, ignoring his friend's proffered hand. 'What you got, Comps?'

Compo, arms extended before him, fists clenched, moved them in a clockwise circular motion with his hips making a similar movement, and proceeded to chant, 'Who's got the goods? Compo's got the goods. Who's got the goods? Compo's got the goods.'

Grinning, Taffy mimicked Compo's crazy dance for a minute and repeated his earlier question, 'What you got?'

Compo dropped his arms and falling back onto his computer chair, moved the mouse and grinning said, 'Ta da!'

Taffy looked at the screen, which looked similar to the one they'd witnessed earlier. 'What's it mean?'

'JayRay's come up trumps. They got CCTV footage from inside Kennedy's solicitors office dated *before* he went into his coma as well as afterwards. Want to see?'

Before Taffy could reply, Compo pressed play and they were transported once more into Russell Allison-Hinton's opulent office. Compo tapped the screen, his fingertip landing on the face of a handsome, well-built man. 'That's Sean Kennedy.'

Taffy leaned in for a better look. 'You're right. God, who'd have believed it?'

Compo flicked the screen right where Kennedy's face was, 'Still think he looks a sleazy bastard. Can't believe Alice fell for him.' He flicked the screen again, 'Smarmy bastard.' With a last glower at Kennedy he turned to Taffy, 'Seems this solicitor records all his meetings and uploads them to a server between Uzbekistan and Romania after sending it bouncing round the world.'

'And this helps us how?'

'Because, my guy implemented a deep search for various key words – two of them being 'Alice' and 'Cooper' – and it threw this up.' Compo cracked his fingers together. It was this sort of stuff that made him love his job. 'Listen.'

Sean Kennedy:	'Well?'
Allison – Hinton:	'It's all set up. Big H is on side. You finish her off and he'll back your self-defence plea. It'll all lead back to Cooper and you can be off sunning it in Barbados.'
Sean Kennedy.	'Shame really. Our DC Alice Cooper was a good lay.' He shrugged, a huge grin covering his face 'Hey ho. That's life. There'll be plenty more where she came from.' He winked, 'I'll just make sure I get shiggy shiggy with her tonight – a final date.'

Compo paused the recording, 'See the time date?'

Taffy nodded. 'The day before the raid that ended with Kennedy in a coma and Alice in pieces.'

Compo prodded himself in the chest. 'Then we put her back together again. Gus and the team.'

Taffy looked at the screen and then at Compo, 'It's really good Comps. It implicates Sean Kennedy and his solicitor in the whole drug and weapon's trafficking and might even clear Alice of all wrong doing. But…' he shrugged, 'how can we use it to clear her name when we got it illegally?'

Compo stood up and grabbed sheaves of paper from the printer behind Taffy. 'These are only a few of the documents showing a paper trail between this solicitor and Kennedy extending as far as Barbados. The rest I've encrypted and saved to the cloud, but there's more than enough evidence there to show that Sean Kennedy planned all of this and implicated Alice on purpose.'

Taffy skimmed through the documents, his grin widening as he read more and more. He looked at Compo. 'But Comps this is all fine and well, but we still got it illegally. We can't use it.'

Compo grinned, 'No you're right, *we* can't, but if someone was to anonymously send an encrypted file with all this information to the prosecution and Alice's defence team, then well… it would be grounds for a search warrant, wouldn't it? Alice is coming home.'

Taffy crashed the heel of his hand against his forehead, 'Why the hell didn't I think of that, Comps. Genius, pure bloody genius.'

Compo stuffed some tortillas in his mouth as Taffy reached for his mobile. 'Time to share the good news with Gus, eh?'

When the phone was answered, Taffy spoke in a rush. 'Oh, it's you Ma'am. Got good news. We got the bastard – Kennedy – we got him, or should I say Comps did. Alice is coming home. She's innocent.'

He listened for a minute frowning, 'Hospital? … Manchester? … Dead?'

Compo stopped, handful of tortillas half way to his mouth. His heart plummeted. What had happened to Gus? They'd only just cleared Alice's name and now Gus was dead.

Before Taffy had a chance to speak, Compo fell backwards into his chair and slammed a can of coke at the wall. Half empty, its contents fizzed and spurted onto the paintwork as the can fell to the ground. 'He's dead?'

Taffy grabbed Compo by the shoulders and shook him. 'Not Gus, idiot. Gus is fine – well not exactly fine – he's been stabbed, but he'll be okay. No, it's one of Daniel Farrier's kidnappers who's dead. Not Gus.'

Compo, blinked, swallowed and then smiled. 'Not Gus?'

'Uh, Uh, definitely *not* Gus'

Thinking that his heart would explode, Compo placed his heel on the floor and did a wheelie on his chair. 'Fuckin bossed it Taffs! Fuckin bossed it.'

Chapter 59

I t had taken hours to get from Epsom to Harrow and by the time they parked up, Kennedy was more than ready to slit the driver's throat. The idiot had talked no-stop for the entire journey and Kennedy had had about enough. However, they had come to an agreement. Nothing like a little avarice to break a man's moral compass and Wasyl was nothing if not avaricious. An hour ago, Sean had phoned through and asked Allison-Hinton to meet him at his office. Sleazy stuck up bastard had tried to fob him off using the weather as an excuse, but Kennedy was having none of it. A gentle reminder that he knew where his kids went to school and where his wife played tennis was enough to have old Allison-Hinton grabbing his coat and hot-footing it to his offices.

From the car, Sean could see a faint light through the frosted glass and was glad that he wouldn't have to wait for the solicitor. He swung open the back door and was relieved when Wasyl pushed open the driver's door and helped him to his feet. Tosser probably wanted a tip – well he could sing for it. No way was he getting any more than what they'd agreed. Sean stood for a moment balancing against the door. His chest was tight and every breath of cold air he took made it crackle. His limbs protested every time he tried to move them and the thought of the short walk to the entrance was enough to make him sweat. His phlegmy cough rattled like a snake and as he spluttered red globules landed on the pristine snow. He wiped the back of his hand over his mouth and tried to pull his coat up around his ears. It was a futile gesture because the wind had picked up again and there was no escape from it.

'Help.' The word was ripped from his mouth by the wind and transported away like a fading echo. He tried again, his throat rasping with the effort. 'Help.'

This time the driver heard and moved closer. Sean rested his hand on the man's arm and step-by-arduous-step, they approached the door. His clumsy feet – like blocks of ice – upset his balance, but the weedy driver was stronger than he looked and, after what seemed like an age, he deposited Sean on the doorstep.

The office wasn't locked, so Sean pushed the door open. 'Wait here.' The two words took all the effort he had left and he was rewarded by a coughing fit that threatened to deposit his lungs on the carpet of Russell Alison-Hinton's reception area.

Dragging one foot at a time, Kennedy stumbled in, the warmth from the fan heater above the door adding to his existing temperature and making sweat gather across his upper lip. Allison-Hinton's office door was closed, but he was expecting Sean. What he wasn't expecting was the little gift Sean had for him. Forcing himself to traverse the short area from the reception to the solicitor's closed office door, Kennedy picked his way towards it. Once there, he leaned on it, using the time to regain his breath before twisting the knob and entering.

The light was almost blinding after the subdued shadowy dim lights from the reception. Sean blinked, trying to clear the little flashes of yellow and red that blighted his vison. Allison-Hinton was sitting behind his desk, his face taut and angry. *Oh, so that's how you want to play it?* Sean didn't care. He was here for one reason only – Allison-Hinton's petty strops were irrelevant.

Kennedy made his way to the chair opposite the desk and fell into it.

'For God's sake, what's happened to you?' Allison- Hinton's voice had an edge of distaste to it and Sean wanted to smack him for it.

'You fucked up.'

The solicitor tutted. 'You came here to tell me *that*?'

'No' said Sean, 'I came here to give you something.'

'Oh yes, what? More orders to do your dirty work for you or rather to pay someone else to do it.'

Sean smiled. *Old Russell's being a bit bolshie all of a sudden when in actual fact he should be shitting his posh pants.* 'Oh, you underestimate me, Russell. No more orders. Just here to terminate our relationship – to absolve you of all responsibility for my affairs.'

Hinton-Allison's mouth twitched. 'Really? Found someone better have you?'

Sean shrugged, his throat was dry 'Something like that. Can I have some water please?'

Allison-Hinton sighed, but he reached over and filled a glass from the crystal decanter that stood on a tray on his desk. He stood and circled the desk, arm extended. As he approached, his mouth screwed up and he placed his other hand over his mouth, 'Good God you stink, Kennedy. Like garbage or worse. Where have you been?'

'You wouldn't want to know, Russell. Believe me, you wouldn't.' He covered his mouth with one hand and began to cough, as if his insides were going to erupt onto the carpet. His entire body wracked from the inside out and he thought his bones were going to splinter into a million pieces.

Allison-Hinton, seemingly managing to overcome his distaste, moved to Kennedy's side and bent over, pushing the glass of water towards him. 'For God's sake, here drink this.'

Kennedy stopped coughing and his arm snaked out, his fingers gripping Allison-Hinton's wrist in a pincer hold with a strength that his frail frame belied. Before the solicitor had the chance to pull away, Kennedy yanked him closer and with a swift upper jab, rammed the knife he had concealed by his side right into the other man's heart.

Spent now, Kennedy fell back against the soft cushions, trying to catch his breath. His entire body was on fire, shaking and aching. Sweat wafted up to his nostrils, mixed with something else, something more feral. He glanced down at the floor where Allison-Hinton lay, his hands cupping the stiletto blade that protruded from his chest. A balloon of ruby red expanded across the cream carpet. Sean found it quite beautiful as it spread, pinkish tinged at the outer edge progressing to a deeper robust hue as it reached the body. The solicitor's breathing was fragmented, his eyes fluttering, making Sean think of that saying about butterfly wings in the rainforests. 'I don't suffer fools gladly, Russell. You should have known that.'

Russell's eyes opened and red bubbles gathered at the corner of his mouth. 'You're fucked, Kennedy.'

Kennedy laughed, 'No, Russell, old boy – on the contrary, it's you who's fucked.'

The door opened, and assuming it was his driver, Kennedy said, 'Help me up.' A gasp and a waft of Dolce and Gabanna displaced both his body odour and the abattoir smell coming from Allison-Hinton. He tilted his head till he could see the receptionist, fingers over her mouth, wide eyes latched onto the solicitor's bleeding body. 'Well, hallo there.'

She retched and tried to back away. But seconds later she was pushed in front of Sean, her face pale, her hands shaking. Sean grinned. *This was an unexpected bonus.* He gestured for the driver to release her. *Not like she had anywhere to run to.* She had her tits out again today and Sean fleetingly wondered if she had a thing going with Old Russell boy – *not any fucking more!*

Her eyes were once more pinned to her boss' body, her chesty gasps making her tits heave like some voluptuous silent movie heroine. The effort it had taken to deal with Allison-Hinton swept over Sean and his limbs began to shake. An annoying tic fluttered by his eye and his vision blurred. All he wanted was to be out of here, even if it meant another struggle with The Beast from the East. He sighed and, voice hoarse, said. 'Lock her in the boot and then come back for me.'

The driver dragged her from the room, stumbling on her high heels, leaving Kennedy alone. He closed his eyes. His body was giving up on him. He couldn't breathe, his temperature was sky high – *pneumonia?* The only thing he had left to do now, was to make sure Cooper was dealt with. When they got away from here he'd put out a few feelers, get things set up.

The door opened again and Sean shuddered. The thought of moving from his comfy seat was almost too much, but he had to do it. Had to finish this. A flurry of activity, bodies rushing into the room, voices. 'Clear!'

'Clear!'

Someone dressed all in black was kneeling beside Allison-Hinton.

'Slight pulse.'

'…paramedics.'

'Sean Kennedy we are arresting you for…'

He blinked up at the officer towering over him, trying to make sense of what had happened. How could they have got here? How did they know what he'd done? But wait they weren't arresting him for the solicitor – not yet anyway. They were banging on about subverting the course of justice, implicating a police officer, drugs, weapons.

A triumphant shout from another officer 'Got it! Just like we were told. Everything's recorded. Just need to unencrypt it.'

The officer who was reading him his rights grinned, 'Looks like we've got you, with bells on, Kennedy.' To another officer, 'Get the paramedics in here. Don't want this fucker dying on us, do we?'

Chapter 60

11:30 Manchester General

'Mum, I'm fine, really. Just a scratch.' Gus held the phone away from his ear and grimaced at Nancy, 'Why'd you have to tell them, Nance?'

Nancy splayed her hands before her, 'Right, like I was going to flirt with the wrath of your mum. She'd have killed me if I hadn't told her. Just be thankful, I didn't spill the beans 'till *after* we'd rescued you.'

Gus held the phone closer to his ear. His mum was still scolding him, words like 'irresponsible', 'waiting for back-up', 'letting the professionals deal with these situations' were fired at him in his mother's staccato tones. The only blessing was that at least he didn't have to face her ire in person. Perhaps by the time he got back to Bradford, she'd have calmed down. This was an unlikely possibility. His mum was nothing if not tenacious and Gus had really pissed her off this time. Hell, she seemed to think he should update her every time he took the slightest risk. If it were up to her, he'd not be able to shave without giving her a three-day warning so she could hover with the Band Aid in hand.

Christ, he was a grown man, not a damn kid. And as for 'let the professionals do it'? What the hell did she think he was, if not a professional? Some bloody randomer plucked off the street to apprehend Britain's most nefarious killers? Bloody cheek. Yes, he was sorry he'd upset her, sorry he'd worried her. But no damn way was she going to cocoon him in bloody cotton wool. He'd a job to do and do it he would – but now wasn't the time to tell her that. So, he did the only thing he could – he lied. 'Got to go mum, the doctor wants to check over my wound before we go.'

Nancy grinned and shook her finger back and forth, 'Naughty, naughty, Gus.'

He sighed, 'Don't you dare tell her I lied – she's having enough of a go at me without you adding anymore ammunition.'

She handed him a can of Irn Bru, 'As if. I'm not a snitch.'

Gus raised his eyebrows but refrained from answering. 'Any word on Gore?'

'Not looking good, swelling on the brain. He's in theatre now.'

Gus pulled the crutches he'd been given towards him. This was all on him. He'd agreed to co-opt Gore onto the team and then dragged him all the way to Manchester. His mum was right about that. He should have left it to the SCO19s. The end result would probably have been the same but Gore wouldn't be in theatre and he wouldn't be on crutches. Shit, why did he always make these bad calls?

As if sensing Gus' mood, Nancy reached out and stopped him from standing up. 'It's not your fault Gus. If you and Gore hadn't gone to the farmhouse, Daniel may well have already been killed and who knows how many of our lot the Turks would have taken down.'

Gus brushed her hand off and pushed himself to his feet, flinching a little as the stitches across his thigh pulled. *More damn battle scars to add to his existing collection.* 'Going to see Daniel. Got to break the news about Izzie and I want to do it before Gabriella turns up.'

Nancy snorted, 'We know her track record at offering bedside support, Gus. Don't expect her to roll up anytime soon.'

Gus grinned. Nancy was referring to a couple of years earlier when he'd been fighting for his life in Bradford Royal Infirmary.

Gabriella had chosen that moment to desert him. 'Clearly, she thinks more highly of her brother than she ever did of me, because she and Katie have managed to get themselves on a flight from Dublin to Manchester. Weather depending, they should be taking off...' he glanced at his watch, 'now-ish.'

Nancy fell into step behind him as he swung his injured leg along the corridor to the ward's exit. 'I already told Daniel, Gus.'

He stopped, and spun round to face her, 'What the hell, Nance. Why did you do that? He deserved to hear it from me. I'm the SIO.'

'Yes, I know that. However, you're also his brother-in-law,'

As Gus murmured 'ex' under his breath, she wafted her hand at him, 'Yes, yes, I know – ex. But the fact remains that however tenuously you're related, he needs someone to lean on. Someone a little divorced from that initial announcement. Someone he won't forever associate with the worst possible moment of his life.'

With an abrupt nod, Gus continued to walk. Nancy was right and he should thank her for that – but maybe not right now. Instead he posed a question. 'How did he take it?'

Nancy frowned, 'Well, to be honest, better than I expected. If I didn't know otherwise I could have assumed he already knew.' She shrugged, 'Maybe he'd worked it out. Maybe I just confirmed his worst fears.'

'Didn't he seem upset?'

Again Nancy hesitated, 'Upset – no – not upset. I wouldn't say he was upset exactly. Buy hey – everyone handles grief in their own way. Just because he didn't react then doesn't mean he won't react later. Seeing Gabriella might push him over the edge.' She lowered her voice and muttered, 'I know it would me.'

Gus snorted. 'Me too – I'm hoping she'll be too wrapped up in mollycoddling Daniel to give me any grief.'

The two of them sniggered. Gus said, 'Physically, how's he doing?'

'The doctors seem pleased. He's responding to antibiotics. They're removing two fingers but have been able to save his toes. He's not out of the woods but we got to him in time.'

As they approached the side ward where Daniel was, Gus lowered his voice, 'Any word on the Kennedy situation?'

'No, not yet. I'll let you know as soon as I hear more. They were supposed to be raiding the solicitor's this morning.' She tapped her toe on the floor. 'Bit of news from Stanton though.'

Gus eyes' raked Nancy's face. He could tell that the news wasn't good and he braced himself for a body blow. 'Alice? She's back there?'

Nancy chewed on her lower lip and Gus wanted to shake her.

Gus slammed his palm onto the wall, causing a passing registrar to stare at him, before hurrying along, no doubt to alert security. How much more could Alice take? Not only had she been attacked repeatedly, but he'd forsaken her. It had taken Compo to make him waken up. 'Bastards. So she's back in Stanton?' It was easier to use the prison's name than the word prison – made it seem less permanent somehow. 'Have they got her in solitary – guarding her? What precautions are they taking?' His heart had sped up and the anticipation exacerbated the low-level headache that had skulked behind his eyes for the past few hours.

'She wanted to go back to her old cell with her old cellmate. Was adamant. Truth is, Bernadette – her solicitor – is worried about her. She's been uncommunicative, refuses to testify against the rapist or talk. But then…'

Gus' heart sank. There was more. 'Go on.'

She sighed. 'There was some sort of riot, this morning.'

Gus heart thumped against his chest. 'And…'

'The woman, Baby Jane Inflictor of Pain, they call her. The one who attacked Alice in the shower …'

'Say it how it was Nancy.' Gus' tone was angry, 'You mean the animal who bit off her nipple and swallowed it before stabbing her – that one?'

'Yes, that one. Well, seems that, during the riot she was attacked. They're thinking the riot was a distraction. A tactic to get the officers out of the dining area. She was found with her nipple sliced off. Seems she was forced to swallow it.'

For long seconds Gus didn't react, then 'aw Alice.' His cry was strangled in his throat.

Nancy shook her head. 'Seems there's a marked absence of witnesses. Cameras were covered with margarine and nobody, not even Baby Jane, is talking. They're still investigating so even when they dot the 'I's and cross the 'T's, it'll be a few days before she can be released.

Tone hard, Gus turned to the door of Daniel's room and said, 'Well let's hope they keep schtum. She needs to be out of there.' As Nancy made to follow him into Daniel's room, he shook his head. 'I've got this Nance. Go for a coffee, I'll meet you there later.'

The hospital radio played softly in the background when Gus stepped into the room. Daniel was dozing. Strapped up to an intravenous drip, and attached to various monitors that emitted a series of slow steady beats, he looked marginally better than he had last time Gus had seen him. Gus made his way over to the chair by the side of his bed and collapsed onto it. It wasn't comfortable but it was still a welcome respite for his leg, which was throbbing now he'd started to use it.

'Storm Emma will descend and the region will be thrown into further turmoil.'

Further turmoil? Gus didn't think there could be any worse turmoil than what had occurred over the last twelve hours.

As he sat, Gus wondered what his reaction would be if he was the one lying in a hospital bed being told that Patti had been brutally killed. How did you even begin to get over that? He suspected he'd be in bits. He remembered how he'd been when he thought he'd lost his mother last year.

'Winds of over eighty miles per hour are forecast and combined with more snow and freezing showers, conditions will be treacherous throughout Rochdale and Tameside.'

He definitely remembered the range of emotions that fired through his mind, keeping him awake for months after Greg had died. He remembered Billy's little face as Gus had tried to staunch the bleeding and he would never forget Becky, with the knife juddering from her eye. None of these images were going anywhere anytime soon and he suspected Daniel would have a fair few of his own to haunt him.

'... Red alert throughout the country. Emergency services on standby...'

Apart from genuinely wanting to make sure Daniel was okay, Gus was determined to get as much information out of him as he could regarding the information found on Izzie's USB. He was sure that the fact Daniel was MI6 was not coincidental and he wanted to get to the bottom of it. According to Mickey, who'd taken over that side of the investigation, Interpol were arresting Sevket Abaci. Gus didn't expect to be privy to the outcome of that aspect of the investigation and that pissed him off. He liked closure.

Trying to breathe through his mouth so as to avoid the clinical hospital smell, Gus settled down and tried to push his own memories away. He still had to interview the remaining Turkish brother and he wanted to do that before MI6 swung their way up North. He wanted to touch base with Compo and Taffy and most of all he wanted to get down to Epsom to see Alice.

A slight cough alerted him to the fact that Daniel was waking up. 'Hi Daniel. It's me, Gus. Gabriella's on her way. She'll hopefully touch down before the really bad weather hits us.'

Daniel grimaced. 'Can't you put her off, Gus? Can't deal with her right now.'

Gus grinned. 'I know what you mean, but it'd take a better man than me to stop her. Just give in to it. That's all I can advise.'

Silence, bar the sound of Dolly Parton pleading with some lass called Jolene drifting from the hospital radio station, prevailed for a while. Gus eventually broke the quiet. 'Sorry about Izzie.'

Daniel nodded, his face betraying no emotion.

'Did you know she was onto her boss, Daniel?'

The other man shook his head, 'No I didn't – look do we need to do this right now? I'm knackered.'

Gus hardened his voice, 'Look, you're MI6. *You* know the score. We need to get on this quick. We need to know what you know. Sure, it looks like the Turks killed Izzie, but we need to know who gave the orders and why. We need to know who was pulling their strings. Seems like whoever it was they were going to sell it to the highest bidder. We need to know who.'

Daniel closed his eyes and shook his head, 'Can't do it now, Gus. Just can't. Truth is I don't know anything.'

'Are you telling me you weren't in Cyprus keeping an eye on that bio-weapons research?'

Daniel shrugged. 'Confidential.'

'Fuck confidential. This is your fiancée we're talking about. She was killed because of what she'd found out.'

Daniel lifted his hand and waved it, 'Nothing to add, Gus. I don't know anything.'

Gus looked at the man for a moment longer. How the hell could he not want to share what he knew? His fiancée had been killed because she'd stumbled upon a new bio-weapon her boss was developing and Daniel was sitting back. This wasn't the attitude he expected from a spook – James fucking Bond, Daniel most definitely was not. Seething, he stood. 'I'll be back, and Daniel, you better be prepared to talk, okay?'

Daniel smiled, his voice lazy, 'Or what, Gus? Or what?'

Chapter 61

'So, Alice – the upshot is that both your legal team *and* the prosecution were sent a whole barrage of evidence that incriminated Sean Kennedy, not only in the drugs and weapons trafficking that you were incriminated in, but also in setting-up the false trail that led to you.'

Bernie looked at Alice, her smile fading from her lips as Alice continued to look straight ahead. Since first meeting her client before Christmas, Alice had changed. The soft contours of her face had become sharp angles. Her body, thin before, had taken on an edgy hardness that spoke of a relentless prison gym routine. However, it was her eyes that broke Bernie's heart. Gone were the spirited flashes of humour that had once typified the woman. Now they were replaced by a dullness that spoke of a soul broken in two. Guarded and expressionless, Alice Cooper no longer let anyone in. She lay in the bowel of a fortress, friendless and alone. Her body primed to react to threat, her heart inured to kindness.

'You understand what this means, don't you?'

Alice gave a quick nod, her expression saying *I'm not fucking thick.*

With an exaggerated sigh, Bernie pulled a folder across to her and opened it. 'Police raided a solicitor's office in Harrow earlier today and found Sean Kennedy. He had stabbed to death the solicitor, a Russell Allison-Hinton.'

A shutter fell over Alice's face but her expression revealed nothing. With a nonchalance that was surely fake, she began picking her fingernails.

'Sean Kennedy has been admitted to hospital with suspected pneumonia. He has been charged with all of the offences, but it's touch and go whether he will live.'

Alice snorted, her face breaking into a fleeting humourless grin that said 'typical fucking Sean, even at the last gasp he manages to get away with it.'

Bernie sighed again, 'Do you understand all of this Alice?'

Alice nodded.

'Look, if you're not going to speak, there's no point in my staying. You'll be released as soon as the prison riot investigation is finished and all the paperwork is collated. Is there anything you need?'

Alice lifted her head, 'My parents?'

Bernie looked down, 'Evidence was found that Sean Kennedy and his solicitor had contracted surveillance on your parents, Alice. Interpol found the two men contracted with this surveillance. Their throats had been slit outside your parents' house. We are still looking for your parents.'

Something glimmered in Alice's eyes for a mere nano-second and her shoulders seemed to relax. Bernie frowned. *What was that all about?* She reached over and touched the other woman's arm, 'Are you okay, Alice? Really okay?'

Alice lifted her chin and looked straight at her solicitor, 'Why wouldn't I be?'

Chapter 62

12:30 Greater Manchester police, Ashton-Under-Lyne

With Nancy by his side, Gus hobbled through the doors of the red brick police station on Manchester Road. It was very different from The Fort, being large and sprawling, with a newer feel to it – all clinical and bleach. Gus immediately missed the warm sandstone building he was familiar with, its tones of beer overlaid with samosas and bacon with an undernote of yuck. Yeah, The Fort was a monstrosity in the heart of Manningham, but it was *his* monstrosity. Its very presence in the heart of the inner city forced it and its occupants to prove themselves to the communities they represented.

This station, by contrast, felt less homely – less Bradford. Too many people in crisp shirts smelling of fabric conditioner and Christian Dior fragrances. The desk officer was too smart – all pens and forms and filing cabinets. Gus would have welcomed Hardeep's gruff kindness right now – his not so gentle teasing and his pen stuck behind his ear under his turban. This guy looked like a spike up his arse would elicit nothing more than a stern frown. *Bet they didn't have rough sleepers camping on their doorstep, not even in these conditions.* They probably wouldn't invite said rough sleepers in for a warm shower and shelter till they could sort out their meds either. Gus had received a text earlier from Hardeep informing him that Jerry and Dave had been taken in by the Franciscan monks in Manningham and were suitably medicated. At least that was good news.

Nancy went up to the desk where a taciturn officer looked at their details, scoured their faces as if to check they weren't on Manchester's most wanted list and buzzed them through. They were met by Haris – one of the SCO19 officers from the farmhouse who grinned when he saw Gus on crutches. 'Patch you up okay on this side of the Pennines, did they?'

Gus smiled back, 'Yeah they didn't hold my being a Yorkshire lad against me. The Turk talking yet?'

Falling into step beside Gus and Nancy, Haris led them along a long corridor with doors filtering off into larger rooms that held all the hustle and bustle of an active police station. 'Says he'll only speak to you. Mind you, we ran his prints through IAFIS and got a hit. Our man is one Vulcan Narkis. His brother is Furkan Narkis. Both have records for international political and commercial espionage stuff, but not that of the subtle variety. Seems the older brother Vulcan is the leader. Any ideas what made the younger one snap and kill his brother? He's good to go. Had the medics check him over. He's bruised and on pain relief but other than that he's as right as rain.'

Gus shrugged. 'Guess Vulcan just got fed up with being his brother's punch bag.'

'Right, he's in here. Didn't want a solicitor, so he's on his own with one of the uniforms for now. I'll watch from in here but he's all yours. When the weather lets up, he can be transported to Bradford.' Gus smiled his thanks and Nancy opened the door.

Vulcan looked wan, faint acne scars spread across his forehead and on his cheeks. An empty sandwich wrapper, tuna, no mayo, discarded on the table beside him.

Gus, happy to relieve the pressure off his leg, sat down opposite him, depositing his crutches on the floor by his side, with Nancy to his left. 'You okay? Been fed and watered, I see.'

Vulcan looked at the wrappers that Gus pointed to and nodded once. His fingers toyed with a disposable cup that he was systematically ripping apart. His leg drummed on the floor and Gus had to resist the urge to reach out a hand and take the cup from the man.

Nancy, as agreed earlier, leaned back and took an observational role whilst Gus went through the preliminaries regarding who was present and so on. Tape recorder on, Gus leaned forward and rested his arm on the table wishing his head didn't pound so badly.

'Tell me about Izzie Dimou.'

Vulcan tossed the mangled cup on the table and inhaled deeply. 'She is dead.'

Gus kept his tone level and smiled, 'Tell me something I don't know. You said you would only speak to me, so why don't you do just that. It'll be better for you if you do.'

'We were hired to steal her from Romanians.'

Gus nodded, 'The ones who broke into her house?'

Vulcan nodded, 'Yes, we were following them. You say keeping tabs, I think? Jordan Beaumont hired Romanians to capture girl. We were hired to take her from them.'

'Why?'

Vulcan shrugged, 'She had information. Our boss wanted it.'

Although he already suspected what information Izzie had, Gus wanted it on tape, 'What information did Izzie Dimou have?'

'I don't know, it was something worth lot of money to the Syrians and the Russians.' He shrugged, 'Maybe even the Afghanis too. We were going to get paid five hundred thousand.' He looked to the side, 'Could have retired on that, me and Furkan.'

'Where did Izzie get this very valuable information?'

'You haven't worked that out? You British must be slow. It was from University of Nicosia – a bio-weapon.' He tapped the side of his nose with one finger, 'but you know that already, no?'

Gus glanced at Nancy before continuing, 'What happened to the Romanians that Jordan Beaumont hired.'

Vulcan snorted, 'Guess?'

'My guess, having been on the receiving end of your brother's attention and having been told what the Romanians' injuries were, I'd say they got in your brother's way.'

Vulcan started a slow hand clap and then winced, his shoulder clearly causing some pain from when Furkan had hit it with his machete.

'And Jordan Beaumont and his family, what happened to them?'

Vulcan frowned, 'That was a mistake. Furkan let things – how you Brits say – get out of hand? We're not supposed to hurt the wife and daughter, but Furkan not stop.' Vulcan exhaled, his eyes focussing on a memory somewhere over Gus's shoulder before repeating, 'He won't stop.'

'Like he did with Izzie Dimou?' Gus was deliberately swapping his questions up. If he kept splitting the narrative he was more likely to get an honest response.

'Yes, like with Dimou. I try to stop him, but he won't and she die before we got the information we needed. That's always been Vulcan's problem. He enjoy his work too much.'

Gus grimaced. His body still ached from Furkan Narkis' enjoyment of his job and the possibility that Lewis Gore might not survive. It lay heavy with him.

'So, Furkan tortured and raped Marcia and Melissa Beaumont?'

Vulcan looked at the uniformed officer. 'Water, please.' Before turning to Gus and nodding, 'Yes. Again, I could not stop him.'

'So, where is Jordan Beaumont?'

'Saddleworth Moor – somewhere.' Vulcan shrugged. His earlier demeanour was changing. As Gus continued his questions, he sensed that the other man was becoming more sure of himself and that puzzled him. Why would Vulcan begin to get cocky? At the farmhouse he'd been nervous and agitated.

Concerned enough about his brother spiralling out of control, to kill him. *So, what had changed?*

Vulcan continued, 'Furkan left him to freeze there. Some dog walker will find him when snow goes away. I think it not far from road.' He shrugged and gave a hoarse rattling laugh that dislodged phlegm from his throat. He howked it into his mouth, chewed it round a bit and, with an exaggerated wink to Nancy, he spat it into what was left of the cup he'd been shredding earlier.

To give Nancy her due, she didn't flinch. Gus could have told the idiot that she'd seen much worse than that and wouldn't be fazed by the Turk's coarseness

With his best disinterested expression, Gus said 'Why Beaumont? What did you need from him?'

Vulcan looked at Gus as though he was thick. 'Daniel Farrier, of course. We wanted *him*. Romanians had taken him, but again Furkan was too quick to kill them and we didn't get the information we need. So, we went straight to the boss.'

'So Beaumont employed the Romanians?'

'Exactly.'

'… and you needed Izzie's information from Daniel Farrier?'

Vulcan raised his head, a huge grin splitting his bruised face in two, 'Fool. Farrier not have information. If he did none of this would happen.'

What? Gus frowned and Vulcan burst into growls of laughter, 'You British are so aptal! – stupid! You cannot see what's in front of your faces. Salaklar!'

The last word was spat at Gus, leaving him in little doubt that it was an insult. Gus took a moment to consider this information and then bent down, picked up his crutches and hobbled from the room, leaving Nancy to terminate the interview.

Chapter 63

Everyone was subdued – that was often the case after a riot. Alice was pleased to have some time to relax. Some time to reflect. Not so much on what she'd done to Baby Jane, but on what she still had to do.

All the prisoners in her wing were confined to their cells pending an investigation into the riot. *Good luck with that!* In Alice's experience it was unlikely that the screws' efforts would uncover anything incriminating and that offered her neither relief, nor regret. *At what point did I stop thinking of them as officers and start referring to them as screws? As one of them and not one of us?* She pursed her lips... hmm that was easy. It was when they became a symptom of everything she'd always railed against. When they'd shown their true colours. Made a mockery of everything she'd worked so hard for her entire adult life. Now, she was reconciled to the uncertainty her future held. As long as her parents were safe nothing else mattered.

She tried to think about Compo and Gus – to imagine them, to summon up some gratitude to them, but she just couldn't. She was dead from the inside and every thought was grey and drab. Even when she'd dealt with Baby Jane, it had been in monochrome – a series of sepia images filtering through her head with her acting them out like a robot. It didn't *touch* her. Didn't make her happy or sad, or angry. It all just 'was'.

She lay back on her lumpy cell bed, her ears tuned into the sound of her cell mate's breathing in the bunk above her. The contour of Lulu's frame curved downwards above her. Alice had some serious thinking to do. She still had to fulfil her promise to Lulu. There was no escape from that. Alice had given her word and Lulu had kept her side of the bargain. Still, it wasn't what she wanted. Not really. Well she supposed it wasn't. Right now, it was difficult for her to get a handle on what was what.

Lulu turned over, snoring lightly and Alice smiled. She owed Lulu big time, so she didn't grudge her this last request. How could she? She wouldn't be alive right now if not for Lulu and, more importantly, neither would her parents. She was ready to do what was needed. But for now, she'd wait and breathe and try to connect with something good.

She snuck her hand under the mattress and pulled out two things. The first item, she tucked up her sleeve. The second, she flattened out and studied. It was a photo of her in shorts and a t-shirt with her parents. Over the years she'd often noticed that in her friends' photos they had either crowded round their parents like one amorphous bundle of love or else been engulfed between them. In Alice's family photos, her parents were always together, holding hands or wrapped around each other, with Alice standing slightly to the side, just outside their bubble. She didn't mind that. That's just how it was. They were co-dependent and Alice wasn't. She never had been, not even as a child. That didn't mean she loved them less than, say, Gus loved his parents or, indeed, that they loved her less. It was just their way. She placed a finger to her lips and then pressed the same finger once on each of her parents' faces, before placing the photo on her pillow. Now, all she could do was wait.

14:45
The siren blasted – three long blasts to signify the end of lock-down. The wing erupted in a cacophony of catcalls and drum rolls against the doors. It had been hours and the stir crazy were rearing their heads. Cynical Alice reckoned some scientist or

other had come up with a formula to say just how long they could maintain a lock down without the stir-crazy erupting into a wholescale massacre. The scientist had clearly never been in prison. Never experienced a loss of privilege or how that could affect the brain. Some of these women were sick. Sick and desperate. Alice shrugged. Hell, maybe *she* was one of them. She shrugged again and this time accompanied it with a short laugh. No damn *maybe* about it. She *was* one of them now. After a lockdown, the incidents of suicide attempts, fights and aggression against officers increased dramatically. You'd think they'd have sussed that out by now.

Alice swung her legs off the bed and stood up. A glance at her cell mate told her that Lulu was ready.

'No getting all squirmy on me Alice, eh?'

Alice's lips quirked. 'No, not squirmy, Lulu. I don't do squirmy.'

Lulu reached out her hand and Alice took it, 'No, too much style for squirmy. Just you do it for me. Get it done and we're quits. '

Alice nodded.

'Oh, and as for Baby Jane? She got what she deserved. No thinking about that anymore. No dwelling on it like you do. Let it go.'

'It's gone Lul. Already gone.'

Lulu patted Alice's hand. 'That's my girl. Knew as soon as I clapped eyes on you that you'd do good. Just remember one thing. It's not your reactions that define you, Alice Cooper. It's what's in here.' And she lifted her fist and slammed it against her own chest. 'You get me?'

Alice squeezed her hand, 'I get ya, Lul. I get ya.'

'Well, girl, what ya waiting for? They'll be opening them doors in a minute or two.'

Now that it was time, a rush of blood flooded Alice's face. Her hands dripped sweat and her heart thumped against her chest making the wound – where her nipple had been – throb. It was time, and despite all her mental preparations, she'd never been less prepared for anything in her life.

14:55

When the female officer opened the cell, Alice lay with her back to the door, her head cocooned under her duvet.

'Get up, Cooper. You heard the siren, Get to your feet. You too Lul. Come on.'

Alice heard the clatter of the prison officer's baton against the wall. *As if the siren wasn't loud enough.* Rolling onto her back, making a show of pulling the duvet off her head, Alice glared at the officer. 'Come on Lul. Get up. Don't want to give her the excuse to insist on a strip search, do we?'

She rolled her duvet down to her toes and swung her legs round, ready to stand up. 'Phew, for fuck's sake Lul, you puked up again?'

The officer was over by the side of the bunks in seconds, pushing Alice back onto her bunk and reaching out to pull at Lulu's still figure. Lulu's arm flopped over the side of the bed, the tourniquet and needle still in place. As the officer jumped back, a bent spoon, a lighter and a plastic bag with a few white granules fell to the floor. Straight away she was on her radio calling for back-up and paramedics, her baton out and pointed in Alice's direction, 'Stay right where you are, Cooper.'

The lock-down siren blared and amidst the cat calls and jeers from the other prisoners as they were herded back into their cells, Alice jumped to her feet, ran to the toilet she'd shared with Lulu for months and vomited.

Chapter 64

Gus was getting fed-up with negotiating icy paths on his crutches. The slight thaw made it harder for him and, despite Nancy's attempts at parking as near to the kerb as possible, he still had to negotiate the equivalent of skating rinks with the added encumbrance of a throbbing thigh and two aluminium legs with well-worn rubber on the bottom. However, he'd more on his mind than the weather. Vulcan should be panicking. He'd been cowed by his brother – frightened even during their time at the farmhouse. When he'd killed him, he'd been devastated. A few hours later, without the benefit of a solicitor, he was cocky as shit. What the hell was Gus missing?

As Nancy drove, he ignored yet another call from Gabriella, who – according to the stringent voicemails she'd left – fully expected him to arrange transport between the airport and the hospital. *Who did she think she was? Queen of Manchester – surely even Gabriella knew that position was reserved for Arianna Grande?* He hit delete and ignored the incoming from Katie. For God's sake couldn't the pair of them negotiate a taxi? Not once had either of them asked about him, or Gore for that matter. No, it was all about Daniel and what he'd been through. Granted, Gabriella's brother had been through a lot, but Gore was in serious trouble and, for heaven's sake, Gus was Katie's brother. Didn't that count for anything? *First mum has a go at me and now Katie's being an idiot.*

The only member of his family who hadn't lashed out at him was his dad. That might happen yet though. Patti had been her usual understated self; concerned, relieved and calm. *Thank God for sanity!* He'd give anything to get back home to Bingo and Patti. He cursed. Going back to Bradford wasn't going to be an easy option either, not with Zarqa at his house refusing to return home – and then there were Alice's parents to deal with. Patti had told him they were at Mo's and how they'd arrived there.

Gus risked a quick glance at Nancy. He hadn't told her about *that* yet either. She was still pissed off with him for '*acting like Spiderman without the Spandex*' and he had the feeling that she wasn't going to be right happy to discover that Alice's parents had been deposited at Mo's. She'd want to know exactly *why* two dead men had been discovered outside the Cooper's Greek home after the Coopers had somehow been mysteriously deposited at Mo's. He was hoping to be able to gloss over the whole stealth operation thing but had his doubts he'd be able to. At least the death of the Coopers' stalkers couldn't be landed at Alice's doorstep. Her alibi, for once, was cast iron – or so he hoped.

One thing at a time. Daniel Farrier! Or rather *two* things – Daniel Farrier *and* Vulcan Narkis. What the hell was going on there? He pumped in a number and seconds later was connected to Compo.

'It's you, Boss. You okay? Me and Taffy were worried, like.'

Gus opened his mouth to speak, only to hear Compo relaying what must have been fairly obvious to anyone listening, 'It's Gus, Taffy. Think he's okay. No, don't know what he wants, I'll ask. Hey Gus, Taffy says are you okay and...' Muffled conversation. 'Oh yeah, what do you want?'

Nancy grinned like some coated-up, bobble-hatted Cheshire cat with a scarf covering most of her grin. Gus frowned. It was almost as if the painkillers they'd given him were hallucinogenic – it was like he'd been dropped into a winter version of *Alice in*

Wonderland with Compo cast as the Mad Hatter or landed in a parallel universe where everyone was setting out to piss him off and stand in his way. A wave of tiredness swept over him and in that instant, he wanted to just hand the phone to Nancy and say 'you deal with these lunatics, I'm going to sleep for a month. Wake me up when everything in my life is normal.' Instead, he did what he always did and took a deep breath, counted to ten and hoped that his tone would not betray his frustration. 'Compo, I'd love to chat, but truth is I'm a wee bit strapped for time. Need you to get me everything you can on Daniel Farrier and Vulcan and Furkan Narkis. Don't care how deep or how dark you need to go. I need what's beneath the surface.'

Something in his tone must have penetrated Compo's fugue of nonsense, because he responded briskly and to the point, 'Ahead of you there, Gus. Should have something for you in the next half hour. MI6 won't know what's hit them.'

Beside him, Nancy began singing 'la la la, da de da – not listening – can't hear any of this. Not happening – this conversation is not happening.'

'Eh, Comps?'

'Yeah, I'll delete this convo too. Next time use the phone I gave you for this sort of stuff, boss.' And he hung up.

Gus looked out the window, hoping that Nancy hadn't quite caught the last bit of the conversation. *No such luck!*

'So, the last thing I *didn't* hear was that you and Compo have some sort of burner phone for when you're asking him to breach protocol?'

Eyes fixed on the passing scenery as they drove through Ashton-Under-Lyne main street, Gus shrugged. 'No idea what you're talking about, Nance. None at all.' And he flicked on the radio, allowing tales of icy doom and gloom to flit over him for the rest of the journey. The Beast from the East had plagued this investigation from the start and he'd had about as much snow as he could stomach.

Nancy's phone rang and she gave him the nod to put it on speaker.

'DCI Nancy Chalmers here, with DI Gus McGuire.'

'Hi Nancy, it's Bernadette, is it okay to talk?'

Nancy smiled and mouthed 'Alice's solicitor' to Gus. *Like I don't damn well know that!*

'Got some good news for us, have you? Alice got the all clear to go?'

There was a moment's silence, which had Gus and Nancy exchanging worried looks. 'Well, there's been a development. Alice's cellmate was found dead of a heroin overdose during lockdown after the riot when Baby Jane was attacked.'

'So?' Nancy's tone was the bark of a feral dog. 'That's got nothing to do with our Alice. These things happen every week – no, every damn day in prisons.'

Gus' own hackles rose and he rolled his head in a circular motion trying to release the tension in his neck.

The solicitor continued, her tone matter of fact, 'Lulu was not a heroin user, so...' her sentence dangled.

Nancy inhaled sharply, 'So, what? They think Alice did it? I thought she got on well with her cell mate. Were there signs of a struggle?'

'No, no struggle. It's just... well, after the Baby Jane incident, which they suspect was facilitated by Lulu, the prison officers think that Alice is implicated. They think Alice sliced off Baby Jane's nipple, that Lulu had set the riot up for Jane to finish off Alice but it all went to pot.'

A ball of fire in Gus' stomach tried to make its escape, burning up his oesophagus, before being swallowed back down to simmer in his gut. He'd had Compo run a check on Lulu when Alice first bunked up with her and the idea that she'd facilitated the riot in order for Alice to get her revenge on Baby Jane was certainly within the bounds of possibility. Alice wouldn't repay Lulu by killing her – that made no sense. Yet the pressure of impending doom fanned the flicker in his belly once more and he could feel the flames licking and lapping – scorching under his ribcage.

Nancy tutted. 'Rubbish! If there was no struggle, then it's clear that Lulu overdosed on her own. She was getting on a bit, wasn't she? Have they any evidence to back up their weird and wonderful theories?'

Bernadette sighed, 'Lulu was ill – really ill. She was arthritic and could barely move. She was weak and her body was wreaked with cancer. Easy pickings for Alice. The only thing in Al's favour, so far, is that nobody is corroborating the prison's theory.'

Fuck, things are getting worse! Gus grabbed a can of Irn Bru, popped the can and took a long slurp. *Maybe that will cool my stomach.* Thank God Nancy didn't know about Alice's parents. Gus had put things together in his own mind. Lulu hadn't wanted to suffer a long, drawn out painful death in prison and had initiated a deal with Alice. *Oh Alice, what the fuck have you done?*

Chapter 65

15:35 Holmfield Court

Taffy, driven by the desire for something more substantial than crisps, muffins and chocolate bars, had braved the elements and walked to Nando's in City Park for a take-out. The very thought of actual cooked food made him salivate and as a result he'd ordered a hell of a lot more food than he would normally. He was about to amend his order when he remembered Compo's voracious appetite and realised that the food would be hoovered up in no time and that unless he dug in quickly, Compo would eat the lion's share. *Boy did that lad have an iron clad metabolism.*

It had been good to get out in the fresh air. The stuffiness of the flat didn't seem to faze Compo, perhaps he'd been a bat in a previous lifetime. However, Taffy was desperate for fresh air and the feel of the cold on his cheeks. Mind you, now that he was nearly back, he was looking forward to the cosiness of Compo's flat, despite the eerie 'dead pop stars shriney' thing going on. Soon as he'd walked through the front door, he could hear the whirr and purr of Compo's printer, but what hit him first was the stagnant farty, body-odoury whiff that slapped him in the face, so his first action was to open a window and light the aromatic pine candle. *Thanks Mrs McGuire, you're a life saver,* before turning to set out the food on the coffee table.

He turned to tell Compo to bring his one plate and a bowl and stopped. He was getting very used to Compo's different facial expressions so, when he saw him absent-mindedly ram a handful of crisps into his mouth and then forget to chew, it was a pretty sure-fire bet that something was up. 'Spill.'

Compo chewed, swallowed the crisps and picked up a ream of paper from the printer. Using his stockinged feet, he propelled his chair over to the coffee table. Stuffing the sheets of paper under his arm, he began to open the various containers Taffy had set out, grabbing bits of chicken from one and breaking off bits of a burger from another. With a sigh, Taffy departed to the kitchen, grabbed the plate, the bowl and a knife and spoon then returned to the small living room. He pushed the plate towards his friend and grabbed the pile of papers, before they were dropped onto the floor. Experience had shown that until Compo had refuelled there would be little point in talking about whatever had upset his equilibrium. So, leaving Compo to 'deal' in his own special way, Taffy nabbed the comfy chair, noting that over the last couple of days he'd made a Taffy shaped indentation in it and began to flick through the paperwork.

Most of it was MI6 related documentation that Taffy had no intention of asking Compo how he'd accessed it. Suffice it to say that as soon as this case was over, he would be shredding these memories along with the actual paperwork – he'd leave Compo to erase any digital trail. It seemed that Daniel Farrier had indeed been tasked with keeping an eye on the goings-on in the science labs, particularly the research into bio-weaponry. Taffy had met Daniel and Izzie with Gus and had considered him non-descript and quite likeable. Some of the encrypted email exchanges between Farrier, codenamed Salamis – no doubt after his supposed archaeological interest in restoring the ancient site – and his handler, Salamhand – *no guesses for the origins of this pseudonym* – put paid to that idea.

November 16th 2017 02:30

Salamis:
Dimou is easy prey – one of those needy, desperate for any male attention sort of women. Not very demanding but good enough to scratch any itches. She's very trusting, but having said that, she's a bit of a prude when it comes to talking shop out of hours. Might need to go a bit further than I'd like. Might need to get the old engagement ring out of storage. Her ex, Gianno Doukus, has his eye on me – so I am unable to get a true feel for the labs. Can't ask too many questions. Abaci is definitely working on something dodgy, but I need more time to gain access – to slowly build trust.

Salamhand:
Do what you have to. That's the only rule. We need to know what Abaci has got, but more importantly whose payroll he's on. Just do it.

January 2018 04:45

Salamis:
Loving this job. Couldn't be easier if I tried. Now that we're engaged, Dimou has shared her reservations re Abaci – not specifics, just a general ill ease. Getting the info more than makes up for having to screw an inanimate object.

Salamhand:
Good job. Think of England… and me and you'll get it up.

Taffy wanted to vomit. He'd seen what had been done to Izzie Dimou and Farrier's subterfuge and his obvious disdain for the dead woman he'd strung along so cavalierly was horrid. No wonder Compo was upset. Taffy put the papers aside and grabbed a peri-peri chicken burger before it disappeared. Compo was munching his way methodically through whatever was on the table, his eyes were glazed as he stared off into middle distance. Taffy wasn't entirely sure Compo realised the other man was still there. 'Comps?'

No response. 'Comps?' A bit louder this time.

Compo started and looked at Taffy, 'Fucking piece of shit. To think I was going to go to his stag do? Wish Gus had left him to freeze to death in that damn farmhouse. How could he? How the fuck could he do that? Pretend he loved her? Set her up like that and then…?' He chucked the half-eaten burger on the table and jumped to his feet, marching out of the room and into the hallway.

From where he sat, Taffy watched as Compo strode to the end of the hallway and turned to the first framed photo. He stretched his hand out and touched his index finger to it. His lips moved, but Taffy couldn't hear what he said. Compo moved on to the next poster and repeated the process, continuing along the wall till he got to the one closest to the door. Only then were Compo's words audible, 'Too young to die, too good to live. Too troubled to survive.'

The words sent a shaft of ice through Taffy's body – as if he was freezing from the toes up. They were like a mantra, but not one like the Sikh mediation mantra his parents did or the ones he heard at the temple. No, the one that Compo had clearly practised and repeated many times before seemed doomlike – prophetic almost. *What did it mean? Should he mention this to Gus? But they'd agreed, 'what happens in Compo's stays at Compo's.'*

Compo walked into the small living room and marched past Taffy straight to his workstation. 'Come on. Let's get this bastard nailed.'

Grabbing the rest of the paperwork, Taffy jumped to his feet and sat in the other office chair, 'I'll just go through the rest of this, shall I?'

Compo shook his head. 'No, don't bother. All that paperwork tells us is that Farrier was a knob. He used Izzie Dimou and was screwing his handler at the same time and he was working for MI6 to get information about Professor Abaci's dirty deals. It's enough to make your skin crawl, but that's not the half of it. At least with all that crap.' He waved his hand at the papers that Taffy held. 'You could say he was working in the national interest, even if his methods were immoral. Look at this though. This is some other world crap and we need to let Gus know pronto.'

As Taffy leaned forward the thought crossed his mind that perhaps, if whatever Compo was about to show him was so important, he shouldn't have spent the last half hour eating Nando's and performing strange mantras with his poster collection. However, as soon as he began to read the stuff that was on the screen all he could think was *Holy Shit!*

He glanced at Compo, who nodded, his face, despite the smear of extra hot peri-peri sauce on his cheek, looking more serious than he had ever seen. Taffy swallowed. 'Encrypted burner phone?'

Compo inclined his head and lifted an innocuous phone from the shelf above his workstation. Fingers speeding over the screen, he composed a text and hit send.

Chapter 66

16:15 North Manchester General Hospital

The dark had settled in, the sky heavy with snow yet to fall. Many of the parking spaces at the hospital were taken up with mucky piles of snow, rendering them unusable and they were just doing their second circuit of the carpark when Gus felt a vibration in his back pocket. A quick glance at Nancy informed him she was unaware of it, as she continued to moan about inconsiderate hospital visitors' parking over two spaces, the snow and parking charges. He had to get away from her for enough time to see what Compo had decided was too sensitive to be sent to his normal phone. With his pain medication wearing off, the familiar pressure of one of his headaches bore down on him. It would become so intense as if his skull was being compressed by giant pliers. He could have done without the added worry of Compo's text, so he popped an Ibuprofen and swigged it back with the dregs from his can of Irn Bru.

Pointing to a space right next to the entrance, he said 'Drop me there and you go park up. I can't walk very far in this weather with crutches. I'll wait inside for you.' He needed to get away from her for just a few minutes – just long enough to rehydrate and deal with the text before she came back. Much as he loved Nancy, she could be a phenomenal pain in the backside at times and, right now, he was in the position of having to put up with it – at least until he worked his way out of her bad books again. However, he had no intention of involving her in Compo's deep diving on the expedition on the darknet. As soon as Nancy drove out of sight, Gus accessed his encrypted phone and dialled Compo's number.

Ten minutes, later sitting on the leather-covered bench near the entrance, a cone of water in one hand and his crutches balanced between his legs, Gus observed the comings and goings. North Manchester General differed only a little from Bradford Royal Infirmary. The ethnic make-up of the patients and the staff was similar, the hustle and bustle familiar and the range of injuries and ailments echoed Gus' memories of his last visit to BRI. He hated it. Instead of relieving the throb in his head, he could sense the pressure increasing with each passing second.

Compo's revelations hammered away at his brain and his skull was ready to splinter into a trillion shards. Gulps of air hitched in his chest and around him noise became echoey and distant, as if it was filtered through a funnel. He dropped the half-filled cone of water and pressed both his palms onto the leather bench. If he made a connection to the seat he'd be okay. If he willed himself to reconnect with the world he'd be fine. It was too late though. He couldn't press hard enough onto the seat, so he lifted one hand and clawed his fingers against his wound. The pain brought tears to his eyes, yet still he was falling… and then Nancy was there. Perching beside him, pulling his hand away from his thigh injury, talking low and soft and gentle. The fuzz behind his eyes lessened, his chest muscles slackened and breathing was easier.

He glanced round and cursed. His panic attack had secured him a sizeable audience and as well as the sweat dotted across his brow, the sensation of a wine-coloured flush spreading through his cheeks made him want to scream 'What the fuck are you looking at?' He didn't need to because Nancy was there, in his corner – his friend as well as his boss.

'Seen enough have you? Go on, piss off. Mind your own business.'

Her words brought a smile to Gus' lips. She didn't swear often but when she did she put it to good use.

'You okay, Gus? Panic attack?'

What makes you think that? A year ago Gus would have shrugged and tried to laugh it off, but he'd grown stronger since then. The corner of his mouth quirked up and he nodded, 'Yep. Bastard of a panic attack this time. Should have realised I was due one. Been a busy few days.'

Nancy prodded him on the arm. 'See, this is what happens when you go prancing off on your own, like Batman and his Incredible Hunk sidekick.'

Despite himself, Gus grinned at her description of Gore as the Incredible *Hunk*. He was a good-looking bugger, but Nancy was on a roll.

'Worrying everyone, going in unarmed, not waiting for back up. This has got to stop.' And she punctuated each of the final five words with a bony prod on Gus' arm.

She had a point. Gus acknowledged that, but did she have to prod him so damn hard? Did she have to choose this precise moment to go off on one? Her reference to Gore had reminded him that they didn't know how his operation had gone. But Nancy was still wittering on, all loud and annoying again.

'Just as well the operation was a success…'

Gus frowned, rewound, 'You telling me Gore's out of the woods?'

With an elongated sigh and an eyeroll that would have been the envy of any self-respecting, stroppy teenager, Nancy tutted. 'I've just been telling you. They managed to relieve the pressure on his brain and he's back in the high dependency unit. They're cautiously optimistic he'll be okay. Sandra has requested he be transported to Bradford or Leeds as soon as he's able as she can't get here with the little one.' She lifted her hand, index finger extended again, but before she recommenced her prodding, Gus slipped his arms into the crutch cuffs and pushed up onto his feet, 'Come on Nancy. No time for your blame fest. Let's go see what Daniel Farrier has to offer.'

Chapter 67

16:25 North Manchester General Hospital

The information Compo had given him was still as sharp as acid in his gullet. If anyone other than Compo had given him this intelligence, Gus would have knocked it back. However, he would trust Compo with his life – unpalatable though it may be, Compo's foray into the dark web had paid huge, if unexpected, dividends. Despite his headache, the cumbersome crutches and the crowds of people thronging the corridors, Gus set off at a pace towards the side ward where Daniel Farrier was and aware of the looks Nancy kept throwing in his direction. He said 'How long before MI6 swoop in on their broomsticks – or maybe it'll be the Death Star?'

Nancy shrugged, 'Couple of hours tops, I reckon. They'd have already been here if it wasn't for the deterioration in conditions in the South of the country.'

Right, long enough! Pulling to a stop outside the door, Gus nodded at the uniformed officer who'd been put on guard duty outside and paused. He could hear Gabriella's voice, loud and domineering, accompanied by a lower rumble that was Daniel and the occasional offering from his sister drifting from inside the room. This wasn't ideal, he'd much prefer to do this interview with just him and Nancy present. But it'd take too long to convince Gabriella to leave. When had he ever managed to convince her to do anything he wanted? And the last thing he needed was for MI6 to storm in and sweep Daniel away before he could put the evidence before him – get an explanation.

Hands on her hips, Nancy glared at him. 'What the hell is wrong with you? You've got a face like a gnarled old Rottweiler and it's not just the after-effects of your little 'do' earlier.'

'Little do' indeed! Damn woman's too perceptive for her own good. He leaned on the wall next to the door and spoke in quiet but urgent tones. 'Nance, you got to go with me on this one, ok? You just need to trust me.'

Her chest heaved as she inhaled and abruptly released the air with an audible whoosh. 'Compo?'

Gus inclined his head, 'Yeah, Compo.'

Nancy tapped her booted foot on the floor and flung her hands in the air, 'Okay. Go for it Gus.'

He could have kissed her. Nancy was trusting him with not only his own reputation, but hers too. Smile tight, he bobbed his head once, pushed himself away from the wall, straightened his body as much as he could and entered the room.

'Where have you been? We had to make our way from the airport – cost us an arm and a leg!' Gabriella sat next to her brother, arms folded across her chest, dark eyes accusing.

Katie jumped to her feet and rushed to meet him, guiding him to the chair that she'd vacated on the other side of Daniel. 'God, Gus. Daniel didn't say you were so badly hurt.'

Gabriella snorted, 'He's not exactly bed ridden, is he?'

Before Gus had the chance to retort, Nancy cut through Gabriella's continued moaning. 'You always were a nasty little bitch. Some things haven't changed. For your information, Danny boy here would have been dead if not for Gus and, just so we're clear,' she pointed at Gus' thigh as he settled onto the plastic chair, 'an inch in the wrong direction and you'd be attending his funeral right now, not feeding grapes to your brother.'

As Gabriella, red faced, opened her mouth to respond, Katie moved to her side and placed her hands on her partner's shoulders, 'Let's call a damn truce Gaby. None of this is Gus' fault and you are behaving like a bitch.'

Gus tensed in anticipation of the inevitable eruption, but it never came. Instead, Gabriella raised one hand to cover Katie's where it lay on her shoulder and smiled. 'You're right, sweetie.' And with an inconsequential shrug she added, 'Sorry Gus.'

Gus and Nancy exchanged surprised glances and Gus pulled his chair closer to the bed. 'Got some more questions to ask you, if that's okay.'

Daniel rolled his eyes in an exaggerated manner and spoke to his sister. 'He's just not letting me off the hook. Izzie's dead, yet he's still hassling me.'

Gus glared at Gabriella before she had a chance to reply and was pleased when instead of speaking, she bit her lip and patted Daniel's arm. 'Just a few questions – it's not like you've anywhere else to be, is it?'

Katie cleared her throat, 'Before you start, Gaby and I will go and grab a coffee.' She turned to her partner and all but manhandled her out of the room. Gus could have kissed her for that. Katie was nobody's fool and she'd clearly interpreted Gus' tone correctly – this was going to be good.

He waited till his sister and ex-wife had left the room and Nancy had settled on the other side of the bed before beginning. 'Bank account in the Cayman Islands is looking good, Danny boy. MI6 is paying big bucks these days.'

It was only a fleeting flicker – gone almost before it began – but it was enough to confirm that Compo's intelligence was accurate. Daniel played with the monitor attached to the middle finger on his good hand – the one with the fingers intact and said, 'You lost me there. Never been to the Cayman Islands.'

Gus took out his burner phone and consulted the information Compo had texted him, 'You see, I don't believe you. We've got a trail that leads from Russia to you, round the houses through the streets – a bit like Wee Willie Winkie – and straight into a Cayman bank account to the tune of three million US Dollars.' Gus looked at Nancy. 'Shame he's trussed up in a hospital bed, or no doubt he'd be en route to sunnier climes.'

Nancy snorted and nudged Daniel's poorly hand.

Gus smiled as Daniel jumped wincing – *maybe in need of a morphine top up – poor sod!* 'Then there's the intercepted emails. Gus pretended to be flipping through his phone. 'Oh yeah – here's one – to Furkan Narkis – encrypted and wiped, but – when you've got a shit-hot team, you've got a shit-hot team. Yep – says here you hired them to find out where Izzie was keeping the formula.' Gus leaned back, ignoring the twinge across his shoulders that warned him the crutches were forcing him to use muscles he'd forgotten he had. His eyes were gritty, his vision blurred until he blinked. He had to keep on top of this. Had to see it through. 'Words like 'torture' and 'do what it takes' and 'Russians getting antsy' – care to explain?'

Daniel, face pale – looked from Nancy to Gus, 'No, no, you got it all wrong. I work with MI6, just trying to trap the Turks – they were the ones going to sell it to the Syrians.'

'Ah,' Gus shook his head and tutted, 'See that's not what Vulcan's telling us.'

Daniel snorted. 'Phew, you believe that piece of scum?'

'Well, you see it's not just 'that piece of scum,' is it? There's also that wee matter of the recovered messages between you and a certain Grigory Dobrynin of Russia's Main Intelligence Directorate detailing the payment schedule and exchange thereof of the bio-weapon formula. You got your eye on the big bucks and Izzie was just a pawn in your game.' Gus let the disgust show on his face.

But Daniel wasn't giving up just yet. 'Good try. But way off the mark. I'm an MI6 agent. You wouldn't understand the complexities of an undercover operation if it hit you in the face. You with your big friend, bumbling in like an idiot to a scene that I had perfectly under control. You fucked up, McGuire.

You – not me. No one will ever believe any of the crap you think you have on me.'

Gus looked at Nancy, his smile steady, his eyes direct. 'Read him his rights. We'll let the CPS decide, shall we? We've got the evidence.'

Nancy had just finished arresting Daniel when the door burst open and two suited men strode in. *Who the hell do they think they are – CID?* They flashed their badges, 'MI6, we'll take things from here.'

Nancy stepped in front of Gus with a warning look. 'I'm afraid we've just arrested this man and so he stays in our custody for now.'

As Nancy uttered her sentence, two things happened. First Gabriella came into the room, her face flushing, eyes wild as she glared at Gus. 'What the hell do you think you're doing? He's just lost his fiancée and he nearly died. Are you crazy?'

The larger of the two MI6 men, pushed forward, infringing on Nancy's personal space.

Nancy glared up at him, her voice lowered to a growl, 'Do not try to intimidate me. He. Is. Our. Prisoner.' Her lips set in a thin line, her hands straight by her side, her posture rigid, claiming every inch of height she had.

'MI6 trumps local police,' said big man.

Nancy stepped into his space, 'Not when the charge is murder. Tell your boss, I'll be in touch, but for now he's ours.'

There was a two-minute standoff, which to Gus seemed to last for hours. The big man nodded and motioned to his partner. They stepped out of the room and Gus could hear them talking on the phone. He turned to Gabriella and Katie, arms splayed, 'I can explain.'

Gabriella rushed at him, her hands fisted and began to punch his face, his chest and his arms, while sobbing. 'You just can't move on, can you, Gus. You can't let it go. You've got to take it out on my brother, don't you?'

Gus' arms in his crutches, fingers gripping the hand-bars to steady himself, put up no resistance. *How could she think that of him?* His cheekbone throbbed, his lip burst, but still he stood there until, at last – Katie and Nancy galvanised into action – dragged Gabriella away from him. As Gus looked at her, Katie wrapped her arms round a weeping Gabriella, her gaze venomous as she looked at Gus.

Nancy stepped close to them. 'The situation is far more complicated than you are aware of – just back off.' She turned and called the uniformed officer in. 'Escort these two out of here. They're pissing me off big time.'

Gus, shaking, barely able to stand even with the support of his crutches, watched as his sister and ex-wife left the room. Their last glances were venomous and directed at him. Gabriella's words to her brother were, 'Don't worry, Danny. We'll sort this out. Stay strong.'

As the door swung shut behind them, Nancy phoned through to the head of SCO19 team and asked for armed guards to be deployed twenty-four-seven to guard Daniel Farrier until they could move him to BRI.

'You're making a big mistake, McGuire. A huge one. Do you really want to lose your sister because of this?'

A flashback to the previous year, when Alice was being taken away by London police officers because of Sean Kennedy's treachery and the image of the body of a young girl discarded down a valley in Bradford because of a police officer's treachery, rocked him. He dropped his right crutch to the floor and slammed his fist into Daniel Farrier's supercilious face. 'Fuck you, Farrier.'

As the two MI6 agents rushed back in, Nancy yanked the sheet off Farrier's bed and yelled, 'You shouldn't have attacked my officer.' She turned to the agents and said, 'Help my officer to a chair, this one pummelled him, look at his face – it's swelling up.'

With armed guards – one outside and one inside Daniel Farrier's side room – in place, Nancy was en route to a FaceTime meeting in Greater Manchester with the head of MI6 regarding Daniel Farrier's move to the dark side. Detective Chief Superintendent Bashir had been unable to accompany Nancy but had issued strict instructions to be kept updated. Compo had encrypted and set up various firewalls and so on before sending all he'd scavenged to Nancy and Gus from an anonymous source that hinted at being from inside Russia itself. Somehow, he'd even managed to play with the times so that it looked like they'd received the anonymous information just after noon. According to Compo, he'd shut every back door that could lead to him, but in all honesty, Nancy doubted MI6 would be focussing anywhere other than Russia. This was a huge embarrassment to them and Nancy, still narked that they wouldn't give her full access to Farrier's file from the start, was prepared to draw as much blood and mortification as she could.

'It stands up to scrutiny, doesn't it? All Compo's stuff?'

Gus nodded. All he wanted to do was nip in to see Lewis, his fellow officer, before they were both flown back to Bradford in the lull of the storm. Then sleep, sleep and more sleep. He'd tried to put the look on Katie's face as she dragged Gabriella from Daniel's room to the back of his mind, but it kept coming back to him. They'd made huge strides forward in their relationship since Gabriella and Katie's betrayal – most of it down to his mum's tenacious insistence. Now, he couldn't see a way forward for him and his sister. Not after this. What else could he have done though? Let a murdering scumbag go scot free? No chance. He'd seen enough coppers get off with corruption and even atrocities and it sickened him. No, he'd done the right thing and he'd rather live without his sister than with a knife slicing his soul for the rest of his life.

Tuesday

Chapter 68

Patti had assumed Gus would sleep well, however experience had taught him that sheer exhaustion, emotional and physical trauma and a body that was slowly turning into a bruised rainbow, would not secure him the respite he needed. He was right. He'd spent the night tossing and turning, trying not to wake Patti. With Zarqa in the spare room, in the early hours of the morning, he'd had no choice but to take his demons and Bingo downstairs to the living room couch. At least here he had Greg to talk to share the things he could never burden Patti with.

Huddled in a fleece, watching the flames in the stove, Gus tried to block out the recurring images that troubled him. Alice – all venom and hatred, Izzie Dimou and Marcia Beaumont's tortured bodies, Missy Beaumont's empty staring eyes when he'd studied her through the window at North Manchester General, the two dead Romanians, Vulcan Narkis' shocked expression when he'd killed his brother, the crazed expression on Furkan Narkis' face as he raised his machete in the air, ready to strike Gus down, Lewis Gore motionless and bleeding out, Daniel Farrier, shivering and vulnerable and later, arrogant and taunting. Gabriella and Katie's expressions, Compo's disappointment, Taffy's optimism.

So many people all relying on him. Expecting him to make it okay, to do the right thing. *Sometimes it's just too much, Greg – too fucking much! Sometimes I get it wrong – like I did with you and then... people end up dead!* He looked up at Greg's painting above the fireplace. The reptiles so intricately laced through Bob Marley's dreads put him in mind of his life. So many things interweaving, complicating things… and so much grief – sometimes too much to bear. He couldn't get comfortable on the sofa. His leg was giving him gyp. Every bruise throbbed, his ribs hurt – he was a wreck and what's more he looked like one too. When he'd seen his swollen face staring back at him from the bathroom mirror earlier, it had given him a jolt. *God knows how mum will react when she sees me.* Huge bags hung like pendulums beneath faded blue eyes – *where has the spark gone?* The parts where Gabriella had punched him were turning an angry mauve and his lip was split. He'd let Patti assume it was the Narkis' who were responsible for that – no point in fuelling an already-over-ignited fire. His nose was still swollen from before and he looked like he should be locked up – *maybe he should. Maybe everyone would be safer that way. Maybe he could do an exchange for Alice?*

According to Nancy, MI6 had received all of Compo's encrypted intelligence implicating Daniel Farrier in everything from Izzie Dimou's abduction and subsequent death to stealing the bio-weapon Sevket Abaci had been developing for the Syrians, in order to sell it to the Russians. With that end in mind, MI6 had pulled rank and demanded to 'deal' with Daniel Farrier. Under orders from Number Ten, Nancy had no choice but to comply. 'Truth is,' she'd said, 'it would be more bother than its worth for us to prosecute him. This way we're distanced from it all.'

Gus had to agree. Compo had worked hard and dug deep. The last thing Gus wanted was for Comps to be held accountable. Best rid of Farrier. Then he'd only have to deal with the aftermath of Gabriella and Katie's accusations. They didn't even have to worry about Vulcan Narkis as MI6 had swept him off to London too – Gus didn't fancy Vulcan's chances at the hands of the spooks.

He was just contemplating grabbing a whisky when the living room door opened and a shadowy figure crept in. In the semi dark, he recognised Zarqa. She wore long sleeved pyjamas and had pulled the sleeves down and was gripping them in the palm of her hands as she sunk into the armchair next to the couch, folding her legs under her, so that she was barely visible. She pulled one of the throws that Patti had dotted around the living room over her. In silence, he watched her hook an arm around a cushion and try to get comfy. 'Can't sleep, eh?'

When she jumped, Gus swung his legs round, raked his hands through his dreads and, waving bye-bye to a nice single malt, asked, 'Hot chocolate?'

Zarqa grinned, 'I'll make it though, yours is always crap.'

Gus pressed his palms to his heart and grinned, 'Ouch.'

Zarqa flicked on a lamp and grimaced, 'God, Gus. You look rough. Not surprised Patti kicked you out the bed.'

With a laugh catching in his throat, Gus swatted his god-daughter, on the arm – 'Bitch.'

Limping to the kitchen, he wondered what exactly a good godfather did in these sorts of circumstances. Did he wait for her to talk, or did he plough in and try to mediate? *Fuck, I'm so out of touch!*

As if aware of his predicament, Zarqa filled a pan with milk and put it on the cooker to boil. 'I know what went on you know Gus. '

Gus, head on one side, quirked an eyebrow. 'You do?'

She nodded. 'Yeah, courtesy of some tosser at mosque school.'

Not the time to admonish her language. Instead he watched as she spooned coco powder and sugar into the milk and began to whisk it in the way he'd seen her mother do countless times and waited to find out exactly what Zarqa had found out from a tosser at mosque school. *But when he found out who the little scrote was he'd have a thing or two to say to him.* When it came, it was worse than Gus had anticipated. Zarqa's whisking became more agitated as she spoke, tears fell from her eyes and dripped into the droplets of spilt milk.

'He's not my fucking dad.' She glanced at Gus, her mouth screwed up like she was chewing a lime. 'But of course you knew that, didn't you?'

Right up his spine and along his shoulders, Gus could feel an army of rats, tails swishing, teeth gnawing and nipping at him as they progressed up to his skull, ready to bite if he put a foot wrong. *This was serious godfather stuff. Where the hell are you when we need you eh, Greg? Oh fuck – forgot – I bloody stabbed you to death, didn't I?'*

The sound of the milk hissing as it overflowed and killed the gas, followed by the acrid smell of burning, jolted Gus to his feet. He reached over and switched the knob off and he and Zarqa stared at each other – her dark eyes full of pain and accusation.

Gus closed his eyes momentarily then looked straight into Zarqa's. 'Yes, I knew that. You need to talk to your dad.'

A rough little half cough, half cry caught in Zarqa's throat. 'Not my dad, remember?'

Gus swallowed, his throat was dry and he really needed that whisky now. Instead he flicked the switch on the kettle. 'Biologically no… but he is in all the ways that matter.'

Unprepared for Zarqa's anger, he flinched when – fists clenched – she stepped right up to him and yelled in his face, 'Don't give me that crap. He killed my dad, didn't he?'

Gus froze. *Fucking little tosser, I'll castrate him.* This wasn't his story to tell, what the hell was he supposed to do?

Zarqa flounced away from him spinning on her heel, her hands raking through her straight black hair. 'It's true. It's fucking true.'

She made to storm out of the living room, but Gus grabbed her arm, ignoring the wrenching pain in his thigh as he over stretched. 'You need to speak to your dad…' her chin lifted, her lips thinning. *God she's so full of rage.* 'Mo. You need to speak to Mo and your mum. This isn't my story to tell.'

'No,' she said pulling her arm away, 'It wasn't fucking Javid at mosque's story either, was it?' She raged out of the kitchen, through the living room, slamming the door behind her. Gus heard her thumping upstairs followed by the spare room door slamming, then muffled tears. *Fuck I'm not equipped for this godparent shit.* He picked up his phone and punched in Mo's number.

Chapter 69

'It wasn't like that, Zarqa.' Mo's voice was low, his hands stretched beseechingly towards his daughter. 'You've only got half the story.'

'Duh, and whose fault is that?'

Mo glanced at Naila who sat at the kitchen table, tears teeming down her face, her hands clenched together in her lap. What must she be feeling right now? This must be hell for her. Their daughter dragging up the past, throwing it in her face, like she was some sort of whore. His voice was sharper when he next spoke, 'Apologise! Apologise to your mum right now.'

Zarqa's face reddened, her lips curled in an ugly snarl. 'Apologise? To her? What for? For saying it like it is? For calling her a whore? Fuck's sake *Mo,* let's call a spade a spade, huh? She was fifteen when she had me – *fifteen.* That's younger than I am now. She trapped my dad and you killed him.'

Mo exhaled. Her calling him Mo instead of Dad drove a stake straight through his heart. On the one hand he itched to slap her, on the other he wanted to sweep her up, cocoon her in his love and absorb all the hurt and venom. How had she become this monster? Where was the sweet baby he'd held in his arms minutes after she was born? The toddler who used to make him give her piggy back rides all over the house, the big sister who loved teaching her siblings new things and reading them bedtime stories? This wasn't her. If he believed in Jinns, he'd assume she was possessed by a malignant one, however he knew it was anger, rage and hurt that drove her – that made her lash out. He wanted to put his arms round Naila, stand in front of her, fend off every poison dart Zarqa fired at her. However, they'd agreed earlier they'd show a united front, but they would *not* create a physical barrier; a wall that would exclude Zarqa, make her feel outside their love. So he stayed where he was feeling increasingly helpless.

Naila, stood up, arms stretched to embrace their daughter. 'He was never your Dad – *Never*. He was a paedophile, a rapist and an abuser. Your dad – your real dad, the one that matters – this one,' she pointed to Mo, 'all he ever did was defend *me*.'

Zarqa brushed off Naila's arms. 'So, I'm just the cuckoo in the nest – the fucking cuckoo. The one nobody wants. The one you keep trying to replace with all your other brats.'

'No, No, Zarqa. That's not true. We love you. You're our daughter and we love you.' Mo could see his words were having no impact on his daughter. With every passing second he could feel her pulling away from them, erecting barriers, hating them. As Naila pleaded with her, trying to explain about her forced marriage to her forty-year-old cousin Waseem, how Waseem had raped her, how he – Mo – had tried to protect her, how the community; her parents, her family, had turned their backs on them.

A vision from his past crashed into his head. The events of that day played like a silent film in his mind, eerily detached from sound or emotions.

Lister Park! – the bandstand – autumn wind howling, rain thrashing, he and Naila trying to find shelter, Naila pregnant with Zarqa. Mo desperate to protect the love of his life, – both of them kids – too young, yet unable to let their love die – sixteen and scared. Waseem had turned up with Naila's brothers and her father. Screaming, yelling, grabbing at Naila, tears streaking her face, her mouth open, one arm cupping her bump, pleading, begging Mo for help. He'd stepped forward, grabbed her and let go with a fist from the second step of the bandstand. Waseem on the step below him – slipped – maybe wet leaves? Feet cycling out of control. CRAAAASH! For a second, everyone stood looking at him as his white prayer hat turned red.

Mo had grabbed Naila and they'd run, her brothers in pursuit. Together they had run down the steps into the Mughal Gardens. Naila stumbled, fell to her knees and then they were on her, her brother Majid, grabbing her by the scruff of the neck, dragging her over to the water pools, thrusting her head in, holding her down. Splashing. Yanking her back up. Gasping for air. Crying for Mo. Thrusting her back under. Meanwhile, Mo curled in a foetal position. Daanish and Jaffer kicking; kicking his head, his ribs, his legs. The knife – Daanish? Jaffer? Sirens, paramedics and all the time Naila screaming, crying.

Zarqa screamed, her face a screwed-up ball of venom as she pushed past her mum, firing daggers at Mo. 'I don't believe you. I hate you both. You're not my fucking dad and I'll never forgive you.'

Chapter 70

It was strange to be back in Bradford and even stranger to be back in The Fort, but it felt good. Just like coming home. Gus watched the snow falling outside the window and wondered what Alice was doing. Nancy had told him she was in the clear. Lulu had left a suicide note, saying she couldn't go on any longer, that she didn't want to die of cancer in prison and that she'd bought the heroin from Baby Jane. Now, Alice's parents were heading down to collect their daughter. Gus and Mo had sworn them to secrecy about how they'd ended up at Mo's and Compo had 'created' a legitimate trail logging their journey from Athens to Bradford, starting before any bodies were discovered outside their home. Greek police had put their deaths down to a vendetta type killing.

Gus wasn't sure he could face her. How could he, when he'd let her down so badly? When he'd given up on her, when she needed him most. He swung his chair away from the window and began shuffling papers around his desk. He'd been doing that for hours and had achieved a big fat zilch. Compo and Taffy were industriously filing and tying up loose ends. And Nancy was no doubt bemoaning the fact that MI6 were refusing to share any information with her about Daniel Farrier. Gus couldn't care less about that. As far as he was concerned, Daniel Farrier could rot in hell – maybe they'd lock him in the Tower of London.

Taffy began to get ready to go home and Gus smiled. Taffy ad Compo had bonded over the last few days. It was good for both of them. Compo needed someone to take him out of himself, to help him connect to the outside world. And Taffy needed someone who would let him take the lead – someone who would instil confidence in his abilities. Normally, that role fell to Alice but, hell, Compo was doing a grand job of it in her absence. He waved bye to Taffy and picked up yet another file only to be disturbed by Compo clearing his throat. Gus hadn't heard him cross to his desk and jumped.

'Boss, gotta say this. Just the once and then it's forgotten okay?'

Gus frowned, unsure where Compo was going. 'It's about Alice.'

Gus nodded, his heart sinking. He deserved to be berated over his lack of faith in Alice, but that didn't make it any the less painful. 'Yeah.'

'It stays between you and me, okay?'

Gus frowned. 'What stays between you and me?'

Compo wiped the back of his hand over his nose. 'You know – that stuff the whole Kennedy stuff. We just forget it, right?'

'Oh, you mean the stuff you dug up on Kennedy, yeah that's our secret, no probs Comps.'

Compo pulled his beanie off his head and twisted it in his hands. 'No, not *that*. The other stuff – *you!* You not believing in her. You'd a load on. Sampson and all of that – loads of stuff. You didn't really believe Al had done it. I know you didn't.'

Gus' heart contracted. *Aw Compo!* No matter how easy it would be to accept Compo's version of events, Gus couldn't do it. He'd never be able to live with himself if he wasn't honest. 'The truth is Comps, at the time I did believe it. I really did. I let her down big time and I'll never ever forget it. I can't lie about it, pretend it didn't happen. I don't know what I was thinking, but I did believe it.'

Compo frowned, put his hat back on and kicked the leg of Gus' table. 'Thing is, Gus… Dun't matter about what *you* feel.

It's about *Al*, in't it? So, you just swallow all that shit you've just said to me. She dun't need to ever hear that, you get me?' His look was ferocious, his eyes sparking, his lips in a tight line that brooked no argument.

Fuck, this team never ceases to amaze me. He stood up, spat on the palm of his hand and then extended it to Compo. 'For Alice.'

Compo grinned, spat on his own palm and gripped Gus' hand and shook. 'For Alice.'

He turned and walked back to his work station. 'Wouldn't mind a Raja's pizza – just to seal the deal like.'

Gus laughed, picked up the phone and dialled. You got to keep the team fed, after all.

Epilogue

Three Weeks Later

Nab Wood Cemetery

Gus waited outside the crematorium, fingers linked with Patti's. His thigh was still tight when he moved, but thankfully the relentless cold had abated. Aside from that, he could have done without being here today. Tomorrow he had to give his statement to Internal Affairs regarding his decision not to await backup before entering the farmhouse on Saddleworth Moor. Nancy had assured him it would be a formality, so why were his palms sweating? Why couldn't he take it all in his stride like Gore? The big man's stock phrase was 'what's done is done. We did what we had to and we're alright.'

Gus wasn't entirely sure his friend *was* alright. Gore had lost weight and his right arm wasn't functioning quite as well as it had done. He had many months of physiotherapy before him, yet he was persistently upbeat. Gus wished he had some of Gore's happy pills to keep him going.

With his Mum, Dad, Taffy, Compo, Mo and Naila grouped around him, Gus was reassured. This wouldn't be easy – course it wouldn't. However, with the support of his friends and family it would be bearable – survivable, and he and Patti could go back to his house and recover. Naila looked pale – washed out and Mo had lost weight. *Looks like things with Zarqa are no better.* He was aware that his friends had had showed up, not to mourn the deceased, but to support him and Gus was thankful for it. When the hearse drew up, Gus inhaled sharply. This was the second funeral in the same number of days and he'd had second thoughts about attending this one. Izzie Dimou's cremation the previous day had been sad – only he, his parents, Nancy, Compo and Taffy were there. What a way to leave this earth. Poor Izzie had nobody to mourn her. When the purple curtains had closed and they'd turned to leave the crematorium he'd spotted a figure, head bowed, sitting at the back of the small chapel. It was Gianni Doukus, Izzie's ex-boyfriend. At least someone who loved her had been there to see her off on her final journey.

Today's funeral, although not as tragic as Izzie's – in Gus' mind at least – would be only slightly better attended. Staring straight ahead as the undertakers removed Daniel Farrier's coffin from the vehicle, Gus struggled not to kick it. Another black vehicle pulled up behind the hearse and Gabriella and Katie got out. Corrine McGuire moved forward and slipped her hand into Gus' other hand and squeezed. He sent a tight smile in her direction and then focussed his attention on the two women.

Katie gave a slight nod and linked her arm through her partner's. Gabriella's cheeks were hollow, her face ashen with crease marks spreading out over her forehead as she stepped towards Gus. Aware of a pulse ticking by his right eye, Gus braced himself. Last time they'd met Gabriella had rained a barrage of punches on him. *Would she do the same today?*

Gabriella's gaze drifted over the huddle of people waiting to enter the chapel. 'Bring reinforcements did you, Gus?'

Gus shook his head. 'We're all family and friends here. We're here to support you and Katie.'

With a snort, Gaby pursed her lips. 'Yeah, right.' Her gaze landed on Patti, who moved closer to Gus, touching his arm with her free hand. Gabriella shrugged in a 'you can have him' sort of way.

'The trouble with you Gus is that you're too damn *moral*. Too set on doing the right thing that you never stop to look at the consequences of those around you. You're always too busy saving the underdog, bringing the villains to justice – no thought for those you care about.'

His voice was thick as he spoke. 'It's what I am.'

Gabriella nodded, a tear in her eye and turned to Patti. 'There'll come a time for you too, when playing second fiddle to his morals will be too high a price to pay for your own sanity.' Before Patti could respond, she turned back to Gus. 'You're here because of your twisted sense of justice. You're here because it's the right thing to do, regardless…' she paused, 'well… you know I'm right.'

Gus inclined his head. No point in lying or trying to or wrapping it up like something it wasn't, Gabriella had got it spot on.

'Daniel did wrong, but he was my brother.'

Gus swallowed the retort that 'did wrong' was rather an understatement for everything Daniel Farrier had done.

'He had to be punished – I'm not saying he didn't. But *you* drove him to *this*. The way you were with him in the hospital, the way you gloated, taunted him, *that's* why he took that damn pill, took his own life. *You* forced him into that corner. You, with your self- righteous gloating, you did this to him, just like you did with Greg. You…' she took a step forward and prodded him in the chest. '*You* killed my brother. You left him no choice and for that I won't forgive you.' She turned and walked into the chapel followed by Katie who cast a single backward glance in her brother's direction.

Gus exhaled. He wasn't to blame for Daniel Farrier's death. On a logical level he was aware of that. However, Gabriella's words still stung. Later, when things had died down a bit, perhaps she'd wonder who gave her brother that cyanide capsule. Maybe she'd realise in whose interests it had been for

Daniel Farrier to disappear off this mortal coil quietly without the blaze of publicity a huge trial would bring.

He leaned over, kissed his mother's cheek, shook his dad's hand and said, 'We'll go. You go in, she'll need someone.'

As he and Patti walked back to his car, he saw a lone figure leaning on the bonnet. His heart accelerated and, with an apologetic look at Patti who grinned, he sped up only to ground to a halt two feet away from Alice. What did you say to someone who'd been through everything she'd been through? Someone he'd believed could do all the things Sean Kennedy had done? Someone he'd betrayed?

He held his hands out in front of him, and swallowed hard. She was so small, so skinny. Her hair had started to grow back but the hollows in her cheeks and her sunken eyes were still there. She looked like a holocaust victim – all jaggy bones and pallor. He swallowed and opened his mouth. Then closed it again.

'For fuck's sake, Gus. You look like shit.' Her lips tugged up into a shadow of the smile he was used to. The one he'd missed all these months.

How could he ever have doubted her? He stepped forward and pulled her into a gentle hug, ignoring her moaning. 'Shut up and just let me hug you, Al. Just once.'

'Wuss.' She said extricating herself.

Gus grinned, 'You got me. You gonna take some time?'

She nodded and pointed behind her. Her Mini was parked a few cars away with her parents inside. 'We're going to Greece for a while. Nancy's giving me time to think my options through.' She shuffled her feet. 'Thing is Gus, don't think I'll be back. Too many memories and stuff, you know?'

Gus' heart hammered, the tic at his temple increased. He'd realised this was a possibility and he'd made a promise to himself that he wouldn't pressurise her. He thrust his hands in his pockets and shrugged, 'Take all the time you need, Al.

The decision has to be yours, but I'll not replace you till you say so, okay?'

Alice nodded, stepped forward on tiptoes and kissed his cheek before turning to Patti. 'Look after him. He's a keeper.' She spun on her heel, marched over to her beloved Mini and drove off.

Acknowledgements

As usual, I have to give a massive 'shout out' to the incredible Bloodhound Books team. They are phenomenal and I'm proud to be part of their kennels. My editors, Ben Adams and Heather Fitt, are indefatigable and always have their eyes on the ball. As ever, my family have been with me on this journey and continue to inspire and support me. The Bloodhound Pups are generous with their knowledge and support. A special shout out to Pat Young and her daughter Stef for *'that'* input – you know the bits I mean.

The bloggers, book groups and reviewers humble me with their dedication to supporting and encouraging us authors. You are an invaluable link to our readers. Love you all!

My Leeds Trinity University writing buddies are inspirational, awesome and damn hard taskmasters – thanks to Andrea, Jo, John, Kathleen, Sam, Stephanie and Suzanne for putting up with me. Toria Forsyth-Moser, whose perception and thoughtfulness, combined with her energy and wit makes sure I'm on the right track – a huge thank you! My Leeds Trinity University PhD compadres keep me sane, assist in my research and offer advice.

I have had help and guidance from a few experts in their field and want to give them a shout out: Claire Vilarrubi whose detailed information on women's prisons was invaluable, Henna Mistry who generously shared her knowledge of weight lifting and training reps.

However, my biggest thanks must go to you, the reader, without whom writing would be an incomplete process. If you enjoyed *Unspoken Truths*, please leave a review. You've no idea how much we authors treasure your words of wisdom.

Three delightful readers offered their names for my nefarious use in exchange for a charitable donation: Izzie Dimou's in aid of MIND charity, Jordan Beaumont's in aid of Cancer Research and Russell Allison-Hinton's in aid of Longlands Care Farm. A special shout out to Russell whose name was nominated as a birthday gift. Happy Birthday in December, Russell!

As ever any mistakes are mine and so I apologise in advance. I have taken odd bits of creative licence and created a few new places… forgive me… it was all in order to enhance the story.